Night Huntress

"Yasmine Galenorn is a hot new star in the world of urban fantasy. The Otherworld series is wonderfully entertaining."
—Jayne Ann Krentz

"Yasmine Galenorn is a powerhouse author; a master of the craft who is taking the industry by storm, and for good reason." —Maggie Shayne, *New York Times* bestselling author

"Yasmine Galenorn hits the stars with *Night Huntress*. Urban Fantasy at its best!"
—Stella Cameron, *New York Times* bestselling author

"A thrilling ride from start to finish."
—*The Romance Readers Connection*

"Fascinating and eminently enjoyable from the first page to the last . . . *Night Huntress* rocks! Don't miss it!"
—*Romance Reviews Today*

"Love and betrayal play large roles in *Night Huntress*, and as the story unfolds, the action will sweep fans along for this fast-moving ride." —*Darque Reviews*

Dragon Wytch

"Action and sexy sensuality make this book hot to the touch."
—*Romantic Times* (four stars)

"Ms. Galenorn has a great gift for spinning a compelling story. The supernatural action is a great blend of both fresh and familiar, the characters are each charming in their own way, the heroine's love life is scorching, and the worlds they all live in are well-defined." —*Darque Reviews*

"This is the kind of series that even those who do not care for the supernatural will find a very good read."
—*Affaire de Coeur*

"If you're looking for an out-of-this-world enchanting tale of magic and passion, *Dragon Wytch* is the story for you. I will be recommending this wickedly bewitching tale to everyone I know!" —*Dark Angel Reviews*

DARKLING

"The most fulfilling journey of self-discovery to date in the Otherworld series . . . An eclectic blend that works well."
—*Booklist*

"Galenorn does a remarkable job of delving into the psyches and fears of her characters. As this series matures, so do her heroines. The sex sizzles and the danger fascinates."
—*Romantic Times*

"The story is nonstop action and has deep, dark plots that kept me up reading long past my bedtime. Here be Dark Fantasy with a unique twist. YES!" —*Huntress Book Reviews*

CHANGELING

"The second in Galenorn's D'Artigo Sisters series ratchets up the danger and romantic entanglements. Along with the quirky humor and characters readers have come to expect is a moving tale of a woman more comfortable in her cat skin than in her human form, looking to find her place in the world." —*Booklist*

"Galenorn's thrilling supernatural series is gritty and dangerous, but it's the tumultuous relationships between all the various characters that give it depth and heart. Vivid, sexy, and mesmerizing, Galenorn's novel hits the paranormal sweet spot." —*Romantic Times*

"I absolutely loved it!" —*Fresh Fiction*

"Yasmine Galenorn has created another winner . . . *Changeling* is a can't-miss read destined to hold a special place on your keeper shelf." —*Romance Reviews Today*

continued . . .

Witchling

Titles by Yasmine Galenorn

The Otherworld Series

WITCHLING
CHANGELING
DARKLING
DRAGON WYTCH
NIGHT HUNTRESS
DEMON MISTRESS
BONE MAGIC
HARVEST HUNTING

The Indigo Court Series

NIGHT MYST

Anthologies

INKED
NEVER AFTER

Berkley Prime Crime titles by Yasmine Galenorn

GHOST OF A CHANCE
LEGEND OF THE JADE DRAGON
MURDER UNDER A MYSTIC MOON
A HARVEST OF BONES
ONE HEX OF A WEDDING

* * *

Yasmine Galenorn writing as India Ink

SCENT TO HER GRAVE
A BLUSH WITH DEATH
GLOSSED AND FOUND

HARVEST HUNTING

An Otherworld Novel

YASMINE GALENORN

JOVE BOOKS, NEW YORK

THE BERKLEY PUBLISHING GROUP
Published by the Penguin Group
Penguin Group (USA) Inc.
375 Hudson Street, New York, New York 10014, USA

Penguin Group (Canada), 90 Eglinton Avenue East, Suite 700, Toronto, Ontario M4P 2Y3, Canada
(a division of Pearson Penguin Canada Inc.)
Penguin Books Ltd., 80 Strand, London WC2R 0RL, England
Penguin Group Ireland, 25 St. Stephen's Green, Dublin 2, Ireland (a division of Penguin Books Ltd.)
Penguin Group (Australia), 250 Camberwell Road, Camberwell, Victoria 3124, Australia
(a division of Pearson Australia Group Pty. Ltd.)
Penguin Books India Pvt. Ltd., 11 Community Centre, Panchsheel Park, New Delhi—110 017, India
Penguin Group (NZ), 67 Apollo Drive, Rosedale, North Shore 0632, New Zealand
(a division of Pearson New Zealand Ltd.)
Penguin Books (South Africa) (Pty.) Ltd., 24 Sturdee Avenue, Rosebank, Johannesburg 2196,
South Africa

Penguin Books Ltd., Registered Offices: 80 Strand, London WC2R 0RL, England

This is a work of fiction. Names, characters, places, and incidents either are the product of the author's imagination or are used fictitiously, and any resemblance to actual persons, living or dead, business establishments, events, or locales is entirely coincidental. The publisher does not have any control over and does not have any responsibility for author or third-party websites or their content.

HARVEST HUNTING

A Jove Book / published by arrangement with the author

PRINTING HISTORY
Jove mass-market edition / November 2010

Copyright © 2010 by Yasmine Galenorn.
Excerpt from *Blood Wyne* copyright © by Yasmine Galenorn.
Cover art by Tony Mauro.
Cover design by Rita Frangie.

ISBN: 978-0-515-14853-4

JOVE®
Jove Books are published by The Berkley Publishing Group,
a division of Penguin Group (USA) Inc.,
375 Hudson Street, New York, New York 10014.
JOVE® is a registered trademark of Penguin Group (USA) Inc.
The "J" design is a trademark of Penguin Group (USA) Inc.

PRINTED IN THE UNITED STATES OF AMERICA

10 9 8 7 6 5 4 3 2 1

Dedicated to
the spirit of the autumn,
the Autumn Lord,
and all of those who walk the path of the Harvest.

ACKNOWLEDGMENTS

Thank you to my agent, Meredith Bernstein, and to my editor, Kate Seaver: the best team I could have. To Tony Mauro, the most talented cover artist *ever*. To my husband, Samwise, and my friends Maura Anderson and Jo Yantz, all of whom help me hold on to the edge of sanity! To my assistant, J. L. Anderson, without whom I'd be frantic. To my little "Galenorn Gurlz"—Meerclar, the senior, and our newest babies: Calypso, Brighid, and Morgana. To the fur babies we lost to old age and illness: Pakhit, Tara, and Luna. Most reverent devotion to Ukko, Rauni, Mielikki, and Tapio, my spiritual guardians.

Thank you to my readers—both old and new. Your support helps keep us writers in ink and fuels our love of storytelling, and believe me, I appreciate each and every wonderful note you send, whether it be via Twitter, MySpace, e-mail, or snail mail. You can find me on the Net at Galenorn En/Visions: www .galenorn.com. I'm on Facebook, Twitter, and MySpace—the links are on my site. If you write to me through snail mail (see website for address or write via publisher), please enclose a self-addressed stamped envelope with your letter if you would like a reply. Promo goodies are available—see my site for info.

Bright Blessings,
The Painted Panther
Yasmine Galenorn

You cannot run with the hare and hunt with the hounds.

—FIFTEENTH-CENTURY PROVERB

All things on earth point home in old October; sailors to sea, travellers to walls and fences, hunters to field and hollow and the long voice of the hounds, the lover to the love he has forsaken.

—THOMAS WOLFE

CHAPTER 1

My nose quivered. Something smelled wonderful. I followed the scent through the crowded hall until I found myself standing next to the buffet table.

My sister Menolly and I had just stood beside our sister Camille as she married her third husband. Three—count 'em—three husbands. Simultaneously. Trillian had been decked out as the best goth groom ever, wearing black leather pants that matched the obsidian gleam of his skin, a black mesh tank, and a velvet cloak the color of blood.

Morio and Smoky were dressed in what they had worn to *their* wedding with Camille: Smoky was in his long white trench with a blue and gold vest, a pale blue button-down shirt, tight white jeans, and his ankle-length silver hair coiling around him like dancing serpents. Morio wore a red and gold kimono with a dress sword hanging from his side, and his hair rippled down his back.

And of course my sister looked good enough to eat, her raven hair glistening against her gossamer priestess robes, so sheer I could see her bra and panties through them. Now that she was an official priestess of the Moon Mother, she was expected to don ceremonial garb for most important occasions.

The four of them had gathered before Iris, who again presided, and together they underwent a variant of the Soul Symbiont ritual designed to bring Trillian into their fold. Menolly and I were wearing gowns—hers of black with shimmering crystals, mine of gold—and stood as witnesses again.

Now we were into the celebration part of the affair.

I glanced at the calendar on the wall. October 22, and we were well on our way to Samhain, the festival of the dead. It had been a month, almost to the day, since we'd unsuccessfully raided Stacia Bonecrusher's safe house.

Thinking about Stacia forced me to face another thought, one I'd been trying to avoid. I glanced across the room at Chase Johnson. The detective was sitting at a table by himself, watching the celebration with a quizzical look on his face. Unable to help myself, I headed in his direction. He watched me approach, his expression carefully sliding into neutral. I took the chair opposite him.

"It's a beautiful wedding." I nervously played with the napkin resting on the table next to me. "Don't you think?"

"Yes, lovely." He blinked, long and slow, and I wondered what he was really thinking. "Camille seemed a little stressed, though. What's up with that?" Even though his tone was normal, I knew there was nothing normal about Chase. Not anymore.

"Our father refused to attend the wedding. Not only does he disapprove of her marrying Trillian, but his official stance is that she's turned her back on her duties for the Otherworld Intelligence Agency by becoming a priestess and agreeing to enter Aeval's court. He refuses to condone her behavior by showing up, and the day she actually pledges under Aeval's rule . . . I'm afraid of what's going to happen."

"Turned her back on her duties? That doesn't seem fair, considering all she's done for the OIA. I know Sephreh's your father, but damn, that's cold." He sipped his champagne, sounding more himself than he had the entire past month.

I glanced at the fading scars on his hands. His body had healed remarkably fast from the deep knife wounds that had laced his skin and punctured several of his organs. But it would take a long, long time for him to heal from the potion that had saved his life. The Nectar of Life had torn his entire world apart and put it back together in a crazy new patchwork. Our relationship was on rocky ground, at best.

"When she promised to train under Morgaine, and *especially* when she agreed to dedicate herself to Aeval's Dark Court, Father took it as a personal insult. But Camille doesn't have a choice; she's under direct order from the Moon Mother herself."

"Yeah, I got that," he said, fiddling with his glass.

"She did everything for us when our mother died, and without her, the family would have been ripped to shreds. Father was extremely cruel to her the last time they spoke, and I'm pissed off that he didn't show today. Our cousin Shamas has been trying to fill the void, but it's just not the same."

"What did he say?" Chase played with his goblet. "By the way, will alcohol hurt me . . . *now*? I haven't had a drink since before the accident."

"No, you'll be fine. You can still eat and drink anything you want. It's not like you were turned into a vampire." I stared at my hands. As loyal as I was to our father, I couldn't blind myself to the truth. "At his last visit, things went from bad to worse. By the time he left, Camille was on the sofa, curled up in a ball, sobbing. Smoky came in at the point when Sephreh threatened to disinherit her. In turn, Smoky threatened to shift into his dragon self and crisp our father."

"Crap. The fallout from that can't be good."

"Things were at a standstill until Menolly stepped in, told Father to go home and Smoky to chill. But definitely *Not Pretty*. Not at all."

"A mess, all the way around, then." Chase morosely picked up his champagne flute and downed the last of the sparkling wine. "And so . . . here we sit." He stared across the table at me, his gaze unreadable. "I don't know what to say, Delilah. I don't even have a clue on how to start."

Part of me wanted to cry. Nothing seemed to be working out the way we hoped it would. The world had gone to hell in a handbasket for all of us. I blinked back my tears.

"How about you start by telling me how you're doing? We've only talked three times in the past two weeks." I didn't mention that we'd barely kissed since he'd healed up and returned to duty.

Chase contemplated the question, looking at me through those limpid, soulful eyes. They'd only grown more luminous since he'd drunk the Nectar of Life. His aura had shifted. Some spark, some force I couldn't put my finger on, was changing him.

"How can I answer that, when *I* don't even know? What am I supposed to do? Jump up and shout, '*Rah rah*, now I'll outlive everybody I've ever known in my life'?" He slammed the goblet on the table so hard it almost broke.

Stung, I blinked back the tears. "Giving you the Nectar of Life was the only option we had—unless you prefer the thought of dying."

Shifting in his seat, Chase let out a long sigh. "Yeah, I know. I know. And believe me, I am grateful. But damn, this stuff does a number on your head. It's more than the realization that I'm going to live a thousand years. There's something . . . nebulous . . . about it. The nectar ripped open a part of me—I feel exposed, unable to put the pieces back together again. And I'm afraid to look too deeply at what's happening." He slowly reached out and took my hand.

I stared at him for a moment, but he remained silent. Both Camille and Chase had come through the autumn equinox worn and weary, covered with blood. Camille had bathed in the blood of the black unicorn as she sealed a fate with which the Moon Mother challenged her: sacrificing the horned beast to his phoenixlike destiny while on the Hunt of her life. And then she'd been thrown under the wheels of Aeval, and would soon be forced to descend into the realms once ruled by the ancient Unseelie Queen.

And Chase . . . no less life-shaking. He'd been bathed in his own blood and was now—by human terms—practically immortal.

"Whenever you're ready to talk about it—"

"What? You'll play shrink to the mutant?" He shot me a nasty look.

"*No.* I'll listen. As your *girlfriend*." I stared at him, the virulence of his anger rankling me. "Chase, this isn't fair. We'd planned on you drinking the nectar anyway, and now you sound like you're blaming me for what's happened."

"I know! And I'm sorry—I don't mean to. But you told me

that the ritual required preparation, and now I understand why. I'm *not human* anymore. I don't know who—or *what*—I am. A thousand fucking years to look forward to, and *I have no idea what to do with them.*"

Fed up and too tired to deal with his angst as well as my own, I pushed back my chair. "I guess . . . it's hard for me to understand what you're going through. I'm trying—I really am. But until you can figure it out, you don't seem to need me around."

"Wait! It's just . . . oh hell, I don't know what to say." He slumped back in his chair. "I want to say that everything's okay. I feel like I should be thinking that wow—now my girl-friend and I can be together for centuries. But Delilah . . . I have to tell you the truth. I don't know if I'm ready for that kind of commitment now that the opportunity is actually here."

The tears stung behind my eyes, but I blinked them back. "It would seem that Sharah is doing a better job taking care of you than I am."

The elfin medic who worked alongside Chase in the Faerie-Human Crime Scene Investigations unit had been overseeing his care as the potion worked its way through his system, changing every cell, altering his very DNA.

Chase snorted. "Maybe that's because she's *not* taking care of me. Sharah is offering me advice, but she's not cod-dling me or treating me like some freak who needs kid glove handling." A look of pain crossed his face, and he dropped his head to his hands and rubbed his forehead. "I'm sorry. I'm sorry, Delilah. I love you, I really do, but right now I'm no good to either one of us."

My stomach churning, I sat on the edge of my chair again. "Yeah, I know you feel that way. But Chase, please, don't shut me out."

"I need to be on my own for a bit. To think about things. Besides, Camille needs you more than I do now. Her life's a mess, too. And Henry . . . poor Henry doesn't even have a life anymore. Go enjoy the party. Be there for your sister. She deserves the support. And if you meet somebody and you *want* them, I won't ask questions."

I tried to protest, but he shook his head and, feeling abruptly shoved out of the nest, I scurried toward the door, biting the

tears back. Chase was right about one thing: our friend Henry
Jeffries had fared worst of all. He'd been working in Camille's
bookshop—the Indigo Crescent—when the demons broke in.
They killed him and blew up a good part of the shop in order
to warn us off. We still hadn't gotten the smell of smoke out
of the walls.

As I neared the door, a voice echoed from behind me.

"Delilah, you okay?"

When I turned, I saw Vanzir, the lanky dream chaser demon
bound to my sisters and me. Over the past seven months, we'd
slowly been forging a friendship. Menolly and Vanzir hung
out a lot. Vanzir and I talked from time to time. Camille kept
her distance, but she was growing less leery of him as the
weeks wore on.

Vanzir's eyes whirled, a kaleidoscope of colors without
any names. His David Bowie goblin-king hair was spiked
and platinum, and he looked uncomfortable out of his leather
pants and ripped tank. But he made the tux and tails work.

I shrugged and said, "I guess."

"*You guess*, my ass. What's wrong? You sense anything
wrong out there? Demons?" Vanzir leaned against the wall in
front of me, giving me the once-over. I realized he didn't have
a clue as to what was bothering me.

"*Men.* Even you demons are clueless." As he stared at me, I
shook my head and pushed past him. "I'm going to take a run
outside. I need some air."

"What? What did I say?"

As Vanzir let out a snort, I sidled to the door, slipping out
while everyone was focused on toasting the happy . . . well,
not *couple* . . . The happy marriage. Camille would understand. She'd forgive me for skipping out. Because pretty
much, only she and Menolly knew what I was going through.
What we were *all* going through.

Rhyne Wood Reception Hall was in one of the larger parks,
and the city leased it out for celebrations and parties. Camille
had decided to hold the reception here because—unlike her
impromptu marriage to Smoky and Morio—this one had been
planned, with over a hundred guests. And those numbers took

space. Rhyne Wood had a dance floor, a nice big kitchen, and catering staff.

Situated in Fireweed Park, the mansion was a small part of the thousand-acre wilderness buttressing the shore of Puget Sound. I stayed away from the perimeter of the butte overlooking the inlet. I hated water and had no intention of accidentally going over the edge. But there were plenty of paths and trees and bushes in which to lose myself. As soon as I was far enough away from the mansion to comfortably feel out of sight, I shifted into my tabby self, my primary Were form. Everybody always thought it hurt, but really, if I went slowly, it didn't. Just a blur and a haze as life shifted perceptions.

Free of clothing—except for a bright blue collar—I took off, racing into the undergrowth, reveling in the scents that flowed like hot chocolate on a cold autumn night. And it *was* cold, but my fur kept me warm and cozy. My worries floated away as I bounded through the rain-sparkling grass, romping in the misty evening, chasing the few moths still braving the rain.

I leapt at one, an Anna's Blue, and caught it in my mouth. With a quick *nom nom*, I swallowed and wrinkled my nose as the featherlight wings tickled my throat. A moment later, a rustling in the grass distracted me, and I raced in the direction of a thicket of alder trees surrounded by dense huckleberry bushes.

I knew enough not to get too near the bushes—they had nice, sharp thorns perfect for snagging my tail. But whatever was hiding there, I could smell, and the scent set my pulse to racing. I wanted to chase, to stretch my legs and feel the thrill of the hunt. I needed to rip things apart, to act out my aggression. And whatever was in the bushes, I might be able to play cat and mouse with it.

As I skirted the huckleberry, the rustling grew louder, and then out popped another . . . *cat*?

Puzzled, I cocked my head, staring at the creature. *Not cat.* But what the hell was it? Fluffy, bushy tail, cute, dark with light stripe . . . I knew I'd seen one somewhere, but I couldn't remember where. Wondering if it might be friendly, I took a hesitant step toward it, and its big, bushy tail fluttered in the wind. The plume of fur was so pretty and tempting that I forgot my manners and pounced.

The creature swung around, turning its butt toward me. *Oh shit! Skunk!*

Just as I remembered what it was, it took aim, shook its ass, and a wide spray came shooting toward me. I yowled and bounded away, but not before getting drenched by the foul-smelling perfume. At least it managed to miss my eyes, but I didn't wait around for the skunk to get in a second shot. I hightailed it back toward the mansion.

As I reached the steps, I slowed, sneezing violently. What the hell was I supposed to do? If I ran in there as a cat, I'd stink up the joint. If I ran in as myself, it would be worse, because I'd be bigger, hence, giving off more of the odor. I paced nervously in front of the steps, wanting the nasty scent gone. *Now.*

Luck was with me. Vanzir was standing there, watching me. As I stared at him, eyes wide and praying he wouldn't start laughing, he slipped back through the door. A moment later, he reappeared, Iris and Bruce in tow. Iris glanced around, her nose wrinkling, and I let out a plaintive yowl.

"Oh good heavens!" Iris shoved her flute of champagne into Bruce's hand and came racing down the stairs, a look of horror on her face. She stopped just out of reach. "You poor thing. Oh dear, how are we going to get you home?"

Just then, Rozurial slipped outside. He looked at Vanzir, then Bruce, who was still holding the champagne, and then down at Iris and me.

"That's not who I think it is, is it?" He barely muffled his laughter, and I hissed at him. "Oh, yeah, babe. You have a little BO problem, know that?"

"What should we do with her?" Bruce asked.

Iris stared at me, cocking her head, and I could see the wheels turning. "Rozurial, you take her home through the Ionyc Sea. I'll head home with Bruce in the car, and we'll get her cleaned up."

She leaned down and shook her finger at me. It was tempting, but I had learned not to swat Iris while in cat form. She wasn't above scruffing me and holding me off the floor, even though she was barely four feet tall.

"Listen to me, Delilah, and I know you can understand me, so you'd better do as I say. Don't you dare turn back into yourself until we take care of this. I guarantee it will be far worse with all six foot one of you skunked, rather than just yourself as a little pussycat. Got it?"

I stared at her and blinked. If I disobeyed her on this one, she'd have my hide. Slowly, I let out a complacent meow.

"Good. Now, Rozurial, you take her home. And I don't want to hear any fuss about it—*just do it*. Honey, will you let Camille know where we're going?" Iris motioned to Bruce, who hurried back inside.

"I'll come with," Vanzir said to her. "I'm not all that comfortable in a tux."

"Good. I can use your help."

Roz picked me up, and I snuggled against the incubus, rubbing my chin on his chest. I had the feeling I wasn't going to like what Iris had in store for me, and I wanted comfort. Purring loudly, I gave him my best *good-kitty* look, and he snorted, rubbing my ears.

"Eat it up, beauty. Eat it up. Come, you'll be safe enough, just don't try to jump out of my arms." And in the blink of an eye, we leapt into the Ionyc Sea and crossed a world to travel fifteen miles.

Roz set me down outside, warning me not to enter the house until Iris had tended to me. "I'll be back in a moment to keep an eye on you, though smelling like you do, I doubt anybody's going to be a bother."

He vanished into the studio-cum-shed that he shared with Vanzir and my cousin Shamas. With Camille's three men staying with us now, and Bruce shacking up with Iris part of the time, we had built ourselves quite the extended family.

I tried to sniff out if there were any enemies near, but the scent of skunk infiltrated every pore. My eyes hurt, my nose hurt, my throat hurt, and I was queasy. It felt like the mother of all hairballs was churning in my stomach. I hunched near the porch, trying to avoid being seen by any would-be heroes of the animal world.

Roz came back after awhile, dressed in a pair of skintight jeans and a muscle shirt, and he sprawled on the ground near me, on his back, staring up at the stars, his long curly hair spreading on the ground beneath him.

"Look at the sky, fuzzball." He ruffled my head. "Look at all the stars whirling around . . . I've walked among them, you know." His voice dropped and took on a sinuous cadence. Even in cat form, I found it soothing and seductive.

"I've danced through the aurora borealis, skated my way through the Ionyc Lands. When I was searching for Dredge, I followed any and every lead, wherever the wind blew me. I journeyed from the Northlands to the Southern Wastes, from Valhalla to the gates of Hel, looking for that motherfucker. I've seen so much beauty and terror in my life that you'd think nothing would faze me . . . but the stars . . . they're still the ultimate treasure. Pristine, luminous, and always out of reach."

He rolled over on his stomach and plucked a long blade of grass, tickling my belly as I stretched out beside him. "I know you're worried about Chase. But, Delilah, you have to let go, if that's what he needs. The Nectar of Life plays havoc with humans when they aren't prepared. You saved his life, but he lost something he wasn't ready to lose. His mortality—in the human sense—is a huge part of what makes humans . . . well . . . human. When you have such a short time to live, you make the most of it. Now, you need to stand back and let Sharah help him. She knows what to do."

I knew he was speaking the truth; I just didn't want to hear it. But he was right. Camille and Menolly had been telling me that for days, but coming from them, it felt like sisterly meddling instead of advice. I let out a little yowl.

"Yeah, I know you know, and I know you don't like it, but take my advice this time, okay? I understand what it means to have life ripped apart and drastically changed."

And I knew that Roz did understand. He'd lost his family to Dredge, he'd lost his wife when Zeus and Hera decided to use them both as pawns. He'd been changed from Fae to incubus in the blink of an eye. Chase's life had been turned upside down in that same fraction of a second, though not as harshly as Roz's.

A car pulled into the driveway. Bruce and his driver. And Iris. They jumped out, and I saw they'd brought Vanzir home, too. Probably a good thing. He wasn't the most decorous guest, and I had a feeling he'd be happier here than hanging out till late at a party where most of the guests avoided him.

Iris ran inside, and in less than ten minutes, she dashed down from the back porch, wearing a rubber apron over what I recognized as a dress she kept for the grungiest chores. She stood over me, hands on her hips.

"Well, I don't know how you got yourself in this fix, but let's take care of you." She leaned over and scooped me up in her arms, her nose twitching. "You reek, girl. What did you say to that skunk?"

I wanted to protest—*it hadn't been my fault; I hadn't done anything.* But I knew that Iris would call me on it. Truth was, I'd invaded the skunk's territory and threatened it by pouncing.

Holding me against one hip, Iris carried me up the back steps and into the enclosed porch, where I saw something so horrible that I squirmed, desperately trying to get away: a bath full of what looked like dark, thick water.

Iris struggled, her thick rubber gloves losing their purchase on me. The minute her grip weakened, I bolted for the door to the kitchen, which was standing open.

"Come back here! Delilah, get your fuzzy butt back here *right now*!"

I galloped toward the stairs, but before I could get there, Vanzir was standing in front of me, snickering. Faster than I could blink, he reached out and snagged me up.

"Gotchya, puddy tat."

I squirmed, but he held fast and carried me at arm's length to the porch, where he unceremoniously dumped me in the water. Iris slammed the door so I couldn't get into the house again. Resigned, I huffed and patiently waited. I was already wet; I might as well let her give me the bath. The scent of tomato juice cocktail broke through the smell filtering into my nostrils, and I took a cautious lick of the water.

Not bad, not bad.

Iris began to scrub me with the juice, and I hated to admit it, but it felt good. I detested the smell of skunk—it was making me nauseated—and if Iris thought that a bath in V8 would help, then I'd let her bathe me. I even relented enough to let her scrub my tummy. She took off my collar, and I suddenly felt naked. After all, that collar contained my clothing. When I changed back, if it wasn't on me, my clothes wouldn't be either.

After about ten minutes Iris motioned to Roz, and they moved to the side, leaving Vanzir to hold me in the tub.

"Puddy tat like her bath? Puddy happy?" he crooned.

Good for you I know you're just teasing, I thought. *Or you'd be dead by now.* Vanzir was our slave, and if we chose, he'd die. Enslaving him had been the only way to keep from killing him when he defected to us in the first place, and there was no undoing the deed. He was ours. Forever.

I settled for chomping on his thumb. He raised his eyebrows, but that David Bowie–Ziggy Stardust platinum shag barely moved. I wondered how much gel he used to get it to stay in place.

Iris and Roz came back, and she lifted me out of the bath and dipped me in a bucket of warm, clear water to rinse off the tomato juice.

"Uh-oh," she said.

That didn't sound good.

"Oh Mama." Roz let out a snort. "She's not going to like that at all. I wonder if . . . will it translate over?"

What? Will what translate over? What the hell was going on?

"Delilah, honey, I think you better shift back now. Vanzir, would you fetch a towel? She's not going to want those clothes, I guarantee you that. What a pity—your beautiful gown. You'll have to replace it."

My gown! Oh no! I hadn't even thought about that, but Iris was right; the skunk had ruined my most elegant evening dress. My *only* evening dress.

She sat me down, and I sniffed the air. Hey—what the hell? I still smelled like skunk! Letting out a huff, I shook my head, and water flew everywhere. Iris jumped back.

"I know you're not happy, but please—mind your manners. I would prefer to smell as little like skunk as possible. Now, here's the towel. Boys, be nice and quit teasing her."

She took the large beach towel from Vanzir, who was grinning ear to ear by now. Oh, he was going to get his. Iris held one end while Roz held the other. She stared pointedly at both of them until they averted their eyes. Normally I wouldn't give a damn, but right now I was in a pissy mood, and the Talon-haltija knew it.

I shifted back slowly, because I was in no mood for any nasty muscle spasms, and the slower I shifted, the easier it went. As I stood up, feeling rank, I wrapped the towel around me. Iris's gaze traveled up to my face.

"Oh my stars," she whispered, her eyes wide. "I had *no idea* that was going to happen."

"What? What's going on? If somebody doesn't tell me soon, I'm turning back into a cat and going on a shredding binge."

"Hey, Red," Vanzir said, once again ruffling my hair. Only this time he had to reach up to do it.

Red?

"No. . . . no . . . you don't mean what I think you mean, do you?" I took off for the bathroom, the smell of skunk with a side of tomato following me.

As I flipped on the light and stared in the mirror, I let out a groan. My beautiful golden hair was now rife with brilliant highlights. I looked like Ronald McDonald, only tiger-striped. The tomato juice had dyed the lighter parts of my hair, and now I was a patchwork of pink, rust, and burnt orange. And none of it looked good.

"Fuck! Fuck, fuck, *fuck me*."

Iris peeked around the corner. "I'm so sorry, Delilah. I had no idea tomato juice would do that. And it didn't take care of the smell, either."

"I reek, and my hair looks like a dye bomb went off in it!"

I dropped to the edge of the tub. I loved my hair. It wasn't fancy, it wasn't anything super special, but it was mine. Now I looked like I was doing a bad Lil' Kim impersonation.

"Well, hop in the shower; maybe you can scrub some of the skunk scent off. Meanwhile, I'll see what I can find out. I've never had to deal with this before—no one I've ever known got skunked. Not that I remember." She headed out of the bathroom, muttering to herself.

I grimaced, then looked at myself in the mirror again. I'd always loved the combination of my emerald eyes and golden hair, but now I looked like I'd gone punk. Bad. Very bad. Splotches of pink to orange dappled the gold, and even where it hadn't, my natural color had become brassy. And not only my hair up top had decided to turn calico, but everywhere on my body. Eyebrows, razor stubble on my legs, and . . . oh yah, I had a burning bush, all right. For the first time in my life, I foresaw begging Camille to teach me how to go Brazilian.

"Crap. One more thing to deal with." But right now, I needed to focus on getting the stench off me.

"Here we go," Iris said, coming back with a basin filled with a bottle of hydrogen peroxide, a box of baking soda, and some dish soap. "Fill the bathtub."

Mutely, I did as she ordered, backing off as she poured a cup of the baking soda into the churning water. Then she added the quart of peroxide and about a quarter cup of dish soap. I stared at the briny bath and gingerly stepped in when she gave me a little shove.

Far from a nice, fresh, minty bubble bath, which I'd willingly take, this felt more like she was scrubbing off the last seven years of skin. By the time we finished washing me and my hair, I was bright pink from the vigorous use of the loofah. As I rinsed off under the shower spray, I could still smell the skunk, but at least it was muted. *A little.*

"Oh, dear," she said, looking up at me.

Wordlessly, I peeked in the mirror. Now, in addition to pink, orange, and brassy blonde, I had platinum patches from the peroxide. Down below, too.

"Crap," I said again, shaking my head. "What can we do about my hair?"

Iris bit her lip. I'd never seen her look quite so remorseful. "I'm not sure. I have no idea how hair dye would react on you, given your half-Fae heritage. *Especially* after the peroxide bath. Let me do some research on spells. Maybe there's something we can do magically."

"Forget about asking Camille to touch my head," I muttered. "I remember perfectly well what happened when she tried to make herself invisible. She was nekkid for a week and couldn't do a thing about it. And didn't even *know* it until somebody told her that her clothes were invisible."

A knock on the door interrupted us. I wrapped the towel around me, and Iris answered. It was Vanzir.

"Delilah—it's Luke, from the bar. He wants to talk to you."

Luke? Luke was a werewolf who worked at the Wayfarer Bar & Grill, owned by my sister Menolly. He occasionally came over to dinner, but if he was here instead of on duty, there must be something wrong.

I stared down at my towel-wrapped torso. At six one, I was

lean, though not gaunt by *any* shape of the imagination. You couldn't see my bones—they were all covered by a nice layer of muscle.

"He'll have to deal with me being half-dressed. I'm not climbing into any of my clothes till I find something that will prevent the skunk smell from spreading to them."

Wandering out into the foyer, I nodded at the tall, lanky werewolf who slouched against one wall. Luke could be mistaken for a cowboy except for the scar that laced its way down his cheek. A faint smile flickered across his lips. The ponytail that hung down his back was tidy but gave me the impression that his hair was fly-away and tousled by nature.

He touched the hat he wore. "Miss Delilah, how you doing? Ran into a skunk, did you?"

"That obvious?"

"Between your . . . perfume, and the new dye job up top, yeah. I bet Iris used tomato juice to no effect?" A lazy smile took the place of the worried look as he flashed a wink at Iris. She blushed.

I nodded. "Yeah, something like that. And then some quasi-crazy peroxide mix. You don't happen to have a cure, do you?"

"Maybe," he said. "At least for the scent. I'll have to go back to my apartment to get it. Learned to make it years ago when I was still running with the Pack. We found out firsthand that tomato juice did a number on light-colored fur. But first, I need your services, if you're willing."

"My services?" I started to bristle, suddenly all too aware of my semi-naked state.

"You're a PI, aren't you?" He was doing his best to keep his eyes on my face, though I saw them drop a couple times, then swiftly scan back up to look me in the eye. Kind of cute, actually. He was blushing. And, mingling with the skunk, the tomato juice, and the chemical scent of the peroxide, I could smell his musk, though not so thick as to indicate arousal. But he liked women, that was for sure.

"Oh. Um . . . yeah." I edged into the living room and nodded for him to follow me. "Have a seat. What do you need?"

Luke edged onto the sofa while I curled up in the rocking chair, making sure nothing was showing that shouldn't. Before I could sit down, Iris slipped in and spread a grungy sheet beneath me. Great. I was beginning to feel like Typhoid Mary.

"My sister's missing."

"I didn't know you had a sister," I said.

He nodded. "Amber was moving up here. She said that she'd had a vision, that she needed to live in Seattle for some reason. A few weeks back, she left the Pack, which is a big no-no unless you're excommunicated like I was."

"Did she say why?" I was beginning to wonder about lycanthropes—the Were system wasn't the same in all species, and I'd heard rumors that among the wolves, rules were very patriarchal. Not conducive to free-thinking females.

"Yeah . . . I'll tell you why in a moment. Anyway, she called when she hit town this afternoon. She was going to check in, then rest a bit and meet me at the bar around eight. But she never showed. I called the cops, but they won't put out missing person reports on Supes for forty-eight hours, which is bullshit. My sister came all the way from Arizona, and I'm worried. I checked with the hotel. They said she checked in at two P.M., but they haven't heard from her since."

"Any chance she got caught up visiting someone else?" Interested now, I pulled a notebook off the end table next to me and began to jot down notes.

Luke shook his head. "Nope. She doesn't *know* anybody else here, but she was adamant about being summoned to this area. That's the word she used—summoned. I'm especially worried because she's pregnant. A werewolf who is seven months pregnant just doesn't disappear. She should be nesting, creating the lair for the pups . . . or children, so to speak." His voice belied his calm exterior, and I could hear the panic welling just below the surface.

"What's her last name, and do you have a picture of her?"

He handed over a faded picture from his wallet. As I took it from his hands, I noticed the calluses that had long embedded themselves into his fingers and palms. This man had seen hard work, harder than he was doing at the bar, and his skin was covered with faded scars.

I took the picture and gazed at the young woman staring back at me. She looked about twenty-five—misleading, of course, given the long-lived nature of the Supe Community.

She had Luke's eyes. Feral and yet . . . a yearning hidden behind the wariness. Long, wheat-colored hair drifted down her shoulders, honey-kissed and vibrant. She was beautiful, luminous, and dangerous.

"Her name is Amber. Amber Johansen. We haven't seen each other in years."

He left something unspoken. Something that told me Luke had a suspicion about what had happened.

"What do you think is going on?" I caught his attention, turning on my glamour, willing him to open up.

He sucked in a deep breath and let it out slowly, locking his gaze on mine without flinching. "I think that rat's ass she calls a husband came after her. She told me over the phone that she was being followed down there, and my guess is he's trying to *convince* her to come back to the Pack. His ego—the ego of the Pack—neither takes it well when their women leave. Rice is an abusive motherfucker, and I'm afraid he'll track her down and kill her."

And then, slowly, he crumbled. "Amber's the only family I've got."

"We'll find her," I said, sliding my hand over his. "We'll do everything we can to find her." But inside, I was praying we weren't too late.

CHAPTER 2

At that moment, the front door opened, and Menolly wandered in, her arm around Nerissa, who was obviously three sheets to the wind. They were both laughing, and my sister's fangs were down, but one look at Nerissa reassured me that Menolly hadn't slipped. Menolly gently deposited her in one of the armchairs and gave her a kiss on the cheek, then turned around.

"What the hell are you doing here? Is everything okay at the bar?" She stared at Luke in that uncanny, unblinking way she had. I could hardly wait until she actually took a long look at me. I could just imagine what was going to come out of her mouth, and none of it would be complimentary.

Luke shrugged. "Chrysandra's covering for me. I needed to talk to your sister . . . and you, if you want to listen."

He mouthed off at her now and then, and she smacked him down from time to time, but they got along a lot better than most werewolves and vampires. Luke was a damned good bartender, and my sister was a damned good boss.

"What's up?" Menolly folded her feet under her, sitting in the corner of the sofa. She stopped, sniffed the air, and looked at me. "Is that *you*? What the hell are you doing . . ." She stared, then let out a strangled laugh. "Oh my fucking gods, what happened to your hair?"

I grimaced. "About that . . . yeah. Me. Skunk. Tomato juice. Peroxide and baking soda. I've turned into a flaming orange calico, sans the black splotches, as you can see. Iris is researching whether hair dye will make it worse."

"I'm glad I don't have to breathe." Menolly laughed again.

"I can help with the smell, I believe," Luke said, leaning back in his chair. "But I ain't even gonna try to touch that mop on your head."

Blinking at him, I frowned. "Yeah, I have a bad feeling I'm stuck with it until it grows out."

Menolly stifled a snort. I flashed her a nasty look, but she shrugged. "What? It's funny—and if anybody can pull off the look, you can."

"Right, that and a dime will buy you the Brooklyn Bridge." I let out a long sigh. "What about Nerissa? Shouldn't you take care of her? She looks about ready to pass out. How much did you—she—drink, anyway?"

Menolly flashed me a toothy grin. "I think she downed a bottle of champagne on her own. Camille and her harem will be home pretty soon, by the way. They stuck around to say good night to some of the stragglers. But before she gets here, I better warn you: Tread carefully around the whole issue of our illustrious father's bailing on her wedding to Trillian. It hit her hard. I heard her talking to Iris earlier, and she was trying not to cry."

"Crap. Why couldn't he have played the good guy this time? He's never been this mean to Camille."

"Yeah, he's never turned his back on her except when she first came out about being involved with Trillian. For him to do so now after all she's done for the agency and our family, it fucking sucks. I'm so pissed at him; he can shove his attitude right up his tight—"

"You're talking about our father!" Wrong or not, I couldn't help but stand up for him. It was ingrained in my nature, even though my heart wasn't holding much in the way of his defense this time.

"I don't care if I'm talking about Zeus. He had no right to do that to her." She tossed a look at Nerissa. "She'll be okay. She's comfy. Where's Vanzir?"

"He went out to the studio," Iris said.

She nodded. "Okay, so Luke—tell me what's going down."

As Luke ran down the info about his missing sister, I stared at the window. Menolly was right. Father ignoring Camille, after all we'd been through in the past year, was worse than a slap in the face.

So who am I? Some days, I'm not sure myself, not any longer—things have shifted so much over the past year or so. I used to think life and people were relatively good, now I live in a war zone and pretty much have discarded the naïve attitude I first toted Earthside. Most of the FBHs—full-blooded humans—walking down the street don't realize it, but their lives, their world, is in danger. I'm just one of the very few warriors on the vanguard, trying to prevent disaster.

I never would have described myself as a soldier a year ago. An agent, yes, for the Otherworld Intelligence Agency, but not a soldier. But we've all become warriors, my sisters and me and our friends, and we're fighting a horde of demons intent on breaking through the portals that separate the worlds.

Shadow Wing, the leader of the Subterranean Realms, intends to make both Earth and Otherworld his private stomping ground by gathering the spirit seals—an ancient artifact that was broken into nine sections and scattered to prevent the worlds of Fae and Earth from being accessed by the monsters from the Subterranean Realms. But the seals are surfacing again, and it's a race as to who can find them first: the demon lord or us. As of right now, we're standing in the way, trying to keep the floodgates closed.

My name is Delilah D'Artigo, and I'm a werecat. But I've also discovered another side to my shifting nature. A black panther self emerges when coaxed by my master—the Autumn Lord, one of the Harvestmen. He marked me as his only living Death Maiden, and someday, I'm destined to bear his child. My panther side is feral, fierce, and I'm beginning to love rather than fear her. She's becoming a part of me in a way that I never thought possible. I'm owning my predator nature—both in housecat and big cat. I have a twin—Arial—who died at birth, and she comes, a ghost leopard by nature, to help me at times. I can feel her near; she's a guardian and watches over me. I only wish that someday, we could really sit down and talk.

My sisters—Menolly, a vampire, and Camille, a Moon Witch recently promoted to priestess—and I are half-human, half-Fae, and our heritage short-circuits our powers at all the wrong times. Let's just say we've never won any employee-of-the-month awards, and not for lack of trying.

Our mother, Maria D'Artigo, a human, fell in love with our father, who is one of the Sidhe. She followed him back to Otherworld during the tail end of World War II. They married, had an exquisite romance, and she gave birth to us. Camille first, then a couple years later me, then another couple years, Menolly. We look in our early twenties to humans. Maturity wise, we're right about there, too, though we've grown up fast the past couple of years. But we're all around sixty-some Earthside years old.

When we were fairly young, Mother died. She fell from a horse. Camille took over and tried to fill her shoes, a daunting task for any young girl. And around thirteen years ago, ES time, Menolly was transformed into a vampire. But we always were sure of our father. Until this past month, he was a rock, and we were certain of his support. Now, things are changing, the Wheel is turning, and nothing is what it seems anymore.

And we've run out of time to adjust. The cards have been dealt, and we're in a life-and-death tournament from which there's no exit.

Menolly sat back, staring at Luke. "We'll do everything we can to find her. And if her fucking jerk of a husband is after her, we'll make certain he doesn't try it again." Abusive men didn't last long around her, often becoming her dinner. She fed on the lowlifes and violent criminals of the world.

Luke gave her a thin smile. "Thanks, boss. I don't want to seem like an overprotective brother, but the fact is that Amber's never been in a big city before, and I can't help but be worried."

Menolly leaned forward, the ivory beads in her cornrows clicking. Her hair was the color of burnished copper, and she was as petite as I was tall.

"Luke, can I ask you something?"

"Sure, what?"

"Why didn't the Pack do something about her husband, if he was abusing her?" Menolly frowned, tapping her nails on the arm of the chair.

He sighed. "That was one of the reasons I left. Well, actually, I was excommunicated. I don't talk about it much. The males of the Zone Red Pack are extreme alphas—in a bad way. I couldn't take it."

"What happened?" I asked, suddenly thinking that there was a whole lot more depth to Luke than I'd assumed.

"I was in love with a girl—Marla. We wanted to get married, but the Packmaster gave her to someone who beat the crap out of her and passed her around to his buddies. I tried to sneak out, take her with me, and they caught us. There was a big fight . . . it was a bad scene. She's dead now, and I'm a pariah. I can never go back. I defied the law of the Packmaster."

Neither Menolly nor I said a word, just waited. His eyes echoed the pain in his voice, and I felt like I'd overstepped my boundaries.

He pushed himself to his feet. "I gave Delilah all the information about Amber that I could think of. Tomorrow I'll bring the skunk scent remover to the bar. Delilah, you can pick it up there."

He nodded, again tapping his hat, and I flushed, looking at him. It had been over a month since I'd had sex, and he was lean, lanky, and all male. But he didn't even blink an eye my way, and truthfully, I was relieved. I was so confused over Chase. And Zach, the werepuma I'd slept with twice and who had saved Chase's life, was taking far longer to heal up from his injuries than anybody had first thought. Last time I'd gone to visit him at the rehabilitation center where he was staying, he'd refused to see me, and we hadn't spoken in over a month, even though I'd tried calling every week.

Menolly saw Luke out while I sorted through the notes. When she came back, I looked up, and she smiled softly at me. Her eyes had once been a gorgeous blue, but the further she sank into her new life as a vampire, the grayer they became and now—now they were almost silver.

"You're horny, aren't you?" She let out a sigh. "That's the

trouble with getting involved with somebody. You begin to need them . . . and then . . ." With a glance over at Nerissa, she shrugged. "And then you can't imagine them not being in your life."

It was then I noticed a gold band on her right index finger. I pointed to it. "That's new. Just when and where did you get it?" I held her gaze, and she narrowed her eyes and gave a little huff. If she was voluntarily breathing, I knew I'd gotten under her skin. *Go, me!*

"Oh, all right. Nerissa gave it to me. It's . . . a promise ring. It symbolizes that we're off the market, at least as far as other women go. Guys—eh, they come and go, but . . . with women? We're exclusive. I bought her one to match." She gently reached over and lifted the werepuma's hand, and I saw a duplicate band. Both were engraved with Celtic knot work. I caught my breath and looked into my sister's eyes.

Menolly had come so far from the torture and rape she'd undergone before being killed and thrust into life as a vampire. She was happy now, for the most part, and she'd actually opened herself up to love—of whatever sort she could handle at this point.

I reached out and took her other hand and brought it to my cheek, and for the first time I didn't flinch at the coldness. As I pressed my lips to her fingers, I glanced up and saw bloody tears sliding down Menolly's cheeks. She silently opened her arms, and I slid inside them as she enfolded me to her chest.

"I'm sorry—I'm so sorry. I tried for so long to just accept you like Camille did without reservations, but I was afraid . . . And now . . ."

"And now you're not," she whispered.

"And now . . . I'm not," I said, realizing it was true. The fear of her death and rebirth had fallen away like a shroud, leaving only Menolly standing in front of me. My sister, unveiled in her new life, happy and radiant and no longer the monster Dredge had turned her into—the monster I still remembered when she was sent home to kill us, when Camille chased me out the window to protect me.

As she slowly released me and I sat back, Menolly grimaced. "I'm so happy. But Kitten, you have to promise to do something for me."

"What?" I asked, breathless, wondering if she wanted a better apology for my hesitance all those years.

"Do something about that mop." She pointed to my hair.

Iris meandered in, clad in a silk kimono. Her hair was tousled, loose and falling to her ankles in a golden rain of silk strands. And her cheeks were rosy, with an afterglow impossible to hide.

Milkmaids gone wild, I thought impulsively. Grinning, I waggled my finger at her. "You and Bruce been busy?"

"Hush you," she said, scolding me. "None of your business, girl. But I will tell you that I did some checking. I'm not comfortable using hair dye, at least not right now. After the peroxide, it would fry your hair and probably muck it up worse than it is."

"Well, I don't want that." I frowned, not at all happy. "Hell." I glanced over at Menolly. "You're right, I need to do *something*—I can't just leave it like this. Maybe it's time for a change." I motioned to Iris. "Get your scissors."

"What? You're kidding." She stared at me like I was crazy.

"Just do it. I want it short and edgy. If I'm going to have punk hair, I'm going all the way. And this way it will grow out my normal color, and I can just trim the ends a little bit till all the mismatched patches are gone."

Menolly giggled. "You're really going to do it, Kitten? I bet you won't go through with it."

I snorted. "Watch me. Fire up *Jerry Springer*, haul out the Cheetos; we're having a party."

Menolly obligingly brought me a bowl of the orange crispy puffs I loved so much, along with a glass of milk, and then, after cajoling Nerissa to sprawl out on the sofa where the gorgeous golden-haired Amazon promptly passed out, she folded her legs and hovered up toward the ceiling, tossing me the remote.

As I channel-surfed, Iris brought out her kit and bade me sit on the hassock in front of her. She still had to stand on a stepstool since I was so tall.

"Can you make it stylish?"

"I know what you want, girl. Just hold still."

The first cut was torture—I heard the clip of the scissors and shuddered as Iris handed me a fistful of blotched hair. But as I stared at it, it occurred to me that maybe this wasn't a bad idea at all. I would have looked hideous; the hair was frizzed from the peroxide and baking soda.

As she snipped her way across my head, razoring in some parts, I began to look forward to the difference. Hell, I *felt* different—something about losing my fear of Menolly's vampirism had opened the desire to make big changes, to sacrifice the parts of myself that made me uncertain and frightened. I was tired of being timid, of being hesitant.

"Almost done," Iris said, whisking off my neck.

My head felt so much lighter, and my neck felt oddly exposed, now that I had nothing to cover it up. "Can I see?"

"Give me a moment." She vanished for a moment, hurrying back with a tube of hair gel, a spritzer bottle, and a blow dryer. She misted my hair and rubbed a little of the gel on her hands, then began teasing it, then brought the blow dryer to bear for a few moments, after which she stood back. "Okay, take a look."

I stood up slowly and approached the mirror over the fireplace. As I stared at my reflection, I almost didn't recognize myself. I was six one, and the new haircut made me look even taller. It was so different—still a patchwork of color, but now it was cute, sassy, bitchy—even a little badass.

"I like it," I said, tilting my head this way and that. The tattoo in the middle of my forehead glimmered from beneath the bangs sweeping to the side. The black crescent-sickle marked me as belonging to the Autumn Lord. I slowly reached up and felt it. The pulsing energy never left me, and over the past few months it had begun to grow stronger. I had the feeling something was coming my way, something big and scary, but strangely, I felt comforted.

As I stared at myself in the mirror, I began to phase out—my face flashing between myself and my panther self. I steeled myself, knowing what was coming.

And then, Hi'ran was there. The Autumn Lord stood behind me. Menolly and Iris couldn't see him, but he was there for me, smiling with those pale full lips, his long dark hair cascading down his shoulders in a trail of frost and silver.

He put his hands on my shoulders, and I leaned back against him. The energy running through his fingers made me want to fall into his arms.

"I was thinking about you tonight. I sensed you needed me."

Hi'ran leaned down—he was so very, very tall, and his cloak was black, covered with a wash of fiery autumn leaves that continually fell from the wreath around his head. As his face neared mine, I stared at my reflection in his unblinking eyes, surrounded by the sparkle of stars echoed through the abyss.

I inhaled his scent. Bonfires and graveyard dust, old musty books, ink long dried and yellowed paper, the scent of mold and decay and toadstools and moss . . . it all swirled around me, an intoxicating blend that set my heart to racing.

"I'm sad," I whispered. "I'm losing my love. So much is happening, and I don't think he and I can make it through the approaching storms."

"You aren't losing your love," Hi'ran whispered, his breath a gust of chilly autumn air on my skin. "You're making room. Keep your eyes open, my sweet. Keep your mind open. Remember the curve of my lips, the scent of old leather and autumn carnivals, the frost that lingers on my breath. Listen for the song your mark sings when I'm near."

And with that, he leaned down and blew on the shining black crescent, and a vibration ran through me that played me like a harp, string by string. I let out a long gasp, wanting him, wanting to give up my breath to him, and he turned me around and slowly lowered his lips onto mine, enfolding me in his arms.

The world began to spin, a vortex of life and death and blood and bones, of leaves in a whirlwind, and all I could taste on his tongue were cognac and juniper and smoked venison stew. As I sank into the kiss, an ice-filled fire raced through me, filling every crevice, every niche, and my breasts began to tingle, igniting every point along my body.

As I pressed against him, he slid one leg between my knees, and I opened to him, but he did not reach for me, just let me rub gently against him as he sucked my life out with a single gasp and then—as I fought for breath—he pressed his lips to mine again and blew me gently back into my body and I came, moaning softly.

Spinning, the orgasm spread through me like melted butter, warm and vibrant, as smooth as glowing lava, crackling like a hearth fire. I gasped as he nuzzled my neck, his tongue playing each and every nerve in my body.

"My living bride, my living bride," he whispered, his hands carefully holding me by the waist. "I can't take you. Not yet—if I did, you'd die. But I want you. There will be a way . . . and then, one day, you'll join me in my world."

"You said you wanted me to bear your heir—how can I if you can't . . . if we can't . . ." I stared into his eyes, caught in the power of his spell.

"Oh, trust me, it *will* happen but not quite the way you expect. Until then, cry no more, my lovely panther. Cry no more." And then Hi'ran backed away, and I reached for him. It seemed so simple in his world—it was life or death. He was one of the Harvestmen, an avatar of Death, and it would be easier just to walk into his world.

He shook his head. "No, it's not your time. You have *so much* to do before I can think of claiming you to sit at my side. But I'll always be with you, always feel you, always know what you're thinking." And then, in the blink of an eye, he was gone.

"Delilah? Delilah? Are you okay?"

Menolly's voice echoed through me, bringing me back to myself. I turned, and she gasped and jumped back, her fangs lowering. Catching hold of herself, she closed her mouth.

"I'm . . ." I blushed, wondering if I'd put on a show in front of them, but Iris saw my fear and shook her head.

"Don't try to explain," Iris said, stepping in. "We can feel it on you. You've been with *him*? You were in a trance."

I nodded. "Yes." Slowly, I brought my hand to my neck where my skin still tingled from the touch of his tongue.

Menolly leaned closer to me and gave me a long look. "That was some message, by the look of your neck."

I glanced back in the mirror and saw the massive hickey spreading across where he'd kissed me. "Uh, yeah . . . I guess it was." I smiled then, blushing.

And then it all fell away, and I dropped to the floor, done in by the night, still smelling of skunk, with punked hair, and awaiting the arrival of . . . well, wherever it was the Autumn Lord was planning.

"Things are such a mess. Chase has changed so much since he took the Nectar of Life—"

"You and Camille saved his life. He would have died without it." Iris bustled around, cleaning up the scattered strands of hair.

"Well, he's not thanking me now. I think the reality of what it means is starting to hit him. And the lack of preparation—let me tell you, *that ain't helping matters any*. I feel like something's looming over me. The Autumn Lord has plans . . ." I couldn't speak Hi'ran's name aloud to anyone but him—it was a secret forged between us and kept solely for my use.

"What did Chase say?"

I shook my head. "Honestly, I blocked it out. He was so stiff, so aloof. Right now I can't deal with his angst. That makes me a bad girlfriend, right?"

"No, that makes you half-human. If you were full-Fae, he'd be long gone by now." Iris sat on the ottoman next to me. "Honey, Chase needs more help than you can give him. Let Sharah work her magic. She has the training to deal with matters like this."

"I guess he's in better hands with her. I'll back off." The thought still stung, but I couldn't waste any more energy. I was exhausted by trying to help when my help wasn't welcome.

As we sat there, a tableau illuminated by the Tiffany-style lamps that Morio had found in a thrift shop, the door opened, and Camille's laughter echoed through the hall. I slowly picked myself off the floor and moved to one of the chairs, but still, when she darted into the room, she took one look at my face as she tossed her cloak over the back of the rocking chair and sat down beside me, grabbing my hand.

"What's going on? Bad news? Was there news from home?"

That was her way of asking if our father had left a message through the Whispering Mirror. Reluctant to burst her bubble, I gave her a quick shake of the head. "No hon, no messages. Not that I know of."

She stopped short, staring at me. "What the fuck happened to your hair?" And then she burst out laughing. "I love it—you're so punk! You look great! But man, Iris was right." Waving her hand in front of her face, she grimaced. "You got skunked bad, babe."

"Yeah, but it was worse before." As I stood up, Camille's men came trooping in. At least they were polite enough to avoid commenting on my brand-new do and perfume, though I noticed Smoky's lips curl into a smile, and Morio's nose twitched. Trillian just offered to take the tray of debris from Iris and carry it into the kitchen for her.

"So . . . you going to keep it that way?" Camille walked around me, studying my hair. "I like it. Makes you seem more seasoned."

I smiled softly. "I don't know. Maybe. Everything's changing, everything's moving."

As I looked in the mirror again, my image flashed. It was as if my panther self and my tabby self were superimposed over my face, and all sides of myself began to merge, blending together as the tattoo on my forehead glistened and flared brilliant red, then back to the shimmering black. A wave of heat rushed through me, and I grabbed the nearest chair to steady myself.

"Hell . . . what was that?" My entire body felt on fire, and I dropped my head back as I started to sweat. It was almost the same confusion I felt the first time I shifted into my black panther form, but this was less transformational energy and more . . . like I was a pillar of fire.

"Crap—what the . . . what's happening?" And then everything went dark, and the last thing I felt was the floor coming up to meet me.

CHAPTER 3

Blinking, I sat up, looking around. I was standing in a forest full of wild, overgrown bushes and undergrowth. The trees were incredibly tall, rising far into the sky, towering beyond my sight. Cedar, fir, oak, alder, and birch—their trunks were thick with moss and toadstools, and lacework moss dripped from the boughs, swaying in the faint breeze that wafted past me. The deciduous trees were covered with a medley of red and orange leaves, burnished gold and yellow, and from every branch dripped the last vestiges of some autumn rainstorm.

I stood, examining myself, but I seemed to be okay. No bumps, bruises, or cuts. I glanced around, wondering if I was dreaming. I seemed to be standing on a path that led deep into the forest, and a compulsion drove me to take off jogging down it. Wherever I was, there was something ahead waiting for me.

I raced along, my speed picking up as I ran. The trees flew by in a blur, and I realized how much I was enjoying the movement. My body felt so alive, zinging with energy, full with the chase. My muscles rejoiced, stretching, moving, pumping full with the blood that flowed through the veins in my body.

The sky was somewhere between twilight and dusk here—wherever *here* was—and even in the dim light, I had no problem seeing the scattered limbs and boughs that littered the trail. As I ran, I began to notice that I wasn't out of breath. Nor was I tiring. I leapt over rocks the size of my head and hurdled a fallen trunk blocking the path before coming to where I could see the end of the trail.

The drive to run slowed, but the summons forward was no less strong. I headed toward the opening leading out of the woodland. At the edge of the tree line, I found myself staring into a dark circle—a grove of sorts, and in the center rested a circle of bronze, engraved with runes and symbols I could not read.

I approached it slowly, holding my breath, waiting to see what would happen. Magic filled this place; it surrounded me like a crackling vortex, and even though I wasn't familiar with its workings, I could sense it racing through me, along my skin like a flurry of pinpricks, making the hair on my arms stand on end.

And then, as I watched, a figure appeared on the dais. It was a man dressed in a dark suit. He was young—he couldn't be over thirty—and a lost, confused look spread across his face. I frowned. What the hell was I supposed to do now?

As I watched him, a soft voice whispered from behind me.

"Training day, darling."

I whirled to find myself facing a petite woman dressed in a long, sheer robe the color of the twilight sky. Her hair was burnished copper, the same color as Menolly's, and it curled past her shoulders in thick waves. A wreath of autumn leaves ringed her head. I caught my breath—on her forehead was the same Mark I bore, the same tattoo. Only hers flared with a brilliant flame that burned brightly in the center of the crescent. And on her arms—intricate vines and leaves inked in vivid black and orange twined their way up her skin, glimmering tattoos mirroring the black of the crescent on our foreheads.

"You . . . you're . . ."

"A Death Maiden, like you. And yet, not like you. I am dead, yes, and yet as tangible and corporeal as you are." Her gaze met mine as she swept over me like a scanner, taking me in, examining me, and—I felt—finding me wanting. I blushed and stared at my feet.

"My name is Greta, and I've been assigned to be your

trainer." She reached out, and her fingers brushed my chin. Greta could barely top five feet, but the power in her touch nearly knocked me flat.

"Tra . . . trainer?" The confidence I'd felt earlier seemed to flow away as her energy slammed into me. Like the Autumn Lord, and yet, not. She was steeped in his energy, but she didn't carry the season in her wake—instead she was . . . *the huntress*. The hunter, the hound after the fox, the tiger after the gazelle, the cat after the mouse.

"Our Master has declared it time to begin your formal training. You are the only living Death Maiden who has ever graced his stable; therefore you must be trained cautiously and with care. I am the leader of the Death Maidens and the best choice to help you adjust to your duties."

She circled the dais, staring at the man.

"I didn't realize I had to train for anything. He summons me and tells me what to do." I was so caught off guard that I didn't realize she was creeping up on me. And then she was there, standing beside me, barely as tall as my shoulder.

"No more. Your training begins in earnest with me. Tonight, you learn what it truly means to be a Death Maiden. You watch. You listen. You feel. You begin your journey toward realizing the full potential of just what you are becoming."

Before I could speak, she reached up and brushed her fingers over my mouth. "Silence. Speak not. Hush and be still."

And I was still.

Greta moved toward the dais, toward the kneeling man. She leaned over the bronze circle. A frightened glimmer filled his eyes and he backed away, but a force—one I could feel from where I stood—kept his knees locked on the dais, and he struggled, trying to free himself.

"No, no, no, my friend." Greta whispered, and her voice echoed through the glade, a trill of sex and desire and love. "Do you know who I am?"

He bit his lip. "I'm not ready. I'm not ready to go." He swallowed, and when he spoke again, the tremor had faded. "It can't be my time."

"But it is. The natural balance demands it. The Harvestmen have sent me. You are a *brave man*, you have saved many lives today, but to balance the scales, the web demands your own death." Greta's voice danced in a singsong manner, tripping over her words. "Ronald Wyndhym Niece, I come for your soul."

And then he was crying. "But I helped save them—I did everything I could, and now . . ."

As I watched, Greta stroked his face and murmured something I couldn't catch. The tears dried instantly, and he looked up at her, a grateful and beautiful light filling his face. She leaned down, kissed him gently, then harder, and he opened his arms to her. As she slid against him, he embraced her, and their kiss turned long and luxurious.

I let out a long sigh, aware that I was getting aroused watching them.

Greta stroked his back, his arms, and the jacket was suddenly gone, and then she was holding him to her, and he was bare-chested—the shirt had vanished somewhere along with the jacket. I opened my lips slightly, sensing their passion, sensing the taste of his soul in my mouth . . .

She motioned for me, and I was at her side in three strides. She clasped my hand in hers, and I could feel the sensations run through her to him, making every touch explode in a minor death. I began to lose myself in the energy, sucked as deep as his soul, and as she drew him out through his mouth, inhaling his essence into her body, breathing his soul out through the pores, I shuddered and came, quickly and without warning, and dropped to the ground, stunned.

With one last moan, he slumped in her arms, then transformed into a pillar of white mist and floated up toward the heavens.

Ron Wyndham Niece was dead.

Greta turned to me. "This is your first lesson: What it means to harvest the soul of a hero. He journeys to spend a while by the side of those who do great things with their lives and sacrifice their own in the process."

I blinked. "You killed him?"

"No, he was shot by the bullet of the armed gunman who would have killed a busload of people—except that Ron Niece was there to prevent it. He rushed the attacker, and in the scuffle, he was shot. Rather than his soul passing by unnoticed, the lords of Valhalla called for him. Since the Valkyries only gather the souls of true warriors—and not all heroes are warriors—they asked the Autumn Lord to allow one of us to harvest him before he could get away. He will sit with honor in the great halls for a time."

"Do you harvest all souls with a kiss?" I didn't know if I was going to like that. What if I had to harvest a demon and kiss him? Like Karvanak or someone equally filthy? Or some perv?

She gave me a sudden shy smile. "Heroes are given a death that removes the pain and loss they both remember and fear. Our kiss leads them into the afterlife in the most pleasant of ways. You will see that we give other souls—ones with less to be proud of in their lives—*distinctly less* enjoyable transitions. But to answer another unspoken question: yes, sometimes we do kill for the Harvestmen when they request it."

I stared at her, realizing what she was saying. We truly were the harvest women for the Autumn Lord. We could make the transition easy or—I had no doubt—deathly painful.

Shuddering to think what infractions might befit the latter, I looked back at the dais. "Do we always come here to do our work?"

Greta sat down on the edge of the bronze circle. It was no longer glowing. "No, not always. But this is the easiest way to train you. When you travel to where our chosen actually are, you must contend with seeing everyone gathered around them, even though they can't see you. It is . . . difficult . . . at first, to see the spouses sobbing or the emergency workers who so desperately want to keep our chosen bound to life."

"How do you deal with it when there's so much pain attached to the death? When you know it's going to hurt the ones left behind?" I couldn't imagine ripping the life out of someone whose wife or girlfriend or children might be watching. "How do you harden yourself enough so it doesn't hurt?"

She shook her head. "You are new to the life, and being alive gives you an added disadvantage. You have not passed through the veil; you're still vibrant with the flush of youth." With a sigh, she reached out and closed her ghostly hand around my fingers. Unlike Menolly, her touch was not cold, but warm and invigorating.

"Help me understand."

It was futile to resist; this was my fate, and one day I might be sitting here holding some young woman's hand, teaching her what it meant to work for Hi'ran. He was my destiny, I might as well accept and embrace it. Whatever amount of time remained between now and the day I joined his harem, I'd eventually end up here, beside Greta.

She squeezed my fingers. "You seem so resigned. I know what you are fighting in your world—worlds, rather. I know what you face. So much, and yet it won't matter a whit once you join us. But for now, just know that you will learn. I promise to help you. And soon, you will understand what it's like to breathe the breath out of one of the chosen."

"Tell me. I want to know. It's important for me to learn correctly. This is a sacred trust, and I don't want to make any mistakes."

The tattoos on her arms flared as she squeezed my hand. "When you breathe out their lives, you can touch their souls. You feel them and rock them and cradle them. The ones who are violent, we don't entangle—we have no need unless we want to reassure ourselves that they are truly the monsters the gods say they are. But Ronald—I felt every inch of him, I felt his love and his sorrow, his memories. His joys and his disappointments. I washed them clean for him and left him ready to leave the world. We give solace to those who have done something with their lives, who have made a difference. We give them the gift of a blessed transition."

I let her words sink in, and for just a moment—I understood. Then the feeling faded but left behind a touch of balm to soothe my worry and fear.

"When your service with the Autumn Lord ends, you will be free to go home to your ancestors, you know," she added.

This was news to me. "What do you mean? I thought we served him forever."

"Oh no, my dear. You serve a term and then—unless there's something special he wants from you—you will be released to your own journey. So take heart, there is a chance you will not be pledged to him forever in the afterlife. And truly, he is a sensual and . . . giving . . . partner."

With that, she stood and motioned to the path. "Run now. Run like the wind. I will come for you again on the next waning moon, and you shall take the helm as we continue our lessons. For now, go back to your life. Live. Enjoy."

And I was off and running. I don't remember how long I ran, but I began to feel sleepy. *It wouldn't hurt me to just lie down a little and rest,* I thought. So I shifted into black panther form, curled beneath a tree, and fell soundly asleep with only the wind to keep me company.

"Delilah? Delilah? Wake up!" Iris's voice echoed through the fog filling my brain.

"Kitten? Kitten—come on. Please wake up." Menolly's voice joined her, and I felt myself blink as she yanked me to my feet and helped me sit down in a nearby chair. "You okay? What the hell happened?"

Camille was rushing into the room with a cool cloth, which she pressed to the back of my neck. "You felt hot, like you were burning up."

I shook my head, trying to focus. "I . . . I . . ." Part of me didn't want to tell them. What had happened would take me some time to come to grips with, but with what we were facing, none of us could afford to keep secrets anymore. Just like when Camille was shoved into her priestess role and would soon be undergoing a rite to induct her into Aeval's court of Night, so, too, this could have ramifications that might affect all of us, not just me.

"I just had my first training lesson as a Death Maiden."

The men and Iris broke out talking, their words falling over one another. My sisters, on the other hand, stared at me mute, both looking terrified. I realized what they were thinking.

"No, no . . . I'm not going to die soon. But apparently I have to be trained in my duties. It's going to be one hell of a journey, I can tell you that." I blinked, realizing that it was no longer a feeling: My life was about to change, and change drastically. Hi'ran had gone easy with me until now, but no more.

As the others quieted down, I dished out what had happened. "It was incredible watching her with the man," I said, whispering. "We truly do *harvest* the dead. He was on his way out and didn't want to go; he was resisting. She made it easy for him."

"I wonder . . ." Iris crossed over to the television and turned on the news. She flipped through the stations until she came to the local cable news channel, and we watched as the story unfolded.

Trevor Willis, the local-boy-makes-good-as-anchor-star, came on, his expression suitably grave. Behind him was plastered a picture of the man in the suit whom I'd seen in the grove.

"Ronald Niece, a local man, died tonight after saving the lives of fifteen fellow bus passengers. Police say that an armed gunman—identified as Shane Wilson Thatcher—intended to gun down the entire bus, according to a note they found in his house.

"His plans were thwarted when Niece—an accountant by day, black belt karate teacher by night—noticed the gun as Thatcher aimed at the driver. Niece managed to knock Thatcher off balance long enough for the driver to stop and open the back doors.

"As people were exiting the bus, Thatcher recovered his hold on the gun long enough to shoot Niece five times. The driver hit Thatcher over the head with a lead pipe he was carrying under his seat. Unfortunately, though paramedics did everything they could, Ronald Niece died en route to the hospital. Bus passengers and the driver are calling him a hero. Niece is survived by—"

Iris flipped off the TV. "How horrible. You'd think with all the problems facing the world, people would find better ways of taking it out on each other. I've been around for a thousand years, and I still find it incredible what people—Fae or human—will do to each other." Her eyes were misty, and she wiped the back of her hand across them.

I stared at the TV. "That was him. He walks in the halls of Valhalla now. Warriors are applauding him; the gods look favorably on him. And he saved fifteen lives tonight that might otherwise be walking in the spirit realm now. I don't think that's a bad way to end your life, even if the end comes too short."

As I'd watched Greta soothe his fear, I'd realized that she—we—performed a valuable service in so many ways. No one who'd been such a hero deserved to take their last breath in fear. He deserved a passionate and lovely welcome, and the Death Maidens could offer him one.

"Delilah, what's happening to your arms?" Camille frowned, pointing.

I glanced down at my skin. There, a faint shadow started at my wrists, working its way up to encircle both forearms in the shape of a vine. *Like Greta's tattoos.* As I watched, the vines reached my elbows and stopped, the leaves springing forth from them—maple and oak. The color was muted, like plum bruises, but the images were definitely there. My arms tingled, though not uncomfortably so, as something inside whispered, *"First lesson . . ."*

"Greta—she had tattoos like this on her arm, but they were brilliant black and orange. But they were the same shape and pattern."

"I wonder if they'll get darker the longer you train with her." Menolly brushed her fingers over my arms, then shook her head. "I don't feel anything. Camille, Iris?"

Camille held her hands over my arm and closed her eyes. After a moment she shivered. "It's his energy, all right. The energy of harvest, of bonfires, and cold autumn nights. I think Menolly's right—these aren't finished yet. I guess you're being marked, like I was by the Moon Mother." She nodded toward her back. The two tattoos emblazoned on her shoulder blades glimmered beneath the sheer material. They designated her Moon Witch and priestess.

Sucking in a deep breath, I closed my eyes, weary. "So many paths to walk . . . but this is mine." The thought of being tattooed didn't frighten me, and indeed—Greta's arms had been beautiful, lovely and wild. And Hi'ran might be one of the Harvestmen, but he was brilliant and as compassionate as he could be frightening.

I straightened my shoulders, proud to be under his rule. My liege walked the paths of shadow, and now, so did I. A little bit of the weight that I'd been carrying for months fell away.

Camille and Menolly knelt by my side, Camille on my left, Menolly on my right. They took my hands, and we sat there in silence. What lay ahead we could not know; we were each facing new challenges, new trials, but we were together.

"We'll walk the journey all the way through, hand in hand,"

Camille said, giving me a slow smile. "My own descent into the realms of the Harvestmen lies through magic and worship. Yours—through duty to an Elemental Lord. And Menolly walks the journey in body. None of us is immune to the shadows, and I think we just have to get used to it. We walk in the darkness, not in the light."

I gazed at my arms, then back at them, feeling a whole lot less alone. "It's true—we have shifted. Shadow Wing saw to that. I wish we could find Stacia. The longer she's out there, the more worried I get."

The Bonecrusher had eluded us for far too long now. But every lead we traced came up empty. We knew there had to be a leak somewhere—someone feeding her information—but we couldn't figure out who was ratting us out. And Stacia was doing a good job of playing her cards close to the table.

"I'm worried that by the time she makes her move, she'll be right on top of us, and we won't have a chance to react."

"We can't do anything about it tonight. Tomorrow's another day." Menolly stood up, pulling me to my feet. "You should get some sleep for now. You've had a long day. Camille, too."

"What's on the agenda for tomorrow?" Iris led the way to the kitchen. We'd developed the habit of gathering around the kitchen table—all of us—and having tea before bedtime. It gave us a close to the day, a moment to breathe.

Camille grabbed the steno pad from the table beneath the wall phone. She hadn't changed out of her priestess robes yet, and they left nothing to the imagination under the glare of the overhead light. Rozurial was checking her out, but the moment Smoky entered the room, his eyes were right back on the tea he was helping Iris fix. Roz had become Iris's unofficial sous-chef in the kitchen and had a surprising knack for cooking.

Menolly was the only one of us still bright-eyed. She hovered up by the ceiling, her favorite place to hang out. The guys sprawled out on the various benches and chairs we'd managed to accumulate around the huge oak table.

Smoky had bought us a new one when it was apparent that the old table wasn't going to do the trick for the number of people living on our land. The new table was gigantic, and there was barely room to squeeze past it in order to get to the stove and counters. The kitchen itself was huge, but the dining area had shrunk in relation to the size of the furniture, and the guys were talking about building an addition—expanding the kitchen and dining area.

Surprisingly, all of the men were handy with a hammer, and over the past month, they had taken care of all the little odd jobs the house needed, including storm windows being installed in place of single-pane.

Camille dropped the steno pad on the table and glanced through the page. "How did everyone do today with what we'd planned out? Not much on the agenda but the wedding."

"Shouldn't we just have our tea and call it a night?" Trillian asked, flashing Camille a suggestive look. Tonight she was all his, and we all knew it. He'd made sure everyone knew it.

Trillian had also proven to be a surprise. Ever since he returned from the war, he'd still been his arrogant self but more willing to help and less combative. He was a strong proponent of Iris's nightly tea parties, and was now addicted to Earl Grey tea with lemon and honey, which he preferred drinking from a bone china cup. Definitely a side of the Svartan that nobody outside of the kitchen would ever guess.

Camille shook her head. "Have to do the agenda stuff. We've gotten to the point where we need to keep track of things. But yeah, not much on here for today. What about tomorrow?"

"I want to start checking into the disappearance of Luke's sister," I said. "I could use some help. What's going on down at the shop?"

She frowned, and a pale light passed through those gorgeous violet eyes of hers. "They're almost done with the remodeling. We can open back up in three weeks. I'm not sure how I feel about it, though. Every time I go in there, I'm going to be thinking about how Henry died."

"That will ease. And you know he'd want you to use that money he left you to expand the shop like he'd planned." Iris patted her shoulder. "Everything will be fine."

Henry had left Camille a considerable sum of money, surprising us all.

"I thought everything would be fine when I hired him to work for me. But look what happened. Now he's dead and . . ." Camille let out long sigh. "Never mind. At least I've found somebody skilled in martial arts to take over managing it for me. I miss being there every day, but with the constant threat from Shadow Wing . . ." Again, her words drifted off.

Vanzir leaned back in his chair. "You won't be sorry you hired Giselle. She knows her stuff. You wait and see—I promise."

I glanced over at him, and he gave me a quick wink. Once in a while Vanzir let down his guard, and a little bit of humanity showed through that demon heart of his. He'd found Giselle for Camille without being asked. The she-demon was part of the Demon Underground and had been living Earthside for thirty years. Carter, our main contact to the Earthside demonic forces, had also vouched for her. Giselle was anti–Shadow Wing, and she hated snakes. And anything to do with snakes. Including Stacia Bonecrusher.

"I'm holding you to that promise," Camille muttered. "My customers expect someone who understands the nature of books."

I cleared my throat. "Let's get this wrapped up." I popped a couple Oreos as Iris and Roz passed around teacups and a plate of cookies. "So, will you have time to help me tomorrow? To look for Amber, I mean?"

Camille nodded. "Yeah, but the guys are busy, I think."

Smoky leaned over her and swiped a couple of the cookies. "Morio is coming with me out to my barrow to do some autumn cleaning, and I need to check on Georgio."

"What about you?" I looked up at Trillian.

He shrugged. "Sorry. I'm taking care of some work around the house for Iris that needs to be done before winter hits."

With a sigh, I turned to Rozurial. "I suppose you're busy, too?"

The incubus shook his head. "Vanzir and I are scouting out another lead on the Bonecrusher. Probably another false alarm, but we have to make certain. We can't let anything go by that might give us a clue to her whereabouts."

"How the hell can a demon general of her stature get lost in this city, I want to know? And that's rhetorical." Camille jotted everybody's plans down on the steno pad as a noise from the living room broke the silence.

"Sounds like Nerissa's coming around," I said, and Menolly nodded, lightly touching back down to the floor. She was through the arch before I finished speaking.

"I guess that's it. Menolly will be sleeping, and Shamas

will be working, of course. Iris—what about you?" Camille
put down her pen and looked up at the house sprite.

Iris shrugged. "Typical day. Take care of Maggie, clean up
around here, and then Bruce and I will finish harvesting the
last of the herbs for the season."

"I guess that covers it," I said as the phone rang. Being
closest, I answered. "Hello?"

Chase's voice rang over the line. "Delilah, we have a problem."

"What?" Whenever Chase called late at night with a problem, it was usually a doozy.

"There's mayhem down on the docks near Exo Reed's
joint—the Halcyon Hotel & Nightclub. Big fight going down.
I need as many of you as I can get down there. ASAP." The
phone slammed down in my ear.

I turned to the others, groaning. "Nobody's going to bed.
We've got trouble at Exo Reed's. Chase needs us. Iris—you
and Bruce stay with Maggie and Nerissa. Everybody else, get
changed double time, and let's hit the road."

A glance at the clock made me wince. We were all tired,
but we had to be ready 24/7 when it came to phone calls in the
middle of the night. I just prayed that we weren't going into a
major battle against Stacia tonight. We needed to find her, yes,
but man, I just did not want to face her smelling like skunk,
worn out, and grungy.

CHAPTER 4

"Crap, and double crap." I slid into a pair of ripped jeans and an old sweater. "I'm going in there reeking, and anything with half a nose will smell me."

I shimmied the pants up over my thighs and pulled on the sweater. As I shook my head and looked in the mirror, I caught my breath. With the dark olive sweater and the black jeans, my new spiked-up multicolored hair lit up the green of my eyes like never before. For a moment, I didn't recognize myself.

"Whoa." I turned, first one way, then the other. I looked like I had balls now. Kick-ass, no-more-tears balls. And it looked good.

"Get a move on!" Menolly's voice echoed from downstairs, and I shook myself out of my reverie and grabbed Lysanthra, my dagger, and carefully slid her into my boot sheath. She and I had a wonderful relationship, and I never went into a fight without her now.

I raced down the stairs just in time to see Camille and the guys come out of their room, and surprise number two in the dress department: no skirt. Camille was in a black velvet jumpsuit with flared legs. A silver belt rode low around her waist, and granny boots completed the retro sixties vision. She looked like Catwoman or Emma Peel, only with better cleavage. The guys were wearing jeans and tops easy to fight in, and we clattered down the stairs together.

Menolly had changed out of her gown and was wearing jeans, a turtleneck, and a denim jacket. Roz had on his usual duster-cum-armory. Vanzir was rocker-chic, of course, and we headed out to the cars without a word as Iris bolted the door behind us.

We split up into three groups. Camille and her men jumped in her Lexus, Roz rode shotgun with Menolly in her Jag, and Vanzir hopped into the passenger seat of my Jeep. Following Camille, we eased out onto the road and headed for the docks and the Halcyon Hotel.

Exo Reed was a werewolf—a presiding member of the Loco Lobos Pack. He was also a stable member of both the Supe Community and the city at large. A psychedelic redneck with a penchant for business, he ran his hotel to cater to Supes of all kinds.

He had, however, instituted a stronger screening process after Dredge—my sister's horrific sire—had infiltrated the hotel, and we totally trashed a suite trying to stake him. After we'd dusted Dredge and done a number on Exo's hotel, Exo had hired a seer to ferret out troublemakers. Now his hotel was always full with Supes who wanted an extra measure of protection while staying there.

The streets of the Belles-Faire District passed by in darkness. There was still quite a bit of undeveloped land out in this area, and some of the Fae were beginning to buy it up to keep it safe. Most of those living in the suburb didn't realize it was happening, but the quiet coup was often discussed in our Supe Community meetings, where we planned out ways to smooth interactions between our people and the FBHs.

I glanced over at Vanzir, who was staring out the side window. "You okay? You seem uncommonly quiet tonight." Usually, the demon had no problem voicing his opinion on anything from music to politics.

He shrugged. "Yeah. I'm fine."

"You don't seem it."

He let out a snort. "And you would be one to talk?" Then, with a sigh of exasperation, he said, "Listen, I'm sorry for being dense at the party. I know you're going through a hard time, and for what it's worth, I think you're handling this whole mess with Johnson really well."

Blinking, I almost swerved. A compliment from slave boy? Almost unheard of. But I didn't want to make a big deal about it because he sounded genuinely concerned, and catching Vanzir in a moment free from sarcasm was like catching Santa Claus on a diet.

"Thanks," I said, slowly mulling over what else to say. "It's been hard—we've had a rocky time from the start."

"He's not your type."

I shot Vanzir a look out of the corner of my eye. "Why?"

"Even though he's taken the Nectar of Life, he's still not your type. He'll come to resent you eventually. I'm not questioning whether he loves you," he said, holding up his hand. "What I *am* questioning is the long-term viability of a relationship with someone not born into your world. I think you stepped outside the box too far. You're simply not human enough for it to work with an FBH, long-lived or not."

"Do you think Smoky will regret being with Camille? He's dragon, and they're as different from the Fae as we are from FBHs." I wanted to hear his answer.

He frowned. "Probably not. They are soul bound, and that makes a huge difference. But you know—as well as I do—that a full-blooded human cannot bind souls with those from other worlds. They can only soul-bind to themselves. You and your sisters only have the ability because of your father's bloodline."

I pressed my lips together. The same thought had eaten at me since the beginning of my affair with Chase. I loved him in so many ways, but sleeping with Zachary had unleashed a need in myself to mate with someone who understood my predator nature.

I wasn't just a woman who put on a catsuit once in awhile. I was part-Fae, part-human, part-feline, all Death Maiden. I was as much myself when I was a panther or tabby as when I walked on two legs.

As we pulled up in front of Exo Reed's hotel right then, I silently leapt out of the car. Vanzir let the matter drop, and we raced forward. Camille and her crew joined us, and Menolly and Roz fell in stride.

Camille tapped me on the arm. She looked beat. "Kitten, I'm dead meat on the hoof, and I just can't deal with keeping things straight. Take the lead tonight?"

I grinned at her. "You are anything but dead meat, but yeah, I don't mind taking charge." I pushed in front and led the way into the hotel.

Chase and a group of officers from the Faerie-Human Crime Scene Investigations unit were waiting just inside the door. I paused, waiting for him to notice us. As we stood there, loud crashing noises came from the stairwell and the floor above us. Crap, it sounded like a brigade on riot patrol.

Chase glanced over, saw us, and motioned us closer. As I stepped into the light, he blinked. "Your hair." He stopped, then he saw my tattoos as I pulled off my jacket. "Your arms . . ." He shook his head, then said, "Time enough for that later. Thank God you're finally here. We've got mayhem going on, and people are hurt."

I glanced back at Camille and Menolly, who both straightened their shoulders. We were in for a fight, so it was time to pick up the energy. Camille accepted a candy bar from Morio, who handed me one, too. We scarfed down the sugar for an extra boost of energy.

"What have we got?" Trillian asked, fingering his short sword.

Chase frowned. "For the most part goblins. They're tearing up the joint." He motioned to Exo, who was standing by his side.

"About half an hour ago, bunch of goblins came bursting into the lobby and decided to make themselves at home," Exo said. "I told security to keep an eye on them, a good thing. The brutes got drunk and tried to carry off a couple of the beta werewolves—and *not* the women."

"They tried to carry off beta males? What the . . . ?" That was odd. Goblins usually went for women, whom they could sell on the slave market back in Otherworld.

"Yeah—go figure. My bouncers put a stop to it, and the brutes started tearing up the joint. A group of them headed upstairs, and the rest are in the lounge, tossing tables, breaking anything in sight, and drinking all my booze. My security guards can't handle them. I've got one man down. I think he's dead."

"Damn," I whispered.

"It gets worse." The look on Chase's face stopped me cold. "Exo said they're led by a couple of Tregarts—the demons went upstairs."

He closed his eyes for just a second, but I saw the worry in his look. Tregarts had nearly ended his life and were ultimately responsible for us giving him the Nectar of Life. One of the demonic human look-alikes had ripped Chase to ribbons with a blood dagger, a blade specifically enchanted to keep the victim's blood from clotting. We'd almost been too late.

And then it hit me: Chase was afraid. Which meant he'd be a hindrance in battle. I tapped him on the shoulder.

"Would you coordinate the troops? And get as many people out of the hotel as you can. Take some of the less seasoned officers and start evacuating the areas you can safely reach."

"Bullshit. You're giving me make-work." Pausing, Chase cocked his head. "I guess I am a liability," he said softly. "I'll do as you ask, but Delilah, don't soft-pedal me. I may be fucked up, but never patronize me again." He flashed me a dark look.

I bit my lip, piercing the skin with one of my fangs. Shit. But there wasn't any time to argue. I swung around to the others.

"Split up. Camille, you, Morio, and Smoky come with me. We'll tackle the lounge. Trillian, you, Roz, and Vanzir follow Menolly and head upstairs." I didn't want to separate Camille and Morio—they were becoming more and more bound with their magic, and together, they made a formidable foe.

The others nodded and peeled off, following Menolly toward the stairs. I turned to the double doors leading into the refurbished lounge. Last time we'd been here, it had been a psychedelic nightmare.

"You guys ready? With all the screaming and thumping there, I doubt they've heard us."

"Ready," Camille said, and as I watched her, I could feel the swathe of energy descending around her. But it wasn't from the Black Unicorn's horn—she had so thoroughly discharged the horn when she was in Otherworld that it was taking two full dark moon cycles to recharge.

Morio put his hands on her shoulders, steadying her. He arranged his bag so that it was out of the way—he carried his skull familiar wherever he went because without it, he couldn't return to human form when he turned into a fox—and nodded. Smoky cracked his knuckles and gave me a thin smile.

"Let's go. And remember: No mercy, no compassion, because the goblins won't have any." I slid Lysanthra out of my boot sheath and glanced at them, then slammed open the door.

As we burst through the opening, I scanned the room. It was filled with shadowy figures illuminated by what remained of the dim light from broken sconces and overheads. From what I could see, we were facing a good twenty figures. Goblins. Drunk goblins. Oh goody. Sober goblins were bad enough, but hyped up on booze, they'd be feeling their oats. Goblins with an attitude: *so not attractive*.

The dining hall was a mess—overturned tables and chairs everywhere, broken glass from behind the bar, holes dotted the walls, and it smelled like someone had put out a fire in the smelliest way imaginable—the stench of urine was strong. With all the strong odors, I could barely smell the skunk.

The shouts of fighting abruptly stopped as all eyes turned to us. I held my breath, waiting for that moment, waiting for the inner urge that would propel me forward. Always before a battle, there was the deciding nudge, the prime moment when all hell broke loose. And it always came before I thought I was ready.

But this time, as I surveyed the enemy, I felt a quiet confidence. Fear, yes, but confidence. Lysanthra hummed in my hand, and I felt her shiver of anticipation. She loved a good fight, and when her edge cut into our opponents and she tasted blood, Lysanthra sang. And her song boosted my energy.

And then someone—perhaps it was a goblin, perhaps it was one of us—made a slight move, and the tableau crumbled and we were into the battle.

I raced forward, straight toward one of the biggest goblins I could see. Our policy was to start with the toughest, which generally scared the weakest ones into submission or to run away.

The brute was at least my height, but he outweighed me by

fifty pounds. A surge of adrenaline flooded my body. Goblins were butt-ugly, their leathery skin protecting them like good armor. His hair hung in makeshift dreads, and he arched one eyebrow as I moved in, a sick look of pleasure crossing his face.

Camille let out a scream—a battle cry of sorts—and joined hands with Morio. They were weaving a web of magic impossible to ignore. Smoky slipped past them, rumbling like an earthquake, and as he met one of the goblins, his nails grew into long, razor-sharp claws, and his hair lashed out like a bullwhip, striking the creature in the face with a loud *snap*. He swiped a long gash along the demon's torso and then leapt back before the creature could touch him.

My opponent engaged me, and we circled one another. I noticed an entry—he'd let his guard down by a fraction, just enough for me to dart in and thrust. I lunged at him, Lysanthra singing in my hand, and landed a stab to his lower torso. He bellowed as I pulled back, my blade bloody.

The goblin brought his hands up, clasping them together overhead. I looked for his weapon, then realized too late that he was casting a spell. Oh shit—a goblin mage, and I didn't have anything to counter magic!

I darted away as he thrust out his palms and a lick of flame shot toward me. Dodging the fire by mere inches, the heat singed me as the column of fire passed by. Now I had the upper hand. I took advantage of his position, bringing Lysanthra down across his forearms. He screamed as I slashed long gashes across both arms and, as he staggered back, I pressed on to drive Lysanthra into his chest, through a gap in his leather jerkin.

The goblin fell back, yanking me along as I held on to my dagger. I landed atop him and promptly slid the blade out of his body. His eyes were flickering—I could still see life—and grimly, I brought my blade across his throat, severing from side to side. Confident he was dead, I leapt up to gauge my position.

Camille and Morio were spreading something through the goblins—I could tell that much, though I wasn't sure just what they were doing. A web, a net of shadow seemed to be gliding over a group of five of them, dark and thick, oozing like poison. The goblins stared at my sister and her husband, petrified.

The looks on their faces shook me, and I wondered what the hell Camille and Morio were up to. But there wasn't time for more than a fleeting thought. Smoky had downed another two and was onto another.

I turned to the next and tapped my blade against my thigh. "Come on, boy, let's get it on."

He said something in Calouk, but I didn't bother trying to translate. I raced toward him full-tilt with a loud shriek. The goblin swung to meet me, his short sword parrying my attack.

Our blades whistled, singing as they cut through the air. I managed to deflect his blows each time, but he was getting the upper hand.

Just then, a noise startled me, and I turned to see a goblin who'd been hiding behind a tipped-over table careening my way, his serrated blade outstretched. I threw Lysanthra at him and dove out of the way. As he stumbled past, my blade lodged in his stomach.

I whirled and gave him a massive kick on his backside. He went plummeting to the ground, driving my dagger through him.

The smell of blood was thick and nasty as I quickly kicked him over and grabbed the hilt of my blade, yanking it out of his body. Turning, I was just in time to meet another goblin, but his blade was already whistling down. As I ducked, trying to roll out of the way, I heard the clang of metal against metal, and for a moment, found myself staring at eyes gleaming at me, out of a dark shadow. The goblin's blade had been deflected before it could reach me and, with a grunt, he fell to the ground, bleeding from the heart.

I scrambled up, startled, feeling a rush of chill wind pass by, the scent of graveyards and bonfires riding high on it. *Hi'ran?* His energy lingered around me, a comforting embrace, and yet . . . and yet . . . it was not him. I whirled toward the dark cloud, but in that moment, it dissipated.

"What the . . . who are you?" I shouted at the vanishing shadow, but it was gone, as if it had never been.

"What did you say, Kitten?" Camille's voice sliced through my thoughts.

I wiped my blade on the dead goblin's tunic, realizing the room had become silent around us. Camille, Smoky, Morio, and I were the only ones standing. The air reeked of blood and death, and a shiver ran down my back. I wavered a moment, feeling Panther rise. She wanted to hunt, to join the fight, to follow whoever it was who had killed the last goblin, but there was no one left for her to battle. I pushed the desire down, whispering to myself, soothing the big cat trapped within.

As the others joined me, I saw that Smoky, in his white and pale blue, was spotless as usual. Morio and Camille were as blood-spattered as I was.

"Aren't we all just a delightful mess?" I asked, glancing at them. "Except you, Dragon Boy. Someday you have to tell us your secret. You're family now."

He merely grinned.

Morio slid his arm around Camille's waist. "At least we took care of this mess."

Camille nodded but glanced at me. "Who were you talking to a minute ago?"

Kicking the goblin, I shrugged. "I . . . don't know." For some reason I couldn't bring myself to talk about it. "Let's go see if the others need us."

Smoky frowned. "I suggest we advise Exo Reed to dispose of the bodies. Permanently. Lately the undead seem to have had a thing for Seattle, and we don't want a bunch of goblin zombies—or worse—running around."

"Reanimation," Morio said. He glanced at Camille. "Not that we'd know anything about that."

She stifled a laugh that sounded mildly hysterical, and we headed out of the room. Exo was standing there beside Chase, who gave me a tight smile.

"All done," I said. "Exo, you'd better burn those bodies unless you want trouble. Don't chance them ending up on their feet again. Ash them."

The werewolf nodded, his face serious behind the Elton John glasses he'd taken to wearing. "I'll call my cousin. He's got space on his land for a bonfire." He glanced at the double doors. "I guess it's too much to hope that the room's in one piece."

I stared at him, feeling sorry for the hotel owner. He was

just trying to do his job. Goblin invasion had not been on the menu. But my thoughts kept running back to the strange shadow who had saved my life. Who the hell had it been, if it wasn't Hi'ran?

"Um . . . no. I'm sorry. Not a chance."

He sighed. "I didn't think so."

A noise on the stairwell announced Menolly, Roz, and Vanzir as they came trooping down the steps. They were covered with blood, and Menolly's mouth was slick with the red stuff. Looked like she'd had an after-dinner snack. Or maybe it was her dinner. It was then that I noticed she was dragging somebody behind her. One of the two Tregarts—all trussed up and nowhere to go.

"You captured one? You think they have any information worth knowing?" Camille hurried over to her.

Menolly grinned, her smile all too scary. "Who knows? But I'm going to find out."

I turned to Chase, who was gazing at me, looking . . . somewhere between lost and angry. "Looks like we're done here," I said. Then, because I couldn't stop myself, I added, "Won't you come back home with me? It's been so long . . ."

He chewed on his lip, which was looking terribly chapped. After a moment, he shrugged. "I suppose we should talk." He didn't look overjoyed.

Keeping my hurt feelings to myself, I forced a smile. *Enthusiastic much. Not.* But best to keep my mouth shut. I glanced over at the others. They were trundling the demon out to Menolly's car. I turned back to Chase. "Are you going to ride with me or—"

"I'll follow in my car," he said abruptly. "Just in case . . . you know, I get a call or need to leave or something."

"Yeah, fine." Again, I forced a smile and leaned in for a kiss, but he turned his head, and my lips slid off his cheek. I headed out to my Jeep.

Menolly took the demon down to the Wayfarer. She, Vanzir, and Rozurial told the rest of us to go straight home.

"We'll find out anything he has to say. Don't wait up." Her eyes were frosty gray, and I took one look at her set jaw and nodded.

I knew that no sounds would penetrate out of that little safe room we had hidden there, and no magic could make it in or out, no demon or anything else could teleport through the barriers. It was our end-of-the-world room, essentially. And once in there, with Menolly and Vanzir especially, the Tregart would give up his secrets.

I arrived home before Chase and rushed up to my room, where I swept all the dirty laundry into the closet, made sure my kitty box was clean so it didn't stink up the place, and stripped off the bloody clothes. I tossed them. Blood and skunk pretty much guaranteed their demise.

Hopping in the shower, I hosed myself off and then decided to sacrifice a Victoria's secret forest green chemise. It had lace around the bust, and even though I wasn't anywhere near Camille's size, I filled it out nicely.

I wandered over to the window, staring out into the blustery night. Maybe once we were alone, in bed, Chase would loosen up, lose some of the worry that had been plaguing him. Maybe he'd reach out to me. Or let me reach out to him.

Leaning back against the headboard, I pulled the blanket up to my neck. The room was chilly, but I loved it. My bedroom was normally a mess—I fully admitted to being a slob—but it had charm. I'd filled it with cat toys and Hello Kitty posters and stacks of magazines and my computer desk where I spent a lot of my time poring over the Net. I'd bought a personal TV but still preferred watching my shows downstairs where I usually could snag Menolly or Camille into joining me.

My hair felt odd, and I shook my head, again wondering at how light and angular the new cut made me feel. And what would Chase think of it, when he had time to really look at me? What would he think of my tattoos?

Strangely enough, I realized I wasn't too concerned. If he didn't like them, it wasn't the end of the world. My hair would grow back. And maybe I'd decide to keep it like this. Or maybe I'd grow it long again, like it had been when I was younger. And the tattoos were already a part of me, delineating my calling. They were here to stay and it felt like they'd always been there.

After awhile, I heard a car outside and caught my breath. I peeked out the window, and sure enough, there was Chase. He was staring up at the house, hands in pockets, standing next to his SUV. The look on his face was pensive.

After a good five minutes, he began to move toward the porch, and I backed away from the window. Iris was still up, making soup for the next day, and she'd let him in.

As I waited for the doorbell, I ran through the possible scenarios in my mind. Chase would come up, and everything would work out—the tension would melt away, and he'd take me in his arms and we'd make love.

Or maybe . . . he'd be too nervous and push me away. Or he'd find me unattractive, my hair and—oh gods, the skunk stench! I still smelled like skunk. I'd grown accustomed to it over the evening, but now, horrified, I realized that Chase was going to walk through that door, and I'd smell like rotten eggs. What the fuck to do?

And then there was a tap on my door, and it opened slightly. Chase peeked through, and I forgot everything—hair, skunk, all the tension of the past month, and rushed into his arms, crying.

CHAPTER 5

➜•➜

"Delilah—what's wrong? Why are you crying? What's . . . what's that *smell*?" Chase kissed my nose chastely, then pushed me back to stare in my eyes. We were the same height, which made it pretty nice when we needed to have heart-to-hearts. Though we hadn't been doing much of that for the past month.

I stared at him. How to start? How to say, *What the fuck has been going on with you?* without sounding accusatory? I stepped back, and he gingerly sat on the edge of the bed.

"I smell like skunk. I got skunked. That's what happened to my hair, too. Iris tried to wash me in tomato juice in cat form and the juice dyed it . . . bad. Then we tried a peroxide formula to get the scent out and it made it worse. So I told her to punk me. The cut will grow out faster, and we'll be able to trim the bad color off easier. Do you hate it?"

For the first time in a long while, he laughed. "Oh Delilah, leave it to you. No, I don't hate your hair—it's different but kind of pretty. Edgy, I'd call it." He stopped. "But what's going on with your arms?"

"I had my first lesson with another Death Maiden tonight. These are the results. They'll darken and change as I go along."

"Then I was right," he said softly.

"Right about what?"

Chase shook his head. "Never mind. Leave it for now. They're pretty. Lovely, really. You are growing more and more into your father's side of the family, aren't you?" Before I could answer, he continued, "I'm sorry about the skunk, but the smell will go away, won't it?"

"Luke—from the Wayfarer—has a deodorizer he's going to give me, and that should take care of the problem. Won't bring my hair back, but what the hell." I flashed him a slow smile. Now that I'd gotten him to laugh, maybe the tension would back off. "So, do I smell bad enough that you don't want to touch me?"

He frowned. "No . . . no . . . though I don't dare get that scent on this suit. Too expensive." He paused, then added, "Oh hell. I'm sorry, Delilah. You deserve an explanation for why I've been so aloof . . ."

My heart caught in my throat. *If he's been lying to me again . . .*

"Is Erika back?" I whispered.

He looked up at me slowly, then shook his head. "No, she's not. And I haven't been sleeping around. I wouldn't lie to you again. But we need to talk. We promised to be honest with each other."

The look in his eyes made me want to cry. Haunted, alone, nervous—I could read him like a book. But there was something else, something that I couldn't pin down. And I had a strong feeling I wasn't going to like what he had to say.

"What is it? What's going on?"

Fumbling with the hem of his jacket, he shook his head.

"You know I've been going through all this stuff, trying to sort out what's happening to my life, right? But what you—and your sisters—don't know is that the Nectar of Life opened me up. I'm feeling things, sensing things on such an intense level that I don't know how to deal with them. It's like a door opened up, and I stepped into a whole new world. Sharah says that the potion catalyzed my psychic senses and that I'm starting to evolve some sort of power. She thinks I'm going to end up a pretty strong psychic."

Whoa. I hadn't expected to hear this, and part of me was hurt that he hadn't come to me with it first, but I pushed away the feeling. At least he'd gone to *somebody* with it instead of hiding it. Crossing to his side, I sat next to him and took his hand in mine.

"I don't know what to say. Camille speculated this might happen—she's sensed something in you over the years. A glimmer of power . . . we just have no idea where you got it from. Maybe your parents or grandparents?"

He nodded. "I've wondered now and then . . . and I don't know where it comes from either. I guarantee you it wasn't my mother, and I really don't know any of our relatives—she saw to that. Can you understand that I'm just . . . there are so many things . . ."

"Shush . . . I understand. I really do. But maybe, if you'd let me help you, I could release some of that tension." I reached for his shirt and begin to unbutton it, but he caught my hands in his, pulling them away from his chest.

"Delilah, there's more. I thought it was too early to say anything, so I've been staying away, examining my feelings. I wanted to wait, wanted to see what if I was just afraid. But I guess I'd better just tell you."

Puzzled, I stopped. More? Okay, so I knew that he'd been having a difficult time with the transition, but what else was hiding behind those limpid pools of chocolate that passed for eyes?

"What's going on, Chase? Did you . . . are you . . . gay?" That was the only thing I could think of that might account for him putting distance between us.

"Gay?" He blinked. "No, sweetie. Trust me, I'm not. The thing is . . . here's the thing . . . you see . . ."

"Just spit it out." Whatever it was, knowing had to be better than facing uncertainty.

He let out a long sigh. "During the past month, I've been thinking about so many things. I need to take some time. Get to know myself now that this has happened. Now that I've got far longer than another forty or fifty years to spend with my own company. I need space and time to adjust to . . . well, my new life."

I didn't like where this was going. The expression drained off my face. "You want to break up? Are you sure there's no one else?"

He stroked my cheek, smiling sadly. "I haven't cheated on you; I haven't lied to you. There's no one else. I just honestly don't think I can cope with *any* relationship right now *and* deal with everything else, too. For now, I need space."

Boom. Godzilla hit dead center, and I toppled like Tokyo.

I forced myself to stare at the floor. If I stared at the floor, then I'd be okay. "When you say *for now . . .*"

"I mean *for now*. For however long it takes me to come to grips with this. Maybe I'll wake up tomorrow and be okay. Maybe it will take twenty years. Forty. I don't know. I'm so confused. I love you—please know that—but there's so much . . ." He trailed off, and I held up my hand.

"No. Don't say it. Don't even try to explain right now. I need to process this." I walked over to my closet, where I retrieved my favorite terrycloth robe. Not giving a damn about the scent of skunk, I slid it over the chemise, suddenly feeling shy. As I turned back to stare at Chase, the look in his eyes told me just how close he was to running scared. I could see it on his face; I could feel it in his silent plea for understanding.

"Delilah, please don't walk away from me? Don't hate me?" He fell back on the bed, staring at the ceiling, looking so forlorn that I wanted to race into his arms, to comfort him. But he didn't want me. Or maybe he did, but felt too guilty over wanting space from the emotional side of us.

"You know," I said slowly, "you have my permission to sleep with other women, if that's what you need." He had agreed to an open relationship; maybe we could still make this work.

But as he slowly sat up, I saw the flush creeping up his cheeks. "Can't you understand? I don't necessarily *want* to sleep with anybody else. It's that I can't handle thinking about anyone else's feelings until I know what my own feelings are."

Don't say it . . . don't say you want to break up. Please, let me hold on to the possibility that we'll be okay for one more day . . . but am I ready to wait for you? I love you, but am I truly in love with you? I thought so . . . but am I wrong?

He turned a bleak face to me and held out his arms. I sank into his embrace, gently kissing his eyes, his nose, his lips. He slid his arms around me and pulled me to him, parting my lips with his tongue as he kissed me deep and long and dark.

I slid my hands over his chest, and he let me unbutton his

shirt. As he slipped out of his jacket, then his pants and shirt, I drank in the sight. Chase was my first love, but it was time to grow, to move on, to explore what waited for me in the future. And truly, if I was to bear the Autumn Lord's child someday and Chase was still with me, how would he handle that? How could any man who hadn't grown up in my world?

Chase pushed my robe back, and I let it slip to the ground. The scent of skunk seemed to fade, or perhaps I was growing used to it. Chase didn't mention it, and as I stepped out of my chemise and stood there, naked in the dim light of the candle, he reached out and ran his fingertips over my body, over my breasts, over my stomach. I shivered, quickening to his touch.

His body still bore the scars of where he'd been injured— and they were fierce and still red, long gashes where the Tregarts had savaged him. I knelt by his side, kissed the markings, gently let my tears fall on them and bathe them.

I couldn't help it. I blurted out, "If we could have only given you the Nectar of Life before you were hurt. If we could have gone through the ritual. Would it have made any difference?"

Chase knelt beside me and took me in his arms again. "Delilah, I love you—I do. But so many things have happened, and I feel like everything I believed or knew has been turned upside down. I have a thousand years to think about my mistakes now. Even with the proper rituals, I think we'd still be here, together in this moment, facing the same issue."

I slid onto his lap, sitting there, feeling him press against me. He wanted me, that much I knew, but his expressions waged war on his face. I could feel it in the way he touched me.

"You've never talked about this, but when Karvanak held you captive, what happened to you, Chase? Could that have something to do with all of this?" I'd never broached the subject before, but as I gazed into his eyes, I thought it was time to tread on sacred ground.

Chase slowly said, "Karvanak tortured me, yes. He knows how to avoid leaving marks. No one would ever know if they were to examine my body. And I'll never tell anybody what fully happened. Not even you. But he couldn't break me. And you know why?"

"Why?"

"The thought that you and your sisters were so bravely

facing an evil like him—and far worse—made me strong. I kept thinking, *If they can go through this, I can.* But my need for time and space comes from more than the Nectar of Life. More than Karvanak. Even more than the fact that I can't stand the idea that you might get hurt. Or caught. Or killed. The mark you wear on your forehead . . ."

He gently reached out and ran his finger over the tattoo on my forehead, then gently traced the ones on my arms. "These mean you belong to someone else—someone who will always and forever come first. Someone I can't ever hope to compare to or to stand up to. And now that my psychic side is opening up, I can feel him there. I can feel him in your aura, and I can't compete with that. You belong to the gods, Delilah. You never belonged to me. I've only been borrowing you."

His honesty—his brutal, gentle honesty—overwhelmed me, and I burst into tears. "I don't want to let go, but I can hear it in your voice. You're leaving me."

"I'm leaving you before you have to leave me. I think it's easier this way." He kissed me then, kissed away my tears, kissed me into forgetting the pain, kissed me until I couldn't stand the tension but slid onto his lap, straddling him. We made love with desperate urgency, but even as his warm flesh filled me, even as I tried to capture and hold every single feeling, I could feel him slipping away from me.

And as I rode him, loving at first and then angry because we were ending, I channeled my sorrow and tears into the act. My heart was breaking, yet all along, I knew this would happen. Furious at the inevitability of my life, I came when he did, came with tears instead of joy, came sobbing his name, even as he clenched my waist and groaned.

After, there was nothing much to say. I stared mutely at him, wondering what to do next. Chase solved the problem for me.

"I have to get back to HQ. I've got to get some sleep. I wish I could stay but—" His words were awkward but gentle.

"Don't," I said, scuffing the floor. I wanted a shower, wanted to wash away the memory of the night. "Don't say it."

He rubbed his head, pinching the bridge of his nose. "I'm sorry. I'm so sorry. Do you hate me?"

Shaking my head, I could only shrug. "How can I hate

you? You didn't screw up this time, Johnson. You told me what you needed. You were honest. I hate what's happening, but I can't . . . I can't hate *you*. You're *Chase*."

He dressed as I wrapped a towel around myself. "Delilah— maybe things will work out in a way we don't expect. Maybe in the future . . . when I get my head together . . ." Pausing, he stopped himself. "I'm kidding myself. I'm not going to ask you to wait for me. That's just wrong, when neither one of us knows what's going to happen."

I shrugged, resigned. "I belong to the Autumn Lord. You're right; eventually, he's going to summon me and get me with his child. Until the day you can live with that, we don't stand a chance. But if you *can* live with that . . ."

He bit his lip, then let out a long sigh. "I can't. I know myself. I'm sorry, but I can't. I'd always feel second-best."

Ducking my head, I nodded. "Yeah, and true or not—and it's not—that's not fair to you. Then I guess it's over."

With a sniffle, he quietly said, "Usually the woman says this, but . . . can we still be friends? And Delilah . . . when you find someone else . . . I'll be happy for you."

His voice was so plaintive, and the look on his face so hopeful, that I broke into a tearful smile. "Just try to stop me from being your friend. Johnson, I love you, and in their own ways, Camille and Menolly do, too. You're part of the family, really. Of course we're friends. And maybe . . . maybe now without the strain of being lovers, we can be closer than ever."

And then a feeling resounded through me, straight from my heart to my lips. "Chase, will you become my blood brother? I want to know we'll always be there for one another. It won't bind you to a relationship with me as a lover, just as a friend, and you'll know I'll always be there for you."

Chase ducked his head, blushing. "You mean it? You're not just trying to make me feel better?"

I nodded. I meant it, all right, with every fiber of my being. "I'd never make that kind of a pledge out of pity or guilt."

Hunting around, I found my dagger and washed her off carefully. Then, motioning for him to sit on the bed, I held up my hand and sliced a clean, short cut on the palm. Chase held out his hand, and I did the same, then, tossing the dagger on the bed, I clasped his palm, our cuts pressed together.

"Johnson, I pledge to you my loyalty, my friendship, and my love. I'll always have your back, as long as it doesn't interfere with my other oaths."

He shivered. "Delilah, you'll be my sister, my blood-bound friend, and I'll always be here for you. I offer you my loyalty, friendship . . . and my love."

As our palms touched, a tear rolled down his cheek, and I gently leaned in and kissed it away. The salt tickled my tongue.

"I guess I'd better head out." He glanced at his watch. "It's going on two, and I have to be up at seven."

"Did you want to sleep here? You'd get at least an extra hour of sleep that way." I didn't want to see him go. It was over, yes, but I didn't want to see him turn and walk out the door.

He paused. "Would that be weird?"

"No, no. Stay and sleep over. One last night." I glanced at my bed. "Since I still reek of skunk, you can have the bed, and I'll sleep in one of the cat beds. Much easier to replace than a mattress."

Once again, he loosened his shirt and slid out of his pants. "Thanks, Delilah. Just . . . thank you."

I slipped into the bathroom and out of my nightgown and took another quick shower, then dried off and transformed into Tabby. As I padded back into the bedroom, I saw that Chase was in bed, already asleep. He was breathing softly, and he'd put the cat bed on my side of the mattress. I let out a soft mew, my heart breaking again. Leaping up on the bed, I climbed into the cushioned nest, circled three times, and slept.

When I awoke, he was already gone. I shifted back into two-legged form and saw that he'd left a note for me. It was a simple, "See you later . . . Sis . . ." but it hit me in the gut, and I slid to the floor, weeping softly.

A moment later, the door opened after a light tap, and Camille peeked in. "Delilah, you need to get up . . . Delilah? Honey? What's wrong?" She raced over to kneel by my side. "Are you okay? Is it about your hair? Were you hurt in the fight? Are you in pain?"

"No—no . . . none of that." I let her cuddle me and then

leaned away, not wanting to smell up her pretty dress. "Last night Chase came back. We talked. It's over. We broke up."

"What? How did this happen?" A shocked look on her face, she bundled me up and into my robe and led me downstairs. "You need some food. Come on, you can tell me over breakfast. The guys are out right now, so it's just you and me and Iris."

The kitchen was thick with the scent of pancakes and syrup and eggs and bacon. Camille handed me a plate and took one for herself, and we loaded the food on as Iris finished making coffee.

"You look like death warmed over, girl," she said.

"I feel like it. Sit with us—I want to tell you both something." When they were sitting at the table, and we were eating breakfast, I told them about my night with Chase. Everything.

A shaft of sunlight peeked through the clouds then, splashing through the window to fall across the table, and the late autumn light bathed the room in a golden glow. I closed my eyes for a moment, enjoying the sudden quietude the light brought to the room. But all too quickly, it vanished as the clouds moved in again.

"Wow. So . . . just . . . wow." Camille put down her fork and stared at me. "The Nectar of Life hit him hard. I feel sorry for the man."

Iris smiled softly. "It makes sense, my dear. Think if you were expecting another thirty or forty years of life, and then you're mortally wounded. And the only thing that saves your life—that can possibly save you—suddenly throws you into staring at a thousand or more years stretching out in front of you now. Such a thing is bound to mess with the mind, especially when he wasn't properly prepared for it."

I hung my head. "Why do I feel like a failure, then?"

Camille grabbed my hand. "No—don't say that. Not every relationship is going to work. And you . . . Delilah, you're incredible. Chase just needs time to figure out his new life now."

I stared at her. It all made sense, but that didn't make it any easier to hear.

"Yeah, I guess you're right," I said. "And I guess I just make it harder on him, with all the issues facing us."

"I think Chase needs to simplify his life right now. Let's face it: You can never be the *little woman* who waits at home for him at night with dinner and his slippers. You're not just eye candy; you're not here to stroke his ego," Iris said. "And right now, even *that* is probably even more than he can handle."

"Thank you . . ." After a moment, I added, "I'll be okay. It hurts, but when I think about it like this, it makes so much sense." I looked up, my gut twisted in knots. "I guess my dance card's wide open again."

Just then the door opened, and Vanzir and Rozurial came traipsing into the kitchen. They looked weary, but their eyes widened when they saw the spread on the table.

"Wash your hands," Iris said automatically.

After obliging her, Rozurial set two plates on the table, while Vanzir got the silverware from the drawer. They scooted in beside us.

"Were you by chance up when Menolly came home?" Roz asked.

Camille shook her head. "No, I don't think any of us were. What happened with the Tregart you took down to the Wayfarer?"

Vanzir shook his head. "You don't want to know. We had quite a fight on our hands, but we might have managed to obtain some useful information."

"Such as?" I handed them the platter with the scrambled eggs and bacon.

Roz speared four sausages and scooped some of the eggs onto his dish and offered the rest to Vanzir. There were plenty of pancakes left, and when their plates were full, they leaned back, eying the three of us.

"Stacia Bonecrusher is so deep in hiding, I don't know how we're going to find her. But there are apparently rumors going around that she's running a training camp for recruits. And you can bet that Trytian's recruits are there, too." Vanzir bit into the pancake, which he ate without syrup, and chewed thoughtfully.

"Where's it supposed to be located?" A long shot, but I had to ask.

Swallowing a mouthful of eggs, Roz shook his head. "Are you kidding? She's not stupid. I have no idea, and neither did the Tregart we captured last night. He wasn't part of the Bone-crusher's army . . . he managed to cross through the Demon Gate when Stacia entered Earthside. He and his buddy went

AWOL from the Subterranean Realms. I suppose we should start searching for the camp."

"But is that a good idea?" I asked.

Camille pushed her empty plate to the side and leaned her elbows on the table. "Um, how is it *not* a good idea, Kitten?"

I frowned. "The thing is—we waste time on chasing her training camp right now, we lose time on finding the sixth spirit seal. You know as well as I do that Stacia's cloaked. Not to mention, say we find this camp? We're going to need more help before we can take on a camp full of demons. She's out to annihilate Shadow Wing, so right now she's focused and centered and not paying attention to us. Shouldn't we quietly go about finding the sixth spirit seal? She may be looking for the seals, too, but I guarantee you, her attention is centered on building up her army against her boss."

Camille frowned but nodded. Roz and Vanzir looked at each other like I'd just grown another head.

"Don't be so surprised. I do have a brain, you know."

Roz laughed, then leaned back. "Good observation, Miss Kitty. And might I say, you don't reek quite as bad this morning."

"Stick to the point, bud. Stick to the point." I wrinkled my nose. "I'll be getting the deodorizer from Luke today. But seriously, what do you guys think about tracking down the spirit seal first?"

Camille sucked on her lip. "That's a tempting idea. Only then we have to turn it over to Queen Asteria, and with her new idea to use them with the Keraastar Knights, I'm afraid of what's going to happen."

"What do you think she's doing with the seals?" I asked. Camille was the only one who Queen Asteria had told about it, and I still wasn't clear on the plan.

"She's up to something. Like I mentioned before, she's gathered Venus the Moon Child, Tam Lin, and Benjamin to her to form the basis of what she's calling the Keraastar Knights. From what I can tell, she's giving them back the seals and means to create some magical warrior force to fight against Shadow Wing. I'm not sure what prompted her to do this, but whatever it was, it had to be big. I'm almost afraid to find out."

"That's right." I almost wished I hadn't asked. The idea was insane, but you don't tell an Elfin Queen she's nuts.

"She shook her head. "The whole thing scares me, actually. But back to the matter at hand. Vanzir and Roz, can you spend the day researching any potential place where we should begin looking for the next spirit seal?"

She paused, then looked at the Demon Twins. "By the way, what happened to the Tregart we captured?"

Vanzir looked her straight in the eye. "He's dead."

She nodded. I said nothing. There was nothing more to say about that particular matter. We all knew there was no other choice.

I pushed back my chair. "Sounds good. Okay, Roz, Vanzir, take a hike after you eat. Be careful; don't let anybody know what you're looking for. Camille, let's get dressed and head down to the bar and get me de-stinkafied. While we're there, remember to ask if Luke has a picture of Amber's husband Rice. Then we'll hit the hotel and find out what we can about her."

Camille and the others stood. As we waved to Iris and headed out of the kitchen, I could feel life shifting and turning. Off one roller coaster and onto another.

CHAPTER 6

≈≈≈

Luke was at the bar early, mainly because we'd called and asked him to meet us there. He handed me a spray bottle with a homemade label on it.

"Go into Menolly's office, strip, and spray yourself with it from head to toe, including your hair. The smell should dissipate for the most part." He waved me off, and I headed for Menolly's office.

I pulled off my clothes and squirted myself silly with the stuff. Immediately, I noticed a difference for the better as the skunk smell faded. After a moment, I decided to spray down my clothes, too. Wonder of wonders, it worked, and a whole lot faster than I thought. I might still have a cool punk do, but at least I didn't reek. I slipped back into my clothes, then stopped. On Menolly's desk was a cream-colored envelope with a large crimson dagger printed on it and Menolly's name written in large, sloping letters across the front.

Peeking out the door, I made sure Camille was busy with Luke, then slipped into Menolly's chair and gingerly picked up the letter. It had already been opened, so all I had to do was slide the pages out and look at what it said. My conscience tweaked a little, but I figured hell, she'd do the same if she was worried about me. And the dagger on the front of that envelope worried me.

A note card slid out—the fancy ones invitations were sent on—and I held it by the edges and flipped it open. The card simply read:

To Ms. Menolly D'Artigo,

I summon the pleasure of your company, to be spent as my companion for the Winter Solstice Vampire Ball, to be held at the Clockwork Club on the evening of December 17th. My limousine will arrive for you at precisely eleven P.M., at your home, to bring you to the club. No RSVP necessary—I trust you will comply.

Roman

What the fuck? Who was Roman? The name seemed familiar, but I couldn't place it, although I knew I'd heard it before. I slipped the note back in the envelope and replaced it on her desk. That she hadn't told us about this made me wonder all the more.

"Delilah?" Luke's voice echoed through the door. "You okay?"

Hastily, I zipped up my pants and tucked in my sweater and, grabbing the spray bottle, I opened the door.

"Yah, just did my clothes, too. Even if it fades them, it's got to be better than the smell they were accumulating. You should market this stuff—it's a miracle. Hey, did Camille ask you about a picture of Amber's husband?"

He walked me to the front, frowning. "No, should she have?"

"Should she have what?" Camille asked. "And who's she?"

"The picture—remember? We need a picture of Amber's husband, if possible. I thought you asked Luke for one on the phone this morning when you called him."

"Damn it, I forgot—"

Luke stopped her. "That's okay. I happen to have a picture of the two of them together in my wallet. You can have it." He pulled out his wallet and fished out the picture. "Here you go—that's Rice, her husband. Fucking scumbag."

"So you said," I murmured, taking the picture. "Okay,

we're heading over to the hotel now." Stopping as we headed for the door, I turned back to the werewolf. "Luke, have there been any ... strange ... vampires around the bar lately? Or other denizens that seem ... out of place. Wealthy, maybe?"

He frowned, leaning on the bar, his biceps bulging through the shirt. Oh yeah, the man had muscles. "You know, someone came in the other night who I thought might be vampire, but I wasn't sure. He delivered a note for your sister. That who you talking about?"

I shrugged, not wanting him to think it over so much that he mentioned my curiosity to Menolly. "Nah, probably not. But thanks just the same."

Camille tugged on my arm, but I shook my head and led the way out of the bar. When we were outside, I pulled my jacket tighter against the gusting wind and led the way to my Jeep. We jumped in, and after fastening seat belts, Camille turned to me.

"So what was that all about?"

"Just this—I found a note on Menolly's desk. It was an invitation ... no—make that a demand—that she go to a vampire ball at the Clockwork Club with someone named Roman. Fancy paper, parchment, sloping calligraphy. If it was delivered by a man in a limousine, then he's probably rich."

She turned over the thought in her mind—I could almost see the wheels grinding away. Then she snapped her fingers. "Roman! I remember her mentioning him. He's some ancient vampire that she went to see when we were investigating Sabele's disappearance. I think she said he's even older than Dredge was. Which means ... he's very powerful. What the fuck does he want with Menolly? I mean, I love her, but he's like ... what ... a rock star among vampires?"

"I don't know, but I have a very odd feeling about it, and I want to know what the hell's going on. We can't afford to keep secrets anymore." I turned the ignition and pulled out of the parking spot as the rain hit again, and speeding along the glistening city streets, we were off for the hotel.

Amber had checked in at the Jefferson Inn, a moderately priced hotel with a standard diner attached. Families on

vacation stayed here, people dumped unwanted relatives here
during holiday visits, and salesmen who weren't making
enough to afford the Hyatt scored rooms at the inn.

Luke had told us that Amber was paid up for several
days, so we wandered over to the registration desk. Camille
unmasked her glamour, and we leaned across the counter.

"Yes, may I help you?" The clerk turned around and blinked.
Twice. His harried expression dropped away as Camille let out
a brilliant smile.

"We need some information, and you're just the man who
can help us." She winked, and he blushed. Yep, bottle her sex
appeal, and we could rule the world. That, together with Luke's
deodorizer, were two of the best inventions since sliced bread.

"What do you want to know?" He leaned over the counter
to meet her gaze, and his eyes grew big and dark and wide
as he breathed in the pheromones coming off of my sister.
He inhaled deeply and held his breath, closing his eyes for a
moment.

"We need information on Amber Johansen, who checked
into the hotel yesterday. Do you know who we're talking
about? She's seven months pregnant."

I held out the picture of Amber and her husband. "And have
you seen the man who's with her in this picture?"

The clerk stared at the photographs for a moment, then
slowly nodded. "That's her—I recognize her. I don't know if
he's been around."

"Can you give us a passkey and her room number? We
need to check on Amber and make certain she's okay. And of
course, we know you'll keep this our little secret." Camille
smiled again and licked her lips.

The clerk just about fell over himself coding another key
card for the room. He handed it over and let out a long sigh.

"Room 422. Just bring it back when you're done, please."
He cocked his head and looked expectantly at Camille. She
languorously kissed her fingertips and blew the kiss to him.
He let out a happy shudder, and I quickly looked away. Some
men were so easy . . .

We headed for the elevator before anybody saw us. When
we stepped out onto the fourth floor, room 422 was right
around the corner. I listened at the door. No sound. After a

moment, I stood back and nodded. Camille moved in, slid the card in the lock, and it clicked. As she opened the door, she pulled to the side, and I pushed through first, slamming my hand against the light switch.

Light flooded the room, but it was empty. Camille peeked in the bathroom, then relaxed and shut the door.

"Nobody here."

"Maybe not now, but someone was." I opened the dresser and checked the drawers. Scattered tops, a couple pregnancy skirts, some underwear . . . Amber had been here, all right. "Check the closet. Suitcase?"

Camille pushed open the flimsy folding door that covered the closet. "Suitcase, check, and two pairs of shoes. Also, one coat."

I frowned. It was far too chilly for someone from Arizona to wander around Seattle without her coat in late October. Especially if she was pregnant. "Do you see her purse anywhere?"

"Here it is, behind the bed, near the wall. How odd," Camille said. "No woman tosses her purse on the floor behind her bed."

She handed it to me, and I sorted through it. "Her ID is here, her driver's license, medication—she's on something . . . probably for her pregnancy. Let me see . . . wallet is empty, but credit cards are still there." I looked over at her where she sat on the bed and added, "This doesn't look good."

She paused, then cocked her head. "I get a really strange energy from this room, Kitten. All tingly with magic—but I can't identify it."

I couldn't pick up energy the way my sister could, but I had the same feeling, and it stemmed purely from my gut. "Where's it coming from?"

Camille closed her eyes and held out her hands. "The . . . minibar? How odd." As she knelt to open the door to the miniature refrigerator, a loud pop sounded, and a cloud of *something* wafted through the room.

"What the fuck?" Camille jumped back, choking so hard I thought she was going to cough her lungs out. "I . . . dizzy . . ." She reached for the dresser to steady herself and then crumpled to the ground.

"Camille!" I hurried over to her side, but the minute I got

near, my eyes began to water, and I couldn't focus on what I was about to do. *Magic*. It had to be some sort of magic from whatever had come blowing out of that minibar.

I stumbled away and leaned on the bed, breathing deeply, shaking my head. After a moment, the fog began to dissipate, and I opened the window, trying to get it to disperse, then grabbed my cell phone.

Glancing over at Camille, who was still stretched out on the floor, comatose, I quickly punched in the number for the FH-CSI, then the extension for Sharah. She was on the line almost immediately—must be a slow day—and I told her what had happened and gave the address.

"Please keep breathing, please . . ." I could see the gentle rise and fall of my sister's breast, reassuring me that at least she was alive. Whatever hit her seemed to be clearing out on the currents of fresh, cold air, but I didn't dare chance getting near her again, of both of us hitting the deck.

Ten minutes later, a discreet knock on the door sounded. It was Sharah. She must have busted ass to get there.

"It's Camille," I said, pointing to her prone figure. "She opened the minibar, something went poof, and she went down. When I went in to get her, she was out like a light, and I started to get so disoriented I couldn't stay near her."

Sharah nodded and put on a simple gas mask, then crept over to Camille and pulled her out of the area, dragging her to the bed, where I helped lift her onto the sheets. Sharah checked her over quickly.

"She seems okay. If she doesn't wake up by the time I'm done here, we'll take her back to the hospital." She headed over to the minibar. Gingerly, she peeked inside. "Magical trap, all right, timed to go off when the door opened." She touched it gingerly with gloved hands. "Hard to tell what this is for. I think we'd better take Camille and go back to head-quarters while I dissect this."

While she finished detaching the trap from where it had been connected to the cabinet, I scoured the rest of the room but found nothing. While waiting for her to finish, I ran down what we were doing here.

"I'm wondering—werewolves don't deal with magic much, so what the hell was Rice doing with a magical trap?"

Sharah nodded slowly. "You're right. Lycanthropes, above all Weres, detest magic and don't like being around it. If he's like a typical werewolf, her husband wouldn't use a magical trap unless he was forced. We'd better get this back to HQ and analyze it. And Camille seems no closer to coming around. That concerns me." She flipped open her cell phone and quietly spoke into it for a moment. "Shamas will be here in a moment with a stretcher."

For the first time since she'd passed out, I began to really worry. "You think she'll come around, don't you?"

"I'm sure she'll be okay. We just have to find out what this crap is."

"Hell." I sank on the bed next to Camille and clasped one of her hands. She was cold—not death-cold, but cold. Silently, I gathered a blanket and spread it over her. After a moment, I looked up to find Sharah watching me.

"Chase told me you guys broke up last night. Are you okay?" She blushed. "I don't mean to pry, but he was so quiet this morning that I was worried."

Stung by the fact that she was the one getting to watch over him, I let out a short huff. "Yeah, I'm just dandy. I guess this is one of the perks of being a soldier on the front line. Life changes in an instant. And even when you save the day, you sometimes lose the battle. Save his life and lose him . . . don't save his life and lose him. Either way, *I lose*."

Sharah winced. "I'm sorry. I'm so sorry. He loves you, I know he does, but remember: His entire life has been thrown into a tailspin, and being mortal—"

"Not so mortal now, as he reminded me last night. Listen, I appreciate the pep talk, but right now it's the last thing I need. I accept that he can't handle a relationship, but I expect him to realize that he's not the only one affected by this. We saved his life. He was going to go through the transformation anyway. Suddenly, he can't wait to get away from me."

She laid a gentle hand on my shoulder. "The last I'll say on the matter: It's not just you he can't wait to get away from. He's trying to get away from his own thoughts. Just remember when you were a child and felt like you didn't belong—"

I jumped up. "You leave my childhood out of this." Sharah might be Queen Asteria's niece, but that didn't give her the right to intrude on my sorrow. At her bewildered look, I stopped, aware of my misplaced anger. I wasn't mad at her. I was angry at the situation. "I'm so sorry, Sharah. I'm just a wreck right now. Where the fuck is Shamas?"

Blinking, she cleared her throat. "He'll be here in a moment. Um . . . can I ask what happened to your hair? I like it."

She meant it; that much I could tell. And she was trying to calm me down, which rankled, but I decided to take the high road: something I didn't always do. I forced a smile to my lips. "Thanks, it was a gift from a skunk. Indirectly."

"Well, it's shocking, but I think it suits you."

Just then Shamas knocked on the door. The clerk was behind him, and I took him to the side and reassured him that everything would be fine while Sharah and Shamas loaded Camille onto the stretcher. By the time we were ready to rumble, the clerk had offered me a free night, if I came in later. I had the feeling he was hoping to be included in that stay, so I politely declined.

We headed to the parking lot, where we lifted the stretcher into the medic unit. As I stared at the closing doors, it hit me that Camille might really be in trouble. A bubble of tears caught in my throat, and I swung into my Jeep and started the engine. If this was how the Samhain season was starting, I wasn't sure I wanted to see any more of it.

At the FH-CSI, of course I ran into Chase first thing. It couldn't happen any other way, with my luck. He stood beside me as Sharah wheeled Camille into one of the examining rooms and put his arm around my shoulders. I wanted to lean into his embrace so badly it hurt, but I kept myself upright. No more relying on him, blood brother or not. It was time I stood on my own two feet.

"She'll be okay. Trust me," he whispered.

"Yeah. Well, I don't know what you're offering for a guarantee, but I sure as hell hope you're right." I told him what happened.

"So Amber's been missing—"

"About twenty-four hours or so now. Luke is frantic, and things aren't looking good." I crossed my arms and stared at the doors that were closed on my sister. "If there was one magical trap, there were probably others that we didn't find. One could have knocked out Amber like it did Camille."

Chase jotted down a few notes. "While it's not SOP to process a missing person report on a Supe for forty-eight hours, I'll have Shamas get on this today."

Tired and heart sore, I flashed him a soft smile. "Thanks. That's the best news I've had in ages." I sucked in a deep breath and stared at the door to Camille's room, waiting for some news—any news.

"Come on, I'll buy you a glass of milk." Chase motioned toward the lunchroom.

I pressed my lips together and shook my head. "I want to wait here—"

"It could be awhile. Come on. Remember—we're . . . buddies?"

That stung. It stung hard and deep, even though I knew he didn't mean it to. He was trying, in his own clumsy way, to comfort me. We headed toward the lunchroom, where he plugged a dollar in the vending machine and handed me a carton of milk. Another dollar, and he handed me a package of Cheetos.

We sat at one of the tables. The room was comfortable; Chase made sure his employees felt at home, that was for sure. A cot in the corner offered a place for a quick nap in case one of the officers was required to stick around on call.

Chase opened the refrigerator and pulled out a sack lunch. I watched as he emptied it on the table in front of him. Bologna sandwich, pudding cup, an apple . . . He bit into the sandwich while I munched on the Cheetos. He'd been right—my stomach rumbled, and I realized I was starving.

"You think she'll be okay?" I finally managed to ask.

"You know Sharah can work wonders. Camille will be fine. I know it," he said, but he didn't sound so sure. He pulled out his notebook. "Let me make certain I have all the details right before I send Shamas out hunting for . . . Amber, is it? Amber Johanson?"

I nodded and ran through the events again. After I finished, Chase stared at the page, then nodded. "Let me get this over to his desk right now—and let me get a photocopy of that picture. I'll be back in a moment." As he stood up, Sharah entered the room.

"Delilah, you can come with me now. Camille's going to be okay, though she's still a little out of it."

Chase touched me lightly on the arm. "I'll meet you in there."

Sharah led me back to the medical unit and through the doors leading to the ER. Along the way, she shook her head. "She's awake, but the spell wreaked havoc with her magical senses. She should be okay, but that was one heck of a jolt she got."

"What the hell was it? Do you know yet? Even getting near the residue made me dizzy."

Camille was sitting, propped up in a bed, and Sharah was right; she looked out of it. She was breathing rapidly and shivering even under the blanket, and her eyes were darker and narrowed, like those of a frightened cat's.

Chase came through the doors and handed me back the photo. He took one look at Camille and said, "Crap," as he pushed past us and strode over to her. "I've seen you take some nasty bumps, but I've never seen you look like this."

Sharah slid onto a stool and flipped open the chart. "That's because she was so disoriented, she couldn't even open her eyes until a few minutes ago. Once we figured out what was wrong, we gave her a drug to counter the effects of the magic. Apparently she was conscious the entire time. Camille—try to say something now."

"I . . . I . . . wh-wh-what the fuck happ—. . . happened?" Her teeth were chattering, as if she was freezing.

"What did happen? I know whatever it was almost knocked me for a loop when I started over to see if she was okay." I frowned, hoping that whatever it was wouldn't have any long-term effects.

"One of our techs figured out the trap. Think ecstasy or roofies, only magical. Geared toward *werewolves* in specific. Though any Were will react to it," Sharah added, looking at me. "Which is why you felt so disoriented even near the remains."

I mulled this over. "If I was a werewolf . . ."

She nodded slowly. "If you were a werewolf, you would

have been done in by a mere whiff. Camille reacted the way she did because, although she's not a Were, she's a witch, and her magic is incompatible with the effects of this magic. But a werewolf like your friend Amber . . . she'd be immediately pliable and under control if she caught a whiff or two of this crap."

"Well, hell." I frowned. "Who created this spell? Could a werewolf have done it? Or, I guess the question is, *would* a werewolf have done it?"

Sharah's lips tightened. She motioned to Chase to shut the door. After he'd done so, she flipped through her notes. "A werewolf would have to be a sociopath to do something like this. Seriously. The ingredients that make up that spell compound—the gas that burst out—contain some heavy-duty dark magic. And not like Camille's death magic, not dark in that way. We're talking sorcery here."

"Oh, my gods. What are you trying to say?" I had a feeling in the pit of my stomach I wasn't going to want to hear what she had to say.

"I'm saying that the person who created this is a sadist. Has to be. I had Mallen analyze it, and he was just as shocked as I was to see the results."

"What's it contain?" Camille managed to push herself to a full sitting position. She looked like she was starting to snap out of it.

Sharah's face was drawn, and she paled even further. "This is bad, guys. The herbs—not so much, but the other ingredients needed to give it a punch are pretty gruesome. Valerian, marijuana, chamomile, and grain alcohol . . . all standard for a controlling gas—and a couple of them dangerous enough on their own. But then we found desiccated scent gland extract from a male alpha lycanthrope added to the mix. *And* powdered pituitary gland—also from an alpha werewolf. Male, because of the amount and the trace smell. Mallen said he's seen this sort of thing before. I'm going to bring him in and have him explain it to you."

She disappeared out the door, and I looked over at Chase, who shook his head. "I don't know what it means, either," he said.

Pale and shaky, Camille forced herself to sit up and slide

her feet over the edge of the bed, clinging to the side rails. "I know what it takes to make that crap. I've heard of it, though it's not allowed in most covens or coteries."

"Wouldn't we have heard about it being used around Seattle?" I asked.

"I'm not so sure. But—"

Sharah entered the room again, followed by Mallen. She nodded for him to go ahead. "Go for it."

Mallen gave us a brief smile, then launched into an explanation. "What we're dealing with here is known by several terms. Wolf Briar, for one, and on the streets it goes by the nickname 'hair of the wolf.' As Sharah said, it's a combination of herbs and desiccated adrenal glands and the powdered pituitary glands of an alpha werewolf."

"They'd have to be killed, wouldn't they, to extract those glands?" I was beginning to understand the underlying issue.

"Oh yes, but there's more. Not only are they killed and dissected to retrieve the glands, but they're enraged before death to heighten the flow of adrenaline and testosterone." Mallen, an elf, was probably far older than we were, but he barely looked old enough to shave. When he spoke, his presence was quietly commanding.

Chase looked confused. "What does that mean?"

"It means that most of these cases involve imprisoning male werewolves, goading them into fight-or-flight stances, and then murdering them. Most likely involves torture, as well." Mallen had a look of faint distaste on his face. Elves were good at keeping their emotions close. That look alone told me he was upset.

Camille let out a little snarl. "Fucking pervs. But how can they possibly be capturing enough alpha males? Wouldn't somebody notice?"

A question we'd all been thinking, by the nods Sharah and Chase gave her. But Mallen shook his head.

"Here's where it gets even worse. Some sorcerers—and usually sorcerers are the ones who conjure this evil mess—have devised ways to force a beta male into temporary alpha status. Nobody notices the lone werewolf who vanishes, or the raggle-taggle whipping boy of the Pack who suddenly disappears. Happens all the time—low wolf on the ladder strikes out to make a life on his own rather than get shoved around. Most of the lycanthrope Packs are hierarchal to a bureaucratic degree. And most are highly patriarchal. You catch one of these betas, feed him enough steroids, and boom, you have a forced alpha male."

I sucked on my bottom lip, thinking. "How long does the Wolf Briar last? Does it travel well?"

Mallen shook his head. "No, this is one of the brews that you have to use right away, in order to preserve the energy of the glands."

"So, for example, someone couldn't bring it all the way from Arizona and be sure it will still work?" If Rice had stooped to using Wolf Briar, knowing what its ingredients were, then he'd most likely have brought it with him.

"No. My guess? Locally made in the past few days. There's probably a dead werewolf body hanging around somewhere. If you can find the corpse, you'll find he's been dissected."

Camille winced. "People are extremely good at getting rid of bodies when it suits their needs, and we can be sure that this won't be the first time the sorcerer in question has stooped to making it. These potions are tricky and take many years to learn how to craft. We're going to be looking for someone skilled. A necromancer wouldn't bother with this crap. But a *sorcerer*, seeing the chance for good money . . ."

"Magic shop?" I asked. "We should start dropping in around town trying to find someone who fits the bill."

"Right." She nodded. "But skip the neo-pagan FBH shops. They wouldn't have the know-how or skill, though perhaps a strega might. But the sorcerers—they're another matter. And we can't rule out that it might be someone from OW or from the Sub Realms."

"Meanwhile, where is Amber?" I turned back to Mallen. "Just what will Wolf Briar do to a female werewolf? And a pregnant one, at that?"

"Make her pliable. What it does to any non-alpha male and any female is amp up the innate reflex to obey authority that werewolves are born with."

I glanced at Camille. "So we can be sure that the Wolf Briar made Amber passively obey whoever kidnapped her. You know, Rice might have used it to avoid creating a scene."

Camille paused before gingerly trying to stand up. She dropped back on the bed. "Fuck, this stuff is bad. We need to establish whether Rice is still in Arizona. Of course, he could be working through someone else, but I think it would behoove us to find out where he is. He may be abusive, and he might want Amber back, but would a werewolf really chance challenging the Pack leader by using something so anathema to his race?"

"It doesn't make sense, does it?" With that thought, I let out a long sigh. "You think you're ready to head home for now? We need Menolly's input, and maybe the boys have found out something about the sixth spirit seal."

Camille nodded, turning to Sharah. "Am I cleared to go?"

Sharah checked her over once more, quickly. "You look okay. Call me if you have any signs of a relapse. Meanwhile—a lot of fresh air and water to get the residual Wolf Briar out of your system, and you rest tonight. *No gallivanting around.*"

Chase promised to stay in contact, and we headed out to my Jeep. As I helped Camille into the passenger side from the wheelchair—Sharah wouldn't let her walk to the car—she winced and rubbed her temples.

"Headache?" I lightly massaged her neck, and she sucked in a deep breath, then slowly let it out again.

"Yeah, aftereffects. Sharah warned me I might have a few periods of dizziness and that I could use a good solid night of sleep."

"We'll make sure you get it." I swung into the driver's seat and fastened my seat belt. Frowning, I shook my head. "This sucks. This all sucks. I wish we could just chuck it all and go home to Otherworld and settle down on a farm and I could raise rabbits and animals, and you could worship the Moon Mother, and Menolly could . . . well . . . she could do whatever she wanted to do."

"Do you really wish that, though?" Camille asked. "Would you truly change things with the Autumn Lord if you had the chance? I'm a priestess now, I'm going to have to start training with Morgaine, and I'm pledging myself to Aeval's court, which will most likely make Father boot me out of the family. But . . . I wouldn't trade it for a cozy cottage and a flower garden. Those things would be nice, but I don't think I'd turn back the clock, except for Shadow Wing. I'd really rather not be fighting him and his cronies."

As I maneuvered the Jeep out of the parking lot, I thought about what she'd just said. "I don't know. I can't answer—not yet. Let me think about it for a while. In the meantime, what next?"

Camille frowned. "We go home and figure out what to do next. I also think that someone should pay a visit to Carter this evening and talk to him about Stacia, the training camp, and the best way to proceed. He seems to have his finger on the pulse of the Demonkin, and I trust him. In fact, let's do that before we go home."

"Are you *nuts*? Look at the shape you're in. Sharah would kill you. And do you really want to visit Carter without taking Vanzir? Don't you think that's a little dangerous?" To be honest, I was intrigued. Carter fascinated me.

"I'll be okay, I won't do anything strenuous, and we'll go home right afterward." She fell silent, then said, "How are you doing now? You know . . . after seeing Chase."

I flipped on my left blinker, and we turned onto the freeway, heading toward Carter's. He didn't live far from the FH-CSI building, not in relative terms. Barring bad traffic, we'd end up in his neighborhood in ten minutes.

"I'm trying to keep calm about the whole thing. There's nothing I can do. If I tried to hang on to Chase, he'd come to resent me. If I argue and fight, then our connection with Chase will be strained, and that would not be a good thing. It was bad enough when I caught him with Erika."

Erika had been trouble . . . or rather, Chase had gotten himself in trouble *with* her. A little voice in the back of my head whispered that, regardless of the fact that I'd forgiven him for lying to me, regardless of the fact that I'd decided to give our relationship another try, my trust in him had been permanently damaged.

The fact that he'd slept with her wasn't the problem—it was the fact that he hid it, that he lied to me about it. I was beginning to think that maybe I wasn't cut out for a monogamous relationship. Camille certainly wasn't. Menolly wasn't. Maybe I was more my father's daughter than I'd tried to believe.

Camille let out a slow sigh. "I'm going to say something, and then I'm going to leave it alone. I'm pretty sure you'll get an earful from Menolly when she gets you alone next and finds out what happened."

I grimaced, but they were my sisters, and we nosed our way into each other's lives all the time. "Go on."

"I honestly don't believe you were ever set up to make it with Chase. You've had a good run. You both gave it a good try, but I predict that the day he finds a woman willing to stay at home, have his children, and not make waves is the day he'll really fall in love. Chase is a decent man, he's a damned good cop, but he can't give you what you need, Kitten. Not for *all* of your sides. And unlike my three men, I don't think he's truly willing to share you—not in the long run."

She paused, then—as I remained silent—continued. "You're a two-faced Were. More than that, you're a *Death Maiden*, for the sake of the gods. As much as you want him to enter your world, even with the Nectar of Life, and even if he finds his own power, he'll never be able to match you. Not unless his powers blow him sky-high. Better this happens now than twenty years down the line. Better this happens now, before you have a child with him."

I stared at the road, watching the asphalt grind beneath the wheels of my Jeep. With every passing inch, with every foot of pavement that disappeared beneath us, I knew she was right. I'd known all along, which is why I felt conflicted when it came to Zachary and my sexual attraction toward him.

"What's your opinion about Zach?" I asked quietly.

"You really want to hear?"

I nodded. "Yeah, give it to me."

"He's too frightened to be your mate. He's scared. He doesn't want to be out on the front line, and it wouldn't be fair to put him there. Last time we did . . ." Her voice trailed off.

I blinked back tears. "Just say it: Last time we took him with us on a fight, he almost got killed, and he's still in a wheelchair. Just part of our collateral damage," I added bitterly. "He won't even talk to me now, you know. He won't answer the phone when I call; he won't allow them to bring me back to his rehab room to see him in person."

"That is his choice, Kitten, not yours." She leaned her head against the back of the seat. "Of course, you feel horrible about his injuries. We all do. And I know you find him attractive, but be honest, Kitten. *You don't love him.* That's plain to see. If you did, you would have left Chase for him."

"Yes but . . . we put him in danger."

"True, but it was *his* choice to go with us. He was hurt saving Chase's life—an action *he* decided to take. He is a hero, and a bad accident happened. But just because he was seriously injured doesn't mean you owe him your life. *You can't love him just because he's paralyzed.* That wouldn't be fair to either of you. And you know Zach wouldn't want you that way."

Hot tears welled up in my eyes. I blinked them away. I had never, ever vocalized how I felt about Zachary Lyonnesse's injuries, but Camille hit the nail on the head. I felt guilty because I enjoyed him in bed, but I couldn't fall in love with him. I felt guilty because he was hurt and in a wheelchair. I felt guilty because he wanted me to choose him . . . and now I was free, but I couldn't do it.

"How'd you get to be so smart?" I muttered as I swerved onto the exit that would lead us to Carter's home.

"I'm married to three men. I may not know how to run your computer all that well, I may not be able to kick ass like Menolly, my magic may be fucked-up part of the time, but trust me on this: *I know men.* And I know *you.*"

She laughed, throaty and full and rich, and my tension slid away like melting butter on a cob of corn. I inhaled a deep breath and willed the guilt to wash away, willed the pain to fade.

"So, even though Chase and I are . . . just friends now, you're saying that it's okay that I don't turn to Zach." I glanced over at her quickly, then back to the road. She was smiling.

"Think about it: Would you want to be picked by someone, knowing you were their second choice? In the long run, he'd hate you for it."

"That makes sense. For a while, I felt that Chase had chosen me only after you told him in no uncertain terms that he'd never taste your pussy."

"Oh no, you *didn't*!" She coughed, laughing. "I can't believe you just said that, Miss Priss."

I laughed along with her. "Hey, it's the truth," I said as I turned onto the street leading to Carter's. "Now, let's go have a chat with the demonmeister and then get you home."

And everything was okay. I might be alone again, but I wasn't lonely. I had my sisters and my friends with me.

CHAPTER 7

Carter opened the door, much to my surprise. It was usually his foster daughter Kim who bade us enter. She was half-succubus, half-human—in particular: of Chinese ancestry. Her mother—a full succubus—had abandoned her to be sold as a slave. Carter, demon of unknown origin, had bought Kim as a baby and raised her like a daughter. The girl was mute, though no one knew why, and she doted on her foster father, keeping house for him in the basement apartment of the ten-story brick building.

A narrow stairwell led to the apartment, but Carter had hired a powerful witch to erect a permanent grid of protection around the front of his home and the sidewalk and parking spaces near it. We could park in front of his place and never once worry about our cars being vandalized. I ended up half-carrying Camille down the steps, afraid she'd fall if I didn't.

I glanced around. "Where's Kim? She okay?"

If he looked surprised to see us, he didn't indicate it. His red hair was in shocking disarray, but it was for effect, carefully groomed, and the long, curved horns rolled back off his head, coiling like an impala's. Carter wore a brace on one knee and walked with a cane, but he was always elegant and suave.

"She's out shopping," he said. Bidding us to sit, he excused himself for a moment and slipped through the door that led to the kitchen.

Carter was an excellent host, and his living room was nothing less than an old-fashioned parlor, with richly upholstered sofa and chairs and solid, handcrafted tables. In one corner stood a huge desk where he did his research. An elaborate computer setup covered one entire side of it.

Camille and I sat down, gingerly looking around. This was the first time we'd been here without Vanzir accompanying us, and I could tell she was just as intimidated as I was. Carter's powers remained unknown—at least to us—and I wasn't sure I wanted to find out just what they were. At least, not the hard way. He was on our side, but with demons, you never knew.

Carter returned from the other room pushing a double-decker tea cart. Steaming tea and a plate of petit fours nestled on the top rack. On the lower, I caught a glimpse of two kittens, curled together, grooming each other. While both were predominantly white, one had cream markings on her and the other, a few splotches of black. Their hair was soft and medium-long and they were striking in their looks, solid for their age.

"You have cats!" For some reason this fact surprised me. Camille looked around, and I pointed to the tea cart.

He nodded. "Aegean cats, yes. They like people. Feel free to pet them. The cream and white is Roxy, the black and white, Lara."

"Oh, how adorable! Look, Delilah!" Camille scooped up the cream one and snuggled her face against its fur.

I gave her a long look. "Not a good idea for *me* to pet them. *You* pet them. Have fun." Although they were kittens, there was always the chance my Tabby self would get bent out of shape and protest. I smiled softly, wishing I could snuggle them, too, but better to err on the side of their safety.

Camille turned to me. "Oh, I wish we could have a few of these around."

The look on her face sparked off a twinge of guilt, and I sighed. "If you stand ready, then hand one to me, and I'll see how it goes." I bit my lip, and she gently placed the black-and-white kitten in my hands and hovered over me.

The fur was so soft and the face so winsome. Even though

a few of my defenses began to rise, I slipped under the kitten's spell. I was about to hand it back to her when the baby let out a loud screech, startling me, and I quickly set it on the sofa. Before I knew what I was doing, I abruptly shifted into my tabby self and leapt up beside it. That mew had been a *need-Mommy* cry, and there was no mommy in sight.

I grabbed the kitten by the scruff of the neck and jumped onto the floor, carrying it with me as I crawled beneath a nearby end table. I gently held the baby down with one paw as I began to groom her face.

"Hold still," I told her. "You need a good grooming, and you haven't been doing it right."

The kitten didn't say anything, but she stared at me with such huge eyes that I found myself wanting to do everything I could to protect her. She began to purr, and I groomed harder. When Camille leaned down to haul me out, I growled. I knew my sister wasn't going to hurt her, but no way in hell were they taking this kitten away from me.

"Delilah, Delilah? Honey? You have to change back. Please, don't make us drag you out of there," Camille said, holding out the other squirming kitten in her hands. "This little girl needs her sister. *Come on out, Delilah. Now.*"

Something about her tone caught my attention. Her voice was compelling, and though I didn't want to listen, I had to obey. I tried to resist, but finally I gave in and slunk out from beneath the end table. The kitten followed me, batting my tail happily, and I didn't even swat it. I didn't even *want* to swat it.

While Carter corralled the kittens and put them in a play-pen, Camille caught me up. She sat me on the sofa and wag-gled her finger at me. I batted it, and she laughed, petting me gently. As I relaxed, I realized that I was ready to change back and gently leapt out of her lap and off the sofa, crossing to an open spot on the floor.

I shifted again, slowly this time to avoid the swift kick in the muscles transforming too fast produced. The cramps from sudden shifting could be worse than a bad lactic acid buildup. I knelt on the floor until the chance for spasms had passed, then glanced up to see both Camille and Carter grinning at me.

Carter let out a soft chuckle when I cleared my throat. "Thank you for making my afternoon so amusing. Life in your household must be fun," he said. "Well, my kittens are safe, and I trust you are all right, Delilah?"

I nodded, trying to figure out what had just happened. Normally I went after other cats, spoiling for a fight. "I guess their age makes a big difference."

Camille's eyes lit up. "Maybe this means we could have a couple babies? You could be their surrogate mother and—"

Hating to burst her bubble, I shook my head. "We'd better think about it long and hard. We don't know how Maggie might react to them. For all we know, she might try to eat them."

"No she wouldn't. Not our Maggie! She adores you when you're in cat form and would spend all day playing with you if we let her." Camille folded her arms, looking crushed.

"Maybe we can figure something out," I said. "Confine them to your rooms till they grow up or something like that. We'll talk later." Feeling, for once, the older sister, I patted her arm. "I know how much you love cats, and I promise, I'll spend more time in my cat form for you until we figure out what to do."

"Sorry about all that—an ongoing struggle in our household." Camille let out a sigh, then turned to Carter and told him about the goblins and the Tregarts. "So now we have a rumor about Stacia running a training camp for demons. Have you heard anything?"

Carter nodded. "Vaguely, but nothing I can confirm yet. I'll assign someone to look into it, and the minute we find out anything, I'll let you know. At least you've verified that she entered through a Demon Gate. Do you think the Tregart was lying or withheld anything?"

"No." Camille sighed. "There's no question that Menolly, Vanzir, and Roz got every shred of info out of the Tregart they could. If he was part of it, they'd know. Between the three, they have some pretty nasty . . . tactics."

She paused, and we looked at one another. Neither one of us was willing to use the word *torture*, though I knew it weighed heavily on both our minds, especially after the talk with Mallen and Sharah about the Wolf Briar.

Carter's eyes took on a luminous hue. He smiled softly.

"Sometimes, what has to be done in a war is regrettable. I

have seen this more times than I care to recount." He paused, then added, "I never told you why I left the Subterranean Realms, have I?" Dipping his head, his horns flashed in the soft glow of the light.

"No," I said. Camille shook her head. "We never felt it our place to pry, but if you want to tell us, we'd like to hear."

Carter leaned back in his chair, pressing his fingertips together as he regarded us soberly. "I am one of the sons of Hyperion—a Greek Titan who watches over the sun and the stars. He mated with a demoness, and she bore a litter of thirteen of us. We lived with my father for a time, then my mother summoned us to the land of Hades within the Subterranean Realms, and Father sent us to her. She sought to use our paternity to her own advantage. All it bought her was a swift and ugly death."

I stared at him. Carter was the son of a Titan and had twelve brothers and sisters? The Titans predated the Greek gods—in fact, they were responsible for the rise of the gods and had warred with them greatly over the years. We were in the presence of a deity, for all intents and purposes. I didn't know whether to kneel or bow, so I settled for neither.

"After my mother was killed, I led my brothers and sisters back to Hyperion. He took us in, taught us the art of observation. We learned to watch, to listen, to be patient. Then he sent us to enter the realm of mortals in order to record the interactions of the Demonkin with the human world. The gods, in rare form, agreed with the Titans that this would be a worthy pursuit and set Athena and Mercury to guide us. We formed a network and began training others to be our eyes and ears in various parts of the world, and they report only to us."

"Who are those you train? Are there many? Are they all demon?"

He shook his head. "We run a far bigger network than you would think. Some are part-demon like myself, others Fae. Still others are races you can barely begin to comprehend. We stay hidden unless we feel it necessary to reveal ourselves. I think it's time you girls know about us. You're fighting a war that could easily turn a page in human history, and it directly involves the Demonkin. The Demonica Vacana Society is keenly interested in what will happen in this Earthside battle."

Carter's cards were finally on the table. I wasn't sure just what to say. But it explained a great deal and made me feel better about interacting with him.

"What do you want from us?" Camille asked.

He shrugged. "Your friendship. Your stories. I want you to tell me what happens so that I can record it for the future. I am a historian, you see, when it comes down to it. While I'm not pledged to refrain from interfering, my main focus is on recording and sealing the information within the Vacana Archives, deep within the Demonica Catacombs that exist in a cavern on one of the uninhabited islands of the Cyclades."

"Cyclades?" My fingers were itching to get a look at those catacombs and the records stored within.

"A large group of Greek islands in the Aegean Sea."

"Why do you help us?" I asked, wondering why he would even care. If his job was to record and keep track of what was happening, would our fate really matter to him?

He smiled then, softly again, and leaned forward. "My dear girl, I care more than you can possibly think. Like the children of my father—the ancient Greeks—I love all things beautiful and wise. I bequeathed my life over to order, to making sense of the present and keeping track of the past so the future may learn. I also know a father's love for his daughter. My feelings for Kim alone fuel me with the desire to keep this world running, as faulty as it is, without interference from my mother's people."

His face lit up, and the look in his eyes made me smile. He cared. He really gave a damn.

"What do you recommend we do, as far as Stacia's training camp?"

Carter shook his head. "I concur with you, Delilah. Don't seek it out at this time. Not unless you want them to take notice of you. My advice? Locate the next spirit seal." He glanced at his watch. "I hate to rush this, but I have a new client coming in twenty minutes, and I need to prepare for him."

We stood, and he ushered us out. Once we were back in my Jeep, Camille and I sat there, overwhelmed by what he'd told us.

"So." I finally broke the ice. "Carter's older than the gods."

"Not necessarily, but he's sort of a cousin of the gods,"

Camille said. "Can you imagine the wealth of information he has within his grasp?"

"I'd pay one hell of a price to categorize and log it on my database. We need to preserve this sort of information for the future, too." I could devote a lifetime to studying data and organizing it, but I had the feeling Carter wasn't going to be taking me along with him next time he visited the catacombs.

"What next?"

"Home," I said firmly. "I let you have this visit, but you're going home, and you're going to rest. Besides, we need to scour the city for magical shops, and I can best do that over the phone and the Internet. And you wanted to track down Rice in Arizona to see if he's still there."

"Right." She fished through her purse and pulled out her cell phone. "I'm going to ask Luke to meet us at the house. Menolly will understand." She hit speed dial and after a moment, said, "Chrysandra, is Luke there? Can you put him on?"

As I put the Jeep in gear and we headed toward the freeway, Camille talked Luke into meeting us at the house. Then she called Iris to let her know we'd be there in a few and would she have a good lunch ready. But my mind wasn't on lunch or on the road. It was back in that basement apartment, mulling over the bombshell Carter had dropped on us. I had a million questions for him, but they'd have to wait.

CHAPTER 8

When we pulled into the driveway, I noticed right away there was a strange car there. A four-door Volvo . . . it looked familiar, and yet it didn't. As I hustled Camille up the stairs, helping her as she leaned against the railing, the sound of arguing came blaring from inside.

"What the hell?" I opened the door to a blast of shouting from the living room. Iris hurried over, and I pushed Camille toward her. "Get Camille settled and comfy somewhere, please, and don't let her get out of her chair except to go to the bathroom, please. What the hell's going on in there? Who's yelling?"

Iris looked flustered. "I was about to break it up. Nerissa's going at it with . . ." She paused, staring at the wall beside me.

"You don't want to make eye contact. All right, who is it? Tell me before I go in and find out myself. Forewarned is forearmed." I wasn't in any mood for shouting fests, arguments, or whining.

"Andy Gambit." Iris blinked.

"Gambit? *Gambit?* That little weasel is here?" Camille struggled to push past us toward the living room, but I barred the way.

"I'll take care of this. *You*—go sit in the rocking chair in the kitchen. Iris, please fix her some tea and strap her down if you have to. Then join me. I'll take care of whatever the heck is going on in there."

Without another word, I strode into the living room. Andy Gambit stood there, and I stared at his back for a moment. Yellow journalist extraordinaire, purveyor of sleaze, slander, and innuendo, he was an unassuming little prick, making up for his lack of personality with full-scale assault on anybody belonging to the Supe Community.

My guess is that we'd replaced the blacks, Hispanics, and Asians as his targets. He was also pushing Taggart Jones, a wing nut extremist going head-to-head with Nerissa for the council seat. Jones wanted to revoke all rights that had been extended to the Supe Community and the Fae, and—in his own words—"Drive them freaks right back where they belong. Under a rock."

And if Gambit was arguing with Nerissa, that could only mean . . .

"You fucking freaky cunt," Gambit said as I entered the room, his attention focused on Nerissa. "I knew I'd catch you up. Not only are you one of those damned Weres, you're also a lesbian and into necrophilia. *Corpse slut.* So, you the D'Artigo freak's blood whore? You might as well admit it—"

I grabbed him by the shoulder and whirled him around. Sputtering, he fell back a couple of steps. Towering over him, I leaned down to stare him in the eyes.

"How *dare* you come into our home and assault one of our guests! You looking for trouble? I hope so, because, dude, you found it. You have ten seconds to hit the door before I use you as a battering ram. Get out before I call the cops and have you arrested for trespassing."

He had more balls than I gave him credit for. Before I realized what he was doing, he spit in my face. "Bitch. Freaks—all of you are freaks. You drive men wild and then use them to take over our society! I'll show you just who runs this society— men do. *Earthborn men!*"

Bingo. I glanced at his pants. The man's hard-on was flashing like a tent pole on opening day at the circus. Gambit wanted us, and he was afraid of his desire. I wiped my face and noticed that Nerissa had backed up, her eyes flashing. She wanted to shift, and so did I—into my panther self. And if that happened, we'd both end up ripping out his throat.

I decided to take the lesser of two evils route, and without another word, I dropped him like a used Kleenex. Smacked him dead on center in the nose. He went down, and I couldn't help myself; I added a nice little kick to the groin.

"Delilah—" Nerissa looked like she was barely keeping it together.

"Go get Iris. And hand me the phone."

She obeyed, and I punched in Chase's number. He must have been at his desk, because he answered on the first ring. "Johnson here."

"Chase, gotta problem lying here in my living room."

"Uh-oh," his voice wavered. "I'm not going to like this, am I?"

"Probably not. I just KO'd Andy Gambit. I want a restraining order forbidding him to come on our property—hold on," I said over his groans. Iris had just entered the room.

"Iris," I said, covering the phone. "Did you invite Andy in? Did Nerissa?"

She shook her head. "Are you insane? I'd no more let that ninny in than I would the Bonecrusher. The door was unlocked, and he entered the house without asking just moments before you got home. I was about to evict him when you and Camille came through the door."

"Thanks. Would you make sure he doesn't go anywhere? I'm on the phone to the cops." I uncovered the receiver. "Chase, I also want to charge him with breaking and entering—or trespassing. Whatever you call it when someone enters your home without asking. He barged in, uninvited, and picked a fight with Nerissa."

"I'll have one of the men out there on the double. Meanwhile, you do realize he can quite possibly file charges against you? Did he make any threats at all? Anything you can use to say you feared for your safety?" The sound of his voice told me that he knew I hadn't been afraid.

But . . . maybe . . . "Yeah, well, he called me a bitch, a freak, and told me that he'd show me just who ran this society—earthborn men. I consider that a threat." I licked my lips. "He had a hard-on you couldn't miss . . ."

Chase let out a strangled cough. "Wonderful. Such a lovely example of the male gender. Makes me proud to be a man and all that rot. Okay, we'll see if we can pound it through his head that he'll come out worse for wear if he tries to take you to court. Tell me everything again. And don't leave anything out."

As I finished going over the timeline from when we'd entered the house, the doorbell rang, and Nerissa led in Officer Yugi, the Swedish empath. Iris was holding Andy Gambit at bay with her wand. He was still on the floor, staring suspiciously at the Aqualine crystal. It hummed gently as Iris waved it in his face.

"Chase, I have to go. Yugi's here." I hung up and once again went over what had happened. Nerissa filled in the moments preceding, including the fact that Andy Gambit had pinched her butt. She wanted to press charges for assault, and I pressed them for Gambit's breaking and entering. I also told Yugi that I'd felt threatened in my own home by the pervert and that's why I'd punched him. Yugi hauled Gambit off in handcuffs, the reporter silent after demanding a lawyer.

As we closed the door behind them, I leaned against the wall, shaking my head. "That man has serious issues."

"*That man* is going to be responsible for his own death one of these days." Nerissa let out a little growl. "Somewhere, some Supe just isn't going to cotton to his aspersions and is going to take the dude out. And I won't be standing by his grave crying." She let out a little moan and dropped to the sofa. "Just wait until the next issue of the *Seattle Tattler* comes out. I'll be splashed across the front: 'Lesbian Necrophiliac Werepuma—the *Freaks'* Representative.'"

She said it with a drawn-out accent, and it sounded so funny, I let out a snort. "Ha! He wishes you'd be repping him, but in some other area. Did you see the erection the dude had going on there? Scary—and while he was angry. Even scarier."

Nerissa shuddered. "Yes, I saw it, and it turned my stomach. Why can't these perverts realize we aren't interested? That they don't turn us on with their drooling and slobbering and horny one-liners that need to be retired? We aren't masturbation bait, as much as they'd like to think so. I don't *even* want to know what his fantasies are, but ten to one, we're starring in his own private porn movie. Fucking jerk gives me the creeps. You mark my words, Andy Gambit will end up raping somebody one day. Honestly, I don't *want* men like him thinking about me—in any way, shape, or form."

"Me either," I said softly. "The thought of someone like that fantasizing about me, or worse—touching me—makes me want to barf up a hairball."

"Yeah, it does at that." She shook her golden hair out of the ponytail she'd had it pulled back in. It was tawnier than mine but gorgeous, like a lion's mane. "What happened to Camille? Is she okay? She looks kind of grim."

"She got hit by big bad magic. Tell you about it over lunch—I'd like to wait until Luke gets here."

"Fine by me. That will give me time to catch a shower. Menolly and I have two glorious days to spend together." Her eyes shone. "I hope you don't mind my staying at your house. I know it's full."

"We don't mind—we love having you here." I playfully snatched her hand and pointed to the ring. "I saw this last night. I made Menolly give it up. You guys are so sweet."

With a soft smile, Nerissa rubbed the band encircling her finger. "I guess it's okay to tell you since we're wearing these openly now. Last week we said *the words* for the first time."

I blinked. "Really?"

She nodded. "Really. We don't know where this will lead. We're still playing with men on the side. At least, guys who have it pulled together and aren't like a certain wacked-out paparazzi tabloid freak we both know and hate. But our hearts belong to each other. Menolly's an amazing woman, and I've never felt so close to anyone in my life as I feel toward her. She knows me, inside and out." The look on her face backed up every word.

"Listen . . . let me tell her about Gambit. She's going to find out, but if you tell her, she'll go off half-cocked and wipe the dude off the face of the planet for what he said to you. And that would not be a good thing, as much as we'd like to see it happen."

"Sure," she said with a wistful look. "But I can dream, can't I?" With a laugh, she took off for the hall bath. Nerissa had spent enough time here. She knew where the towels were.

As I stood there, watching the back of the Amazon goddess as she headed down the hall, I could only hope that things worked out better for them than they had for Chase and me. A knock on the door interrupted my thoughts. Iris answered and led Luke in.

"Have you found out anything about Amber?" he asked, scanning the room quickly.

I shook my head. "We have some news, but now more questions. Iris, can you help Camille get her ass in here?"

I motioned for Luke to join me in the living room. He slid into one of the upholstered armchairs and crossed his legs, tapping on the end table with his fingers. *Nervous.* Beneath the scruffy exterior, I could see the glimmer of trouble in his eyes. His long ponytail was neatly caught back, and he looked like he was trying to keep his composure.

Camille slowly made her way to the sofa, looking exhausted. Iris brought her a blanket and then quickly vanished with the promise of tea and cookies.

Luke looked at Camille for a moment, then sniffed the air. "What the hell happened to you? I smell something . . ." He stopped short and growled.

"Wolf Briar." I said the words as gently as I could, but he jerked his head up, his face a wash of fear.

"No . . . *no.* Where the hell did you run into Wolf Briar? I didn't know that crap could affect a non-Were. Unless there's something about Camille that I don't know." He bit his lip and then let out a soft sigh as the words sunk in. "Not . . . Amber?"

"When we went to Amber's room, we found a trap. It exploded all over Camille. Definitely Wolf Briar. Apparently it messes something fierce with magical energy like Camille possesses. Damned stuff paralyzed her. We had to call in the medics."

"And my sister?"

I could tell he was holding his breath, and I shook my head. "We don't know. She's gone. Her clothes are there, her purse and keys. But Amber's gone. A strange magical signature was left behind in the room. We have no idea what's going on." I paused for a moment. "Do you think Rice would use Wolf Briar to capture her?"

Luke winced. "I'd like to say yes, because that scumbag

will use just about any dirty trick in the book . . . but *Wolf Briar* . . ." He shook his head. "I can't imagine a werewolf using it on another werewolf. They'd have to be a psychopath, and while Rice is a sadistic bastard . . ." Wiping his hands on his knees, he finally looked up at me. "I don't know, but I'm not inclined to think so."

"Is there a way to find out if Rice is in Arizona right now? If so, he can't be the one who actually used it, though I suppose he could have hired somebody."

Luke frowned. "I don't have any connections down there anymore. Amber was the only one from the Pack that would talk to me. Except . . ." He frowned, then stood and paced over to the window. "I had one buddy. He's an expatriate from the Pack, too—but he stayed down in the desert. I haven't heard from him in ages, but I can try to contact him. He might be able to find out for us."

As he pulled out his cell phone and began flipping through the contact list, it occurred to me that Luke was very much like us. He was a Windwalker, a nomad without roots. He'd been cast out. We lived between worlds. More and more it seemed like too many people had nothing to anchor themselves to except the family they could create from their friends.

"Hey, while you're looking for his number, what are you doing for Thanksgiving? We're going to be putting on a huge spread here, and you're more than welcome to join us. Your sister, too, once we find her." I wasn't about to put a damper on the offer by hinting that I thought Amber was dead.

"That's a wonderful idea." Camille shifted on the sofa, looking more tired than I'd seen her in a long time. "Damn this stuff. I can't feel my connection to Trillian, Morio, or Smoky—the links are clouded from the Wolf Briar."

Luke glanced up at us over the screen of his phone, his gaze softening. "Thank you—I appreciate the offer. Menolly hinted at it, but I didn't want to barge my way into a family gathering." He stopped. "Here it is. Jason's number. Let me give him a call . . . we haven't talked in over a year."

As he moved to the other side of the room and made his phone call, I motioned to Iris. "Any chance of getting some lunch? Nerissa will be back from her shower soon."

"It's on the stove. I started it when Camille called." The

house sprite bit her lip, then sat down next to Camille. "I am going to need some time off this winter. And I was wondering . . . Camille, could you and Smoky and Roz come with me if there's any way that you can tear yourselves away from here?"

Camille blinked, then sucked in a deep breath. "Is it regarding . . ." She stopped, staring at Iris. It was obvious that she knew something I didn't.

"Yes. I think I've found a way, but it's dangerous, and I need help."

"Hold on here, you two. What's going on?" I asked. "What are you talking about?"

Iris glanced at Camille, who gave her a nod.

"You're going to have to tell Menolly and Delilah at some point, especially if the boys and I accompany you to the Northlands."

"Northlands? You're making a trek all the way to the Northlands? Why?" One look at Iris's face told me she wasn't anticipating it with joy. More like dread. More like *rabid fear*.

"I'll tell you and Menolly later, when the boys are back. I suppose . . . it's time my secrets came out to more than just Camille. And don't yell at her—I asked her to keep my confidence because it doesn't affect the war against Shadow Wing. I needed time to reconcile myself to what I must do."

Wanting nothing more than to prod her secret into the open, I forced my curiosity back to acceptable limits and gracefully refrained from harassing my friend.

"Sure, no problem," I said, reaching out to give her a quick hug. "Whatever you need. I can wait."

"You lie, but you're sweet. You're champing at the bit to know what's going on. But it will hold till later. Right now, let me go get lunch on the table. I hear Nerissa in the hall—make sure she can find the blow-dryer, will you?" And before I could say another word, she vanished back into the kitchen.

Camille shook her head when I turned to her. "Don't even try. Leave it to Iris to tell you herself. But hang on for one hell of a roller-coaster ride. Remember that spell she cast at Stacia Bonecrusher's? When she turned the Tregarts inside out?"

My stomach lurched, but I nodded. "Yeah, I remember. All too vividly."

"It has something to do with her magic—and her past."

Luke rejoined us then. "I talked to Jason. He's still alive, so that's good. Lone werewolves have a rough time walking separate from the Pack. Anyway, he's going to see what he can find out through the grapevine. He wasn't exiled until after he chose to leave, so he's not nearly the pariah that I'm considered."

"Lunch!" Iris called from the kitchen.

I took the roundabout way, stopping in the guest bath to check on Nerissa, but she'd already found the blow-dryer and was squeaky clean and pulled together.

"Ready for something to eat? Iris fixed lunch." I motioned for her to follow me. We wandered into the kitchen, and I glanced at the clock. Three P.M., a little late for lunch but far too early for dinner.

Iris had prepared homemade tomato soup and grilled cheese sandwiches, along with a fruit salad and a dizzying tray of cookies. I clapped my hands.

"Cookies!"

Camille snorted. "You and your cookies."

"I can't help it. I love sweets." And I did. I slid into my chair and dutifully bit into the sandwich and spooned up soup, both delicious, but my eye was on the prize: sugar cookies . . . oh yeah.

As we ate, the door opened, and the Demon Twins came thumping in. They'd left their coats and muddy boots on the back porch and looked chilled. Roz and Vanzir slumped down at the table, and Roz reached for a cookie. Iris slapped his hand smartly.

"Lunch first, and *then* dessert. Wash up, and I'll fix your plates." She hustled to the counter as they contritely shuffled over to the sink, where they washed their hands. Iris rustled up two more bowls of soup and sandwiches.

Roz bit into his sandwich, sighing as he leaned back. "Before you ask," he said between bites, "nothing. Zip. We struck out as to any clue where the other four spirit seals might be hiding."

"Crap. Well, you tried." I picked up my bowl and—despite Iris's shake of the head—chugged down the rest of my soup. "Yum, that was so good I'd like another bowl and another sandwich." Meanwhile, to tide myself over, I snatched a cookie.

Iris glanced at Camille. "You, too?"

"Yes, please. I'd help, but I feel like death warmed over." She frowned at me, and after a second, I caught her meaning.

I jumped up. "Iris, let me do that. You sit down and eat." I took over the stove as the house sprite gratefully slid onto her high stool and began eating. As I raised the spatula and said, "Anybody else?" the front door opened.

"Anybody else what? And what do I smell?" Smoky popped his head in the kitchen. "Food?" His glacial eyes lightened.

"Food, yes. Plenty of soup, and I'm slapping more sandwiches on the griddle." I held sway with the stove as Morio, Smoky, and Trillian wandered in. They hung up their outerwear and gathered around the table. But one look at Camille ended their jovial moods.

"Camille . . . what the fuck happened to you?" Morio was blunt and to the point, and the moment he spoke, the three of them were hanging over her like bees on a flower petal.

"I'll be all right," she said, waving them to sit down again. "Just sit down, and we'll tell you what happened."

"Somebody needs to fill Menolly in on everything when she gets up," I said, flipping the sandwiches as they browned on one side. The smell of melting cheese and buttered, hot bread wafted up, and I realized I was still starving. Our metabolisms ran higher than most FBHs, and it seemed like we were always eating. The food back home in Otherworld generally had more substance to it, and we filled up faster there.

As Camille and I ran through everything that had happened, including Carter's disclosure about his heritage, I reached for more bread.

Trillian crossed the room and took it from me, along with the butter knife. He began to butter the slices and hand them to me, and I gave him a shy smile.

Yep. The same arrogant, cocky man he'd always been, but something had changed, and he was kinder to the rest of us, no longer relegating us to the sidelines whenever Camille was in the room. Whether it was the fact that we were now family or whether he'd gone through something in the war that had changed him, I didn't know and wasn't going to ask. But whatever the cause, it was a pleasant change of pace. Even Menolly had cottoned up to him a bit.

When we finished telling them what had happened, Morio

let out a long sigh. "Wolf Briar. I know of it—and whoever is using it must be stopped. Anyone with a *shred* of decency wouldn't touch it. Hell, this is something only someone as rotten as the Merés would pull." He motioned to Luke. "Have there been any reports of werewolves disappearing lately?"

Luke frowned. "I don't know, to be honest. I'm ostracized from a lot of Packs because they know I'm a pariah at home, and they don't want to get on my old Alpha's bad side."

Nerissa spoke up. "I've got a friend who belongs to the Olympic Wolf Pack. They're unusual in the fact that they run a matrilineal society, and they aren't well accepted by other werewolves. Let me call her and see if she'll talk to us after we finish lunch. She might know something."

I glanced at the clock. "Menolly won't be up for another couple of hours. Luke, would you like to come with Nerissa and me, if we can get an okay on meeting her buddy?"

He shrugged. "As long as she doesn't mind me being there. I wear a mark in my aura of having been excommunicated from the Pack. Most werewolves can pick it up by simply standing near enough to me."

"I didn't know that," I said, wondering just how the energy signature read. I was about to ask Camille to give it a try, but one look at her told me the only thing she was up for right now was a nap. "Can one of you big, strong dorks please carry my sister up to her bed? No fun stuff allowed. She needs her rest. The Wolf Briar played havoc with her senses."

I overrode her protests as Smoky carefully swept her into his arms and headed toward the stairs. "I'll stay with her and make certain she's all right," he said. "Can someone bring me a tray with something to eat when it's ready?"

Trillian nodded. "I'll do it. Then Fox Boy and I'll start in on our project while you watch our wife."

"Project?" Somehow that sounded dangerous.

"We're working on the studio." That was all he would tell me.

"Katrina said she has the afternoon free," Nerissa said, putting her phone away. "As soon as you're finished, let's head out. And Luke, she said you're welcome. She lives here in the city, even though she belongs to a Peninsula Pack."

As I finished up with the sandwiches, I couldn't help but wonder just where this was all leading. We hadn't found out much about Amber. We didn't know where she was. We didn't even know if she was alive. Frustrated, I fixed a tray for Smoky, and Trillian carried it out of the room. As I bit into my second sandwich, I couldn't help but feel that the universe was holding a pissing match over our heads. And I was getting tired of it.

CHAPTER 9

~❧~

It seemed odd, heading out with Nerissa and Luke, when I was so used to handling cases with my sisters. Iris waved from the door, and I waved back, feeling an abrupt sense of loneliness.

The sky was dark, rain looming again, and the wind, chill. I watched as a murder of crows perched in the tall oak near the back of the house. Morgaine, come to spy on us? Shaking the thought off—I was getting paranoid in my not-so-old age—I slowly inhaled a deep breath. The scent of woodsmoke and air made crisp by the sparkling raindrops filled my lungs, followed by the deep, pungent scents of cedar and fir, moss and mildew. This was Hi'ran's season. The Autumn Lord ruled over these months, and once again, I felt a longing to summon him to my side, to talk with him. His presence was becoming oddly soothing, and I felt calm when I thought about him.

A sudden movement caught my attention out of the corner of my eye, but there was no one there. A second later, I felt someone cup my elbow. *Hi'ran?* I could feel his heat, and yet—and yet—again, it wasn't him. Shaking my head but feeling less lonely, I unlocked the Jeep and motioned for the others to get in.

Nerissa called shotgun. She was dressed in a pair of jeans,

a long-sleeved top, and stilettos that brought her to my height. Her golden hair trailed down her back, curling in tendrils that made me smile. She really was beautiful; I could see how Menolly had fallen for her. Luke sat in the backseat, his face a tense slate of worry. He was hunched forward, his elbows resting on his knees.

"Could you please sit back and put on a seat belt. I don't want to be responsible for killing you if we have an accident, the gods forbid."

Blinking, he obeyed without question. As I inched us out of the driveway, I could tell he was struggling with something.

"Are you okay, Luke? Whatever it is, you can tell us."

He shrugged. "It's just . . . as much as I hate Rice, I hope to hell he's not the one who did this. Any member of the Pack who would use Wolf Briar against another member should be shot. I don't want to think about Rice having the balls to use it, especially not against my sister. One thing Sharah didn't mention to you, apparently—and perhaps she doesn't know, we tend to keep a tight rein on the information—is that too much exposure to Wolf Briar can lead to domestication. Ultra-submissiveness. Wolf Briar can turn a Were near the top of the Pack into a groveling slave. Forever." Venom filled his voice.

I winced. "Not good. I didn't know that, and I don't think Sharah does either. I take it you'd prefer that information to be kept quiet?"

He cleared his throat. "Yeah, if you and Nerissa would be so kind. If it leaked out to the general public, do you know what the hate groups would do with it? Or anybody with a beef against a werewolf?"

I could see his point. What if the Freedom's Angels got hold of this information? They'd crossed the line from hate speech into action, and they would have no problem with funding the production of Wolf Briar and using it. Anything to get rid of the object of their fear and disgust.

"So, why does your friend Katrina live in Seattle when her Pack is over on the Peninsula?" I turned onto Greenwood Avenue.

"She works over here, and it's easier for her Pack to keep their paws in the Supe Community Council activities with one member nearby."

We headed north through the Bitter Lake area, then took a right onto Westminster Way, then left again on Dayton. When Dayton intersected Carlyle Hall Road, we curved left and continued along past the Shoreline Community College area, where the woods were still thick and the city took on a greenish hue. Seattle wasn't called the Emerald City just because somebody liked L. Frank Baum's books. Eventually, Carlyle merged into Third Avenue, and shortly after that, 175th Street, where we turned left.

"She lives out there a ways, doesn't she?" Luke said.

"Katrina lives near the sound, on Sixteenth." I quickly turned onto Tenth, and we wound our way through more wooded suburbs, until we came to 167th. From there, it was a short jog, and we were on the right street, the last street before Puget Sound. I slowed as we drove through the cul-de-sac, stopping in front of a modest house that had recently been built at the end of the road.

As I parked, I glanced at the view and thought that, modest or not, this had to have set the werewolf back a pretty penny. Waterfront property—and that included anything with even a remote view of the water—was mega-expensive.

The wind was whipping a froth on the sound as we climbed out of my Jeep. The scent of brine hung heavy as it filtered in, and the screech of seagulls made me nervous. I didn't like the water—most werecats didn't. Even though we were nowhere near any danger of falling in, the mere sight of such a vast expanse of silvery waves unsettled me. I never could figure out what people found so soothing about the water. To me it was all one big scary bathtub.

Luke, on the other hand, lifted his nose into the air and sucked in a deep breath, closing his eyes as the wind whistled past.

"I love this weather," he said. "I love this area. I'd never go back to Arizona, even if the Pack asked me to return."

"Let's go," Nerissa said. "Katrina's waiting for us. I don't know if Luke gave you the rundown, Delilah, but a few pointers: never stare down a werewolf. It's a challenge, and even though Katrina's not an alpha bitch, it will set her on edge. When you greet her, smile, nod, but don't lock gazes."

"Good point," Luke said. "I'm pretty good about controlling

the impulse, but a lot of werewolves haven't been able to master their inner beast."

"I'm glad you told me, because in the feline Were world, it's the opposite."

We headed up the sloping lawn to the house, where Nerissa rang the bell on the freshly painted house. The smell of paint had faded and now mingled with the smells of overturned earth—which meant Katrina probably had a garden—and woodsmoke. A glance at the roof showed she had a chimney and yes—it was puffing away.

The door opened, and a dark-haired, rather intimidating looking woman stood there. I don't know what I'd expected, but it hadn't been to see a woman in a corporate skirt suit, with her hair done up in a bun, wearing wire-framed glasses. She was trim and petite, barely five five I guessed, and her jaw was set strong and firm. In days gone by, she would have been called a *handsome* woman. Her eyes, though, were arresting. Dark, brilliant brown, like molten chocolate, ringed with a circle of topaz.

As she saw Nerissa, a smile washed over her face, and the stern primness turned to warm beauty. "Nessa! Long time, no see. Are these your friends?" She glanced at Luke and me. "Weres, both of you, but you—" She pointed to me. "You have something else in the mix. You're not a typical Were."

Just then a crack of thunder rumbled overhead, and the clouds broke, drenching us with huge, fat raindrops. Nerissa squealed and covered her head as Katrina slipped away from the door and ushered us in.

"Good grief, where are my manners? Get yourselves in here. Come on." She hustled us into the living room near the fireplace. I gasped as I saw the huge bay window that faced Puget Sound. Enough of the obscuring greenery had been cut away for us to be staring out over the huge body of water that Seattle nestled itself against, and the sight was breathtaking, picture-perfect.

"How lovely," I whispered, sinking down onto the window seat that jutted out from the house, providing a panoramic view. With glass and rocks and plenty of ravine between me and the water, I could appreciate the sight. "You have a wonderful home," I added, glancing around.

Polished, rich hardwood floors underscored cream-colored walls, and the built-in shelves and trim matched the color and grain of the floor. The furnishings were dark and heavy, leather and wood, and matched perfectly with the brick of the fireplace. The décor was that of a hunting lodge but upscale and comforting.

I sucked in a deep breath and looked around. *Yuletide,* I thought. It smelled like Midwinter. Sure enough, a jar of blue spruce–scented potpourri rested on an end table next to an oversized chair. Cinnamon sticks poked out of the mix, and cloves, and what I suspected was a dried vanilla bean.

"Thank you," Katrina said, sitting down in a wooden rocking chair that had been covered with a patchwork quilted throw. I had a feeling she'd made it herself.

Nerissa motioned to Luke. "This is Luke—he's the Were who's . . ." She paused, glancing at him, her face flaming.

"What Nerissa is trying to say without offending me is that I'm the Were who's pariah to my Pack. I was excommunicated and turned out on threat of death many years ago." He pulled back his hair, and I gasped as a notched ear came into view. "I bear the mark of the unworthy."

If Katrina was surprised, she didn't show it. Instead, she offered him her hand. "Luke, it's nice to meet you. Welcome to my home."

It was as if some unspoken acceptance ritual had passed between the two, and by the look of relief that washed over his face, I knew I was right.

"And this is Delilah," Nerissa said. "One of Menolly's sisters." When her voice touched on Menolly's name, there was a hint of pride in it, and I repressed a grin. Nerissa had it bad for my little sister, all right.

Katrina shot me a long look. "You're right, she's definitely pretty—but she's not as flamboyant as you mentioned."

"That would be Camille, her other sister," Nerissa said, turning bright red. She glanced over at me, flustered. "Trust me, I don't talk about you guys to everybody," she offered. "Just to my friends. Oh wait—that didn't sound right . . ."

I cleared my throat. "Don't sweat it. As long as you aren't pulling a Jerry Springer on us, it's all good." Turning to Katrina, I said, "So, yes, I'm a two-faced werecat who's half-Fae, half-human. I'm also a Death Maiden. It's no wonder you sense other energy clinging to me."

We settled back, the only sounds the rain pounding down on the roof and slashing against the windows. After a few moments, Nerissa let out a long sigh.

"We have some tricky questions for you, but trust me, we wouldn't ask them if they weren't important."

"Whatever it is, it sounds serious," Katrina said.

"Yeah," I answered. "Lives depend on finding out the information we're seeking. We don't know if you can tell us anything, but we have to try all avenues."

"All right, I'll help you if I can. Please, ask what you need to." She sat up straight, shoulders back, hands primly on her knees, eyes front forward on me.

"Have you ever heard of anything called Wolf Briar?"

Katrina immediately reacted. She blinked, then recoiled, and a look of distaste crossed her face. "Yes . . . yes, I have. It's a hideous drug."

I let out a long breath. "Have you heard of anyone in the area making it? We found a hotel room booby-trapped with it, and it knocked my sister—Camille, who's a witch—on her ass. Lucky for me, I wasn't in aim of the blast. We found one trap that had already been triggered, and we think it was used to kidnap a female, pregnant werewolf. Luke's sister Amber, actually."

"Oh, my Goddess." Katrina made a small sound. Luke echoed it, and I wondered what it signified but didn't have time to ask before Katrina looked up again, furious. "I can't believe someone would do that to a pregnant female. Is she an Alpha Bitch?"

Luke shook his head. "No, she's not. I can't help but wonder if my brother-in-law did it. She left him, came up here from Arizona, and at first I thought that he followed her to take her back. But Wolf Briar . . . I don't know if even Rice would be capable of using such a fucking rotten trick."

"What Pack are they with? Is it the same one you were excommunicated from?" Katrina didn't seem shy in the least.

Luke arched his eyebrows. "Have you ever heard of the Zone Red Wolves?"

Apparently Katrina had. "Great Mother, preserve you. You

escaped alive from them? And you say your sister is married to one of the males?" He nodded, and she bit her lip. "I'm sorry, then. The Zone Reds . . . they hate our Pack, and we've been attacked by a few of their males over the years. We're just lucky they live in Arizona, and we live up here."

"Why would they hate you?" There was so much about Earthside Were politics that I was still learning. The Rainer Puma Pride—from which both Zachary and Nerissa hearkened— didn't like me all that much because of my half-Fae heritage. They claimed I wasn't true Were, and in a sense, they were right, but their righteous indignation rankled more than anything.

Luke clasped his hands between his knees. "The Olympic Wolf Pack is matrilineal in nature—one of the few werewolf Packs to be so. They're run by a council of women, not men, and that goes against a long tradition among the lycanthrope clans, especially a heavily patriarchal clan like the Zone Reds. It's almost considered heresy against the race."

He quickly darted a look at Katrina. "Not that I agree with that mind-set—hell, I was kicked out for my inability to accept the authority of the Packmaster, especially when injustice ruled."

She nodded. "You are no longer Zone Red material. That's a compliment, in my book. But even so, back to your sister . . . the Zone Red wolves are as violent as they are stubborn, but you're right. I don't know if even *they* would be capable of using Wolf Briar."

"If the Zone Red wolves are the worst of the lot, then maybe we're not dealing with werewolves here. Maybe somebody else kidnapped Amber. But who, and why?" Nerissa stood. "Do you mind if I start some tea?"

Katrina blushed. "I'm so sorry—I should have offered. Go right ahead, Ness. I have a feeling your friends have more questions for me."

"That we do." I leaned back in my chair, smiling. I liked Katrina. She seemed with it and together. "So next questions: Have any werewolves, especially male, vanished without a trace over the past months? And do you know of any enemies to the werewolves in this area, besides the hate groups?"

And then it hit me: Exo Reed had said that the goblins and Tregarts were trying to abduct a couple of the beta werewolves. Had they been in on making the Wolf Briar? It was too late to find out, but I made a note to remember to tell the others about my suspicions.

Katrina crossed to the window, staring out at the blustering weather. The trees were whipping in the wind, the firs bending from the tops of their towering spires. Mama Earth was brewing up quite a storm.

"You know, now that I think about it, there might be a couple males missing. I go to the Supe Community meetings, and I met a couple of werewolves there about six months ago. We started getting together once every few weeks, for drinks, to shoot some pool—"

"You shoot pool?" Luke asked, his eyes lighting up.

She shrugged, tossing him a grin over her shoulder. "I may appear to be the local librarian, but that's only for work. I ride a Harley, and I can run the table better than you ever dreamed, I'll bet."

"That sounds like a challenge," he said, his eyes glinting.

"Maybe you'll take me up on it someday," she said, a curl of smile tipping her lips.

From where I was sitting, I could smell Luke. He was interested, all right. And by the lingering look she gave him, so was Katrina. Great! Nerissa and I could go into business as matchmakers. But that didn't help us with Amber.

"Anyway," Katrina continued. "I've been hanging out with them for a while, but last time we met, three of the guys didn't show. Doug Smith, Paulo Franco, and Saz Star Walker. Here, let me get you their phone numbers."

As she opened her Rolodex and began jotting down notes, Nerissa returned, carrying a tray with tea, mugs, and a box of Oreos.

"Now we're talking!" I snagged up three of the cookies and bit into one, the sweet, crumbly taste of chocolate and cream filling my mouth. I could live on cookies . . . if only Iris would let me.

"So here's the information. I haven't had a chance the past week or so to call them and see if everything's all right. We normally don't check in with each other on a regular basis. Casual buddies, nothing more."

"Thanks," I said, folding the paper and sticking it in my

pocket. "So, do you know of any enemies the werewolves might have in this area? Maybe a sorcerer, or wizard or . . . someone of that sort?"

Katrina shook her head. "I'm sorry, I really mostly focus on my own Pack's needs and concerns. We get enough flack from everybody else as it is, and not many werewolves in this area worry about *us*. I can tell you that for sure."

We spent another few minutes making small talk and eating cookies, and then headed out. As we reached the car, Luke paused.

"I'll be right back—I forgot something." He jogged back to the house.

Nerissa and I climbed in and shut the doors against the slashing rain. "Ten to one he asks her on a date," I said, grinning.

"Ten to one she says yes." Nerissa snorted. A moment later, Luke was back and slid into the backseat, fastening his seat belt.

I glanced over my shoulder. "So, she agree to go out with you?"

A long, red blush crept up his cheeks, making him look totally adorable. He ducked his head. "That obvious, huh?"

"Ya think?" Nerissa chuckled. "So dish. Did she say yes?"

With a hiccup that sounded suspiciously like a giggle, Luke nodded. "Yeah, she's going out with me. I can't believe she said yes. Good god, I haven't had a date in years, and I'm scared shitless."

"You should be," Nerissa said as I eased the car back down the street. "That girl's gonna take you for one hell of a ride. Just jump on and grip tight."

We stopped at the FH-CSI headquarters so I could call the potentially missing Weres. I could have used my cell, of course, but it seemed like a good idea to let Chase know about the possibility of other missing Weres. However, he wasn't anywhere to be seen when we got there.

"Yugi, can we use a private room with a phone?"

He motioned me into one of the conference rooms. As I pulled out the piece of paper, Nerissa opened her purse.

"Coke? Candy? I see a couple vending machines out there,

and I know you can't stay away from the sweet stuff." She waved a dollar bill in front of my face.

I pulled out my netbook—a recent purchase that I loved—and flipped it open, starting it up before I called the first number.

"Mean woman. You're a *mean, mean* woman. I think I had enough cookies, actually." I didn't want to admit it, but I was on a sugar high from hell, and my body suddenly didn't like the feeling. "Maybe just some sparkling water if they have it?"

She nodded and headed out the door. Luke pulled out his cell phone and moved to one side. I heard him mumble something and realized he was checking in at the bar. As he flipped it shut, I glanced at him, and he shrugged.

"Chrysandra says it's going to be a heavy night, but they have things covered for now. I have a little time before I have to check in."

"Good. Let me just start with Paulo here." I punched in his number and waited. The phone rang three times, and then a woman answered.

"Hello, my name is Delilah D'Artigo, and I'm trying to get hold of Paulo Franco. Is he available?"

"Who the fuck are you? Are you having an affair with my Paulo? Because let me tell you something. I'm pregnant with his child, so just back off!" She punctuated her outburst with a sob and the sound of harsh tears.

"Wait—please, no. Nothing like that. I assure you, I haven't even met Paulo before, but I needed to ask him some questions." I scrambled to keep her from hanging up—and from believing the worst.

A couple of sobs and a gulp later, she said, "Are you sure? You sure you aren't sniffing around my Paulo?"

"I'm positive. I promise you. This is in regards to a missing werewolf. I was just wondering if he'd heard anything through the grapevine."

I decided it was better to play it safe than to ask why he hadn't shown up to meet Katrina and the gang. On the off chance Katrina had been fooling around with him, I didn't want to bring her name into the matter. But the woman on the phone saved me the trouble.

"Well, you can make that two missing werewolves. Paulo

ain't been home in almost three weeks. I don't know where he is. He's always been jumpy, and when he found out about the baby, he got skittish. But he's going to marry me, and he promised he'd do right by me." Her voice now flat, she sounded defeated and out of steam.

"What's your name? I'd like to come talk to you. Maybe I can help track him down. I'm a private investigator."

Bingo. The promise of help seemed to do the trick.

"You mean it? You'd help me? I don't have much money, but I'll see what I can come up with—"

I caught a sudden image of a rundown apartment, a pregnant werewolf, and the metaphorical wolf at the door. "Don't worry about it. As I said, I'm on the trail of another missing Were. I'll see what I can find out for you, though I can't promise anything."

"Thanks," she said, breathing softer. "My name's Mary. Mary Mae Vegas. I'm Paulo's fiancée."

And with that, I had two missing werewolves on my list. I made an appointment to visit her the next day and took down her address. Then, sipping the water Nerissa bought me, I put in a call to Doug Smith and Saz Star Walker, but struck out. Nobody home. I asked Yugi to run their phone numbers through and get me addresses.

"Sure thing, Delilah. Anything to help out. Give me about ten minutes."

While waiting, I meandered over to Chase's office and stood there, my hand resting on the door molding as I stared through the slatted blinds behind the window. Normally, I'd wander in and leave him a note, but somehow, it now felt off-limits. I wasn't his girlfriend anymore. He wasn't my boyfriend. We were . . . *just friends.* Part of me wanted to cry as I stared at the glassed-in office.

"You okay?" Nerissa asked, slipping up behind me. She gently placed her hand on my shoulder.

"No, not really. Chase and I broke up. The Nectar of Life is having one hell of an effect on him, and he needs to find himself. It seems I'm in the way of him doing that." A hint of bitterness tinged my voice, a bitterness I didn't want to claim. "I understand what he needs to do. I really do . . . but it hurts."

"Yeah, I guess it would. I've always been the one to do the

breaking up, so I can't really say I've been there. Except for Venus." Her voice took on a wistful tone.

"Did you love him?" Venus the Moon Child was the Rainier Puma Pride's shaman, and he was a wild man in more ways than one. But now he was under the protection of Queen Asteria and training as one of the Keraastar Knights, and the Pride was suffering with his absence, from what I'd been able to gather.

"Love him? It's hard not to love Venus, but not romantically. No. But he was . . . he's a powerful man. And power is attractive and addictive." She let out a soft laugh. "But I'm happier now. Menolly and I fit together. And the men? They're just for fun. They aren't for keeps."

I patted her hand. "I'm glad my sister found you. She needs you. More than she'd ever let on."

And I needed someone, too, but as painful as the knowledge was, I knew it wasn't Chase. I'd always love him, but now that we'd parted the sheets, I knew that *we* weren't meant to be. Someone was out there, waiting for the right time to enter my life. And for some reason, the thought scared me spitless. Because as much as I loved Chase, I was beginning to realize I'd never been *in love* with him. I'd been in love with the idea of *being in love*.

"Nerissa, I need to ask you something."

"What?" She let out a soft sigh and leaned against the glass, one knee bent with her foot against the wall.

"Does the Rainier Puma Pride blame me for Zach's condition? Does . . . does *Zach* blame me?" I had to know.

Nerissa let out a low whistle. "I've been waiting for this question, wondering when you'd finally break down and ask." She turned to me and, hands on my shoulders, gave me a little shake. "Girl, anything that happened to Zach was the fault of that fucking Karvanak. Don't blame yourself. I don't. Zach doesn't. He just . . . he needs time alone to heal, to adjust to his new way of life."

I frowned, thoughts cartwheeling through my head. Chase needed time to adjust to living a thousand years beyond what he'd ever expected. Zachary needed time to adjust to living in a body that no longer worked the way it had. And for Camille and me, we were being forced to adjust, to make our transitions now, her with the Dark Fae Queen and the Moon Mother, and me with Greta and the Autumn Lord. A whirl-wind of change, a vortex that threatened to sweep us all up in a tornado. Only we weren't being carried to Oz, but instead, we were careening straight toward the mouth of the Sub Realms, where Shadow Wing waited for us, ready to eat our souls and the soul of the world.

"Oh!" Dizzy, I stumbled. Nerissa caught me up.

"Are you okay?"

I realized I'd forgotten to breathe and sucked in a deep lungful of air. After a moment, my shoulders relaxed, and I shook my head. "Just . . . my thoughts were whirling so fast that the room started to spin. I'll be fine. Really."

And I meant it. I'd be fine—I couldn't walk Chase's path for him, nor Zachary's. I couldn't help Camille shoulder her burden any more than she could take over mine. The only thing I could do was face my own life, my own fate. Without warning, a weight fell away from my shoulders, and I began to breathe easier as I realized how much guilt I'd been shouldering for things over which I had no control.

"You sure you're okay?" Nerissa looked around. "We could go sit down for a moment if you need to."

Shaking my head, I let out a long breath. "Really, I'm fine. Or at least, I will be." As I saw Yugi bustling over, I added, "Say, you never did answer me. Does the Pride blame me?"

Her gaze flickered away from me, and she stared at the wall. "The Rainier Puma Pride doesn't blame you, no. But they blame Zach."

At that point, Yugi arrived.

He cleared his throat and handed me a piece of paper. "Here you go, Delilah. The information you needed." He glanced at Chase's office, then back at me and scuffed his foot on the floor. "I hope I'm not speaking out of place but . . . he misses you. I know he does. Whatever happened, it wasn't easy on him."

I patted the man's shoulder. "Yugi, I didn't send Chase away. *He* broke up with *me*. But we're still friends."

Yugi nodded then, looking relieved. "Okay, well . . . I'd better get back to my desk then. Do you need anything else?"

I shook my head. "No . . . I think we're done for now. Come on." I motioned to Nerissa. "Grab Luke, and let's head out. His truck is at our house, so let's head home so he can get to work. When I go exploring any of these leads, I want Menolly at my back."

As we left the building, I glanced up at the sky. Still pouring, the silver drops thundered down, filling the parking lot and turning it into a pond. I wasn't sure what I was feeling. *Sadness. Relief. Wistfulness. Hope. Loneliness.*

But in the back of my mind lay the tingle of anticipation. With all that we were facing, I felt like there was something on the horizon—something new waiting for just the right moment to appear.

And *that* was rather exciting.

CHAPTER 10

By the time Luke pulled out of our driveway, the sun had just gone down. Menolly should be up I planned on enlisting her help to check out Doug and Saz's places. I had a nasty feeling that I shouldn't go in there alone, and I didn't want to put Nerissa in any danger. As we'd pulled into the driveway, I was relieved to see Morio's Subaru in the driveway. Chances were everybody was home.

Nerissa and I hustled up the walk, dodging puddles and ducking against the rain that thundered incessantly from the dark sky. We clattered up the steps and both let out audible breaths as we darted beneath the porch roof. She was also feline. Neither of us liked water all that much.

I took off my jacket and shook it before opening the door, and she followed suit. As we entered the foyer, the smell of rich beef stew hit us, thick and robust, with onions, wafting through the hall. We never cooked with garlic out of respect for Menolly, but Iris made quick work of every other root vegetable she could get her hands on.

Another scent—fresh corn bread—lingered behind the blast of beef and gravy, and my stomach rumbled, despite all the cookies and crap I'd eaten that afternoon. Pushing through to the kitchen, I saw that Iris was clearing the table, but a big stewpot still bubbled, and there was a stack of cornbread left.

Menolly descended from the ceiling and strode over to Nerissa, hovering to meet her eye to eye. Nerissa slid her arms around Menolly's waist as their lips met, passionate and searching. The werepuma fisted a handful of Menolly's hair and leaned her back, kissing her deeply as her hands slid around to cup Menolly's back and butt. After a moment, with all of us transfixed on the lovers, they broke apart, eyes glazed, Menolly's fangs ever so slightly descended.

Oh yeah, that was hot, all right. I licked my lips, wondering if it was right that I could get so turned on watching my sister kiss somebody. In fact, the thought ran through my head, maybe I should take a peek at some of Nerissa's friends in the Rainier Puma Pride. I wasn't averse to the thought of a woman lover. The opportunity had just never presented itself before.

Menolly snapped her fingers in my face. "Come on, Kitten. Time to eat."

"Huh? Oh . . . yeah." I slid into the chair and accepted a bowl of stew and a piece of bread from Rozurial, who motioned for Iris to stay seated. "Listen, we have some pretty freaky stuff to tell you."

"Camille already told us about this morning." Menolly leaned back in a chair, propping her feet on Vanzir's lap. He arched his eyebrows at her with a smirk but said nothing, leaving the stiletto boots to rest on his thigh. "Wolf Briar. Fucking perverse shit. Luke okay?"

"Better than okay. Luke got himself a date," I said, grinning. "Katrina—Nerissa's friend from the Olympic Wolf Pack—took a fancy to him." Between the two of us, we filled them in on what we'd found out that afternoon.

"Anybody going out to see Franco's fiancée?" Menolly asked.

"I have an appointment with her tomorrow. But tonight, I want to check out Smith's and Star Walker's places. And I don't want to go alone. Menolly, come with?"

"Fuck. I was going to spend the entire night with Nerissa." Menolly rarely pouted, but now she was doing the full lip thing.

"'S okay," Nerissa said, kissing her on the cheek. "I need a nap anyway, if we're going out late, clubbing. You help

Delilah, and I'll catch a couple hours of shut-eye." She hugged
Iris, then grabbed a couple pieces of cornbread. "If you don't
mind, I'll eat these while I'm jumping into my jammies. Is it
okay if I sleep in your playroom again, Delilah?"

When she was staying here and needed to sleep, I loaned
her my playroom on the third floor, where I kept everything
that I needed to make my not-so-inner tabby happy.

Since Nerissa had started staying over on a regular basis,
we'd fixed up a sofa bed there for her, and for Menolly when
they wanted to spend the night together. Menolly wasn't
secure enough about her self-control to take Nerissa down to
her lair, and nobody chided her for it. With vampires there was
always the chance of slipping into the predator without realizing it, and if something during sex set Menolly off, at least this
way there'd be a chance we could step in and protect Nerissa.

"No problem—go for it." I waved her up the stairs. Turning
back, I looked over at Camille, who was still snuggled in the
rocking chair. She looked a little better, but damn, the Wolf
Briar had really hit her hard. "You going to be okay?"

"Yeah, but I still feel like death warmed over." She nodded.
"We need to find out who's making it and put a stop to them.
It's dangerous to far more than just werewolves. If I'd taken a
bigger blast of it, I could still be paralyzed."

Smoky growled. He was sitting by her side, and now he
looked over at me. "You have my help if you want it. There is
dark magic, and then there is this. And if you find out who planted
the blast that hit Camille, I'll remove them from this world."

"I'm sure you will. Who would know about sorcery shops
in town?" I leaned forward, playing with a piece of the cornbread. "Any ideas?"

"Wilbur." Morio slowly raised his head. "Wilbur would
know. Somebody care to go escort him up here? And make
sure he leaves Martin at home."

I groaned. Wilbur, our neighbor, wasn't my favorite person
in the world. A necromancer, he walked on the shady side of
gray, but he'd helped us more than once, and we managed to
form an uneasy truce with him after Menolly broke Martin's
neck and almost pulled his head off.

Martin was Wilbur's ghoul. Martin was long dead but well-
preserved, and looked like a ghoulish accountant and wore a

suit. Wilbur and Martin had a master-servant relationship that I wasn't entirely comfortable contemplating, because at times it seemed a little too chummy, but I wasn't about to ask awkward questions that might tell me more than I wanted to know.

Menolly grumbled. "I suppose I'll go. You guys always send me because you know Wilbur wants to fuck a vampire, and he keeps hoping he'll get lucky." She stood and stretched. "If he gets grabby, I can backhand him from here to Hel. I'll be back in a few with the cavalry." She excused herself and headed out the back door.

I finished my meal and carried the dishes to the sink. As I rinsed them off, there was a knock on the front door. Morio went to answer it and returned with Trenyth—the elfin assistant to Queen Asteria—in tow. Drenched from the downpour between Grandmother Coyote's portal and our house, Trenyth barely smiled, and I knew something was up.

"Something's wrong. Is Father okay?" I motioned for him to take a seat.

Trenyth glanced around the table. "Everyone's here. Good. Wait—where's your sister? Menolly?"

"She'll be back in a few minutes. Is it Father?" Camille leaned forward in the chair, her pale face even whiter.

The emissary sighed. "He's not hurt, so calm yourself with regards to that. But yes, the message is . . . from him." He looked sad, and I wondered what the hell was up. Trenyth had been on the periphery of our lives since we first wiped the floor with Bad-Ass Luke and Shadow Wing's first Degath Squad. We'd developed a friendly though professional rapport with the ancient elf. He was Queen Asteria's right hand, and I had the feeling she'd be lost without him.

We settled him in with a cup of tea and dessert—cookies—which he politely munched on, though I had the feeling they weren't to his liking at all.

"How's Her Majesty doing?" I asked to make conversation.

"Queen Asteria is in good health. She's . . ." he paused, then let out a long sigh, as if he'd been about to say something.

"What is it?" I pushed. Camille sat up, eyeing him cautiously. She glanced over at me and gave a slight shake of the head.

"Nothing. Nothing—just not all plans are going as hoped.

But leave it be. I can say no more on the subject." He took a sip of his tea and stared into the steaming cup, once again quiet.

Ten minutes passed, and the back door opened, Menolly leading Wilbur into the room. The guy looked like a front man for ZZ Top, with a streaming beard, long ratty hair pulled back in a ponytail, and shades on even though the light was long gone. He was big and burly, dressed like a mountain man, but there was a tingle about him that signaled magic. Magic and an overdose of testosterone.

"Now that you're home, I'd like to talk to the three of you alone, please. Then I'll be off. This will just take a few minutes." Trenyth motioned to Smoky and the rest, including Iris. "Please, give us some privacy." The elf's presence was commanding enough that everyone automatically vacated the kitchen.

We waited. Obviously, this was big, or he would have talked to us in front of the others. Finally, after an uncomfortable pause, he pinched the bridge of his nose and winced.

"I hate this." He looked up at us, a stricken expression crossing his face. "I've come to know and respect you girls over the past year. *I like the three of you.* Please know that. I really do. And that makes this even harder."

Uh-oh. Any announcement starting out with *I hate this* couldn't be good. "What's up?" I said quietly.

He sucked in a deep breath and let it out slowly, then pulled a parchment scroll out of his pocket and showed us the seal. Queen Tanaquar. Shit. But why was the elfin ambassador delivering one of the Fae Queen's official documents?

Breaking the seal, he unrolled it and cleared his throat.

"I, Trenyth Vesalya, ambassador for the Queen of Elqaneve— Her Highness Asteria—have been dutifully entrusted by the Crown to deliver an official notice from Queen Tanaquar, friend and ally of the Elfin Throne."

We remained silent, waiting for him to continue.

"Her Majesty, Queen Tanaquar, sends a royal decree to Camille Sepharial te Maria, also known as Camille D'Artigo, daughter of Ambassador Sephreh ob Tanu. She shall hold fast to the terms of this decree."

He paused.

I sat up straight. This was targeted directly at Camille, not at all of us, but that didn't make me feel any better. In fact, it made me feel worse. We handled things better as a team. We were unbreakable together, or at least pretty damned intimidating.

Camille, pale and looking terribly vulnerable, forced herself to lean forward. "Please, continue. Just . . . get it over with. Whatever *it* is."

Trenyth did something I'd never seen him do before. He reached out and took her hand in his, then lifted it to his lips and softly pressed a kiss against her skin. "Very well, my lady." As she slowly withdrew her hand, he unrolled the scroll again.

"Camille te Maria, be it known that if you go forward with your intentions to pledge yourself to the Court of Aeval, the Queen of Darkness, you shall be ostracized from Y'Elestrial, considered pariah unless you recant your change in allegiance. You are to continue in your position of OIA agent inasmuch as the task at hand relates to the spirit seals only.

"Unless this ban is lifted, you may never again set foot within the city limits of Y'Elestrial, nor within the home of Sephreh ob Tanu. You will report to Delilah and Menolly D'Artigo, and they will report to the OIA headquarters. You will follow all orders precisely. You may not contact any member of the Court and Crown on your own, including Sephreh ob Tanu. Nor will the Court and Crown contact you except through an emissary. As a punishment for turning your back on your allegiance, you no longer exist in the Court's eyes."

He put down the parchment and looked at Camille. "And I've one other message, my dear. Again . . . I am so, so sorry. Your father asked me to give you this." He handed her an envelope.

Shaking, she took it. After a moment, she ripped it open and pulled out the single sheet of paper and scanned it.

"Oh!" With a little cry, she dropped it, her hand flying to press against her lips. She was trying not to cry, trying to be strong, but the tears slowly spilled over.

I picked up the paper and read aloud:

"Camille. I'm sorry to have to do this, but duty has always come first with me, and I thought you followed in my footsteps. Apparently I was wrong. If you align yourself with Aeval, you are no longer my daughter. I will disown you. Choose wisely. Your future within the family depends on your actions. You have already proven your lack of loyalty to the Court and Crown by even contemplating such a move. Stay well. I will always love you, but I cannot be your father if you persist in this."

Crumpling the page, I knelt by her side, and she threw herself into my arms, sobbing, as I patted her back.

"Motherfucking peons!" Menolly pounded the table. "I knew better than to trust his conciliatory tone. So you're good enough to find the spirit seals but not good enough to set foot in town? Fuck the bitch and her Court. Tanaquar's likely little better than Lethesanar, and that was to be expected. But after all Camille has done for this family, *for Father*, to see him treat her like this. I disown *him*!"

Trenyth stared at us for a moment, then stood and slowly disengaged Camille from my arms. He turned her to face him, holding her firmly by the shoulders, chucking her chin when she tried to evade his gaze.

"Look at me, Camille. Look me in the eye. I reassure you that Queen Asteria makes no such judgment. You are well-respected in Elqaneve, and you are always welcome in our city. You are welcome in the Queen's chambers. And . . . you are welcome in my home."

"Thank you." She spoke so quietly I could barely hear her.

In a rush, he continued, "I feel like you girls have become my foster daughters. I've never had children, never been married. I'm truly wed to my duty to serve the Crown. But I've watched the three of you bravely face what would cow greater men. I've watched you push through fear and worry to complete your duties as best as you can. I honor that. So I'm offering you my guest rooms, if you ever need a place to stay in Otherworld. And my hospitality and gratitude for what you are doing to save both of these worlds."

And in that moment, the wisdom in his eyes fell away to show compassion, concern, and love. I truly believed he meant everything he said.

Apparently, so did Menolly. "You're all right, Trenyth." She kicked the cupboard, but I could tell her heart wasn't in it. She didn't leave a gaping hole in the wood. "We should all just quit. Tell them to fuck themselves. I knew Father wouldn't follow through with his supposedly new tolerant attitude. And if he lied about tolerating Trillian, then he's lying when he says he accepts me now. If he disowns one of us, he disowns all of us."

Camille dashed aside the tears. She was still shaking, and I knew her heart was broken, but she forced herself to straighten her shoulders. "Will you take a message to Ambassador Sephreh ob Tanu for me, and to the Queen of Y'Elestrial?"

Trenyth nodded. "Of course. Do you wish to write it down?"

"No, you can just tell them to their faces. I trust your memory. Tell Queen Tanaquar I will fulfill my duties as asked. I will report to my sisters. And tell Her Majesty she needn't bother to pay me if I'm such a disappointment. I'll fight against the demons for free if I have to; I care that much about this war."

"And to your father?"

I held my breath, waiting. Menolly's gaze was glued on her.

"Tell him . . . tell the ambassador that I'm sorry he's lost a daughter. Tell him that Camille D'Artigo said: The calling of the Moon Mother is stronger than the power of his approval. And that . . ." her voice broke, but she caught herself. "And that . . . that my duty is to my Goddess, first and foremost. I wish him a long and happy life. Apparently, I shall not be there to share it with him."

And then she turned and walked down the hall toward the bathroom.

Menolly and I looked at each other.

After a pause, I said, "I guess that's it. Tell Father that Menolly and I are pissed as hell and he'd better not contact us in anything but an official capacity for a while. I'd tell him myself through the Whispering Mirror, but I'm too angry and I'd probably shift if I tried to confront him."

"I, myself, have nothing to say to him," Menolly added. "Other than this: I don't need him. I don't want him in my life.

But Trenyth, we aren't mad at you. You just got stuck with a crappy job tonight."

He ducked his head, his cheeks burning. "I wish I hadn't been the one assigned. I was dreading this. And yet, better me than some officious ass." Gathering his robes, he added, "I'd better return now. Please, take care of her. I can't imagine what she must be feeling."

"We will." I saw him out the back door and watched as he crossed the yard. Oh yeah, this was shaping up to be a lovely autumn, all right.

As Menolly went to help Camille, I called everybody back in the kitchen and gestured for them to keep quiet. "I'll tell you about it later, but right now, I think we need to just let sleeping dogs lie." *And give my sister a chance to lick her wounds,* I thought but didn't say.

Menolly and Camille returned. It was obvious that Camille had been crying, but Menolly shot a look around the room that warned, *Back off,* and nobody took a chance on crossing her. Smoky glowered, Trillian and Morio looked worried, but she gave them a small shake of the head, and they kept quiet.

Roz quickly jumped to get everybody's attention off of her. "Yo, Wilbur," he said. "You want anything to eat?"

Wilbur cleared his throat as he plunked down into a chair. "Coffee if you got it, black, strong. And something sweet would not be amiss," he added, staring at Menolly.

She let out an audible hiss. "Hands to yourself, big boy. I told you that on the way here."

"Damn wench smacked me a good one," he said, rubbing his jaw and laughing. "All right, all right, I'll back off. Looks like you've got cookies there—I wouldn't be averse to a couple of those."

I handed him the plate, thinking that if he had his way, all three of us girls would be his personal cookie jar. But none of us were interested. Wilbur was too coarse for our tastes. He bit into the cookie as Roz poured him a cup of tea.

Wilbur glanced at Camille, frowned, then sniffed the air. "Wolf Briar. I can smell it on you. Jangled your senses, didn't it, girl?"

I shot a look at Menolly, wondering if she'd told him about it, but she shook her head. "You can smell the stuff? What else do you know about it?"

He swallowed the mouthful of cookie before answering. "Wolf Briar—I learned about it down in the jungle when I was in Special Ops." We'd recently learned that Wilbur's stint in the military had included a tour in some special operating force, one so top secret it didn't even have a name, though we knew it had been part of the marines.

"You have a lot of werewolves down in the rain forest?" I knew he'd been stationed down in South America, but he never told us just quite where.

"Yeah, actually, we did. There are tribes of shifters down there who make your kind look like puddy tats," he said, motioning to me. "The Jaguar Warriors—deadly and swift, dangerous beyond belief. But they aren't as bad as the canid clans. The Jungle Stalkers are Mexican gray werewolves, and they're skilled hunters but deadly to intruders. But then the coyote shifters moved in from North America, and they're far more unpredictable. They'd just as soon slit your throat as help you out. They used the Wolf Briar to take over some of the Jungle Stalkers clans."

"The *coyote* shifters use Wolf Briar? But don't they feel like they're betraying their cousins?" I'd only met a couple coyote shifters before—one was Siobhan the selkie's friend Marion, who owned the Supe-Urban Café. And she was one of the good guys. Just a few weeks ago, she'd helped Camille and our friend Siobhan escape a crazed stalker Siobhan was running from. I'd never think of her as trying to displace someone else.

"Wait—are coyote shifters technically Weres?" Roz asked.

"Yeah," Wilbur said. "But they often used the term shifter instead. They're a little different than a lot of other Weres. It's said they originated from Great Coyote himself."

"Hmm, a little like the werespiders we fought—they originated from Kyoka the shaman. They weren't a normal adaptation, though." I paused, then cleared my throat. "Coyotes are found in Arizona, right?"

"Just about every state, from what I know." Wilbur frowned. "So, what do you want to know? Elvira here said it was something to do with sorcery shops?"

Menolly hissed at him, and he gave her the finger. Everybody froze. I slowly flickered my gaze toward her. She was staring him down. Not good. Oh—this could be so bad. But then she broke into laughter, startling me and everybody else, including Wilbur—I could see the sweat on his forehead—and I relaxed.

"Wilbur, do you know of any sorcerers who set up a shop in the area? Somebody who maybe could be producing Wolf Briar? It's truly a matter of life and death." Camille leaned forward, still looking shaken but doing what she always did: putting duty first. "Please, if you have any information, tell us."

He eyed her slowly, his gaze running up her body, but for once he wasn't ogling. "I know how bad that crap can be." His voice was gruff, but I sensed a gentleness behind it that I'd never before heard. "Somebody hit me with a load of it once, and it wiped me out for days. Of course, I didn't get no antidote either, but still . . . you look like you got the crap beaten out of you. Okay, babe. Give me a pen and paper. I'll tell you what I know."

I slid a notepad and pen across the table to him, and he jotted down a name and address.

Wilbur shoved the notepad back to me. "This dude, he came into town a few months ago. I heard he was opening up a shop and so decided to see what he had to offer. I was looking for a few rare spell components. But a few seconds through the door, and I nearly passed out."

"What happened?" I met his eyes, thinking that maybe, beneath that rough exterior, Wilbur was okay.

"The energy was so thick in that joint I could barely breathe. Be cautious. Dude's name is Van, and his partner's name is Jaycee. As far as I can tell, they're both sorcerers. I don't know what tradition they follow, but I can tell you this: They're dangerous and chaotic. I got out of there as soon as I could, and I've never been back. I assume the shop is still there."

Crap. If *Wilbur* was afraid to go back, then they must be pretty damned nasty. Wilbur didn't spook easily, and with his skill in necromancy, it would take a buttload of bad energy to scare him. I glanced at the notepad.

"Madame Pompey's Magical Emporium. Wow, that sounds

so . . . so . . . B-grade movie-ish." Images of '60s science fiction gypsy fortune-teller werewolf movies skittered through my head.

"Trust me, we're not talking B-grade anything. These folks are for real, and if there's Wolf Briar being produced around the area, then my bets are on them. There's bad, and then there's *bad*. And those two . . . they walk on the dark side of the fence." Wilbur let out a sharp breath and leaned back in his chair, folding his arms. He shook his head. "I wonder . . ."

"What are you thinking?" Camille winced as she shifted position. "May I please have some more tea?"

Trillian scrambled to pour her another cup.

Wilbur ran his fingers through his beard. "Just . . . Once, down in the jungles, when I was on a mission, I ran across an old shaman from the Jaguar Warriors tribe. He'd wandered away during a vision quest and was a good ten miles from his village. I asked him why he was hiding, and he told me he'd accidentally crossed the borders into Koyanni territory— coyote shifters who made Wolf Briar. That old man could have easily killed almost every one of us with the flick of an eyelash, but he was scared shitless of the Koyanni."

"And?"

"Just this: I wonder if Van and Jaycee have anything to do with coyote shifters. I don't know enough about them to know if they're all like the ones I met when I was in the service, but . . ."

"But it's a good thought to check up on," I finished for him.

Camille cleared her throat. "We know not all of them are like that. Marion isn't. But . . . we can ask her about others in the area, if there's any connection between the shop and the shifters."

"We'll have to be delicate about it," Menolly said. "And being so, it's not a chore for me—I'm too blunt. Camille, tomorrow you and Delilah can take a trip over to the café and check it out. You think you'd be up for that?"

"Sure. I'll be fine. Really." She yawned, and I could tell she was about ready to faint from exhaustion and shock. "I should be good to go then. But for now, I just want to sleep. If anything happens tonight while you guys are checking out the two Weres, let me know. I'll come help if you need—"

"You will not leave this house tonight." Iris motioned to Smoky, who tossed Camille's afghan over his shoulder. "Smoky, get her back up to bed."

As the dragon gathered Camille up in his arms and headed toward the stairs, Trillian followed with a tea tray. Morio turned to me before heading after them. "You need us, the three of us will come help, but if you want your sister to be okay by tomorrow, she needs a full night's sleep. The Wolf Briar really disrupted her system. More than you think."

"It's not just the Wolf Briar." Menolly frowned. "Iris, you go with them. Ask her what Trenyth had to say. But be gentle, or I'll rip out your throats."

I glanced at Morio. "Do you think the Wolf Briar might have done permanent damage? Sharah said it should be out of her system by tomorrow."

"Sharah's an excellent medic, but she doesn't work with magic. Not like Camille and myself." Morio's expression was grave. "I have the feeling Camille's spells may be a little more off-kilter than usual for the next few days. I'm hoping no permanent damage was done, but knowing for sure is a matter of wait and see." He scooted past the table and vanished up the stairs.

"I hope to hell he's wrong and that it's out of her system for good by tomorrow. But you can bet the news from our *beloved father* won't be." Menolly slowly descended to the floor, looking grim. "Shit like this Wolf Briar hurts the entire Supe Community, not just the intended targets. So, you ready? Let's go check out your Weres. I don't want to spend all night on a wild-goose chase. Nerissa and I get so little time together that we want to make the most of every minute."

I grabbed my coat and glanced at the stairs. "I think we should leave the terrible trio with Camille. She needs all the support she can get. Vanzir—Roz? One of you willing to come with?"

Vanzir leapt up. "I will. Roz, you stay and see Wilbur home." He grabbed a heavy denim jacket and followed us out to my Jeep. I insisted on driving. Menolly's Jag was actually fairly uncomfortable for me since I was so tall, and while sports cars seemed like fun toys, it wasn't up to the actual work my Jeep could do.

Menolly rode shotgun; Vanzir climbed in the back. As we headed out into the storm, I wondered how many rain-soaked nights we'd crept into the dark, knowing we were headed into danger, chipping away at the edge of our luck. One of these days it wasn't going to hold.

We'd already lost so much, but there was so much, much more that could crumble beneath our feet. Every step was a question mark. Every move—a domino. And all we could do was make the best decision we could at the time and hope that the entire house of cards didn't come fluttering down around our shoulders.

CHAPTER 11

Menolly grumbled about having to take my Jeep, but I told her to stuff it. Vanzir laughed from the backseat. We headed toward Doug Smith's house—which was located up on Queen Anne Hill, one of the highest hills in Seattle. The neighborhood was somewhat upscale, and I realized that I was surprised a werewolf would have a house there. So much for my own prejudices.

While I drove, peering through the streaming rain that was making my windshield wipers work overtime, Menolly told Vanzir what Trenyth had wanted. Vanzir remained silent for a moment, then cleared his throat.

"I know you love your father, but that's a shitty thing to do. Ten to one, if he's banging the Queen like you say, she convinced him to play along with it." He leaned forward, peering between the front seats. "Camille and I don't have much in common, but she's all right. And she's doing what she needs to be doing. Chances are your daddy just doesn't like the fact that she married Trillian, and when the Queen offered him a good excuse to slam the situation, he ran with it."

What he said made sense. Hell, I'd been thinking the same thing myself for the past hour or so. "I guess we could ask Grandmother Coyote what to do."

Menolly let out a sharp hiss. "Camille already owes Grandmother Coyote payment from last time she talked to her. Remember? The Hag told her that a sacrifice had already begun. Maybe that's what this is."

"I don't think so. I think it was Henry's death, to be honest, but I'd never mention my suspicions to Camille. I wouldn't want her to feel responsible." I swerved to avoid a dog that darted out in the street and, since there were no oncoming cars for now, switched to brights until we got into the city proper.

"She already feels responsible. I don't think she'll ever get over feeling guilty for the old guy's death. But you two hens are overlooking the most important point. The important thing isn't what *started* this mess but *how to deal with it*. Are you going to stand with her, or are you going to let them run over her?" Vanzir slapped the back of the seat behind Menolly. "Either of you bother to let your father know how you really feel about this?"

I darted a quick glance at Menolly, who looked rather nonplussed. And it took a great deal for Menolly to look nonplussed. "We sent messages back to him with Trenyth . . ."

"Messages? Like, *Gee, Daddy, I don't like what you did to my sister?* You two are such a piece of work. How can you be so deadly, so beautiful, and such wimps at the same time? Hah." Vanzir leaned back, crossing his arms, and shook his head. I glanced in the mirror, and he gave me that arched-eyebrow look that says *gotcha*.

"He's right," I said after a minute.

"Yes, but I wasn't going to let him know for a while. Allow me a shred of dignity." Menolly let out a sigh—purely for effect.

Must be nice at times, I thought, to be able to avoid inhaling in the perfume department or the laundry soap aisle. Shaking my head, I brought my mind back to the subject at hand.

"So, are we going to fire up the Whispering Mirror and give Father hell?" I asked softly.

Whistling softly, she nodded. "Looks that way, doesn't it?"

Vanzir laughed gently from the backseat.

As I parked along the street, I had a creepy feeling. Doug's house was a two-story monstrosity with small windows dotting the surface. No lights burned from within, and the yard looked overgrown, even for this time of year. The only light came from the lamp on the front of the house, illuminating the porch steps. Or rather, the stone slab landing that passed for a porch.

As we climbed out of the car, a set of broken stone steps led up to the yard, which sloped up to the house. I glanced at the mailbox on the curb. It was partially ajar, and when I yanked it open, mail spilled out. Frowning, I gathered the letters back up, glanced at the name on them—Doug Smith, so yes, we were in the right place—and shoved the bundle back in the box.

Leaves in burnished shades of copper and brown and yellow littered the overgrown weed patch that passed for a lawn. The walkway itself was cracked, foliage growing through the patches to further push apart the stone path. Ferns and low-growing evergreens ringed the house, nestled beneath the windows and walls.

The house was old, weathered and wind-worn. The paint peeled from the sides, chips as big as my hand missing. The windows opened in, and screens had been nailed over them rather than properly set into place. The front door was located up yet another steep set of stone steps—I counted fourteen of them. An ironwork rail guarded both sides, and I was cautious not to touch it as we climbed the narrow stairs to the landing. The last thing I needed was a nasty burn.

I paused, then pressed the doorbell. We could hear the chimes sounding from within. After a moment with no answer, I pressed the bell again, and pounded on the door. Nada.

Glancing at Menolly, I pulled out my pack of lockpicks. Very few people knew I owned them, but they came in handy, and after being locked in a room by a harpy while a shopkeeper got killed, I'd quietly reassured myself I'd never be stuck in a room again. At least not one with easy-open locks. A moment later, I heard a faint *click*. I turned the knob, and the door swung ajar.

Quietly, I pushed the door open and sidled in, listening for any sound, looking for any movement. But the house felt cold and empty. I motioned for Menolly and Vanzir to follow me. Menolly shut the door behind her.

The hallway was tiled, but the tiles were worn, as was the paint on the walls. This place was badly in need of fixing up.

I edged forward, motioning for them to be quiet. A peek into the darkened living room showed that it was as empty as it seemed.

Vanzir tapped me on the arm and, in the lowest of whispers, said, "Maybe he's asleep?"

I shook my head. "I don't think so. Menolly, why don't you head upstairs and check it out—you're quieter than both of us combined."

As she slipped past me, silent and moving like a shadow, I found myself hoping that Doug Smith would be in his bedroom. Best scenario: He'd wake up and freak out that we were in his house. I'd rather face that than think about potential alternatives.

I motioned to Vanzir. "Quietly—very quietly—check out the living room. I'm heading through there." I nodded to an opening that led into what looked like a large kitchen-dining area. The walls had a stucco texture, and from the décor, I'd say that the house was stuck back in the sixties or perhaps the early seventies.

As I crossed into what was, indeed, the kitchen, I scanned the room. Nobody there. In the dim light filtering in from the backyard where a floodlight shone over the alley, I could see a stack of dirty dishes in the sink, encrusted with dried food. Flies buzzed around the plates.

Curious, I glanced in the fridge. Several open containers on the shelves proved what I thought I'd find. It was impossible to tell what the food had been; a flourishing colony of mold covered the tops of whatever the leftovers had been. A cantaloupe rested on one shelf, falling apart. I shut the door. Menolly wasn't going to find anybody upstairs. That much I knew. Wherever he was, Doug Smith hadn't been home in quite awhile.

Vanzir poked his head through the archway. "Nothing. Menolly's checking out the basement. I think I found the site of a scuffle, but it's hard to tell without turning on the lights."

"Hold on till she gets back. I don't think she's going to find anybody or anything down there." I spotted a roll of paper towels and tore one off, wiping my hands on it. Even touching the dishes in the sink had left me feeling dirty.

Just then, Menolly returned. "Nobody in the house."

"Thanks." I flipped on the light, flooding the room. The kitchen looked worse than I imagined, pots and pans and dishes filling the sink and drain board. A cutting board with a rotten tomato and stinking meat sat on the counter. It looked like someone had been in the middle of fixing dinner when they were suddenly interrupted.

"Go find the light for the living room," I told Vanzir.

We followed him in and, as a dim lamp illuminated the room, I saw what he'd been talking about. A desk sat in the corner, a rundown sofa faced a television, and a bookshelf, overflowing with books, rested against one of the walls. But the room was tidy, if a little threadbare. Except for a spot near the desk. One of the drawers had been yanked out and was upended on the floor, its contents spilling across the rug. A lamp had been knocked over, its bulb broken. And one corner of the desk was clear—with papers scattered around the floor.

I knelt near the mess. Brown spots spattered the beige rug. "Menolly, take a look at this. Ink or . . .?"

She squatted beside me and leaned down, inhaling deeply. Her nostrils flared. "Blood. Those are drops of blood."

"Crap." As we looked farther, we found more of the splatters. "I guess we should call in Chase. This doesn't look good."

"He's going to want to know why we're in the house. Like it or not, we're breaking and entering," Vanzir said. "But . . . I guess we could say we were just worried. Checking up on the guy for a friend. Which is ultimately true. If Nerissa's friend is worried about him . . ."

"Yeah. We may have committed B and E, but that doesn't matter. Whatever happened here . . . so not good. I wonder if there are traces of Wolf Briar around. I can't smell anything. Whatever happened took place a while ago." I stood up and pulled out my cell phone. The FH-CSI headquarters was fourth on speed dial, right after Camille, Menolly, and home.

Chase answered. "Johnson here. What's up?"

"Delilah. We've got a problem, Chase. Besides Amber, we've got at least one other—potentially three more—missing werewolves. And we know this one didn't go without a fight. We found blood on the carpet." I gave him the address and then turned to Vanzir. "Dude, can you go out and bring in the mail? There might be some clue in there."

He nodded, then sprang out of the house.

Menolly shook her head. "So, two down, one to go. Want to make a bet Saz Star Walker isn't going to be home, either?"

We waited, sitting on the porch steps, until Chase and his team pulled up. He frowned as he saw the open door and the lights on in the house. As they came up the steps, I held up my hand.

"Save the lectures. We got word he was missing, and I was asked to look in on him. With that Wolf Briar crap around, we weren't taking any chances. It looks like Doug's been gone awhile." I pointed to the stack of mail. "We just pulled that out of the mailbox, in hopes there might be some clue. And he's not the only one. Franco Paulo, another werewolf, has been gone too long for comfort. His fiancée is freaking. And we need to check on a Saz Star Walker tonight."

Chase and his team spread out through the house, taking fingerprints, looking for evidence, tagging and bagging things. He handed me a pair of gloves. "Now you can help. Check in the desk. Look for an address book. Something to give us next of kin, so we can find out if this is just a robbery."

"Robbery? With blood spatters?" I cocked my head, and he shrugged.

As I nosed through Doug's desk drawers, I thought about the Were's life. The house was fairly sparse. The kitchen showed a place setting for one. No photos on the walls, nothing to show friendship or family. It all seemed rather sad, actually.

Stopping short, I held up a clothbound volume. *What have we here?*

Yep, I thought as I flipped through it, an address book. I sat down and riffled through the pages. First place to look: under the letter *S*. Surely his parents or siblings would be there. But nobody by the name of Smith was listed. However, I did see Saz Star Walker's name. I showed Chase, then went back to *F* and sure enough, Paulo Franco was listed. And Katrina was in the book, too. There were a few other scattered names, including one for the Loco Lobo Lounge—a hangout for members of the Loco Lobo tribe. Exo Reed's Pack. Had Doug been a part of the LLs? Only one way to find out.

I put in a call to the number and, even though it was late, someone answered on the first ring.

"Loco Lobo Lounge. Jimmy Trent here. What can I do you for?"

I cleared my throat. "I'm wondering if Doug Smith is there? Can you page him, please?"

"I could, but I guarantee you he ain't here tonight. I haven't seen him in two weeks." Jimmy sounded distracted, and the music in the background blasted out of the phone so loud it was a wonder he could hear me.

"When was the last time you saw him? My name is Delilah D'Artigo, and I'm on the board of the Supe Community. We need to contact him." If anything, that might pull an answer out of him. And I was right.

"D'Artigo? *The* Delilah D'Artigo?"

"One and the same."

"Doug was in about two weeks ago. Last I saw of him and his buddies."

His buddies? I frowned. "You talking about Paulo Franco and Saz Star Walker by any chance?"

"Yeah. How'd you know? Hey, the guys aren't charged with causing trouble, are they?" He sounded genuinely concerned.

I sighed. "Not that I know of, no. Thank you." As I hung up, all I could think about was that they might not be causing trouble but that they were *in trouble* was beyond doubt. Unless they'd suddenly dropped everything, bled a few drops on Doug's floor, and taken off on a road trip without telling anybody.

Chase tapped me on the knee. I stared at his fingers for a moment, remembering other places his hands had been. Places that had welcomed him in. But now . . . *Oh fuck it.* Best to stop that line of thought.

"What?"

"The mail dates back to three weeks ago." He held up a letter. "This is postmarked the earliest. By the time stamp and city of origin, I'd say . . . yeah, three weeks to the day." He riffled through the envelopes. "Looks mostly like bills. No personal letters. Some ads. A *Penthouse* magazine."

"Three weeks. That coincides pretty much with what Katrina was saying about not seeing her buddies. Tomorrow I'll talk to Paulo's fiancée. What about Saz? Should we stop over at his place tonight?"

Chase began gathering up his gear. "Yeah. I'll tell my crew to stay here, finish, and then be prepared to head out in case Star Walker is missing, too." He followed me outside with the others behind us.

"You okay?" he asked, his voice low.

"Oh, I'm just peachy. I lose my boyfriend, we've got missing werewolves up the yin-yang, and my sister just got disowned by our father all in twenty-four hours. I'm dandy, Chase. Just *dandy*."

"Disowned? Who? Not Camille."

"Yes, Camille. Not only that, she's banned from Y'Elestrial. Don't worry yourself over it. It's our problem, not yours." I knew I sounded bitchy, but I couldn't help it; I was feeling bitchy.

Chase stopped and turned, taking me by the shoulders. He ignored the others as they delicately passed by us.

"Listen, Delilah. This is hard on me, too." He ducked his head. "Don't think it isn't. But I have to figure out what the hell is going to happen in my life now, and I can't do that if I'm worrying about a girlfriend, a lover, or anybody in that capacity. What if I decide I don't like this? What if the Nectar of Life fucks me up for good? I *didn't* have the chance to go through the proper rituals, and I'm having a hard time. Yes, I'm very grateful to still be alive, but this seriously has fucked with my head. Good god, woman, you really don't think I just woke up and thought, *Wow, time to ruin Delilah's life?*"

I caught my breath, shivering. Not only was it getting cold, but his words slapped me like a wet blanket. "No," I said softly. "No. I don't think that. You're right. I'm just . . . things are so weird right now that I don't know what to think. All our foundations are being shaken."

"I'm still here for you—as your friend, as a brother . . . as someone who cares. I just can't take a chance on loving you. I could end up hurting you again, worse. And that would be very bad." He pulled me into his arms, and I leaned against his shoulder.

"Thank you," I mumbled against his shoulder. "I feel so convoluted right now. And there's so much at stake." He held me tight, patting my back, calming me, and finally I eased away from him, staring into his eyes.

Chase gazed back at me. There were sparkles in his eyes that I'd never seen before—magic, a hint of it, crackling back there, waiting to break out. And when it did . . .

"You're right," I said, inhaling a long, slow breath. "You need to concentrate on the changes you're going through. I'm not a weak-willed person. I just miss having you around. But Chase, I'm not begging you to come back, and my life won't end because we're no longer dating. I'm a big girl. I can handle change." Giving him a soft smile, I headed down the sidewalk to my Jeep, where Menolly and Vanzir were waiting.

Chase followed, catching up to me before I opened the driver's door. "Delilah—you know there's nobody else, right? I'm not looking for any other pussycat."

The gentle grin on his face made me laugh.

"There's the smile I know and love. I'll meet you over at Star Walker's. Drive the speed limit, you hear?"

"Aye, aye, sir!" I jumped in the driver's seat, fastened my seat belt, and without a word, took off for Saz's house. Somehow, Chase's humor had managed to break through the gloom, and even though I felt on the verge of tears, I was smiling.

Saz lived in the dregs of town, along junkie row, hooker hangout, whatever you wanted to call it. The back streets that we were navigating were definitely on the wrong side of the tracks. The address Yugi had dug up was a four-plex town house. If Doug's house had seen better days, this dump had seen better centuries. The carport looked two shakes and a nasty gust of wind away from crashing down, and I made certain not to park beneath it. It seemed the other tenants had the same idea—none of the slots were filled, though I saw lights shining in two of the units.

Chase didn't park there either. As he got out of the car, he motioned to me, and I jogged over. "We ran the license plates of the cars in front of Doug's house. Sure enough, one of them was his car. And we found his keys on the desk. No wallet, but that was likely in his pocket. Looks like your buddy got himself abducted, though that's off the record and not an official statement."

Ouch. I didn't want to think about who abducted him . . . or why, though in the back of my mind the words *Wolf Briar* kept repeating themselves over and over again. And the essential ingredient in Wolf Briar . . .

Shaking my head to clear away unwanted thoughts, I motioned to the others, and we headed up the walk after Chase. He motioned for us to stay back—he had the badge, after all—and then knocked at the door. Nothing. He rang the bell. Nothing. After a few minutes, he ordered one of his men to bust it open, and they broke in, Chase holding a special revolver that I recognized as bearing silver bullets—the only kind that worked all too well against werewolves.

After a moment, a light went on, and Yugi motioned for us to enter. We trooped through and stopped in the middle of the foyer. The dingy little apartment would be nondescript except that a struggle had obviously taken place.

Books were scattered on the floor, chairs knocked over, an end table smashed. Blood had dried against one wall and was splattered on the floor. The room was thoroughly trashed, and I blinked as a sudden wash of scent rolled over me. Immediately, I turned tail and raced outside.

"What's wrong?" Chase poked his head through the door.

"You can't smell it?" I winced, my head hurting. "Wolf Briar. The place reeks with it. Whoever took Saz, used Wolf Briar. And I don't think it's been two full weeks—because that crap would have dissipated by now."

As I stared at the open door, a sick feeling raced through my stomach. Someone was picking off beta wolves in the area, and all the evidence pointed toward murder. Before I could react, the stress of the day flattened me like a steamroller, and I turned to the side and vomited over the edge of the landing.

CHAPTER 12

The rest of the evening passed in a blur. The FH-CSI team made an excruciatingly thorough pass through Saz's house, but this time they hit pay dirt, discovering a number and address for his sister. I waited on the periphery, watching them comb the carpets for evidence, take blood scrapings, dust for fingerprints, and do whatever magical procedures it was they did. I knew they were working on a method for tracing magical signatures, but it hadn't been fully developed yet.

Menolly and I leaned against one of the walls, while Vanzir took a turn outside, looking for anything he might be able to find. Two of the officers were conducting a door-to-door, questioning residents for any information they could glean.

"What do you think is going on?" Menolly asked me.

I shook my head. "Want to make a bet somebody's making Wolf Briar and needs beta wolves to pump up on steroids? I have a bad feeing we aren't going to find Saz or Paulo or Doug. At least not alive and in one piece."

"Delilah?" Chase came over, holding a piece of paper. "I was wondering if you would go with me to talk to his sister. It would probably help to have another woman along, and you'll get your info right now instead of relying on what my men and I bring in."

I nodded. "Yeah, but we'll all come. Menolly and Vanzir can stay in the car." I didn't want to ride in his car, alone with him. Not right now.

He nodded. "Here's the address. Let's go. My men can finish up here."

Saz's sister lived in a slightly better section of the city. The lights in her house were on, though we were pushing nine P.M. by now. As I slipped out of the car and joined Chase on the sidewalk, I thought this had to be one of the worst parts of his job.

"You ready?" He straightened his tie and cleared his throat, popping a Listerine strip into his mouth. He handed me one. "When delivering bad news, have good breath. It's bad enough to be associated with bad news. Hygiene counts."

I popped the strip in my mouth, wincing. The taste was too strong, though I liked it, and after a moment as it melted on my tongue, I asked for another. He snorted and handed me the pack.

We headed up the path, climbing the steps to the cottage house, where Chase pressed the doorbell. A moment later, a woman in a pair of sweats answered the door. She had a baby propped on one hip, and in the background, we could hear the sound of shrieking children. They were either having a lot of fun or were pissed as hell.

"I'm Detective Johnson, ma'am." Chase flashed his badge. "Are you Madge Renault?"

She nodded, looking suspiciously at the badge. "Yeah, what is it?"

"Do you have a brother named Saz Star Walker?"

The irritation on her face gave way to fear, and she opened her mouth in an O as she stepped back and motioned us in with a nod. "Is he . . . is Saz in some kind of trouble, Detective?"

We followed her into a tiny living room overflowing with toys. A large dog sniffed at my ankles and let out a sharp yip then ran off to play with three very messy but happy-looking children, who all appeared to be under the age of three. But their looks could be deceptive—Weres aged slower than humans, though for the first fifteen or twenty years they grew at what appeared to be a normal rate. Then the aging process slowed drastically.

She tried to clear off one end of the sofa, and I quickly stepped forward to help. Giving me a grateful smile, Madge retreated to a wooden rocking chair and shifted the baby to her breast, where the child began to feed.

"I'm sorry—but my husband works evenings, and with five kids . . . it's hard to keep things clean." She brushed back a strand of hair from her face, and I caught a look in her eyes that worried me. Madge Renault was reaching a breaking point. I made a note to send out someone from the Supe Community Council to see if there was anything we could do to take the burden off—if only a little. We had been discussing setting up a sliding-scale day care for Weres in the area, and it was about time we followed through.

"Mrs. Renault, I need to ask you some questions about your brother."

The apprehension returned to her face. "Yes. What's wrong? He's okay, isn't he? Saz is a good kid; he doesn't get into much trouble."

Chase shook his head. "As far as I know, he hasn't gotten himself into trouble with the law, Mrs. Renault. The problem is that he seems to be missing, and we found signs of a struggle at his apartment. We're trying to pinpoint the last time anyone talked to him and find out if he said anything that might give us a clue where to find him."

Her face paled, and she motioned for the little girl tugging on her arm to back off. "Saz, missing? No, that can't be. He was just here . . ." she motioned for her purse, and her daughter brought it over to her. Madge pulled out a day planner and flipped it open. "Hell, it's been over a week since I've seen him. Time just gets away from me these days." Lifting her head, she asked, "What do you think has happened to him?"

I forced myself not to flinch. What we thought happened to him was far too gruesome to speculate on. Luckily, Chase saw it the same way.

"We're not sure. Do you know if your brother had any enemies? Anyone out to get him for any reason?"

She slowly shook her head. "Not that I know of . . . oh, he

had his run-ins, but so does every hot-blooded werewolf his age. I don't know . . . our parents are out of state right now on vacation. I hate to worry them until we know for sure that something happened."

"Do you by chance know his blood type?" While Weres' blood was of a different makeup than humans, we still could cross match and classify the types.

"That I can help you with," she said softly. "He was type U-7. Same as me. I needed a transfusion during the birth of my triplets, and he was the only match around." Tears flickered in her eyes. "Find him, please. He's a good boy. He's never been high ranking in the Pack, but he's worked hard for what little he's got. I love him."

Chase nodded. "We'll do our best. Do you know where he likes to hang out, by any chance?"

"The Loco Lobo Lounge—it's a Pack-only joint. And let's see . . . the bowling alley. He bowls a mean game. I don't have time to check out every place my little brother frequents."

"Thank you, then. We'll be in touch with you as soon as we find out anything. Meanwhile, you might want to go over to your brother's apartment. It's . . ." Chase's voice dropped. "I won't lie to you. There's blood, and the place has been trashed."

Madge wavered. "Do you think he's alive?"

Chase glanced at me. I cleared my throat. "We don't know. We hope so, Mrs. Renault. If he is alive, we'll do our best to find him and bring him home."

As we walked away, leaving her with tears trailing down her face, I felt like we'd just piled one more unbearable burden on the woman's shoulders.

"How do you do this?" I asked. "How do you go to them, tell them that their life is about to fall apart? How do you handle it?

He was silent for a moment. Then, "I figure that if *I* do it, at least somebody compassionate will be telling them the bad news. They won't get a callous attitude from me."

It was my turn to be silent. As I climbed back in the Jeep, deep in thought, Chase took off for the FH-CSI headquarters, and I glanced back at Menolly and Vanzir. "Life fucking sucks sometimes," I whispered.

"Yeah, I kind of know that." Menolly smiled, her fangs

descending. "I get to remember that every night and every morning, when the sunset calls, when the daylight chases me into sleep."

Vanzir pointed at his neck. "This creature beneath my skin . . . he kind of underscores your thought, too."

I looked at both of them. "Yeah. I get it. Okay, let's head home for the night. Menolly, you want me to drop you off at the bar?"

She shook her head. "I need to get my Jag. You going to be okay?"

I smiled faintly. "Somehow I can't imagine not being okay anymore. I've got one of the Harvestmen guarding my back. Even if I die, I'm guaranteed a good job in the afterlife, you know?"

My laughter just a tad on the verge of hysterical, I pulled out, and we headed for home.

By the time I got home, I was exhausted. I trudged in and dropped in a chair at the kitchen table. Menolly waved, grabbed her keys, and headed for the bar. Vanzir had stopped at the shed-turned-studio apartment where he, Roz, and Shamas shared quarters.

Iris took one look at me and put on the teakettle. Then, before I could say a word, she plopped Maggie—who was playing with her Barbie that had a replacement head in the form of Yoda—into my arms and began to forage in the cupboards. For once, she said nothing about my junk food habit, just set a bowl of Cheetos in front of me.

I buried my face in Maggie's soft, downy fur. The calico gargoyle was our child, our baby, our pet—all the innocence of the world rolled up into one cute and destructive little package. But even she wouldn't stay that way, and she was—like cats and wolves—a predator at heart. But right now, she was just a baby, laughing and playing with her Yobie doll, as she called it, and shrieking as she ran her fingers through my short spiky hair.

"Deeyaya! Ca-yee-ko!" She seemed delighted with my new style, and I suddenly realized that some of my colors matched her own fur.

"Yes, baby, that's right. Delilah's a calico now!" I laughed then, blowing on her belly and tickling under her chin. We'd finally taught her not to bite, though she still made mistakes at times, but she just shrieked again, laughing. Then, with a yawn so big I could have seen her tonsils—if she had any—she began to close her eyes. I handed her back to Iris.

"I think she's ready for bed."

"Yes, the cream drink puts her to sleep when it's late and she's tuckered out." Iris carried her into her room, where Maggie slept at night, and a few minutes later returned. "Maggie's already asleep. She had a hard day helping me weed the garden and clean house. Of course, her help was more hindrance, but I don't mind. And Trillian and Morio took her out for a walk—they put her on a leash, which I don't think is necessary at this time—she can barely toddle—but it makes them feel more secure. Her leg muscles are starting to strengthen up some. Another year or two, and she'll be waddling around without a problem."

"When is she supposed to start flying?" I asked, picking up one of the Cheetos and blissfully closing my eyes at the tangy taste.

"Oh, not for another ten or twenty years. Her wings won't be big enough till then. In the wilds of Otherworld, the young ones are secluded for the first fifty or so years, and their parents bring them food. But she has to learn quicker than they would, although her body can't grow faster than it's normally supposed to." Iris poured us both tea and sat down near me at the table.

"On one hand she seems to be growing so quickly, and yet . . ." I sighed, thinking of how we were going to deal with a teenaged gargoyle. But we'd have many, many years to worry about that. We just had to stay alive for the present.

"How are you faring tonight?" Iris sipped her tea, inhaling the steam. She motioned for me to do the same.

I lifted the cup, letting the minty smell envelop me. It soothed my headache that was brewing, though it couldn't cure the heaviness in my heart. "I'm probably better off than Camille. I just lost a boyfriend. She lost a father. It's quiet in here, did she go to bed?"

"Aye. A few hours back. Her men made sure she was tucked

in and asleep before ten P.M. They're a good lot, those boys are. They may be a handful at times, but they love her dearly. But you're right. Camille worshiped her father—to have him pull this, it's a dark day for her." She shook her head.

"I'm so pissed at him. I can't even begin to express how mad I am. Menolly and I are going to have to confront him before long." As I sat there, contented to eat Cheetos and watch Iris as she made little snow etchings on the table with her magic—doodles, really—I began to drift. The room grew hazy, and the next thing I knew, I was standing in a misty vapor.

"You're here." The voice and presence felt familiar. I turned but could only see shifting shadows skittering around me.

"I . . . I don't know. What am I doing here? Who are you?" Puzzled, I looked around. I was in the astral, that much was apparent.

Eyes shimmered from the mist, gleaming like those of a cat, but this was no feline energy. It felt like Hi'ran, and yet . . . there was something different. The voice was smoother than his but had the same timbre. "You must be tired. I didn't realize you were so strong at sending."

"Are you . . ." Hi'ran's name would not form on my tongue. "You aren't . . ." My voice fell. "But you feel so much like him. Who are you? Tell me?"

A shadow moved forward; the rush of bonfires came with it, the scent of the autumn wind, boreal and icy, and the silhouette of a man around my height swept me into his arms. Even though I couldn't see him clearly, it felt like the most natural thing in the world.

"Oh, I wish I could take you here. Now . . ." He nuzzled his face in my neck, and I closed my eyes, letting the wash of passion rush over me in one fell swoop. It was like being dragged under dark seas. Welcoming the embrace, I wanted to slide into the sweet taste of restful oblivion.

The shadow kissed me again, and I tasted loganberry wine. He pressed his lips to my neck as his hands searched my body, setting off explosions—a cataclysm of sparks, a rain of *la petite mort*. It suddenly occurred to me that with Hi'ran, even though I'd felt his energy envelop me and stroke me, this was more tangible, actual fingers touching me, hands sliding across my body.

And then, with a shudder, I climaxed. The shadow kissed me again as I caught my breath, feeling renewed and refreshed.

"I'm not sure who you are," I whispered, "but only one other being has made me feel like this."

"Before long . . ." He paused, and I stared at the dark form that smelled of bonfire smoke and oak moss.

"Before long . . . what? Is my death drawing near?" I didn't want to know, and yet—I had to know.

"No, my dear one. No . . . nothing of the sort. But keep your eyes open. Listen to your heart."

"What about . . . the Autumn Lord?"

And then Hi'ran himself was there, strong and looming in back of me, and the shadow faded from view. He enfolded me in his cloak and once again, it was his energy touching mine, not the touch of fingertips.

"While you are mine in the end scheme of things, I am not a jealous master as long as you remember that I *am* your master."

And then—like the wind—he was gone, and I opened my eyes. Iris stared at me, grinning.

"*Him* . . . again?" She could feel the energy. I could see it in her face.

"Yes, him. The Autumn Lord. He makes me feel . . . beautiful and brilliant and powerful. I both fear him and desire him in a way I've never wanted anyone else before. But . . ." How could I explain there had been someone else, someone who felt like Hi'ran but wasn't him? I decided to keep that to myself for now. "I don't feel quite so worn out."

I was tired but no longer heartsick. I felt like I'd just had the mother of all massages, and in a way, I had. Orgasms given by the gods—priceless. I finished my tea and picked up my Cheetos.

"I'm going to go to my room, finish eating these, then sleep for a good eight hours. I'll see you in the morning, dear Iris." As I kissed her, she smiled, but behind that smile I sensed worry. And then I remembered—she was carrying a secret of her own, one that she had yet to tell Menolly and me. "And tomorrow, perhaps you can tell me what's going on with you—why you need to go to the Northlands."

The house sprite dipped her head. "You'll know at some point. But for now, sleep well, my dear. Sleep well."

As I headed upstairs, I pondered what Iris could be keeping secret. It was enough that Camille had promised to visit the Northlands with her—a journey not for the faint of heart. In fact, it was a daunting journey and—with what we knew about Smoky's father and him being on the rampage against my sister and her husband—potentially dangerous.

My thoughts whirling, I slipped into my Hello Kitty nightshirt, flipped on the TV in my room, and settled in for an hour or two of late-night TV and junk food. And I realized that even though the other side of the bed was empty, I wasn't lonely. I felt secure and comfortable, and for once I was glad to be alone with my thoughts. It was a soothing end to an otherwise stressful day.

CHAPTER 13

For once, a beam of sunlight broke through my window the next morning. I woke, blinking against the light, and found that I'd buried not only myself but the mostly empty bowl of Cheetos, a half-eaten Snickers bar, and a bottle of water under the brand-new quilt I'd bought a month ago. The Snickers bar was melted to my pillow. *Delightful.* The water bottle had come open, and I was lying in a wet spot. *Lovely.* The Cheetos had stained the sheets, but against the earthen tones of the comforter, the orange wasn't that noticeable. *One out of three isn't too bad.*

Since I kept a mattress protector beneath the sheets—my hairballs were a constant threat—only the sheet had gotten wet and stained, and remembering Iris's last reminder when she'd dumped my cat box on top of my bed, I stripped the sheet and put it in the hamper. She didn't mind making the beds, but she and my sisters had pounded through my head just how much of a slob I was and how badly I'd abused her services. I was trying to make sure that I helped out more.

I opened the window and immediately slammed it shut. The sun might be shining, but it couldn't be more than forty degrees outside. Digging through my closet, I came out with a pair of brown cords and a green pullover. I slipped my feet into a pair of cowboy boots, spiked up my hair with a dab of gel, and brushed my teeth. Earthside had it all over Otherworld when it came to dental hygiene technology, that was for sure. And being half-human, our teeth weren't as strong as our father's people.

When I was done, I grabbed my purse and headed downstairs. The smell of bacon and eggs drifted up the stairs, and I inhaled deeply, my stomach rumbling. We had a lot to do today, and in the back of my mind, I couldn't forget the fact that every moment her captors had her, the danger to Amber grew.

Iris and Camille were at the table, Maggie in her playpen. The kitchen was otherwise empty. I glanced around.

"Wow. Where is everybody?" The breakfast table was usually jumping. I glanced over to the sink and saw the pile of rinsed dishes. "Looks like everybody's already had a go at the food."

Camille grinned. She looked better. "Trillian, Smoky, and Morio have enlisted Roz and Vanzir to expand the studio into a multiroom apartment. It's not the best weather for building, but I think they can get a lot done today if the rain holds off. The guys certainly could use the room, and now and then I really want my bedroom to myself and the three of them out of the house. Husbands or not, they can be a pain in the ass." She dotted the corners of her lips with her napkin. "When do we head out for Mary Mae's?"

Iris handed me a sandwich of eggs, bacon, and toast. I wolfed it down, feeling oddly energized. My encounter the night before had done more than comfort me. I felt recharged.

"She said to come over around ten A.M."

The phone rang, and she answered. After a moment, she handed it to me.

"Luke here. I just heard from Jason."

"And?"

"Rice has been placed in Arizona. He's not up here. And something else—Jason told me that there's some big to-do going on in the desert down there, among one of the minor Packs."

Damn it, that meant likely Rice had nothing to do with his wife's disappearance, and we were back to square one. "What kind of to-do?"

"A string of deaths occurred in one of the werewolf Packs

down there. Five beta males, all turned up dissected, their scent glands and other organs missing. They've cleared all the rival clans in the lycanthrope community. But there's more. The scent of magic was picked up at one of the bodies—*trickster energy*. Dark trickster energy."

Trickster. There were a few clans that fed on trickster energy. Rabbits, jackals, hyenas . . . coyotes. "Coyotes—coyote shifters. From what Wilbur said, the coyote shifters down in the jungle use Wolf Briar to take over territory and kill off their rivals."

"Fuck. Territory wars?" Luke fell silent for a moment, then said, "Coyotes—the good ones—are helpful to no end. But the bad ones . . . they're dangerous and ruthless. They give Demonkin a run for their money."

"We'd better look into the coyote Packs around here. Although what they might want with Amber is anybody's guess. Nothing against your sister, Luke, but she's a solitary pregnant female, and she's not the Alpha's wife."

"Yeah, I hear you. So how's Camille doing today? The Wolf Briar wear off?"

"She's feeling better. We're going to talk to Paulo's fiancée, and I think we'll also drop in on Marion at the Supe-Urban Café and see what she can tell us. Meanwhile, you try to figure out what the hell a group of coyote shifters would want with your sister."

"The question for the win. I have no idea. I haven't talked to her much over the years, until she called saying she needed to move up here. She sounded slightly crazed, but I thought it was the hormones from the pregnancy. Okay, I'll let you get busy." He hung up, and I stared at the phone before handing it back to Iris.

"This is as bad as fighting the werespiders. We didn't know what they wanted, but in the end, it wasn't anything good." I ran down what Luke had told me about the trickster energy and the werewolf deaths in Arizona.

"Somebody in Arizona is producing Wolf Briar then. And so is someone up here. We have to make three stops today— Marion's, Franco's, and Madame Pompey's Magical Emporium. I hate that we aren't closer to finding Amber," Camille said, carrying her dishes over to the sink and rinsing them off to stack them with the rest. "I keep thinking they're torturing her or that she's already dead. And there's no good way to find out."

"Is there any way you could scry on her? Find out if she's still alive?"

Camille frowned, thinking. "I might. My spell of Finding won't do anything more than point the way if she's being held captive. Unless it backfired and dropped us into the captive's lair."

"Hell, I'd almost go for that—but not without backup. One whiff of the Wolf Briar, and we'd both be down for the count."

"Yeah, about that. Sharah called today, told me be careful because I'm sensitized to it now, and subsequent exposures could cause an allergic reaction—which could be anything from mild to fatal."

"Wonderful. Okay, what about the scrying? Can you do it?"

"Bring me a bowl of water. Use one of the crystal ones." She sat back down at the table, closing her eyes and breathing softly as I prepared the water for her. We had several silver and crystal bowls that both she and Iris used for magic, and I pulled out the clearest one. Then, in a spurt of inspiration, I ran up to her study and found the Tygerian well water from back home in Otherworld. Couldn't hurt to give it a little extra oomph by adding a bit of holy water to the mix.

When I returned, I saw that Camille was holding Amber's picture. A touchstone. I added a cup of the Tygerian water to the tap water, and it spread through the liquid like oil, then blended, and the liquid took on a startling clarity. Cautiously, I wrapped my arms around the massive bowl and carried it over to the table.

Camille let out a long breath, and as I watched, she leaned over the bowl and opened her eyes. She searched the water, face pensive, scanning for—what I didn't know. Magic confounded me, amazed me, and frightened me.

When Camille was wrapped up in the energy, it was as if she belonged to another realm, one that swept her away and consumed her. I couldn't reach where she went. But then again, she couldn't follow me into my realm as tabby and panther. We had our own private kingdoms—the same with Menolly and her bloodlust. And yet, each of us stood stronger together than apart.

A swirl of mist rose from the water, and she gasped and sat back. "Look," she whispered, pointing at the bowl.

I gazed in at the still surface, waiting till the mist cleared. There she was—Amber. She was in a cage, holding on to the bars, a plaintive look on her face and—wait a second.

"What's that around her neck?"

Camille leaned forward, squinting. After a moment, she jerked her head up, a frightened look on her face. "That can't be what I think it is, can it?"

Around the frightened Were's neck was a golden chain, and on the chain a pendant of the clearest topaz, brilliant yellow and sparkling. The setting was ornate, carved, and looked extremely old. And the gem glistened, even in what appeared to be dim light.

"It looks like the others, doesn't it?" I sucked in a deep breath. Could Amber really have what we thought she did? And if so, how the hell did she get hold of a spirit seal?

"Fuck, fuck, fuck." Camille frantically scanned the image again. "I can't make out anything other than that she appears to be in a cell—a cage—and the light there is dim. I have no idea where she is, and I can't see anything to give us a landmark." She slammed the table with her hand. "If she has one of the seals, we have to find her before she's killed."

"What would the coyote shifters want with the spirit seals? Would they even know what they were?"

Camille grabbed her coat. "Iris, we're heading over to Marion's. She should be at her café by now."

I grabbed my jacket and purse. "Right behind you. Let's take my—"

"*Not* your Jeep. The sun may be out, but it's cold and supposed to get colder today. We're taking my Lexus." She held up her keys. I shrugged, giving in before I even bothered arguing, and we headed down the steps.

The Supe-Urban Café was on East Pike, and it was a hangout for Supes of all kinds, but especially Weres. We'd first met Marion—a coyote shifter, the owner—at a Supe Community meeting, and then, a few weeks back, she'd helped Camille and our friend Siobhan escape from a crazed psycho stalking the selkie.

Business was brisk at the café, with nearly every table filled. Scenic photos from around the area covered the walls, landscape shots of Mount Rainier and the city of Seattle—the Space Needle, down at the docks, Seattle Center—urban scenes mingling with the wild. The tables were polished wood, and the chairs were simple but sturdy—wood and green leather.

The smell of hot coffee, chicken soup, and fresh bread lingered in the air, and though we'd just eaten breakfast, the scents were enough to make my stomach growl. We took a table and motioned to Marion, who was behind the counter, making change for a customer.

She meandered over, coffeepot in hand. "Coffee? Biscuits and honey? Cinnamon roll?"

Camille broke into a grin. "What the hell. One of your big biscuits and honey, please. And a Sprite."

"I'll take a cinnamon roll. And if possible, a few minutes of your time. We have a few questions we could use some help on."

Marion nodded. "Let me put in your order, then I'll be right back to talk to you girls." She headed toward the warming shelf and slapped our order up. Then, Sprite in hand, she returned and settled down at our table.

The woman was gaunt, but not for lack of food. Coyote shifters all seemed to be on the thin side, lean and wiry, and most were tough. Marion had curly red hair—almost mahogany—pulled back in a neat ponytail, and her eyes flashed hazel. She was wearing jeans and a T-shirt and a green apron that had the Supe-Urban Café logo embroidered on the corner. Leaning back against the chair, she folded her arms and smiled.

A waitress came in with our order and handed me a gigantic cinnamon roll and Camille what was truly the biggest biscuit I'd ever seen, along with a nice big dab of butter and a miniature pitcher of honey. As the waitress excused herself, Marion motioned for us to eat up.

"What can I do for you?"

Camille glanced at me and nodded as she slathered the biscuit with butter and honey.

I cleared my throat. "This is a delicate situation, Marion.

We don't want to appear accusatory, but a problem has come up, and we'd like your take on it."

Marion glanced around, but everybody seemed involved with their food, drink, books, and conversation. "Okay, what's up?"

I leaned forward and kept my voice low. "We may have a problem with some . . . coyote shifters making Wolf Briar. Or buying it."

"Fuck. Just fuck." She paled, as pale as someone perpetually tanned can turn. "In my office. *Now*. Bring your food."

We followed her past the kitchen, with its steaming pots and pans, to the office in the back, where she dropped into the chair behind her desk and motioned for us to sit. "Now that we're in private, spill it."

I ran down everything that had happened, leaving our speculation about the spirit seal out of the mix. Marion played with a piece of wood she'd been whittling into a figurine as she listened. When we came to the Wolf Briar traps hitting Camille, she leaned forward.

"I'm going to tell you something my people don't talk much about. For one thing, the coyote tribes keep to themselves, and we don't like our secrets to get out. But another: We have some dark cousins among our midst, and to speak of them . . . it's feared we'll invoke them by doing so." She opened a drawer and withdrew a figurine of a coyote. He was standing up, a mask across his face, carrying a bag over his shoulder. "May Coyote Master hear our words and keep them secret," she whispered, touching the statue reverently.

A tingle ran down my back. *Magic.* I may not always pick up on it, but this was tangible and felt comforting—like crawling into a warm bed with a thick quilt. A moment later, the room lay muffled and silent.

"Now we can talk safely, away from prying eyes." Marion glanced at the clock. "The spell should last for about fifteen minutes."

"I didn't know you worked magic." Since werewolves had an innate mistrust of magic, I had just assumed that most coyote shifters would, too. "I thought most canid Weres didn't use magic."

"Werewolves don't, but coyote shifters? Some of the most magical weres around. We run Trickster energy, my feline friend. The great Coyote is inherently magical, and so are those true to his path. But we can talk about that later. I need to tell you something, and this must remain secret—if anyone asks, you didn't find out from me. Got it?" She folded her muscled but lean arms across her chest.

"Got it."

"I'm going to tell you a story. A legend among my people. This, my grandmother told me, in these words, and so I tell you now. You are the first non–coyote shifters to hear this story. At least from me."

"We're honored, and we will not abuse your trust," Camille said.

Marion nodded. "Then I begin. A thousand and a thousand years ago, the Great Trickster gave his people the power to shape-shift into coyotes. It was a gift from him, for his people followed his path and had grown wise from his teachings. And for being so attentive, the Trickster bestowed a special gift upon the leader of the first tribe of shifters, whose name was Nukpana. The gift was a gem, and the gem shone like the sun. Nukpana wore the gem around his neck, a sign of the covenant between the Great Trickster and the shifters."

Camille let out a little gasp but kept her tongue. Oh yeah, this was going just along the direction we wanted to hear. So the Great Trickster had possessed one of the spirit seals. Wonderful.

"The gem strengthened the peoples' powers to dance with chaos and live through the unexpected. But as with all powerful gifts, the gem was two-faced, and Nukpana began to live *for* chaos rather than living *with* it." Marion let out a long sigh. "Nukpana tipped the scales."

I licked my lips. "He began to toy with the balance of order and chaos?"

"Correct. Nukpana began to practice dark magic, and his greed overcame his willingness to live in harmony with others. He used his knowledge of trickery and illusion for power rather than to make his peoples' lives better. Soon, his son rose up with a group of those who were unhappy with the changes, and they forced Nukpana out, driving him into the desert. But there were some enticed by the sorcerer's magic, and they followed him, setting up their own village where they threw themselves into learning the darker arts of chaos. They reverted to *Koyaanisqatsi*—a life out of balance. His descendents are known as the Koyanni."

"I don't think I like where this is going," I said softly.

"The story does not end happily." Marion shook her head. "Your friend is in grave danger if what I suspect is true."

She continued as Camille and I listened, eating our food.

"The Great Trickster tried to turn the Koyanni from their path—it saddened him to see Nukpana use the great gift he'd been given to twist Coyote's teachings. And so as the years went by and Nukpana fell further into the dark path, Coyote sent Akai, one of the Fox Brethren, into their midst to steal the gem and hide it. Nukpana, by now old far beyond any natural life span, abandoned his people and chased the cunning Akai through the centuries. Long after he fell, killed by the dust of time, the heirs of the Koyanni have searched for the gem, hoping that it will help them fulfill what they believe is their destiny. They remain true to the twisted lessons Nukpana taught them, far from their origins, and the Great Trickster still mourns the lost tribe."

"So . . . the Koyanni . . . who followed Nukpana . . ."

"They're considered the lost tribe by the rest of us. They turned from the teachings of the Great Trickster and fell into the shadows. The shadow tribes are scattered across the country now—but I know some live up here. And definitely down in Arizona. They could easily have chased down your friend and captured her, though I haven't the faintest idea of why." Marion shook her head. "The Koyanni are vicious and cruel . . . they use trickery to hurt. They don't honor their word."

"Thank you," I whispered. "Question: You said some of the shadow path tribes are local?"

"Oh yes," Marion said, her voice falling to a whisper. "They live up here, and they're dangerous and magical and enticing. They use illusion to get what they want, and poisons of all sorts. If they wanted your friend, she's dead and painfully so, unless they have a reason to keep her alive."

Camille slid to the front of her chair, and the room seemed to take on a darker feel, as if the spell Marion had invoked was wearing off. "Do you know where they live?"

Marion looked up, meeting our eyes. She shuddered. "They

walk the city streets. No wild places for them. They live in the urban areas; they haunt the suburbs. I don't have an address, but I know they live in the city—I've heard rumors of a house in Belles-Faire, but I don't know exactly where. I'll see if I can find out anything. But you can be sure they've a hand in creating the Wolf Briar."

Feeling like the enemy was all too close for comfort, I thanked her, and we left.

"Let's head over to Mary Mae's." Camille pulled out of the parking lot. "It's close enough to the time she gave you."

"Sure." As we sped along the streets, I finally looked over at her and said, "So Amber has one of the spirit seals. The one Nukpana wore. And now the Koyanni are after her. They must be able to sense it. Nukpana wore it for so long that it must still have some of his energy imprinted on it."

"And they followed her up here—or contacted friends up here—and took her out with Wolf Briar. But why didn't they just steal it off her when she was out in the hotel? Why kidnap her?" Camille shook her head. "There's another piece of the puzzle we aren't getting."

"Yeah, and I don't like it. There—that must be the house." I pointed to a small house set back on a narrow, tidily mowed lawn. Camille parallel parked with an ease I'd never mastered, and we hopped out of the car.

I glanced at the house. Well-kept but ragged. Mary Mae and Paulo might be lower income, but they didn't let that stop them from making the place as homey as possible. As I opened the chain-link gate, I could hear a dog bark—probably the backyard. We headed up the walk, but the place looked silent and too quiet.

Once we were standing on what passed for a porch, I noticed that the door was ajar. I gestured to it with a nod of the head, and Camille caught my gaze. She backed up, and I could tell she was summoning the Moon Mother's energy just in case we needed it. I didn't usually carry my dagger along with me, but I had a tidy little stiletto affixed to my wrist. Chase would have chewed me out if he knew I wore it—the blade was entirely illegal. But that never stopped us before.

I motioned for Camille to step back, and she plastered herself against the side of the house. Raising one booted foot, I slammed the door open and darted in, Camille right behind me. A glance around showed the living room was empty, but Camille tugged on my arm and nodded to the kitchen.

"I hear something," she mouthed.

We raced toward the open archway. I ducked through, and my first impression was one of blood. Everywhere. The walls were stained red, the floor covered in a pool of the thick, viscous fluid. And in the center of the pool—a woman, very pregnant. Very dead. Mary Mae. It had to be.

The scent made me reel, and I felt Panther waver, wanting to come forth.

Camille darted around the blood toward the back door, which was standing open, and disappeared into the backyard. I followed just in time to see her shooting an energy bolt at a thin, gaunt man who was racing for the back fence. It hit him, and he turned, snarling.

I raced past her, flipping the wrist blade open. "Stop right there!"

He pulled something out of his pocket and threw it toward me. The thing exploded on the ground. Wolf Briar. Fuck!

My senses reeling, I screamed for Camille to stay back, but those were the only words I managed to get out before Panther took over and I found myself shifting, transforming. The minute I was on all fours, I bounded after the man, who was clambering over the fence. In one leap, I cleared the chain-link and was on his heels. I chased him down the alley and got in a good swipe. The second swipe took him down, and he rolled over on his back, his eyes wide with fear.

I landed on his chest, growling, knowing I needed to keep him alive, but the scent of the woman's blood was thick on his jacket, and a terrible anger welled up inside—fury that he'd taken her life, her child's life, that he had put my sister in danger. Without thinking, I caught his throat in my teeth.

"No, no—" He tried to break free, his arms wrapping around my neck, but I clenched harder, and he let go. A crazed look filled his eyes, and I saw my own bloodlust reflected back at me—he was a killer, all right, I could feel it in his soul. And I could feel something else, too—he was Were. *A coyote shifter.*

Without realizing what I was doing or how I was doing it, I began to read his thoughts, sensing him lash out at Mary Mae, seeing him thrill as he slashed her life away, feeling his relief that she wouldn't be able to say a word about Paulo. He'd killed her to keep her quiet, and he'd enjoyed every second of it. The man was mad like a devil, and it was *his time to go*.

Startled, I felt Greta next to me, and she gently rubbed my fur as I held him. She knelt beside me and whispered, "No—it's not time for you to learn this. Delilah, back away."

But I ignored her plea and with one garbled growl, I shook the life out of the coyote shifter. As he dropped to the ground, a limp dishrag, I nuzzled him, rolling him over. I felt so alive it terrified me.

CHAPTER 14

By the time I'd licked her blood off of his chest, along with some of his own, Camille found me. She cautiously approached, her hand out.

"Delilah? Delilah, back away. We have to identify him. We have to call Chase because of Mary Mae. It's time to come back, Delilah." Her voice was soothing and yet commanding, and I found myself paying attention to her.

I let out a long huff, wanting to maul the freak some more, but then backed off and—this time slowly—changed back into myself. I still had blood on my face and the taste of it in my mouth, but by now it was part of who I was. Though I still got queasy when I thought of Menolly and how she drank blood, I was losing my squeamishness.

Staring down at the body, I cleared my throat. "He killed her. I know it. I felt it—in my Death Maiden aspect." And even though I said it to soothe myself, in my heart I knew it was true. "The stench of death was on his breath. He killed her, and he enjoyed it."

Camille stared at me for a moment, then nodded. "Stand guard. I've called Chase. I'll go back and wait with Mary Mae's body." She turned to go.

"How did you avoid the Wolf Briar?"

"Thanks to you, I managed to duck out of the way before the vapor caught me. You saved me. That big of a dose could have knocked me out for a good long time. I think I'm going to have to be very careful when we finally go up against this group." She shrugged. "Either that or be prepared to take the consequences. Maybe Wilbur knows of a vaccine or something."

As she headed back to the house, I could hear the faint sound of sirens in the distance.

Chase knelt by the dead shifter. "What do I need to know?" The question was pointed. He did *not* ask me what happened.

"He attacked Mary Mae. We know that much. Her blood's on his hands, and I'm pretty sure the murder weapon will have his prints on it. He must have dropped it in the house. And then he attacked us with Wolf Briar when we went after him. He's a coyote shifter, Chase. He's not human."

"Any way to prove it?" Chase glanced up at me.

Ask Sharah to do a DNA screen. She'll prove it. I chased him, and he turned to put up a fight. I shifted into panther form and . . ." I paused, realizing I could be in real trouble here if we couldn't link him to the murder. I'd basically mowed him down.

Just then, Yugi joined us in the alley, holding up a paper bag. "I've got the murder weapon. Found it just outside the back door. Bloody prints on it. Looks like the guy was doing something with her blood when Camille and Delilah interrupted him."

"Probably harvesting it for something." I let out a long sigh. "These coyote shifters . . . Chase, they aren't like other Weres. They aren't like Marion and her group. They're dangerous and they're deadly and they have no remorse. They don't give a flying fuck about anybody else, and they're power hungry."

"Why did he kill her, do you think? What was his motive?"

"We were coming over to talk to her about Paulo's disappearance. He must have found out and decided to kill her before she could talk to us. We think we know why they kidnapped Amber, and what they want."

I motioned for him to edge away from Yugi. Chase told the FH-CSI team to clean up the scene, and we headed back to the house. Along the way I told him about the Koyanni, shortening it, but keeping the gist.

"So why are they after Amber?"

"Because . . . when Camille did some scrying and Amber's image came up, both of us recognized what she's carrying around her neck. One of the spirit seals—and it must be the one that the Trickster first gave, then took away, from Nukpana's people. Somehow, Amber came across it, and they want it back."

"Crap. You mean a bunch of crazed coyote shifters possess one of the spirit seals? That's as bad as the demons getting hold of it." He leaned against the fence, sighing. "What the hell are we going to do?"

"We check out the magic shop. Meanwhile, you verify that this guy killed Mary Mae for me. I know he did . . . but I want your kind of proof."

"All right. But tell me this: why is Amber still alive if they got what they wanted?"

I shook my head. "That's as much your guess as mine. We have no idea. But we can't press our luck. We have to find her before they decide they don't need her anymore and kill her. And if the seal's truly still around her neck, that means they can't use it right now. I hope."

As I trudged inside, avoiding the lingering traces of Wolf Briar in the air, Chase headed back to Yugi and his team.

Camille was in the living room, sorting through papers on Mary's desk. She looked up as I entered the room and pointed to a large leather-bound book in her hand. "Paulo's Day-Timer. The dude had quite a busy schedule. Appears he was a handyman and kept all of his appointments in here. And he was organized; he checked them off one by one as he finished." She grinned and waited.

I frowned. "How does that help us?"

"*He checked them off when he finished them*—both work and recreation appointments." She waited again, then said, "Cripes . . . Delilah, we can trace back to the last appointment he completed and find out where he was headed next!"

Duh me! I thunked my forehead. "Sorry, still a little blood-crazed from taking down the shifter. Yes, that will be a tremendous help. We can talk to his last contacts and follow the trail from there. Where was the last place he went?"

"Hmm . . . he finished up a job over on Elm Street . . . then . . ." She looked up. "He has an appointment to go jogging in Rodgers Park after that. It's not checked off. Hmm . . ." She picked up the phone and dialed a number. I started to ask who she was calling but after a moment, she said, "Katrina, this is Camille. Do you know who Paulo used to go jogging with?" A pause. "Really? Thanks."

Hanging up, she waited a second, then picked up the receiver and dialed again. "Hello, is this Mrs. Davis? Hi, I'm with Franco Repair, and I'm just following up to make sure that Paulo Franco made the appointment at your house . . . let's see . . . it would have been ten days ago . . . He did? Good, and was everything satisfactory? . . . Oh good. Now, I have one last question, and it may seem strange, but I assure you, I wouldn't ask if it weren't necessary. Did Paulo seem odd in any way? . . . Well, the reason I want to know is because he's missing, and we're trying to trace his steps after he left your house. We know he returned home, but we were hoping he might have said something . . . You weren't? You didn't? Okay, well, thank you for your time."

"Let me guess: he showed up, did the job, nothing unusual, and she really wanted off the phone." I grinned. "Trust me, this is why you ambush people in person. They give a lot more clues to what might have happened if you can see their faces. But I think in this case, she was telling the truth. He wouldn't have checked off her appointment if something had interfered with him on the way home from there."

"I guess . . . we check Rodgers Park? I might be able to cast a trace spell from there." She gathered her things, and we headed out to the car, where I flipped open my netbook and pulled up Google Earth.

"Here it is—not far. Let's head out, and then we'll drop in at the magic shop." I let out a long sigh. "I just keep thinking what those maniacs might want with a spirit seal. And the fact that they're willing to kill in order to cover up their steps isn't a good sign. Not at all."

By the time we hit the park, I was getting sick of chasing down leads only to find they were washouts. We stood on the edge of the green, staring at the forested land. How did we ever expect to find anything here? I shook my head, ready to turn and pack it in when Camille held up her hand.

"Wait. I smell something. It's lingering in the air . . . almost like . . ." She took off at a run, and I followed her. As we headed around a bend in the road toward an opening in the tree line, I started to smell something myself, but for the life of me, couldn't figure out what it was. Like honey, or flowers, or something appealing. Definitely not Wolf Briar.

We slowed as we entered the copse, surrounded by cedar and maple, fir, and here and there an oak tree. The smell of flowers still lingered, drawing us in, and while it wasn't a compulsion as in being charmed, the draw was there.

At another bend, a dirt path forked off to the left, away from the sidewalk, and I took over the lead, motioning to my wrist blade. Camille nodded and slipped behind me.

The path wove through a small glen and then, ahead, we saw an opening—though it didn't look big enough to be a ball field or any such man-made glade. As we came to the edge of the wood and peeked out, there, in the center of a small opening, sat a huge boulder. And atop the boulder rested a creature who looked ethereal, and yet, an edge of danger clung to her.

Her hair was gold, shining in a shaft of cold sunlight that broke through the tree canopy, and she was willowy, tall, and fragile-looking. Yet, when she raised her head and gazed at us with weeping eyes, I could see a cold light behind her stare, an icy, ruthless passion. But she merely motioned for us to enter the glade and pointed to a tree trunk.

We sat, waiting.

After a moment, she spoke. "You are not fully human. You are from the Tribe Who Left?"

Camille and I glanced at one another. That was one way to describe it. "Yes, we're from Otherworld," I said. "Our mother was human. Our father is of the Sidhe. And you are . . . ?"

"Dryad. Earthborn. Bound to this wood. Or what there is left of it." She heaved a great sigh and dried her eyes. "Every day I come here and mourn the loss of the land. And every day I guard what's left of this patch—this *park*, as *they* call it. I observe."

"We smelled your perfume," I said gently. "We didn't mean to intrude on your mourning."

"You smelled my fragrance? Then we have a connection. Only those who connect with me in some way can smell my violets and freshly mown grass. What is it you seek?" She delicately wrapped one leg beneath her, folding her knee and pulling it to her chest as she balanced on the granite rock.

I knew better than to ask her name. Dryads, like flo-raeds, were dangerous and unpredictable. They could also be immensely helpful if they chose to be. "We're seeking information on a man who may have come through this park a fortnight ago. He was a werewolf. He never returned home, and this was the last place he was expected to be. He never checked his appointment off the calendar, so we're wondering if he made it here."

"He would have been jogging, possibly with a friend," Camille added. "We think a coyote shifter might have abducted him."

"Coyote shifter?" The dryad's eyes grew narrow. "You mingle with those scum? Then get the hell out of my garden, or I'll hurt you." As she jumped to her feet, standing atop the rock, a great thorny vine came lunging out of the foliage behind her, aiming right toward us. It looked nasty and dangerous, and the thorns were a good four inches long.

"Wait! Please!" We scrambled off the trunk, and I pushed Camille behind me. "We just want information. We aren't friends of the dark shifters!"

The vine stopped, hesitating. The dryad tapped her foot on the stone. "You say he was a werewolf?"

"Yes," I said, edging back yet another step. The hovering vine made me nervous, and I didn't trust the dryad not to send it whaling away on us. "He was a beta wolf . . . he would have been easy prey for those wielding Wolf Briar."

The vine began to retreat, but only to the edge of the wood. We could still see it. The dryad squatted on the rock, wrapping her arms around her knees. I wondered, briefly, how her flimsy gossamer dress—so sheer it was see-through—could keep her warm in this weather, but she didn't seem bothered by the chill, and I didn't want to chance insulting her with another question.

"Wolf Briar." Her voice was low. "Someone is using Wolf Briar. I smelled it—close to the time you are talking about. It stank up my trees, and I remember trying to hunt down whoever left the trail, but they were quick and not easy to trace. I stopped when I came to the edge of the wood."

"We think the coyote shifters used it to attack our friend. He had a pregnant fiancée. We found her dead today, before she could talk to us. We know the coyote shifters—the Koyanni—killed her to shut her up. They didn't want her to tell us anything that might endanger their plans." I decided to take the chance. "Will you help us? Will you show us where you smelled the Wolf Briar being used?"

She stared at us, unspeaking, for a moment. Then, with a single nod, she jumped off the boulder and motioned for us to follow her as the thick undergrowth next to her parted, revealing a hidden path.

The dryad led us through a winding trail until we came to a small field with a track in the center of it. She pointed. "He was there. I was watching him because he seemed odd, not human, and I watch all who wander the paths. He was alone, by the way. No friend came with him."

"Nobody?"

She shook her head. "None. I was about to leave him be when a group of shifters came off that path across the way." Gesturing, she pointed to one of the sidewalks. "They raced over to him, and I heard a noise and smelled the Wolf Briar. I hid, so I didn't see what happened. When I returned some time later, there was no sign of the werewolf nor the shifters. The Wolf Briar was still drifting on the breeze."

Camille and I headed over to the track. It didn't look well-used, most likely due to the fact that we'd had rain for most of the past two weeks and the track was dirt. Most joggers seemed to prefer the city streets or park sidewalks when they ran in the rain, and Seattle joggers didn't let rainstorms stop them from getting out on the streets.

As we circled the quarter-mile path, I stopped and pointed off to the side nearest the walkway that the dryad had pointed out. Something shiny lay in the grass. We headed over and knelt beside whatever it was.

"A watch," Camille said, lifting it up. She turned it over. "It's inexpensive, but look—an inscription. To Paulo, the love of my life." She paled. "This was Paulo's watch." Standing up, she shaded her eyes and looked to the opposite tree line. I followed suit.

"Something must have been waiting here for him, come out, dragged him off. What's over there?" I turned toward the dryad, who had followed us out onto the grassy meadow.

She frowned for a moment. "Parking lot," she said after a pause. "Cursed machines. Tear up the ground, tear up the earth to lay pavement. Humans need to learn how to walk again."

I didn't say anything, not wanting to get her off on a tangent against cars. I rather liked my Jeep, even though it wasn't the best thing for the environment, and by now, cars were an integral part of human society, although the new hybrids were winning my heart for their attempts to shift away from polluting the world.

"Coyote shifters got him here. Took him to the parking lot . . . this was Paulo's last free stop, I'll bet you." Camille hung her head. "Poor guy. And poor Mary Mae and her baby."

My cell rang, and the dryad jumped back as if she'd been burned. I moved out of her way to answer it. "Yeah?"

"Chase here. We found something you need to see. It's not pleasant."

"What is it?" I was getting tired of *unpleasant*. I could really go for something a little nicer right now. Maybe even downright fun.

"You mean, *who* was it. We think it's the remains of one of your werewolves. I say *think* because what's left isn't in very good shape. Get over here ASAP." And with that, he signed off.

I flipped my phone shut and turned to Camille. "We've been summoned. Chase's men found something." I motioned to the dryad. "We thank you for your help—we really appreciate it. If there's anything you ever need, let us know, and we'll see what we can do."

She blinked. "You mean it?"

Oh great. Earthside Fae were notorious in the way they latched on to the words "thank you" as a promissory note. Usually, it was a good month or two before people called in their markers, and when we were lucky, they said, "Forget about it," and let it go as a favor. But she was serious.

"Yeah. What are you thinking?"

She blinked, then broke into a sly smile. "I could use a new garden to tend. I'm tired of the space closing in on me here. Find me a place where the trees are still wild and free, and I'll move."

Wow. That was unexpected. I choked down my first thought, which was, *Oh yeah, we're great little Santa's helpers,* and forced a smile to my lips. "We'll do our best. It may take a little time. Do you mind cold winters?"

The dryad gave me a look like I had just asked her if she encouraged strip mining. "No . . . does it look like the cold bothers me? You may call me Bluebell. I'll be waiting here for you. Don't take too long. Please." And with that, she vanished into the undergrowth.

Camille shook her head, warning me not to speak. We high-tailed it out to the parking lot, Paulo's watch in hand. Once we were in the car, I told Camille what Chase had said. "I think we don't have to look far to find one of our missing Weres."

She grimaced. "Wonderful. Okay, let's head out. This day just keeps getting worse and worse."

I was all in agreement, though to be honest, after finding Mary Mae's body, I didn't think there'd be much of a *worse* coming, and I prayed I wouldn't be wrong.

CHAPTER 15

The FH-CSI headquarters had become all-too-familiar territory the past couple of days. We pulled into the lot and hustled
inside, heading for Chase's office, but he cut us off before we
could get there, meeting us near the door.

"Come on, we're heading toward the morgue."

We hit the elevator. The second floor of the building—
heading underground—was the arsenal and included a number
of weapons the Seattle government wasn't aware Chase was
stocking. They wouldn't have understood most of them—silver
bullets, garlic bombs, various and sundry custom tricked-out
guns. The elevator glided past the second floor, down to the
third—jail cells for offenders from Otherworld. The fourth
floor was the lowest level as far as I knew, though Chase had
hinted there might be another, but he wouldn't tell me what for.

Fourth floor was the morgue, the in-house laboratory, and
the archives. We stepped out of the car and onto the concrete
floor. Camille let out a long breath. She hated enclosed spaces
and only took the elevator under protest because nobody
else would do the stairs with her, and in this case, the stairs
required specialty clearance badges.

As we followed Chase down the hall, her heels clicked a

staccato tattoo on the floor, and I found myself listening to them, counting away the steps. Chase and I'd been together more since we'd broken up than we had the past few weeks. Somehow, that didn't seem like such a great thing now.

We stopped by a set of double doors leading into the morgue. During a rash of vampire risings last December, when Menolly's sire had come over from Otherworld to destroy her, she'd made mincemeat of the morgue, putting fledglings down. Now, you couldn't even tell that damage had been done.

We entered the antiseptic room, and I focused on quieting my suddenly churning stomach. I was still squeamish about some things, dead bodies included, although they didn't bother me nearly so much as they used to. The shelves were lined with bottles containing rubbery, slippery looking organs and various chemical mixtures. Each was labeled, but I did my best to skip reading what they contained. My stomach couldn't handle placing a name on the gruesome visuals.

Camille and I were facing a long metal table. Mallen was standing beside it, in full gown, mask, cap, and gloves. He looked like a mad elfin scientist, with something in his hands that had to be . . . oh crap, it was. A lung. I looked away.

"Have you determined what we're dealing with?" Chase asked.

"Looks like it was a werewolf, all right." His voice was muffled, but his words were clear enough.

I steeled myself and turned back to face the table. What was left of the body had been dissected—or at least it looked that way now. It had been opened up, cut expertly into thin layers as if somebody had been butterflying a chicken breast, and the layers were folded back, held in place by clips.

"What shape was he in when you found him?"

"Like this—opened up like an envelope. Scent glands are missing. Pituitary gland is missing. Adrenals are gone. Testicles are gone. And the heart is gone. Whoever got to this poor guy is using more than just his scent glands, but I don't know for what. They wouldn't need the heart or testes to make Wolf Briar." He slowly folded the face back over the skull, which had a large slice taken off the top so the brain was showing. "Do you recognize him?"

My stomach lurched, and I winced. "No, but Katrina would, if it's one of her friends. Should we call her?"

"Please. But warn her. We can set it up so she won't see the rest of the body, but there's no way she's going to miss the fact that he's been sliced and diced like your local heifer on slaughtering day." Chase shook his head. "I can't imagine doing this to someone. Harvesting from them."

"There's more than that," Mallen said as Camille stepped over to the landline on the wall to call Nerissa and ask her to contact Katrina. Cell phones didn't work underground.

"What more could there be?" I asked, wondering just how far the coyote shifters would go.

"His arms and legs show signs of being manacled. He was bound by something hard, something tight that bit into his skin. The bruising is consistent with—I'd say, iron or steel manacles. Cuffs. And they were tight. Drug tests are due back in a few minutes. We're specifically looking for steroids."

"Can you imagine . . . you take a beta werewolf, hop him up on steroids till he's in a fighting rage. Manacle him in a cage and intensify his desire to get out. The power and fury that would create is scary to think about."

Unable to look at the remains any longer, I turned away. It wasn't so much disgust or revulsion as imagining what his end had been like. Terrified, most likely cut open while alive to maximize his rage—it made me want to hunt down his murderers and rip them to shreds, slowly.

Camille rejoined the group. "Nerissa's going to bring Katrina down. She's tough—but this isn't going to be easy for her. Maybe you should have some tea waiting for after? Up in the medic unit?"

"Good idea." Chase punched a button on his walkie-talkie and gave orders. "I suppose you can head out now. Unless you want to wait to see what Katrina says about his identity."

I slowly crossed to the table. His arm was to one side, his hand hanging off the edge. Quietly, I ran my fingers over the indentation—a band of pale skin that encircled his wrist, a startling contrast to the darker tone of his arm.

"It's Paulo Franco," I whispered, bringing the watch out of my pocket. The watchband matched perfectly with the markings on his skin. "And here's his watch. We know where they got him; we know when they got him. We know what they did with him. Now we just find out who did this and hunt them down."

Chase took the watch and glanced at the inscription, pressing his lips together as he read. He slid it onto the tray next to a gold ring and what looked like an earring. "Yeah," he said after a moment. "I think you're right."

"Damn it!" I grabbed Camille by the arm. "Let's get the hell over to that magic shop and demand a few answers." As I dragged her to the door, I called back to Chase, "call me on my cell when you have the definite ID, please."

We jogged out to the car. Camille had taken one look at my face, and I could tell she wasn't even going to try to suggest anything else. She just motioned for me to get in and pulled out of the parking lot, making quick time.

As we parked in front of Madam Pompey's Magical Emporium, Inc., she turned to me. "Before you head in there like a hothead, you listen to me," she said. "Wilbur says they're sorcerers. That means they're dangerous and most assuredly more powerful than I am. Do not, under any circumstances, accuse them of Paulo's death or of making the Wolf Briar. Not until we find out just who we're up against."

I stared ahead, sullen, not wanting to listen. "They practically flayed him alive. They killed his fiancée and their unborn child. They have Amber, who has one of the spirit seals. What would you have us do—just wander in and play nice?"

"Exactly. Kitten, I'm working death magic. I know my way around a shop like that. So don't mess it up. We'll find out far more if they don't think we're out to kill them. You got it?"

I knew she was right, though I didn't want to admit it. But I nodded and followed her inside.

The shop was like one of those dark, cobwebby little holes-in-the-wall where you could find the most amazing things tucked away in corner baskets or under a table, or in the half-open drawer of some ancient dresser. Floor-to-ceiling shelves lined the walls, filled with jars of herbs and odd bits of creatures and liquids that I didn't dare speculate on.

In the center of the shop were the tables covered in bones—not human, I hoped—and wands made of metal, crystal, and wood. Decks of tarot cards bordered the tables, surrounding baskets of miniature scrolls radiating a strange light. And behind the front counter were large quart jars filled with powders, some glistening with sparkles, others black as powdered ink.

The scent of dark musk and night-blooming jasmine filtered through the air from long sticks of hand-rolled incense that burned on the counter.

We browsed, Camille turning over a bone here, a spell there, as she surveyed the shop. I tried to tune in to whatever she was listening to, but all I could feel was an annoying static that set me to gritting my teeth. After a while, she picked up what looked like a rib bone from a small animal and a deck of tarot cards, and we headed toward the counter.

The woman who slipped from the curtained room leading into the back was striking, especially for an FBH. A lot of FBH women were gorgeous, beautiful . . . but this woman—she had the spark of magic in her eyes, a dangerous fire that seemed barely contained, ready to lash out. Her hair was raven black, flowing long and straight down her back, and her features were delicate and yet chiseled in stone. She wore a long robe, navy in color and clinging to her body in a lewd way that none of Camille's fetish gear ever did.

She glided to the counter. On one level, I couldn't take my eyes off of her. On another, I understood exactly what Wilbur had been talking about when he said the woman scared him shitless. Even as magic-blind as I could be, the woman was dark, and a shadow oozed out of her aura to permeate the shop.

"May I help you?" Her voice leeched across the counter, tendrils of that same shadowy energy. She stood near the cash register.

Camille sucked in a short breath. "I'd like to buy these, and I have a question. I'm in need of several components that most shops around here won't prepare for me. Do you ever make custom-designed powders and potions?"

The woman blinked. "On occasion, when the price is right, if we have the interest. I can feel your energy, death-priestess. Why don't you make them yourself?" She cocked her head, her gaze focused on Camille.

"I don't have the setup in my home for it, and some of the ingredients are . . . shall we say . . . difficult to procure, and dangerous." Camille let out her glamour fully, catching the woman unaware. "What name shall I call you by?"

"Jaycee," she answered, now totally fixated on my sister. "What are you looking for? We might have it in stock. We keep a select inventory for a few of our regular customers."

"Corpse reanimation powder and demonic sentinel oil." Her voice smooth, Camille ticked off the components like she might be reciting a grocery list. "Snake slither, if you have it."

Jaycee's gaze flared. "I have all three, but we don't keep them here. Not wise to keep substances like that in plain view. I can bring them for you when I come in to work tomorrow."

Camille frowned. "That will work, although I'd rather have them today." She pulled out her purse and paid the woman for the bone and deck. "I'll see you tomorrow—I need an ounce of each."

"You know the snake slither's going to run you a good hundred fifty for an ounce," Jaycee said as we headed to the door.

"I'm not worried," Camille called back over her shoulder.

As soon as we were outside, she hustled me to the car, stopping at a nearby garbage can to dump the tarot deck and bone. "I can't stand having those in my hands. They reek as bad as Demonkin energy."

The minute we were in the car, she turned to me. "We need to find their home address. Wilbur's right. They're the ones making Wolf Briar. I could smell some of the ingredients on her robe, but I'll guarantee you they don't keep it in the shop. And wherever they keep that crap, they're going to be keeping a diary of who brought them the werewolves. Making Wolf Briar's bad, but kidnapping werewolves to harvest their organs? So much worse."

"What about Van?"

"I heard someone in the back and sensed an energy very similar to Jaycee's. Ten to one it was Van. So if they are at work, there's nobody at home to keep watch over things."

"So we break into their house. They may still be holding Doug and Saz—the guys might still be alive. And if we can prove they're making Wolf Briar, we shut them down. We also search for the records that will give us some idea where the coyote shifters live—and *they* have Amber."

"Two birds with one stone, babe." She started the car. "How do we find out where they live?"

"They have to have a business license, and there has to be

a record of who owns that license. Simple enough. Stop at a coffee shop, and I'll go online and look it up. That stuff's all public knowledge."

We pulled into a Starbucks, and while Camille bought cookies and a monster latte, I flipped open my laptop, jacked into the wireless service, and pulled up a browser. I had numerous sites bookmarked where I could dredge up all sorts of goodies on people. Some were pay-per-use, others I'd subscribed to, and still others were public domain. Within five minutes, I had the address of both president and treasurer of Madame Pompey's Magical Emporium, Inc. Van and Jaycee Thomas, and they lived a few miles from our home in Belles-Faire.

"Move it," I said. "I want to get there well before they even think of going home for the day."

Camille grabbed her latte and cookies, and we headed back to the car.

The Thomases lived back off the main road, like we did, on what looked to be a two- or three-acre parcel of land. In the Seattle area, that meant they weren't hurting for money. Camille paused at the edge of the drive.

"Just remember: They may have wards up. Keep your eyes open." She let out a long breath and began to edge forward along the drive. Like most driveways in the area, it was heavily graveled and bordered on both sides by heavy foliage.

I watched nervously as we eased along the road. The sun was beginning to disappear beneath the cloud cover, and the scent of impending rain hung heavy in the air. Huckleberry and thimbleberries reached out from the side to brush the car as Camille focused on staying in the grooved wheel ruts that had been worn into the drive, and I caught sight of a deer poking his head through the undergrowth up a ways to our right.

He was a four-tine buck, and he watched as we quietly drove past. I stared into his eyes and caught a glimpse of something—an intelligence I didn't normally associate with deer. They weren't stupid animals, by any means, but this . . . this was cunning and wile—not normally deer characteristics. I filed away the information in case we needed it later. For all we knew, the Thomases were creating souped-up animals for guardians.

As we rounded a curve, the house was suddenly in front of us. Like our own, it was a rambling Victorian, three stories high. Unlike our house, it was badly in need of repair and would have given the Munsters' house a run for its money. The paint was faded, the weather vane had snapped in two, at least three of the windows were cracked, from what I could see, and the porch sagged dangerously.

"They need to sink some of their money in a visit to Home Depot," Camille said, turning off the engine. "That porch doesn't look stable. Let's head around back and see what we find. I'm pretty sure we tripped a couple wards on the way in, so let's get the fuck in and out, just in case they have a warning system set up at their shop."

We cautiously circled the house, me leading. I wished now that I'd thought to bring my dagger, but the Seattle cops frowned on carrying weapons around in public. I took it when I knew we were heading into a fight, but I didn't go flaunting it on jaunts around the city streets.

The back of the house was no better than the front, but at least the steps up to the back door looked more stable. I gingerly climbed them, testing each with my weight. At the landing, I motioned for Camille to join me while I began to pick the lock.

She kept watch as I eased my picks into the keyhole and fished around. After a moment, I heard a faint click. *Bingo!* We were in. Easing open the door, I edged my way inside, Camille following.

The door led into a small laundry-utility room. The washer and dryer had seen better days, too, and I had the feeling that Van and Jaycee had sunk all of their money into the shop rather than their home. A half door led to the kitchen, and I peeked through the top half, which was open, before turning the knob.

The kitchen was tidy. *Too tidy.* There were no signs that anybody ever ate in this room, no fruit bowl on the counter, no dishes in the sink, no coffeemaker, toaster, or any other appliances. Frowning, I opened the nearest cupboard, while Camille peeked in the refrigerator.

"Nothing," I whispered. "No dishes, no food."

"Nothing here, either."

"Are you sure that they're human?" I asked. "The woman looked almost . . . too vivid to be an FBH, but I thought maybe it was her magic that did it to her."

Camille leaned against the counter. "I don't know. Can't be vampire if they're out in the daylight. But you're right—she did seem terribly vivid, although she responded to my glamour."

"Unless she was faking it." With that unsettling thought, we headed into what turned out to be the living room. Again, all the proper furniture, but no sign that people actually lived there. Everything was tidy, neat, dusted . . . but no personal pictures, no personal effects, nothing that clued us in on just who Van and Jaycee were.

"I don't like this," Camille said. "It's . . . too antiseptic. We have to hurry, though. More than ever, I'm thinking they have some warning system and may be on their way now. And considering what we're *not* finding, I'm feeling awfully uneasy here. Look for a basement. What better place to hide someone?"

We began peeking in doors, looking for steps leading down. The first two I opened led to small rooms—what looked like a parlor, and a bath—again, both with nothing to indicate this was anything but an empty house. But third time's the charm, and I opened the door to find a set of steps. I motioned to Camille. She held up her hand and flipped out her cell phone.

"I'm calling home—letting them know where we are . . . just in case."

I didn't like thinking *just in case*, but it was a good idea. She left a message with Iris, telling her if she didn't hear from us in twenty minutes, to send somebody looking. After she stowed her phone, we headed down the steps.

"This is too reminiscent of when we fought the hellhound for comfort," I whispered as I found a broom—new and untouched—to use for a tapping rod.

"At least this time we haven't caught the scent of Demonkin."

"*Yet*. You can't believe those two haven't been cavorting with demons." Van and Jaycee seemed the perfect couple to call in a demon here or there for favors.

"Believe it or not, not all evil comes from the Sub Realms. There are plenty of evil people in the world, plenty of evil beings in the astral."

I tapped on the first couple of steps with the broom handle. They were stable, so down we went, our conversation falling to the wayside as we descended further into the basement of the house. I glanced around. No cobwebs? That was impossible. Every basement had cobwebs. Unless they had some magical housecleaning service that spiffed everything up with the blink of an eye.

The steps seemed to go on forever—this basement was deep, deeper than our own, which housed Menolly's lair, deeper than the one in which Chase had been imprisoned. But after awhile, we came to a door at the bottom.

I jiggled the handle. "Locked. I don't know if I can pick this one."

Camille held her pen-sized flashlight on the keyhole as I worked it, first one way, then another until finally, the lock sprang.

As the door edged open, a bright flash blinded me, and I cried out, ducking to one side. Camille let out a sharp scream as the wood burst into flames, licking out at us. She turned tail and scrambled away from the stairs, which were acting like a wind tunnel, sucking the flames up toward the top.

I pressed against the wall, and she joined me.

"What do we do? That's magical fire, and I guarantee you, I can't put it out. I don't know how long it will last—"

But even as she spoke, the flames died down, the blast fading. The door was a pile of charred splinters, but the steps and sides of the basement hadn't caught fire at all. I frowned.

"How the hell did that happen?"

"Magical fire can be geared toward one target. My guess, it was aimed at any living thing in its path. The steps aren't alive. The door charred because of the blast, not because of the fire." She gingerly peeked through the hole in the door. "We were lucky. Let's get a move on. I need to check in with Iris in ten minutes."

We climbed through the hole in the door—there was no use trying to open it anymore, considering only the frame was left intact—and found ourselves in a laboratory. Here, it seemed, the Thomases actually lived. Or at least worked.

Benches lined the walls, with beakers and jars, test tubes and powders and Bunsen burners and everything necessary to produce compounds of all sorts. In the center of the room rested a basin large enough to hold a body. Drains were evenly spaced along its length, and what looked to be blood stained the porcelain. I grimaced, realizing they were used to drain away body fluids.

"This is where they make it—the Wolf Briar. They must be working with the coyote shifters—the shifters procure the werewolves and the . . . whatever they are . . . Van and Jaycee do the dissection here. But I don't see any cages, and there doesn't appear to be an inch of wall space leading to any secret chambers.

Camille stared at the basin in horror. "I've had to learn some pretty graphic and repulsive spells lately, but we've never touched someone alive. Raising the dead is one thing . . . killing the living for spell components is another. There's one way to find out if there's anything behind the lab benches."

With one leap, she was at the edge of the first. She took it in hand and heaved, tipping the table so that all the glass crashed to the floor. Fluids mixed with potions, and there were several small explosions and hisses as the reagents combined. In another moment, she'd tipped the table entirely, crashing it to the floor amid the broken glass. Then, grabbing a broken piece of wood, she thumped along the wall behind the overturned lab bench.

"Nothing here," she said, moving on to the next.

"Allow me." I stepped in and sent the next table flying. Again, the crash of glass, the hiss of burning chemicals, and again, nothing behind the walls. And then the frustration of the situation took hold, and we gutted the place like maniacs, tossing beakers, smashing the glass off before sending the tables sliding across the floor.

"This is for Paulo," I growled . . .

"And this is for Mary Mae and her baby . . ."

By the time we'd destroyed the room, Camille motioned to her watch. "I need to call Iris before she sends someone over—"

"Well, well, look what we have here, Jaycee. Visitors. Aren't we lucky they've taken such an interest in our work?"

The voice came from behind us. Startled, I turned. There, just inside the broken door, stood Van and Jaycee. And they looked pissed out of their minds.

CHAPTER 16

~~~

"Oh, crap." I backed up.

Van, who was a nondescript, pale man, stepped forward. His blandness faded as a wave of power rolled toward us. *Shit.* The dude had strength. Camille let out a gasp, and I realized she could feel his energy better than I could.

"He bad?" I asked her softly.

"Yeah . . . bad." She moved toward me.

There was no good way out of this. We couldn't talk our way out of having trashed their lab, that was for sure. I flicked open my wrist blade, jonesing for Lysanthra. But I'd fought before I began carrying her, and I could fight barehanded if necessary.

Camille sucked in a deep breath; I glanced at her. She was invoking the energy of the storm that was starting to break outside. Not only could she call down the Moon Mother, but she could invoke the power of lightning. She had a thing for the forked bolts, and they liked her a bit too much.

Van kept his gaze on us but motioned to Jaycee. "How much do you suppose we'll get for them?"

She looked us up and down, like a couple of fryers. "Two

out of the three? My guess is more than we expect, although we can't press our luck. I don't want the boss thinking we're trying to jack up the price. We're toast if she even remotely believes we're trying to scam her."

"What are you talking about?" I jostled, trying to find just the right position. It was obvious they weren't going to let us waltz out of here.

"Seems a certain demon general we work for has set a pretty price on your pretty heads," Van said. "We've been planning this moment—or one similar—for the past two weeks. Our only concern was that we get to you before the other recruits."

Realization of what he'd just said swept over me, and I wavered—only for a second—before spreading my legs and taking a firm stance. "So you work for the Bonecrusher."

"This is a setup." Camille let out a soft sigh. "The coyote shifters, the Wolf Briar . . . all to gain our attention and bring us to you."

"No, we just lucked out with the stupid shifters. They wanted the Wolf Briar, and they wanted it bad. We decided to use that to bring you out. We knew it would catch your attention sooner or later. You've got your nose into everything in this town. We just had to be patient. In the meanwhile, the more werewolves we captured, the more ingredients we had, and the more personal profit we made. Everything we get from the Wolf Briar is ours to keep." Van shrugged, a pasty grin plastered on his face.

Fuck . . . but we had one thing on our sides. They didn't seem to realize what the coyote shifters were after, which meant they didn't know about Amber or the spirit seal. If Stacia knew we were on the trail of the sixth seal, she'd be right on our asses herself.

"What are you planning to do with us?" I tried to gauge what kind of magic they had at their fingertips. Camille would know better than I, but I couldn't just ask her in front of them. The trapped door had been a harsh reminder that we weren't playing with neophytes.

"Well, that depends on you. On whether you come easily or whether you push your luck." Van stepped forward, a cunning, wicked smile on his lips. "Oh, this is going to be fun, isn't it, Jaycee?"

Jaycee slid behind him, guarding the door. "Yes, my sweet. We're going to have ourselves a lovely time." Her eyes glimmered, sadistic and cruel.

"You ready?" Camille whispered, so low that even I could barely hear her.

I inclined my head, ever so slightly.

"Inch a ways to the left," she said.

As I did, Camille let loose.

Lightning crashed through the side of the house, arcing down through the basement. With a rip and a shriek, the wood splintered as the bolt landed directly in front of Van, missing him by two inches. Thunder jolted the foundation, shifting the ground as the electricity whistled so loud it popped my ears.

Camille moved forward, a dark light filling her eyes. "Want to play some more, little boy?"

Van laughed. "I'd love to play ball . . . here, *catch*." And a ball of light shot out of his hands, directly at her, sizzling. Tendrils emerged from the energy bolt as it zeroed in on my sister.

Camille dodged to the side as I leapt past Van, flipping over his head to land in front of Jaycee. Before she could react, I slammed her in the nose with the palm of my hand, and the sound of breaking cartilage was music to my ears. Blood raced down my hands, and as I jerked back, I grabbed a handful of her hair, ripping it out of her head as I used it as a handle to swing her to the side, smashing her against the wall.

"Bitch." Her voice was muffled from the blood, but she didn't look like she was in any sort of pain. *Not* a good thing.

Shit, what the hell was she? No human could take such a hard punch and not react in *some* way. I decided I wasn't waiting around to find out and sliced through the air, my wrist blade singing as I aimed for her throat.

The next thing I knew, I was moving through mud, my hand inching forward in increments so slow that I might as well be standing still.

Jaycee's eyes burned bright. She laughed softly, and the

blood stopped flowing. It was then that I noticed there were no bruises on her face. None at all.

"You like to play rough?" Jaycee opened her mouth, and the next thing I knew, a coiled vapor launched itself at me from out of her throat. It wrapped itself around my neck.

I tried to wave it off but realized the gas was solidifying—manifesting into flesh, with a grip so tight I was having trouble breathing. A constrictor. Crap!

Digging in with my nails, I tried to dislodge it. Camille let out a scream, and Van's harsh laughter answered in return. I twisted, trying to see what was happening, but the snake tightened again, and spots appeared before my eyes. As I dropped to my knees, the room began to swim in shades of black and gray. Before I could pass out, a movement caught my attention. White wings came flying overhead, and the floor shook again.

And then I was on my side, gasping as the sweet flow of air whistled into my lungs. Voices filled the room. Somebody grabbed me by the hand and dragged me to my feet.

Blinking, I recognized Vanzir—but the next moment, he pushed me to the side and leapt back in a blur of motion. As I tried to make heads or tails out of what was going on, it began to dawn on me that Smoky, Vanzir, Trillian, and Morio were fighting Jaycee and Van, but no sooner had I grasped this fact when the pair vanished. We were alone in the basement.

"Camille! What happened to Camille?" I stumbled forward, looking for my sister, panicked they might have captured her.

"I'm right here, Kitten." She limped around from behind the platform in the middle of the room. Covered with lacerations, she was bleeding from a hundred little cuts on her body.

"What the fuck—?"

"Van pushed me into the glass on the floor and held me down, rolling me on the splinters." She winced. Jagged shards of glass, some barely the size of a thumbtack's point, others as big as a playing card, were embedded in her skin.

"Holy crap, you look horrible."

Smoky took one look at her and let out a huff. He turned to Trillian and Morio. "See that she gets treatment. *Now.*"

"Where are you going?" I asked, suddenly aware of how much was teetering on the edge.

"Where I go is none of your concern." He gave me a frozen look, then vanished into the Ionyc Sea. Oh shit, he was primed to kill.

"You realize what this means, don't you? Stacia's put out a bounty on our heads. Every bad guy worth his salt is going to try to collect." I dropped to sit on one of the steps.

"Yes, I realize that." Camille leaned cautiously against one of the tables, biting her lip. "Our lives are about to get so fucking complicated we'll long for the days we were just fighting Degath Squads. But before we focus on this little goody, we'd damned well better get a line on where the coyote shifters are and get that spirit seal before Stacia figures it out."

"That we can help with." Morio began picking shards out of Camille's flesh. She winced but said nothing as blood tickled down her arms and the backs of her legs. I shuddered to think how long it was going to take to get all the glass out of her. "Marion called the house after you left the café. Apparently, she talked to a friend of hers and . . . long story short: We have an address."

"Thank gods. That's the first real break we've gotten in awhile. So, where the fuck did Jaycee and Van disappear to? And *what* are they?" My mind was spinning with everything that had gone on.

"You still don't recognize them when you see them, do you?" Vanzir shook his head.

"Stop trying to be enigmatic. You don't wear it well," I said, glaring at him. "We don't have time for riddles."

"They're Tregarts. Human looking—but demonic. Add in that they're sorcerers, and you're both lucky to come out alive."

"I thought they smelled close to Demonkin but . . . why didn't I sense them?" Camille stifled a cry as she reached down to yank a particularly nasty looking piece of glass out of her leg. "Cripes, this goddamn stuff hurts. Now I know how it feels to be inside a Cuisinart."

"Most likely, the pair were masked. Sorcerers with the power they have can easily cloak their demonic nature, so don't blame yourself. Though it doesn't look like you went easy on the spell tossing either, toots. You do skylights pretty damned good." Vanzir glanced up at the gaping hole in the wall where the lightning bolt had ripped through, then gave her the once-over. "We'd better get you to the doctor."

"Uh, yeah, I think that might be an opportune suggestion." She began to hobble toward the door, sucking in a deep breath, then stopped. "Every step I take drives some of the shards deeper. The stairs are going to be murder."

"I can take you." Roz leapt to her side and wrapped his arm gently around her waist. "I'll carry you through the Ionyc Sea to the FH-CSI. The rest of you—go plan what you need to do next. I'll see you in a bit."

"Hold on," she said, fishing out her car keys and tossing them to me. "Okay. Let's get this over with."

Roz closed his eyes, and they wavered out of sight. The Ionyc Sea wasn't the ideal way to travel, and both Smoky and Roz only took us with them when it was absolutely necessary, but travel through the frozen astral realms came in handy when necessary.

Vanzir, Trillian, Morio, and I trudged up the stairs. There was nothing left here but destruction. They probably never bothered to use the rest of the house, just the lab in the basement. And the pedestal, where they . . . Images of what was left of Paulo filtered through my mind, and I pressed my lips together. We'd track them down and destroy them. And we'd put a stop to the Koyanni while we were at it.

Outside, I leaned against Camille's Lexus. "Where to? I'd like to have Menolly with me when we go after the coyote shifters. She tends to be real handy in situations where we might have to hold our breath. We have an address, but we're definitely down manpower without her and Smoky. Camille's going to be laid up again, if I don't miss my guess."

"Camille's probably going to be okay to go in unless she contracts an infection from the cuts, but she'll hurt. You know she won't stay home if there's danger to the rest of us. You head over to the FH-CSI building and see how she is. We'll head out and see what we can track down about the address Marion gave us. Drive by, get a look at it . . . anything we can use for an advantage right now." Vanzir motioned for me to take off as he, Morio, and Trillian headed for Morio's SUV.

I gave him a long look. At this point, if there was a way we could remove the soul binder, I'd consider it. Vanzir had earned his place with us, but the enslavement lasted for life. He'd never be free. But we were coming to trust him more and more. With one last glance over my shoulder, I hopped in Camille's car and headed, once again, to the hospital.

Sharah grimaced when she saw me come in. "Again? What's with you two? I think you just like us too much."

"How is she?" I glanced around, looking for any sign of Chase, but if he was here, he was in his office, not in the medic unit.

"We're tweezing out the shards. There are so many that it's going to take a while longer. For the first twenty minutes we used clear strapping tape—plastered it to her skin and then pulled. Brought the majority of the bigger pieces and a lot of smaller slivers off. It's a good thing she shaved her legs recently, I can tell you that." Sharah bit her lip, then said, "I need to talk to you about something. They're working on her, so you're going to have to wait for a while anyway."

Worried they'd found something else wrong with Camille, I followed her as she led me back into her office. "What's wrong? She's going to be okay, isn't she?"

"Camille? Oh, yes—she'll hurt and probably have a number of tiny scars, but she'll be all right. This is something else, something private I needed to ask you." She let out a long breath and sat down—not behind her desk but in the chair next to me. "Delilah, I have something to ask you, and you probably won't like it, but I can't just keep quiet. I have to know."

Sharah was friendly, but she seldom confided in us, and I'd never had a heart-to-heart with her until Chase had been in the ICU.

"What's up? Is something wrong with Chase?"

"That's debatable. We've got a long ways to know how the Nectar of Life will ultimately affect him. But, no, that's not what I wanted to talk about. Not directly. I know you broke up—he told me, and he told me it was his doing, and that it had nothing to do with you." She cleared her throat, looking definitely uncomfortable.

"Uh . . . yeah. He's right on all counts."

"I know he's not ready for a relationship, but do you think . . . when he is . . . are you planning on getting back together with him?" She glanced up at me then, and I saw it in her eyes. I saw the same look I'd felt at the beginning, after the newness wore off and the affection crept in. *Sharah was in love with Chase.*

Hell. How was I supposed to respond? Did I even know the answer to her question? We'd only been separated for a day or two. Was I ready to give up the hope of being with him forever? But as I searched my heart, I knew my response, and it wasn't what I expected to feel.

I reached out and stroked her cheek. "You have feelings for him, don't you?"

She blushed—and on an elf, flaming cheeks were not that attractive—and flinched. Just enough to tell me she was afraid of how I'd react.

"It's okay to tell me how you feel. Please, I'd rather know. After Erika, secrets are *not* my most favorite of pastimes."

"Please, don't think I'm like her—I'd never, ever step in where I wasn't invited." She lowered her gaze to the floor.

"I know you wouldn't. I just . . . meant I'd rather know up front. So, do you love him?"

"Yes," she whispered. "Over the past two years that I've worked with him, I've grown extremely . . . fond of him. I truly see the goodness in his heart, even if he doesn't know what to do with it and bungles it up. He really does love you, Delilah, but I think . . . I think he doesn't know whether he loves himself."

I closed my eyes, listening to my pain. It stung to hear her say she cared about him, but it wasn't the sting of betrayal. It wasn't the sting of abandonment. It was simply the sting of letting go.

"He doesn't know how you feel, does he?"

She shook her head. "And I'll never tell him if you are just on a break. I'd never step in and try to take him from you. And if you are truly through as a couple, I promise you that I won't say a word until he's ready—and that won't be for a while yet. *If ever.*"

Taking her gently by the shoulders, I gazed into her gamin face. She really was beautiful, in a pale and breathless sort of way. Ethereal, even as she was practical. She was brave and strong, but gentle enough to make a man like Chase feel secure.

"Sharah, Chase and I have run our course. We learned from each other, and we'll always be friends. I'll always love him, and he'll probably always love me, but . . . I don't think we'll ever go back to being *in love*. If you feel the time is right, don't stand back because of me. Take a chance and talk to him. You might just be the woman he needs, because *I'm not that person.*"

Her eyes lit up and I thought she was going to cry, and I knew I'd done the right thing. Inside, whispering in my ear, I could hear the boreal wind and on it, Hi'ran whispered, *"Don't fret, my love. You'll never be alone."* And then he fell silent again. I gave her a sad smile.

"I'm going to miss having him around the house as much, but sometimes, no matter how much you love someone, it's just not going to work."

"Yes, I know that." Sharah glanced up at me. "I left someone back in Elqaneve for that very reason. He was . . . too set in his ways. He disapproved of my assignment to come Earthside—he wanted me to stay home and make babies. And I couldn't do that, even though I loved him."

As I sat back and gave her a smile, the pensiveness left her face in a sudden wash, and I saw a woman sitting there who might really be able to make my detective happy. Sharah was safe enough for him, she was stoic and strong-willed, but she wouldn't constantly make him feel like he was running to keep up, like he was compromising himself for his love.

"So," I said after a moment. "Shall we go see how my sister is doing?"

And with that, our discussion was over, and my future with Chase was settled and history.

* * *

Before heading back to the medic unit, I dropped in to Dispatch.

"Chase around?" I wasn't about to tell him what I'd discussed with Sharah, but I wanted to bring him up to speed on Van and Jaycee.

"No," Yugi said. "There's been some sort of explosion at one of the magical shops, and he headed out on the call."

Suddenly feeling chilled, I asked, "Which one?"

Yugi consulted his clipboard. "Madame Pompey's Magical Emporium. Looks like somebody totally trashed the place."

Crap—so *that's* where Smoky had been off to. I decided to keep my mouth shut. No good getting the dragon pissed at me. Especially when he was defending his wife.

Instead, I asked, "I was wondering if Andy Gambit decided to press charges against me?" Might as well kill two birds with one stone, I thought.

Yugi shook his head. "Don't worry about him pressing charges—my men had a little talk with him when we hauled his ass away from your house. But, Delilah, you know he's going to make a hash out of this in the *Seattle Tattler*. That rag's going to mop you up like a sponge."

Grimacing, I nodded. He was right, meaning I'd better double-check when next week's issue hit the mailbox. We subscribed just to keep tabs on what the freak was up to. Usually he was taking potshots at Camille, but this time I knew I'd be on the menu.

"Thanks, Yugi. Tell Chase . . . just tell him I said hello, would you?"

He nodded, and I took off to see how Camille was doing. By the time I got there, she was sitting up, looking a little worse for wear. Her skin looked like she'd tried to shave and nicked herself in a hundred places.

"Maybe Roz's wonder salve can prevent scarring?" I winced as I saw the pile of shards and slivers sitting in the tray next to the table. "Crap, that's nasty. Did they get it all?"

"We think so," Mallen said. "In the end, I resorted to calling in one of the healers who could charm some of the fragments out—she was getting too sore to use the tweezers anymore. We've put a special ointment on that should take care of most of the healing and leave no marks, but there are a couple places we had to stitch up. No taking a bath for two days and *no* picking at scabs!"

As we headed out, Sharah smiled and waved. Her eyes sparkled, and for the first time in weeks, I felt at peace about Chase and me as Camille and I headed out to the car.

CHAPTER 17

By the time we got home, everybody else was there and gathered in the kitchen. It had become our usual hangout for planning strategy. Nerissa was absent—she'd had to go home after her mini-vacation with Menolly, but everybody else was sitting around, drinking tea, eating cookies and chips and whatever else Iris had managed to find for snack time.

I looked over at Smoky, a faint grin on my face, as Camille settled in between him and Trillian. Morio sat to Trillian's left.

"What?" Smoky cleared his throat, cocking his head to one side. "Why are you looking at me like that?"

"I just got wind that a certain magical shop was trashed. Thoroughly." I met his stare. "Did you leave evidence?"

He snorted. "Do I look stupid?"

I wasn't going to answer that. A—he didn't look stupid, he was probably one of the hottest dragons around. B—even if he did, you don't tell a dragon you think they look stupid.

Camille looked from him to me. "What's going on?"

"Your husband took out the magic shop. Van and Jaycee are going to be so pissed. I have the feeling Stacia didn't have them open it just to snag us in. Looked like a good way to establish a foothold here. Now, there's not much left but one big junk heap of shelves, bottles, and merchandise."

Camille turned to Smoky. "Cripes, what am I going to do with you? They're going to know we did it—all the more reason for Stacia to up the bounty to *dead or alive*."

"Which reminds me," Iris said, "have you thought about hiring a few guards for the house? When you're all home, everything is dandy, but during the day, when you're out, with just Maggie and myself here—and Menolly asleep—we're perfect targets. And I don't mind helping out, I don't mind fighting in this war, but it would seem a wise precaution."

"I'll get on it," Camille said, jotting down a note on her steno pad.

I covered my ears and rested my head on the table, not wanting to think about all the crap we were facing. After a moment, a hand ran down my back, patting me lightly. I looked up, glaring, and found Roz staring down at me, a soft smile on his face.

"Too much?"

I nodded. "Too much of everything. The past few days have been insane. The only good thing that's come out of it has been Camille's wedding." As I glanced over, staring at her sitting with her husbands, a thought occurred to me.

"Smoky! You could solve one of our minor problems for us." I beamed at him. "Make your sister-in-law happy, would you?"

"How so?" He looked worried. "You don't want me to start catching game for the house or anything, do you? Because dragon-scorched meat doesn't taste so good to humans and their ilk."

"That steak you caught me when I first came to your barrow was delicious, sweetheart." Camille patted his hand. "He's lying—his game is always prime choice—"

"Oh for Pete's sake . . . no, I am not asking you to play mighty hunter. But Camille and I promised a dryad we'd find her another home—one with more wild land she could spread out on. What say we turn her loose on your land?"

Camille stared at me. "You're right—that would be perfect!"

"Hold on—both of you. What are you up to now, and what sort of creature do you want to turn loose on my land? I just got rid of Titania and that insufferable Morgaine." Smoky looked ready to take a belligerent stance on the subject.

"She's not a Fae Queen, she's just a dryad looking for a wilder place than Rodgers Park. You could make her happy—and help us fulfill our promise." I snickered as Camille grinned and lightly rubbed her hand along his arm.

"Smoky, love, it would make me so grateful if you'd do this," she said.

Smoky let out a low rumble that sounded all too much like a growl and gazed at her hand. "You aren't above bribing me, are you?" he asked, his voice husky. The glacial chill of his eyes swam in a whirl of ice floes and ocean mist. Camille leaned in and kissed him, her lips lingering over his. After a moment, she pulled away, wincing.

"Damn these cuts . . ."

"My love, you never have to hurt yourself to ask a favor from me," he said, wrapping his hand around hers and holding it against his shoulder. He turned back to me. "You have your wish, as long as the Fae understands it's my territory, and she's a guest there. You may take her there whenever you like. Also: I've insured that Georgio and Estelle are taken care of by . . . a couple of my friends. Warn the dryad not to come close to the house."

"Trust me, Bluebell isn't like Wisteria was. That veg-head was a freak." The floraed—an offshoot of the dryads—had been out to kill anybody who stood in the way of wiping out humanity so the plants could take over the world again.

Which brought up thoughts of the demons and the spirit seals. Again. "Trillian, Vanzir, Morio—what did you find out about the address Marion gave us for the coyote shifters?"

Morio pulled out a digital camera and handed it to me. "Can you download these pictures? We thought it might be easier than just going by description."

I grinned at him. "Geek boy! I'll teach you yet."

Pulling out my laptop, I fired it up. As they continued to chat, I plugged in the USB cable to one of my ports on the laptop, then into the camera and punched the "On" button. We'd picked up several cameras of the same type so we'd only have to deal with one brand of software, and kept one at the house, one in each of our cars, and one stayed in Morio's SUV. I was determined that we'd learn to use technology along with our innate magic—it would be the only way we could survive in this society.

As the pictures downloaded, I motioned to Iris. "How long till sundown?"

She glanced at the chart we had tacked up on the wall. "Another two hours—shortly after five. In a week or so, we'll be switching back out of daylight saving time, and she'll be able to get up an hour earlier."

"Then maybe we'd better get some rest. As soon as I finish downloading the photos, we'll take a nap, then go over them when we get up. Menolly will be awake then."

I opened a window and pulled up the folder into which they'd downloaded. The JPEGs were huge, but my computer had been upgraded to handle bigger tasks, and I opened them up, zooming out so I could line them up side by side. Then I plugged in the wall monitor we'd had installed to yet another USB port so the images would feed onto it instead of just my smaller screen. That way everybody could see them.

"Okay, this is all set up for when we need it. Nobody touch my computer, got it?" After they all nodded, I said, "So let's hit the sheets for three hours. Wake-up call at seven P.M., Iris. Camille—you be sure to get some sleep."

And amazingly, they listened to me, and we trudged upstairs for a catnap.

I looked around and realized I was roaming through the streets of Seattle. It was late, and a cold wind was howling in off the bay. I pulled my leather jacket closer around my neck. The stars shimmered overhead in the chill night, and I wished that I'd asked Menolly to come with me.

I was heading toward a building up ahead—why, I wasn't sure, I didn't remember ever seeing it before, but I knew that there was something waiting for me, and I had no choice.

"Hello. You know you're out of body, don't you?" The voice beside me was familiar, and as I turned I saw Greta, walking beside me. She inclined her head.

"We're fast-tracking you. After the incident this morning, we can't wait too long, or you won't be able to control your powers. The *Panteris phir* is helping you learn to control shifting into your panther form, but it won't prevent you from losing your temper and using your Death Maiden abilities before you've been instructed in the proper rituals."

I stared at the sidewalk as we walked. The cracks were filled with snippets of grass and weeds. Nature always found a way. It broke through all man-made structures in time; it reclaimed even as it was destroyed in the never-ending war.

"He killed that woman and her baby. He had to die." The look on the murderer's face still haunted my thoughts. I wasn't sorry he was dead. As Menolly would have said, "One less slime in the gene pool."

"Yes, but when you use your powers as a *Death Maiden*, you must always wait for orders. Either from our Master, or from me." She caught my eye. "Unless His Lordship gave you leave, and I didn't know about it?"

I gazed steadily ahead, not speaking. It wasn't that I wanted to be obstinate, but I didn't want to discuss my relationship with Hi'ran with her. *I* was his only living emissary, *I* was the one he wanted to get with child, and I didn't want to think about him touching the rest of them, even though I knew that I was simply one in a harem of women.

But she must have seen it on my face. "You will never have him all for your own, and he cannot touch you until you are dead. Accept the reality. He's one of the Harvestmen—an Immortal. He's beyond even the gods."

"I know," I whispered. "I'm just lonely. And he makes me feel . . ."

"Please, trust me when I tell you that you're special to him. You are his chosen one. He won't let you remain alone. There are wonderful things waiting for you—long before you enter the realm of the dead. Don't begrudge the rest of us what joy we have. We can never receive the chance he's offering you."

I stopped then, turned to her. No guile or anger flickered in her eyes—simply wistfulness. "You love him, don't you?"

"I do. We all do. Joining the Death Maidens, being chosen to serve *him* is one of the best things that ever happened to me. I met my death willingly because I knew I'd be joining him. My life was horrendous, but now . . . And every one of us will tell you that being his servant is a blessing, not a curse. In fact, that's where we're going. You must realize that you are not acting alone."

"I'm going to meet the rest, aren't I?"

She nodded, a faint smile creeping across her face. "Yes, you will meet your sisters tonight." And then, in a whirl of smoke and mirrors, she caught me up and we raced ahead, a blur in the night, shadows running under the moon, Death Maidens on the prowl.

We might have entered a sheik's palace or a harem out of *One Thousand and One Nights*, or some epic fifties Cecil B. DeMille movie. The room was dimly lit, opulent, and lush, and I realized we were no longer in Seattle but in some distant place, like the glade I'd been in when I first met Greta. Giant pillars, evenly spaced throughout the hall, held up the domed cathedral ceiling.

The walls were invisible, hidden behind sparkling curtains that draped languorously across them, a silken paradise swathed in yellow and red, in pink and ivory, embroidered through with golden threads.

Against one wall, upon a raised dais, dozens of scattered pillows matched the drapes, inviting me to come sink into their splendor, to rest, to dally. Here and there, ornate tables held trays of fruit and pitchers of what smelled like fine wine and mead. Dipping bowls filled with honey, platters of cheese, and freshly baked bread covered the surfaces.

As I turned, I saw one wall covered with a rack containing weapons of every sort. They were polished but used—no decorations here. Urns my height held giant fronds of grass and autumn foliage, and a fireplace big enough to walk into crackled with a fire that filled the room with warmth.

The décor might be stunning, but what caught my eye most were the women. I counted them—twenty-one in all, including myself. Blondes, redheads, brunettes—some with fair skin, others with skin the color of burnished ebony, tall and short, thin, fat . . . mostly human but a few who looked Fae. They were all unique, but one common bond connected them: every one of them looked content.

A few were reading, a small group were discussing something around one of the tables, a pair of taut, muscled women sparred with daggers and swords, but as Greta walked me to the center of the room, all eyes gravitated my way. I held my tongue. This was their home—their abode. I was the guest, and I would let them lead. Within seconds, they gathered around me, chattering brightly.

"You brought her!"

"Good to see you here. It's about time—"

"You're Delilah, right? Delilah of the Fae?"

"You've finally come to meet us!"

The questions and comments came fast and thick, but I sensed no animosity and began to relax. And as I relaxed, I began to talk with these women of the grave, these women who were now my sisters in spirit.

"Yes, I'm Delilah . . . I'm originally from Otherworld, but I'm part human."

"You're still alive, aren't you?" One particularly lithe young woman, Japanese by her looks, and with hair that flowed to her ankles, cocked her head and laughed then. "What funny hair you have. I like it, though."

I grinned. "I got skunked—it's a long story. And yes, I'm still alive."

It felt odd, as they pulled closer, to realize that all of them—all of these seemingly corporeal women—were spirits. But before I could dwell on that thought, I found myself herded over to the pillows where they drew me down and sat around me.

Greta held up her hand, and everyone quieted. She must wield more power than I'd thought.

"I brought Delilah here tonight for several reasons. One, to meet you—so she will realize that she is not alone. We've all walked the path she now walks, and when we died, our Master brought us here, to Haseofon. That's what this place is called, Delilah—*Haseofon, the Abode of the Death Maidens.*"

I rolled the name around on my tongue for a moment, getting used to it. "Is the name private? Can I use it outside of these walls?"

"It is not of great importance. We will not attempt to keep too many secrets between you and your corporeal family." And then she smiled. "Introduce yourselves, please. She may not remember all of our names at once, but part of her training will be to interact with all of you and to learn from you."

And so, one by one, they introduced themselves. Most of

the names went by in a blur, but a few stood out. Eloise, the tall, dark-skinned warrior woman; Lissel, a gorgeous redhead who dropped into a quick curtsy; Fiona, a dark-haired Irish lass; and Mizuki, the Japanese girl who seemed as light on her feet as I did when I was in cat form. And every one of them bore the markings on their forearms that Greta—and I—did. Brilliant swirling leaves and vines of black, orange, rust, and red, tattooing their allegiance to the Autumn Lord.

She turned to me. "There is another you must meet. She is part of our family, although she is not a Death Maiden. You will recognize her."

Of course that sparked my curiosity. I turned in the direction that Greta was pointing, and waited. Out of the shadows, from behind an urn, stepped a carbon copy of myself, only she had hair the color of sable fur, rich and brown. She smiled and held out her arms, and in that moment, I understood. *Arial.* My twin. My leopard sister.

"Arial! Oh Great Mother Bast—my Arial!" And then I was sobbing, in her embrace, holding on for dear life. "I can't believe it's you."

"Yes, it's me," she whispered, and her voice was my own as well. "I live here, when I'm not prowling the astral, keeping an eye on you. The Autumn Lord took me in when I died, and I grew up here, in spirit if not in body."

"But why aren't you with our ancestors in the Land of the Silver Falls?" I managed to force myself to stand back, holding her by the shoulders. "Why aren't you with our mother?"

"That will keep for later—the story is long and involves your own destiny. But for now, just be glad we're together again. Whenever you come here to visit, I'll be able to talk to you. I can't appear as anything but my leopard self when outside of these walls." She laughed, tossing her long hair back over her shoulder. It reached her lower back in a cascade of curls similar to Camille's, but it wasn't nearly so dark or thick. But her forearms were clear of tattoos. She wasn't a Death Maiden; that much was obvious.

Unwilling to let go of her, I wrapped my arm around her waist and turned to Greta. "Bless you . . . I can't repay you for this gift. I don't know what to say."

"Just promise me that you will keep your temper and wait

for my direction next time. It's one thing if you fight to the death against an enemy, but you obliterated his soul, Delilah. You may not realize it, but you sent him directly to the abyss without being told. That could have serious repercussions down the line. Be cautious not to invoke your powers as a Death Maiden to take down your foes unless you have been given leave."

I understood then. She wasn't asking me to keep from fighting. It was *how* I fought that worried her. "I see . . . and I promise. Now, can I spend some time talking to Arial privately?"

Greta laughed. "You have all the time in the world. And you may come any time, though for now you are here in spirit only. But bid your sister farewell for now, for I have lessons to teach you."

Reluctantly, I said good-bye to my twin. Arial turned for one last wave before darting out of the chamber through one of the side doors. I gave Greta a long look. "What does my sister do here? Why is she tied to the Autumn Lord?"

"She has never met him, save at birth. He brought her in, and she spent her first few years as a lovely leopard cub, secure in her life here, adored by all the Death Maidens. We've grown very fond of her. We helped her learn how to take her two-legged form, how to speak, we taught her to read and to play the harpsichord—"

"The harpsichord?"

"I have no idea why she chose that particular instrument, but it's the one to which she gravitated. She sings beautifully and writes poetry. And she acts as our handmaid, helping us when we need it. She's a part of our family, even if she's not a Death Maiden." She paused. "More you will find out in time, but for now . . ."

"Now . . . lessons?"

"Yes. Follow me." She rose, and I followed her through a door to the side and down a long hall. We entered another room, this one sparse, though still beautiful, and in the center, a bench with a thick pillow on it. "Please, take a seat."

"What are you going to teach me?" I asked, taking my place on the pillow.

Greta smiled slyly. "Oh, girl, it's not what *I'm* going to teach you. Whatever you do—do not get off the bench. That is the one rule I give to you, and see that you follow it. You can die if you don't. I'll be back for you in awhile. Until then . . ." Her voice dropped, and she gave me a solemn pat on the shoulder and left the room. I heard a faint click of a lock.

Nervously, I looked around, wondering what was going to happen. The lights dimmed, and the room took on a faint glow around the bench, but everything else fell away, bathed in darkness. I sucked in a deep breath and waited.

A scuttling caught my attention, and I jumped but, remembering Greta's admonishment to stay seated, I forced myself to remain in place. The sound creeped me out; it was the sound of feet skittering around the room. A shadow here, a sudden movement there, and I thought for sure that I saw a jointed leg stretch out from the darkness.

Hell. Werespiders again? I flashed back to the werespiders we'd fought a year before. Kyoka and his hobo spiderlings. Could they really be here? As the noises came nearer, I thought for sure I could hear breathing behind me, and I began to shiver, every hair on my body standing at attention as the rasping grew louder.

Crap. Every instinct screamed, *Move, fool!* But if I moved, would I die? Was this a test of skill? Of strength? Or of obeying the rules? Breath catching in my throat, I poised to leap the minute anything go too close.

Remain calm. Do not move; do not run. Fear is your worst enemy. Fear can annihilate you.

The words echoed in my head, but it wasn't my voice. Once again, I sensed Hi'ran, and yet the voice was smoother than his, like honey, calming and sweet.

I sat on my hands, trying not to cry, trying not to notice the darkness that was narrowing in on me. The circle of light surrounding the bench was growing smaller, the faint glow fading. Something brushed one shoulder, and I jerked around but saw nothing. A tap on my other shoulder, and I lurched to my right. But there was no one there. Nothing to fight, nothing to see.

Breathe in slowly, then exhale. Close your eyes. Reach out with your senses.

Again, the calming voice, steady and deep, smooth silk and honey on my frayed nerves. I obeyed, breathing slowly. One breath at a time. Deliberate, focused, trying to push beyond the fear.

The movements hastened around me, and I pulled my legs off the floor, tucking them beneath me on the bench, wanting nothing more than to shift, to turn into Panther and tackle whatever enemy waited in the darkness. The sound of a thousand scurrying insects rustling against the floorboards taunted, both terrifying me and luring me in.

Listen to me. Reach beyond the fear, move past your gut reaction. Step over the fear with your mind, and don't be afraid to go into the darkness. Follow my voice; follow the cadence of my words, the trail of my thoughts.

His voice became a thread, and I followed. And when the words stopped, the energy remained, and I could suddenly see the signature. So often I'd heard Camille describe doing just this, and I never understood what she was talking about until now. But his voice left a trail of frost, a trail of sparkles, and I hurried after them, journeying with my mind, keeping my body still, forcing myself not to transform, not to shift.

Now, imagine a light, a brilliant light coming from within you. A light that clears away the fog and dust and cobwebs.

I focused on creating a light—on turning on a switch somewhere inside. At first, nothing happened, so I tried harder, urging the light from out of my stomach. Memories of Chase and loneliness immediately rushed through me, and I felt like I was floundering.

Let him go. Let him be what he is now. Walk through the loss and leave it behind. What ties you to the pain?

Thoughts raced through my mind, but a clear voice, from somewhere deep inside, whispered, "I'm afraid of not mattering to anyone." And as soon as I heard it, I recognized the little girl who missed her mother, who always felt more at home with animals than people, who felt like I blended into the background.

That's not me anymore, I thought. *I left her behind a long time ago, but I've been carrying her baggage.* Memories of childhood—of taunts and feeling inferior—passed by, screaming *Windwalker! Windwalker!* at me. The ring of children trying to goad me into shifting into Tabby, the snide looks of our relatives . . .

You are no longer the frightened little girl. You are a strong, capable woman. The rich, velvet voice washed over me, and I knew he spoke the truth.

Smiling, I pushed the memories aside like cobwebs. They were meaningless now. I'd conquered my childhood shyness.

As soon as I let go of that fear, the haunting visions of the werespiders, of Karvanak, of the demons crowded in. But I knew I could hold my own in a fight. As frightening as the creatures were, I knew I could face them and win—or at least take them down with me. I could stand up for myself; I didn't need anyone else to fight my battles for me. This time, I chased them from my heart without coaxing, ordering them to depart.

Suddenly, the room was silent—the sound of scuttling feet gone—and a sliver of brilliance broke through the darkness, filling the dim corners of my heart as the inky void fell away.

Open your eyes. You have learned to pass through the fear intact. You've found your inner light, Delilah, the part of yourself that can slice through the darkness. All Death Maidens must find their light, for they work in the darkness, and the energy must balance. It is harder for you, because you still live, but you've done it. Be proud of yourself, and know that you will never lose that light again.

Slowly, I opened my eyes. The room was lit, and there was nothing to be seen except an empty chamber with a bright light shimmering through it, and I was sitting on a bench in the center. As I let out my breath, I looked down and gasped. The tattoos on my arms had changed. The black shadow was more vivid, and the hints of burnished copper and rust shone within the leaves. My marks were growing stronger, and I guessed with every lesson, the tattoos would darken. Proud that I'd passed, content that I'd faced down the challenge and won, I glanced up to see a glimpse of a shadow in the corner.

"Delilah?" The voice echoed out of the shadows.

I know you. You have been with me before. "You're not Hi'ran, but you bear his energy. You've come to me several times now. Let me see who you are." My pulse began to race, and my heart leapt into my throat. I needed to find out just who he was. I needed to meet him. There was something so familiar, and yet . . . so alien.

And then he stepped out of the corner of the room. His lips

were the first feature I noticed. They curled into a bow, into the most delicate of smiles. I could tell he was a moment away from laughing, and that made the serene smile seem all the more intriguing. I stepped back, my gaze locked with his.

Hi'ran?

No . . . not Hi'ran. And yet—the autumn was there, in his aura, in his energy. I could see it, feel it, practically taste it, like candy corn and caramel apples and pot roast and pumpkin soup.

"*I know you* . . ." I whispered.

The man was tall, but not more than an inch taller than myself. He was muscled, from what I could tell, with a V waist and broad shoulders. His heritage and warm toffee skin suggested that he might be half-Japanese, half-black, but that in itself was impossible to tell, because I had no idea if he was human or not. Definitely not an FBH, though, because he emanated energy like a lighthouse.

His eyes were liquid—like glossy obsidian or flowing ink. They glowed, shimmering with a dappling of stars. A craggy set of scars marked one cheek and his forehead, but rather than mar his looks, they added to them. His hair was the color of honey, amber, and wheat, all streaked together in a shimmering array of high and low lights, and he wore it back in a ponytail.

"You are so beautiful," I whispered, not caring if he heard me. He was the most gorgeous creature I'd ever laid eyes on, scars and all.

He laughed then, and slid off the brown leather coat that hit him mid-calf. Beneath the rich-toned coat he was dressed in a pair of brown cargo pants, a black turtleneck, and around his neck, he wore a pendant of smoky rutilated quartz. He had on motorcycle boots, but there was something . . . and then I noticed.

Frost trickled off the heels. Frost, like the frost of Hi'ran's boots. And when the man gazed up at me, I caught a whiff of bonfires, of smoke, of the early tang of autumn hoarfrost.

Automatically, without a second thought, I stepped in front of him, Hi'ran's words ringing in my head. "*Keep your eyes open, my sweet. Keep your mind open. Remember the curve of my lips, the scent of old leather and autumn carnivals, the frost that lingers on my breath. Listen for the song your Mark sings when I'm near."*

"You can't . . . Could you be . . . ?" But I got no further, for the mark on my forehead started to sing, to play me one chord at a time, as the man reached out to take my hands. Awash in the current of flame that raced between us, I moved toward him, and he held out his arms.

"How . . . ? Who . . . ?"

"Shush . . . let it be what it is, Delilah. He's my Master, too. And we're both his chosen." He pulled me into his arms, and I wrapped my arms around his neck as if it were the most natural thing in the world.

As I gazed into his eyes, I could see the ages long past, the eons gone by for this man—whoever and whatever he might be. I wanted to snuggle deep into his arms and rest, safe from the storms of my life.

He slid his arms around my waist and pulled me close. As his lips sought mine, I was able to think clearly enough just to ask, "What's your name?"

His hands wandering along my thigh, his gaze fastened on my face, he whispered, "Shade. Just call me Shade." And then his lips found mine, and everything in the world slid away except the power of his kiss.

CHAPTER 18

I have no idea how long I stood there, kissing him, pressed against his chest and listening to his heart beat as hard as my own, but after what seemed like forever, his hands began to move, and they slid under my shirt, touching my flesh, and I recognized his touch. He'd kissed me before in shadow form, and I wanted more. I knew, in my heart, with him I could have what I never could have with Hi'ran. With Shade, I could have what I couldn't find with Chase or with Zachary. Shade's energy enveloped me like the haunting strains of a distant waltz, like a storm battering at my senses.

Pulling him down to the bench, I frantically began sliding his turtleneck up to reveal his chest—toned and strong, but also covered with the scars of time. He pulled the shirt off and, eyes luminous, gazed into my face.

"Are you sure you want this?"

"Now, I want you now. I know you, I know you . . ." I could only repeat over and over the thoughts running through my head as I struggled to remove my clothing. He helped, sliding my shirt off as I struggled out of my jeans. I needed him, needed to quench my thirst, needed to be touched, to be loved, to be taken and thoroughly sated in a way I'd never felt before.

Shade said nothing more, but slipped off his boots and his pants. He was golden in his color, reminding me of warm sugar toffee, of a vanilla latte, and I slid my hands down his sides, running them shamelessly around to cup his butt. His muscles were oh, so firm, and he was ready, so ready for me. I wanted to taste him, looked at his cock with hunger, but my fangs reminded me of failed attempts before. My heritage had given me non-retractable fangs, just enough to hurt someone if I made a wrong move.

However, Shade seemed to pick up on my desire. "It's all right. If you want to, I would love it—you can't hurt me as easily as you can a human. Trust me," he whispered.

It was my turn to ask, "Are you sure?"

He nodded, and I knelt in front of him, cautiously licking his erection, the tip of my tongue running up its length to tickle the head. One fang caught a bit of the flesh, but he didn't even wince, and, emboldened, I gave a long, coiling lick around the head of his penis, pressing my lips to the top. I couldn't fully take him in my mouth—it would leave fang marks all the way down—but I sucked lightly with my lips, pursing them around him, enjoying the feel and light, salty taste of him on my tongue.

He moaned and motioned me up. I slid up his body, pressing my breasts against his skin as I did so, feeling his cock press against my groin and stomach.

Shade laid me on the bench and leaned over me, taking one of my nipples in his mouth, sucking, as his fingers trailed down my abs, down to my thatch, where he slid them inside me, kissing me deeply as he did so. His tongue caught on my fangs, but he gently moved it away and continued to probe my mouth, even as he fingered me into a sudden, jolting orgasm that I wasn't ready for. Spiraling, I let out a cry, sharp and jagged, as he moved between my legs and slowly, inch by inch, slid inside me.

Shade was wide and hard, and I felt every inch of him as he entered me. He set up a delicious movement, the friction driving me crazy as he matched his rhythm to mine, and then thought fell away as I looked into his eyes and spun out of control, falling over the cliff into a bliss I'd never felt before. My panther and Tabby both were sailing with me, and for the very first time, all of my selves responded as Shade tore me outside of myself, filled me full with sparkling joy, and set me free from any lingering doubts I had about myself as a woman.

Some time later—I have no idea how long—he reluctantly broke away. "You must return home now," he said, kissing my neck gently. "I don't want you to go, but you can't remain in Haseofon for too long while you are still in body. I can come and go as I please, because of my nature, but you must return to your bed." He cocked his head in a peculiar way that made me want to laugh.

"I thought I was here in spirit."

"No, my dear, your body is here, too, in a way. It has been since you entered this chamber. You are bilocating, in two places at once. It's difficult to maintain, though, and the thread is wearing thin."

"But . . . will I see you again?" I couldn't bear to walk away. Not now, not after I'd just found him. A piece of me had broken away during our lovemaking, and it was with him. And I held a piece of his heart in my own.

"I promise you, my love, I will meet you soon in your world. Keep watch for me." He helped me dress, stopping to kiss me time and again.

My head fuzzy from the rush of emotion and desire, I stared into his eyes. He was different—oh, so different—from both Chase and Zachary. Shade met my eyes, calm, cool, unwavering. And in his gaze, I saw no backpedaling, no hesitation. And in that moment, I understood.

"You are the *one* . . . he will use you to . . ."

"Hush, go now." He pressed his fingers to my lips, and I pressed my nose to his neck, inhaling deeply the scents of pumpkins and apples and spiced rum and woodsmoke.

Our roots ran deep into the same core. Beyond Were and—whatever Shade was—we were bound by the same master, by the same Elemental Lord. We walked the same energy, we understood the thrill of the flame and the pungent odor of freshly tilled harvest soil.

"I choose . . . to take the chance," I whispered. "Come to me soon."

"I will. Until then . . ." He pressed a box into my hand. "This is to remember me by."

I blinked, trying to hold my eyes open, but the room began to spin, and he vanished before I could say another word. I started to look at what he'd given me, but Greta was suddenly at my side, lowering me to the bench. She leaned down and breathed a kiss into my mouth, and everything began to fade. I struggled, not wanting to leave yet, but then I let go and surrendered my will. To her, to Shade, to Hi'ran. To my destiny.

"Delilah? Delilah, wake up." Iris shook me awake, and I blinked against the light flooding from the overhead fixture on the ceiling.

I struggled awake, wiping my hand across my eyes. "Is it . . . seven o'clock already?"

"Seven thirty. I let you sleep a little longer. Both you and Camille needed it. You were dead to the world when I tried to wake you up half an hour ago. Now, come on, get dressed."

I scrambled out of bed, wondering how much of the dream had been real and how much had been wish fulfillment. As I finished fastening my bra and pulled on a pair of jeans and a shirt, Iris made my bed for me.

After a moment, she said, "Delilah—what's this?"

I turned to see she was holding . . . *the box Shade had given me*. No, not a dream at all. "I'm not sure, to tell you the truth. Open it, would you?"

She did, gasping as she flipped the top open. "Look," she said hoarsely.

I finished tucking in my shirt and fed a leather belt through the loops on my jeans, buckling it as I walked back to the bed. The box contained a ring. It was gold, with a faceted smoky quartz. I slowly took the ring out of the box and rested the intricately etched band in the palm of my hand.

With every fiber of my being, I knew that if I put this on, Shade would become a part of my life. Memories of Camille talking about Trillian and how they met flashed by, and for the first time, I understood. I understood the connection they shared and would never again question it.

I looked up to find Iris staring at me, a peculiar look on her face.

"What's going on, Delilah? Where did you get that?"

"Why? Can't it just be a ring?"

She shook her head. "Not with the energy rolling off that band. I recognize that energy. I've felt it before."

I slowly held it up to the light. It sparkled. A ring of promise. A ring of binding. A ring of acceptance and submission to my destiny. A ring of empowerment by *accepting* my destiny. Once I put this on, there was no going back. The only question was: Did I want to know what Iris knew *before or after* I put on the ring? If I hesitated, was I still resisting the inevitable?

Sometimes, I thought, you just have to submit to your life . . . go with the flow, take a chance, leap before you look. In tabby form, I was a free spirit. I bounced and played my way through the day without worrying what waited ahead. In panther form, I did what came naturally—I bounded ahead, fearless.

At what point had I lost that fearlessness in my life as a woman, half-Fae or not? When had I become afraid? Or had I ever been without the fear and doubt? What made me so hesitant in two-legged form when I could let go and just be who I wanted to be as a cat—big or small? When had I first begun to put everyone else's opinions ahead of my own intuition?

I'd learned to break through my inner darkness in that room with Shade, and I'd tasted the passion in a way I could only dream of. Now, was I ready to take a chance? To stride ahead and be the woman I knew I could be?

I looked up at Iris, thinking all of these things, as I slowly slid the ring on the fourth finger of my right hand. No booming chimes or trilling harps sounded, but I'd just signed the pact. I'd jumped at the chance, taken the leap, and nothing would ever be the same.

Iris sat on the edge of my bed. "Oh girl, what have you done? I felt the shift in your aura as plainly as I see it when you change shape. I hope you know what you're doing."

"I do," I said, laughing. "I do. But tell me now—now that I've followed my gut. What sort of creature owns this ring?"

"Come down as soon as you've dressed. Supper is ready,

and the rest are waiting." She stopped at the door, peeking back over her shoulder. "My dear, I'm not sure how or where you met him, but you've just accepted a ring from someone who has part shadow dragon in his lineage—black dragon. And I expect he'll be showing up here soon enough to claim what is now his. Which . . . in case you had any doubt . . . is *you*."

Shadow dragon. The words resonated through me like fire. Yes—that would fit. It fit Shade's energy, his name, and the fact that he served Hi'ran. If Iris was right and he was only part dragon, though, then what about the rest of his background? I resolutely pushed doubt away.

The thought that perhaps shadow dragons and white/silver dragons might not coexist well in the same group also crossed my mind, but again—we would find a way. We had to. And if Shade were half as attentive and helpful as Smoky, we'd have another ally on our hands.

I tossed my nightgown in the laundry hamper and pulled on my boots, taking the stairs two at a time. As I hustled into the kitchen, I saw that Iris wasn't kidding—everybody was gathered around the table, including our cousin Shamas, who was dressed for the night shift.

"Sorry I took so long," I said.

Camille stared at me. "What the fuck? What did you do in the past three hours? Delilah, your aura has totally shifted— it's . . . flaming brilliant."

"And where is the other dragon?" Smoky asked, jumping up and looking around. "I can smell him from here."

I could see this wasn't going to be just my little secret. I glanced at Iris, but she shrugged and mouthed, *I didn't tell them,* so apparently Camille was right, and my aura was playing kaleidoscope. I took a deep breath and held up my hand.

"Yeah, I've got something to tell you. I was going to do so in my own time, but apparently you can sense what's happened. It's complicated, and so much went down while I was out on the astral. I went on a journey while I was asleep, and . . . oh hell, just shut up and listen."

As I spilled out everything that had happened from the time Greta had walked beside me through the city streets to waking up with Shade's ring, the room grew increasingly silent until by the time I finished, a pin dropping would have produced a minor earthquake.

Menolly glanced around. "What are you all staring at her for? We knew something like this was going to happen sooner or later. The Autumn Lord wasn't just going to let her continue going on her merry way without eventually stepping in. I think we should just be grateful that he didn't decide to kill her so she could join them in—what did you say the name of the place was?" Her tone demanded an answer.

"Haseofon." I whispered, giving her a faint smile.

"That's right—in Haseofon. And by the way, if there's any way we could meet our sister face-to-face, it would be nice if you could arrange that." She hovered her way up to the ceiling, where she liked to hang out, and cleared her throat as if to put a lid on the conversation.

Camille spoke more slowly, and I could tell she was weighing every word. "Are you comfortable with what happened?"

I considered the question. Was I comfortable? A week ago, I might have said no. A month ago, a year ago, I would have freaked. But now . . . the answer was there in the forefront.

"Yes, I am. I'm . . . content. I feel more settled than—well, than I ever have. Maybe this was my destiny all along. Maybe I was chosen from birth to become a Death Maiden—that would actually make me proud. I've found my peace with what . . . who . . . I am. Arial was taken to Haseofon when she was a cub, right after her death—so it's not like my connection to the place is totally new."

Smoky let out a loud cough. "May I see your ring?"

I reluctantly tried to take it off my finger, but it wouldn't come. It wasn't too tight, but it wasn't going to budge, either. Rather than say anything, I just held out my hand to him. He glanced into my face, and by the look in his eyes, I could see he knew what had just happened, but he kept silent. Instead, he just took my hand and passed his fingers above the stone.

"Shadow dragon—but not totally. There is another energy mix in this stone, but I sense no evil. Your Shade is not fully dragon. Probably half." He let go of my fingers and sat back. "He and I should be able to coexist if he keeps his focus where it ought to be."

"I know dragons are territorial, but will it really strain you to be in each other's presence?" I stopped. It felt so weird to be talking about this. But in the core of my gut, I *knew* this was only the beginning.

"We'll give it a try. And if things get dicey, we can sort it out then. He sounds reasonable. And I know what it's like to fall for a dragon you barely know." Camille cleared her throat and glanced at Smoky. "I'm the last person who's going to chastise you. Hell, I fell in love so quickly with all three of these louts that my head was spinning. It happens, and when you're *meant* to be together, you know it from the beginning. I'd love to ask you more about Arial and Shade, but we need to get down to business here."

She motioned to my laptop. "Let's see what the pictures have to tell us."

I could tell the guys were dying to ask questions, but with Menolly and Camille at my back, they'd have to leave me alone for now. I smoothly slid into position at the computer and flipped the switch. The first picture Morio had taken came up on the wall screen. He grabbed one of the barbecue skewers to use as a pointer, forgoing the mouse that I offered him.

"Thanks, but I'll do it the old-fashioned way."

We were looking at a house that could have been any other suburban ranch house—huge rambler that stretched across a third of the lot. Two stone walls formed the fence, but it wasn't gated. The house looked reasonably clean, the yard was tended, but there was something I couldn't put my finger on that bothered me.

"Do you realize that the picture was taken in broad daylight, but the curtains are tightly closed? Look at that—not a crack in them. Seems odd, especially since the house has quite a bit of privacy." Iris wandered over to the picture and cocked her head. "Windows are barred if you look closely."

Morio nodded. "Yeah, I noticed that. I didn't want to chance going in there in fox form, but I managed to get close enough to see the bars on the windows. And you're right— I'm almost certain someone was back there, watching out. I doubt if they noticed us. The house is across from a corner store—one of those old mom-and-pop type outfits. We parked there, and I slipped around with the camera while Vanzir and

Roz made pointed entrances and exits from the store." He motioned for me to click to the next image.

Morio had been hiding in a thicket, with ivy fronds and ferns thrusting their way into the picture. We could see a side yard to the right of the house. A gate cordoned off the front yard from the back, and enough of the backyard showed to indicate several sheds back there, as well as a dog kennel. What looked like a very large Rottweiler was chained next to the kennel.

"Friendly or dangerous?" Rottweilers could be either— depending on their owners. Actually, I thought, most dogs were like that. While some breeds had a predisposition to aggressive behavior, it was all in the breeding and training whether a dog ended up a lover or a fighter.

"Oh, I can tell you right now, that dog is not a playmate. He could sense me, I think, and barked the whole time. I got as close as I dared, but if I moved forward any farther, I would have been in their yard instead of the neighbor's. By the way, the neighboring house is for sale, there's no one there, and we can get into the backyard without too much trouble. A lot of cover until you hit the fence, which is stone covered with ivy."

Vanzir cleared his throat. "While Morio was taking pictures around back, we were hanging out by the car. Saw a couple of lean guys come out of the house and drive off in a beat-up VW van. They looked thin but wiry and tough. Don't underestimate them—they can probably throw some nasty punches."

"Do you think they'd risk hiding Doug and Saz in the house? If the guys are still alive, that is? They had to store them somewhere to hype them up before they . . ." I stopped, thinking again about Paulo's remains. "Before they murder them and rip them apart."

"And if they're holding Amber, could she be there, too? Yes, it's a large rambler, but my guess is that this is where they live, not where they stash the bodies, so to speak," Menolly said.

"Only one way to find out," I said. "Any more pictures?"

Morio ran through three more, giving us a little more information on the layout of the neighborhood. "What it comes down to, though, is when we go in, I have no doubt somebody will be there. I'm worried that we might put Amber, Doug, and

Saz's lives in danger if we don't do this right. Which is why we followed the van."

"I could kiss you for that," I said, beaming at him. "But why didn't you say so before and save us time?"

"Every piece of the puzzle counts—every piece could be important. Better to go through this step by step than overlook some information and have somebody pay the price. And from now on, I think we need to keep that in mind. With Stacia putting out bounties on your heads, we can't afford to be lax or stupid or lazy. Because one of these days, somebody tough enough and bad enough is going to come along and take up her offer and manage to snare one of you in a trap. We don't want that to happen."

He let out a long sigh. "I drove. I'll let Roz take over as to what we found. That's why there are still pictures to look at. We took them along the way and when we got there."

"Got where?" Camille asked.

"To a very unlikely compound," Rozurial said as he took the pointer from Morio. "First, these dudes are good at hiding in plain sight. They aren't coyote for nothing, I'll tell you that."

The picture that flashed on the screen showed what looked like a warehouse down by the docks. Small, freestanding, but definitely a warehouse. The sign over the door read EMPORIUM MEATS, and a very realistic-looking delivery truck sat by the side.

"Oh, please tell me they aren't really selling meat. I'd hate to think where they got it and what they put in their hamburger," Camille said.

"Thank you *so much* for the visual, and no—they aren't," Roz countered. "My guess is that if you look in that truck, you're going to find restraints and whatever else they need to transport very angry, very drugged male beta werewolves turned alpha."

"Perfect." I stood, staring at the image. "They really have cloaked themselves in the middle of the city. What about the warehouse?"

"Several entrances—standard front door. Big loading dock in back with doors on both sides. Morio scanned magically for traps, but we were too far away, and we couldn't very well walk up there and ask. The parking lot in back is big enough for about twenty cars—we did some checking and found out that at one time this building did, indeed, house a slaughter-house. So it's got plenty of good setups inside for torture and tearing things apart."

"Then why would Van and Jaycee need to dissect the Weres at their house, if the warehouse had everything necessary?"

"I can answer that," Camille said. "Two reasons. One—magic. Pure and simple. Or rather, not so pure. Think of it as territory. Sorcerers—even witches and mages—all have personal magical signatures. Each of us radiates a unique foot-print on the magical realm, and my guess is that the coyote energy may interfere with Van and Jaycee's sorcery."

"And the second reason?"

"From what we can tell, for some reason, they kept it from the shifters that they're Demonkin. But the basement reeked of energy that—had I been a little more perceptive—would have told me just that fact. They wanted their privacy, and they didn't want to be recognized. And that fact may have saved our butts, since their unwillingness to use the warehouse also seems to have been the one factor that prevented them from finding out about Amber and the spirit seal."

"So what next?" I asked.

"As usual. Go in swinging and do our best not to get killed. There's no way to know what's going on in there without just charging in. Somehow I don't think applying for a job at Emporium Meats is going to net us an invitation into their so-called factory." Menolly rubbed her hands on the legs of her jeans. "I guess that's all she wrote, ladies and gentleman. Shall we hit the streets?"

"Wait a minute. Morio and Camille, you'll both have to be very careful. Chances are they've got a nice little stash of Wolf Briar in there. And all bets are on that they'll use it if they see us coming, in hopes of knocking at least a couple of us out. You two better go in on the tail end and wear masks. That won't interfere with your spell casting, will it?" I frowned, hoping they'd say no.

They didn't make it easy.

"Yeah, actually, it might," Camille said. "The best we can do is go in at the back and run like hell if they let loose with that crap."

"Everybody get your weapons. We have to move, because if they haven't killed Doug and Saz yet, you know they're planning to. And Amber—it's anybody's guess why—and for how long—they plan on keeping her alive." I stood and stretched. We were headed into battle again, and each time, I always wondered if we'd all make it out alive.

CHAPTER 19

The Emporium Meats warehouse was down past the docks, in the Industrial District of Seattle. The warehouse sat smack in the middle of the wasteland existing past the ferry terminals, a mile or so north of Georgetown. Over the years, Georgetown and the surrounding area had taken on an almost schizophrenic quality. On one hand, charming, neo-bohemian shops and houses were scattershot through the district. On the other, gangs wandered the area, poverty seemed all too abundant, and the grittiness of the industry warehouses and factories, along with the train yard and tracks belonging to the BNSF Railway, lent an air of danger to the streets.

As usual, we were taking two cars: my Jeep and Morio's SUV. Menolly, Vanzir, and Roz were riding with me, while Trillian, Smoky, and Camille rode with Morio. I put in a call to Chase to meet us there.

As we headed south on First Avenue, the streets were fairly clear. A few gangbangers—probably the Zeets—were hanging around, but the night was too wet and chilly for much outdoor activity. We passed the piers to the ferries on our right, and the back side of Pike Place Market on our left, and continued along past the Seahawks Stadium and Safeco Field, also on our left.

As the streets wore along, the charm vanished, and the darker, seedier aspect set in. We zoomed along on the overpass leading over the BNSF train yard—a maze of tracks and boxcars in weathered pinks, greens, whites—all colors from so many different companies and places. The thought of being stuck down there, on foot, gave me the creeps.

We weren't just near gang territory but also vampire territory—and not vampires like Menolly, who did their best to keep themselves in check, but vampires like Dominick and Terrance, who led the cry for vamps to quit trying to assimilate and to create their own culture that didn't try to mimic human culture.

Menolly had been tossed out of Vampires Anonymous, the one group where she might have done some good against the fanged dangers, because Wade—the leader of the vampire self-help group—was afraid she'd spoil his bid on becoming regent over the Northwest Vampire Dominion. We hadn't heard lately how his campaign was going, but I had the feeling next time they met, there would be hell to pay on his part.

As the overpass glided back to street level, I pulled into a side parking lot shortly after we passed South Dawson Street. We were parked right next to the Emporium Meats warehouse.

"Here we are. And it looks like we're going to have company." I nodded to the parking lot. There were at least five cars that we could reasonably assume belonged to the shifters.

"Camille and crew are here," Menolly said, as Morio's SUV parked alongside my Jeep. "We're too near Dominick's for comfort."

"Not only that, but take a look across the street—there appears to be a new club in town," Roz said.

We glanced across the darkened road to the neon sign that glowed green. THE ENERGY EXCHANGE. Somehow, I didn't think it was a pay station for Puget Sound Power and Light. No, with a name like that, the joint could dabble in several things, none of them registering good on my internal danger meter.

"I don't like the feel of that," Menolly said. "But I don't think it's vampire."

"No, it's not." I slid out of the driver's seat and stood there, staring at the glowing neon tubes. "There's something . . ."

Just then Morio and Camille wandered over, gazing at the club's sign. "Sorcery. I can feel it."

"You think Van and Jaycee run that joint, too?" Seattle was becoming a scary place to live. Even as more and more Fae were drawn here, so it seemed were the lowlifes of the Supe world.

"I doubt it, since they're Tregart. But I bet they frequent it." Camille glanced over her shoulder at the warehouse. "We'll have to worry about this place later. We need to get into the warehouse and see if they've got Amber and the men."

"How we going to do this?" I considered the building. Morio was right—there was an entrance to either side, and the dock had its own door—as big as the entire loading bay. It operated like a garage door, and I wondered if there was a mechanism on the outer wall to open it.

"My guess is they keep that locked from the inside," Vanzir said, following my gaze. "But the side doors shouldn't be hard to break through. The locks look old, and I doubt if they've bothered to buy new ones. After all, who would ever suspect them?"

"Wilbur told me, when I escorted him home, that coyote shifters are arrogant. They never think anybody's going to be able to keep up with their tricks. So let's give the side door a try." Roz gave me a little push and, in a bad Humphrey Bogart impression, said, "This is your department, doll. How's about you go first?"

I motioned Camille and Morio to the rear. "You two stay back there. We fight better without men down, and Camille sure doesn't need to be caught by a flurry of Wolf Briar again. Menolly, you and Smoky up front with me. Vanzir and Roz, bring up the middle."

Grateful to the moody October night for the rich darkness that surrounded us, I led the way across the parking lot to the concrete steps, up to the walkway that ran the length of the warehouse. Briefly, I wondered if it curved around to the sides, but we didn't have time to check it out. Not right now. I headed over to the left-side door and knelt beside it, flashing a penlight on the lock. It was old and looked like it hadn't been used for some time.

Gesturing for the rest of them to stay there, I tugged on

Menolly's arm, and we bent low, crossing to the right-side door. The lock on this one was oiled and rust-free. Yep, this was the door they used to enter the building. I'd bet the bank on it. Once again, we crossed back to the left, and I hurriedly whispered my thoughts to the others.

"If we go in here, they won't necessarily be expecting us. If we take the lesser-used route, we may buy ourselves time to root around without being caught. And while I expect we're going to have a fight on our hands, I'd prefer to get in, grab Amber and the guys, and get out again before anybody catches us."

It wasn't entirely true—I really wanted to pound the crap out of them, but hey, the less stress, the better. Why make waves that might attract Stacia if we could be sneaky? Granted, we weren't good at sneaky, but we'd give it the old college try once again. Why I thought this time would be any different than usual, I didn't know, but then again, I was always being accused of being an optimist.

Camille nodded. "Good thought. Spring the lock."

I pulled out my picks and began mucking around with the lock. It was simple, no big-assed deadbolt, and it looked like the original that had come with the building. I took out my tension wrench, inserted it in the lock, then slid in the pick as I pressed my ear to the door and began working the pins.

Click. Click. Click. The pins fell into place.

Yeah, I was good at this. It occurred to me that between my glamour and my ability to pick locks, I might do better as a thief rather than a private investigator. Gods knew, I had few enough cases lately. Of course, if I spent more time advertising and hunting for clients, I'd be pulling in more work. Then I'd have to find the time to do it. Content to leave matters as they were, I finished jimmying the lock, and the latch sprang.

"We're good to go," I whispered. "Just try to keep the noise level down." I turned off my penlight and sucked in a deep breath.

And then we headed inside.

The door opened into a long passage that was dimly lit by flickering florescent tubes that ran the length of the hallway. We wouldn't be able to hide in this light, but considering that the corridor was empty, right now it wasn't a worry. I edged through the door, looking for traps, but the place was deserted. Motioning the others in, I glanced down the hall to make sure that we wouldn't be surprised if somebody came around the bend. The corridor ended, turning to the right, but between the turn and us were three doors to worry about—two on the left side and one on the right.

As Morio closed the door behind us, I sucked in a deep breath and did my best to softly creep along the tiled floor. The tile hadn't seen the end of a mop in a long, long time, and the dirt was ground in, years old by the look of it.

When we came to the first door, this one on the left, I pressed my ear against the wood and listened.

Nothing.

I tried the knob, but the door was locked. Thinking that maybe one of these might lead to our missing Weres, I pulled out my pick set again. Two minutes later, the door was open, and we were staring into a room that had a desk and not much else. Except for one hell of a dust bunny problem.

We moved on to the middle door on the right. This one was unlocked, so we listened carefully again, then I cracked it, ever so slightly, and paused. Nothing. No sound, no indication there was anybody in there. I eased the door open another few inches and peeked around the corner. The room was dark but full. Motioning for everybody else to wait outside, I tapped Menolly on the shoulder to follow me.

Deciding to chance it, I pulled out my penlight and sent the narrow beam around the room. It was jammed full of boxes and bags of all sizes. Hmm . . . stockroom? I slid through two stacks of boxes and stopped to examine the lettering on one. It was fully sealed and was marked as containing canned peaches.

"Peaches?" A quick gander around showed the rest of the boxes to be filled with tinned fruits, vegetables, tuna, peanut butter, and a number of other goods. "What, are they planning on this becoming their fallout shelter?"

Menolly poked me in the ribs. "Shush. Who knows what they're up to? But seriously, there's enough food in this room to feed a family of four for a year." She frowned. "They believe in some post-apocalyptic future or something?"

"I don't know." I opened another box that wasn't marked

as food and had simply been shut by tucking the corners of the flaps under one another. *Holy crap!* I jumped back before I could stop myself.

"What?" Menolly leaned in past me to take a look. "Motherfucking pus bucket. What the hell are they planning?"

Staring at us from the depths of the box were sticks of dynamite. Plural. As in, I had no idea how many, but too many to count offhand.

"I have no idea, but I sure don't like the way that looks. They aren't primed for use—the blasting caps must be in a different box, but fuck, this stuff goes bad." I'd already been whispering, but I lowered my voice again. "We don't know how long this has been here. Dynamite degrades. I don't know just how much I trust being in a building full of this crap."

"There's a door on the other side of the room." Menolly nodded in the direction of the opposite wall. "I'll take a quick listen, and then we'll get out of here." She silently glided over to the other door and pressed her ear against it. Then, just as silently, she backed up without opening it and motioned toward the hallway where the others waited.

As she shut the door behind us, I leaned against the wall—the opposite wall, considering that the room we'd just vacated held enough dynamite to take half this building out of commission—and let myself breathe.

"We have to be very careful. The Koyanni apparently like to play with things that go boom. As in dynamite. As in at least one full box in that room. They also have enough food to stock a corner grocery store—looks like they're stockpiling. I have no idea why, but consider them armed and dangerous. And for the sake of the gods, do not send anything that explodes into that room. No lightning bolts, no energy balls, or we could blow this joint sky high."

"There's a door on the other side of the room," Menolly added. "And I heard someone on the other side. I suggest we very quietly make our way down the hall and see what's around the corner."

We slipped down the hall, doing our best to limit our noise, until I reached the end of the corridor. I motioned for them to hold up and inched a look around the edge. The passage turned to the right and continued for the length of what looked like a room before a fork branched off into another hall to the right.

It was hard to tell what was at the opposite end of the corridor—probably another hallway. The building was big but not unending. I nodded for the others to follow me, and we slipped around the corner and headed for the next hallway.

We were almost there when a thin, wiry man came barreling around the corner. He was reading something on a clipboard and ran right into me before bouncing back, openmouthed, as he realized what he was seeing.

"Crap," I said. We were going to be outed by a geek.

But he didn't stand there gawking and yelling like an amateur. No, instead, he whipped out something that fit in the palm of his hand as he let out a loud shout that sounded like a cross between a yip and a howl. So *not* a good sound. But before I could say a word, Morio returned the cry, howling at the top of his lungs even as he began to grow into his full demonic form. Eight feet of humanoid fox demon was a sight to behold.

"Double crap," Menolly said and launched herself forward, but before she could reach the dude, he lifted whatever it was he was holding and pressed a button. And all hell broke loose.

I reached out just in time to meet an oncoming wave of what felt like electricity. Or maybe it was pure joy juice or whatever the fuck, but a thousand stabbing needles forked their way through my body, and I went down like a wet noodle. As I lay convulsing on the floor, Menolly leapt past me and then, before I could hear the satisfying crunch of our enemy's broken bones, she joined me on the floor, her eyes flashing red even as the jolt kept her from moving.

"You die!" Smoky flew past me, and once again, I heard the charge go off, but this time there was the sound of something wet smashing against one wall, and Smoky's raw laughter filled the hall. Meanwhile, Camille helped me stand as the flickering tingles played across my nerves like a freaking torture machine.

"Can you stand? Can you hear me?" She wrapped her arms around me and helped me over to the wall so that I could lean against it. Menolly joined us—apparently the effects didn't last as long if you were already dead.

I nodded, trying to catch my breath. "Yeah . . . yeah . . . I'll be okay. Really." I glanced over to where Smoky was standing, near the end of the hall, keeping guard. The guy was a puddle on the floor, blood pouring out of every orifice he had. Smoky had not only tossed him like garbage, he'd raked him with his claws. So much for the front man.

Camille gingerly picked up the weapon he'd been using and handed it to Roz. "You're the expert on weaponry. What is this?"

"Essentially, a magical Taser," he said. "Sorcery, no doubt." He paused, then gave us a veiled look. "Want to make a bet it has something to do with that new club—the Energy Exchange? Just a gut hunch."

I held out my hand. "Let me see it."

Shaped a lot like a one of the old-fashioned phasers off of the original *Star Trek* shows, it was lighter than it looked. A simple button controlled the trigger, and there was a digital readout that showed the number *ten* in the green LCD display. A small icon was flashing in another window. Meaning it needed to recharge? Or was it ready to shoot?

We were about to find out, because down the hall, a set of double doors to the left flew open, and a group of men rushed out. They were all wiry and thin, and while I didn't see any more of the magical stun guns, at least two of them carried baseball bats, and a third had a very nasty-looking stiletto— and I'm not talking shoes.

"Incoming, and they don't look friendly!" I yelled as I brought the contraption up and aimed it at the leader. He paused. I decided that we weren't going to get out without a fight, and fired.

"Cripes!" Camille let out a shriek, and I heard a commotion, but I didn't have time to look back. The leader was down, but the four other men rushed us, and I knew I couldn't get all of them before they came in swinging.

I tried another shot, but the stun gun sputtered, and I saw a red minus sign in the display. It was out of juice—I didn't need an expert to tell me that. I tossed it to the side and pulled out my dagger just as the first shifter came swinging, bat poised to take out my head.

Moving just in time to avoid getting a concussion, I still managed to get clipped on the arm. He hit me full on the shoulder, and I yelped as he raised his bat for another swing. I took advantage of the opening and darted in, my dagger at the ready. Lysanthra sliced through the air, whistling as she came singing down across his arm, gashing the bicep wide. He let out a shout and dropped the bat as he tried to stanch the blood.

While he was down, I whirled to lend a hand to the others. Smoky had dropped two of the shifters, but I saw why Camille had yelled. She was kneeling beside Trillian, who was woozily sitting up, rubbing his head. Three dead shifters were lying near them, and Vanzir was wiping blood off his knife.

I noticed that my guy was trying to get up and, in a flash, I was behind him, Lysanthra poised at his throat.

"It doesn't get any better than this from here on out, but it could get a *whole* lot worse," I said. "Where are the werewolves? All of them?"

He stared up at me, his eyes narrow. "Bite me, bitch."

"I can do better than that. I can turn into my panther self and rip you to shreds. I can let our friend over there," I nodded to Vanzir, "suck the life force out of you. I can let my sister throw an energy blast into that dynamite you've got and blow this whole fucking place to smithereens. Or you can tell me and maybe . . . just maybe . . . get out intact with your skin." Of course, I thought, I'd be turning him over to the Supe Community Council for charges, but he'd be alive. For a while.

He cleared his throat. "Fuck it . . . in there." He gestured toward the double doors. "There are still guards, though."

"Good boy. Now, time to sleep for a bit." Chase should be outside by now. He knew enough to wait for us to come out instead of barging in on his own. I glanced around. Crap, we didn't have anything to put our prisoners to sleep. "Okay, go nite-nite for a while." And with that, I gave him a good wallop to the back of the head. He conked out with a low groan.

"What you want to do with him?" Vanzir helped me lift him up.

"Take him out back and see if Chase is here yet. Tell him this man is a high-security-risk prisoner for the Supe Community. He'll need to be treated and then locked up. Get your ass back here as soon as you can."

Vanzir tossed the coyote shifter over his shoulder and took off, backtracking the way we'd come.

I motioned to everybody else. "How are you? Trillian, you going to be okay?"

Trillian was rubbing his head but looked steady enough on his feet. "Yeah, got one hell of a headache, but I'll be fine."

"Then let's do this. Our Weres are in there, along with more guards." I headed toward the doors. No use giving the enemy more time to prepare than they already had.

"Should we wait for Vanzir?" Camille asked.

"No, he'll catch up." I wasn't in the mood to take any more time with these bozos than we'd already spent.

We came to the double doors, and I stood back, motioning to Menolly. She grinned and with one massive blow, broke through both, slamming them open with a thunderous noise.

The room was massive, and I wasn't sure just what it had been used for, but giant meat hooks that lined the ceiling gave us a good clue. I stared at them, feeling slightly queasy as I noticed the dried blood dappling the rusty hooks.

There were hundreds, in lines, on what appeared to be some mechanized pulley system. And then I saw something dangling from one of them a little ways down the line. It was a body, skinned from head to toe. Sucking in a deep breath, I turned, wanting to give myself another moment before I took a closer look . . . before I saw that it might be Saz or Doug or . . . even Amber.

The chamber was filled with old stainless steel carts and sinks and . . . near the back, cages. From where I was standing, I could see that at least three of the cages were occupied. And in front of those cages stood four more guards, waiting. We could take them out—even if they had their magical stun guns, we'd push through and exterminate them.

"You know, we can make this a lot simpler," Menolly said. "You guys head over there, away from the door and away from the cages." And within a blink, she was gone. We'd barely complied with her orders when she returned, carrying the box of—oh fucking hell.

"What are you doing with that?" I pointed to the dynamite.

"Making use of their stupidity. It appears to be stable, but they don't have to know that, and they don't have to know that I don't have the blasting caps." She removed a stick, fiddled with it for a second, then started to walk toward the guards, the stick held clearly out in front of her so that they could see it.

"You've got till I get within throwing range to put down your weapons and move to the side. I'm a vampire—one stick of dynamite might tickle, but it's not going to destroy me. But you guys are a little more vulnerable. Think wisely; you only get one chance."

Her voice was so commanding, so clear and resolute, that I found myself backing up. I wasn't sure she actually hadn't found a blasting cap. In fact, I noticed that Roz, Camille, and Trillian took a good step back, too.

The guards bought it hook, line, and sinker. Which was good for us. They dropped their bats—thank gods that only one of those stun guns had been around, and it probably cost a pretty penny—and backed away from the cages, hands up.

As Menolly hustled them into a group, she called over her shoulder, "Go get Chase and some handcuffs. He can take this lot in, too."

Vanzir sped off, while Smoky went to help Menolly keep guard. Roz steeled himself and began to climb a nearby freestanding ladder up to the body on the hook. The rest of us headed over to the cages. Three were occupied. Two men, one woman—Amber. And she did, indeed, have a spirit seal around her neck. I found the keys and unlocked her cage, but she stopped me before I could open the other two.

"They're crazed. They aren't in their right minds, and they'd attack." She rubbed her arms as I unlocked the manacles around her wrists and ankles. "Thank you. I'm Amber—"

"You're Luke's sister. We know. We've been searching for you. And ten to one, those two are hyped up on steroids?"

Amber nodded. "I thought that's what they might be giving them, but I don't know why. Only that . . ." Her voice cracked, and she glanced up at the body that Roz and Vanzir were wrestling down from the meat hook. "Oh, Great Wepwawet. I couldn't see what they were doing to him from my position in the cage. That's why he kept screaming and screaming."

A stricken look washed across her face, and she hung her head. "He was nice to me. He was one of them, but he was nice to me, and they caught him trying to loosen my manacles so that it wouldn't hurt so much. They beat him in front of me and dragged him off, laughing. An hour or so later, I heard him start to scream. Another hour . . . and nothing."

That answered my question. The two men still caged were sure to be Doug and Saz. Paulo had been tortured and murdered. And if Amber was right, then we knew they treated their own just as badly as they treated their enemies. Which would seem to lead to dissent, unless the fear of repercussions won out.

Chase called in his team, and they set about trying to deal with the drug-crazed werewolves and the flayed body. I told him we'd take Amber over to headquarters to get checked out and give her statement. He glanced at the pendant around her neck but said nothing, just nodded.

As we gathered our things—Roz picked up the magical stun gun and stowed it in his belt—and left the building, part of me wanted to see it blow sky high. I had a fleeting desire to come back after everyone was gone and set off the dynamite, to put this place of misery and torture out of commission, but I knew that was better off left a fantasy. I wasn't a barbarian—yet. But I was rapidly learning just how far the enemy could push in order for me to turn into one.

CHAPTER 20

Along the way, Menolly put in a call to Luke and asked him to meet us at the FH-CSI building. She made sure to reassure him that Amber was alive and relatively unscathed.

I glanced at Amber. "Do you know what that necklace is you're wearing?"

She frowned. "I have no idea, but all I could think of was, don't let them have it. There's something about this . . . Ever since I found it in an old trunk that I bought at an antique store, I've known I needed to move here, to be near my brother and his friends. It was the final push that got me to leave Rice." Falling silent for a moment, she stared at her hands. Then, "I suppose Luke has told you all about him?"

"Yeah, you could say that." I didn't want to dis her husband in front of her—that was the straw that drove some women back into abusive relationships. She had to come to that point herself.

"Rice . . . the whole Zone Red Pack has a hard time coming to grips with the modern era. The women of the Pack are demanding more. Demanding to be treated with respect, demanding our rights. Some . . . a lot . . . of the men can't handle it. Alpha werewolf males have a tremendous amount of testosterone, and the tendency to bluster is always there. There are so many fights, almost all of the men in our Pack are scarred. You've seen my brother's scars, right?"

Menolly nodded. "I never asked him about them. He just recently told me about the woman—the one he loved."

"That was a tragic situation. Did he tell you that Marla pissed off the Alpha when she refused him because she was in love with Luke? He basically handed her over to some of the younger alpha males for revenge. She was passed around like a piece of meat, brutally used. Oh hell, I'll just say it like it really was . . . she was gang-raped, and the Pack leader watched and forced Luke to watch. It took every ounce of self-control he had not to kill the Alpha right there."

"Luke said she was killed?" I hated bringing up painful memories, but talking about her past seemed to be calming her down. And it would help her to trust us when we had to take the spirit seal from her.

"Yeah, she was. When Luke tried to sneak her out, the Alpha caught them—he'd sent someone to spy on them. The Alpha killed Marla himself, in front of Luke. Then he scarred my brother and excommunicated him. I wanted to go with him, but I wasn't old enough. Shortly thereafter I was married off to Rice. He offered the most attractive dowry and situation to my father. Rice is bad . . . but it could have been worse."

"You said you bought a trunk that had the necklace in it. Do you . . . are you attached to the pendant? Why do you think the coyote shifters kidnapped you? Did they tell you?" The time had come. We would be at the FH-CSI building soon, and I didn't particularly feel like airing the info in public.

She paused. "The truth is . . . I can't take the damned thing off. It feels like there are voices in my head, and they're coming from the necklace, but when I go to take it off, they start screaming until I put it back on. I haven't felt the same since I first started wearing it. From the start, it wouldn't let me take it off for more than a moment."

I stared at her, thinking about Queen Asteria. What were we going to do?

Then Rozurial said in a low voice, "The Keraastar Knights.

Want to make a bet that . . ." His voice drifted off, but I knew what he was saying. Amber may be making more of a journey than she expected.

"The coyote shifters were after your pendant. Did they try to take it from you?" I couldn't imagine them caring if she went crazy from voices in her head.

She nodded. "Yes, they did. But the minute they put their hands on it, they got shocked. One of them died. And when they tried to make me take it off, the necklace started humming and scared the hell out of them. Why do they want it? What is it? What's going on? And who are you?"

Menolly spoke up. "I'm Menolly D'Artigo, your brother's boss. He asked us to help when you went missing from the hotel. My sisters and I are from Otherworld."

Amber gasped. "I had a dream about Otherworld, even though I've only ever heard of it. I dreamed about a city with cobblestones, and about elves and a circle of people—I have no idea who they were. But there was a werepuma among them, and a young man, and an ancient . . . I guess he was human."

I let out a long sigh. "Amber, there's a lot to explain, but you have to trust us. As long as that necklace is around your neck and you stay here, you're in far greater danger than just from the coyote shifters. There's a demon general out there looking for the spirit seals. And a demon lord in the Subterranean Realms looking for them."

She gasped and cringed back in her seat. "I had no idea."

"My sisters and I—and our friends—are on the forefront of a war even your brother doesn't know about. We're trying to stop Shadow Wing and his army from taking over Earth, and eventually—Otherworld. And that pendant you wear around your neck is an ancient artifact that will make his quest a whole lot easier if he gets hold of you."

Amber was silent the rest of the way to the FH-CSI building. We let her be—she'd been hit by far too much to take in over the past few days, and she needed a little while to just rest after her captivity.

At least now we knew why the coyote shifters hadn't killed her. On one hand, the fact that the spirit seal had bonded itself to her had saved her life. On the other hand, I had the queasy feeling there was nothing we could do except hustle her over to the Elfin Queen, whether Amber wanted to go or not. We couldn't let her run around with one of the seals around her neck.

"So, do we go back and take down the rest of the Koyanni?" Roz leaned back against the seat and folded his arms.

"I'd like to put them out of commission. I'd also like to find out where that little gem of a weapon came from and see if we can do anything about getting them banned. That's fucking dangerous to any Supe out there, and I have the nasty feeling it would kill an FBH."

"Ten to one, our answers are going to be found at the Energy Exchange." Menolly leaned forward and peeked over my shoulder. "And that's Camille's department if it's a magical club."

"Maybe, but she's been beat up a lot the past few days from the Wolf Briar." My cell phone jangled, and I flipped it on, adjusting the Blue Tooth in my ear. I hated the damned thing, but it was the law, and it made sense. "Delilah here. Speak to me."

"Delilah, get your ass back home now. We've got trouble." Iris's voice sounded muffled.

"What's wrong?" I punched the button to put her on speaker.

"Something broke through the wards, and by the way the alarm is sounding, it's big and bad. This isn't any ghoul or zombie meandering through the woods. I put Maggie in Menolly's lair, and I've called Wilbur. He's on his way over." Her voice was trembling. Iris was powerful—far more powerful than we'd originally thought—but she also was a single house sprite alone in the house.

"Crap! We're on our way. You get down in Menolly's lair, too—"

"No time, I hear them breaking in. I'm heading outside—Maggie should be safe where she is. But hurry."

The line went dead. I looked at Amber. "I hope you aren't

hurting too much, because we're making a detour. Roz—call Camille and tell them to get a move on toward home."

And then, flooring the gas, I made a U-turn and headed toward Belles-Faire. We were about fifteen minutes away, thanks to it being late at night with little traffic. I planned to make it in ten at the most.

As we came racing up the driveway, I was terrified what we'd find. The house on fire? Maggie and Iris in the ashes? A horde of Demonkin? Or was it somebody else—had the shifters figured out where we lived and that we'd taken down their operations?

Roz had called Camille, and Morio's SUV was right behind us. Then he'd placed a call to Chase, asking him to send Shamas home. We wanted every hand on deck. Chase had promised to come with him.

I turned off the motor. It was obvious we were here, so no use being sneaky. But for a moment—just a moment—we sat, surveying the house. Roz said, "I'll go in through the Ionyc Sea—they won't be expecting that. I told Camille to have Smoky do the same. We can come in from the top floor and surprise whoever it is that way."

"Good idea." I closed my eyes, reaching for my inner light, reaching to push past the fear so I could be effective. "I need to get out of the car and shift into my panther form. The rest of you—head in. Amber, damn it, we don't dare let you near there—and we can't leave you alone. Vanzir, you have to protect her. With your life. We can't let that spirit seal fall into the wrong hands. So . . . I guess, Menolly—you go in with Camille, Morio, and Trillian."

Speaking of, the three of them were passing by the Jeep. Menolly silently joined them as I turned to look at Amber. "Whatever you do, don't get caught. Run like hell if you have to, but don't let anybody take that necklace. In fact, Vanzir—can you drive?"

He grinned. "I can probably manage it. I don't promise how well."

"This is no laughing matter. Drive her to Grandmother

Coyote's portal and hide with her there. If we don't come along within an hour or so, take her over to Queen Asteria."

"Queen who? Portal? You mean send me to Otherworld?" Amber was beginning to look a little panicked.

"Better than let the demons get hold of you," Vanzir said. "I know. Trust me." He slipped behind the wheel, and I showed him how to start the ignition and which were the brake and gas pedals.

"Just try not to get in an accident, okay? You know the way to get there?"

"Yeah," he said, then softly reached up to cup my chin. "You're getting braver, pussycat. And harder. Like a good soldier must be." And with that, he put the Jeep in reverse and—sputtering in a fit of stop-starts, backed away out of the driveway.

I watched as he went, then inhaled a sharp breath and shifted into panther form. The world looked different as I transformed, and I felt my inner predator rise to the top. Oh, I loved this form, loved prowling the night in panther shape.

Taking a deep breath, I wondered how to summon Arial, and then I knew. Apparently Greta had left me with a residual memory to reach out to Haseofon. Because the next thing I knew, I was walking into the halls in panther form. The others looked at me, but apparently they recognized me even in my Were shape, because they just waved. I glanced around until I found Arial. She was sitting on a pillow, reading a book. I bounded over and nuzzled her.

I need your help. The thought was clear, and she nodded.

"As always. I'm here to help you." She dropped the book and stood, shaking out her sable hair, and then she stepped back and shimmered. I watched transfixed. I'd seen Nerissa change before, and I knew what it was like *to transform*, but watching my sister was another matter altogether. Within seconds, a golden leopard stood there, her spots the color of her hair.

What's wrong?

Somebody's invaded our house—possibly the demons. I need you to go in on the astral and see what you can find out.

Lead me.

I turned and bounded out of Haseofon, Arial on my heels. We raced through the mist and landed right where I'd been standing, in front of the house. I turned to Arial, who gazed up at the house in her ghostly presence.

Can you go in—find out what's going on? I'm going to creep around back.

I'll meet you shortly. She vanished again, quicksilver as a shadow in the night. I gazed after her, wondering what it would have been like if she'd lived. There would have been four of us—and maybe things would be different. Who knew what turns our lives may have taken? But that was conjecture. We were who we were, and at least we knew she was happy and we could contact her. And right now, Iris was in danger, and we had enemies on every side.

I padded through the grass, trying to catch a whiff of our enemies. A sudden cry from the back of the house sliced through the night, and I broke into a run, racing around the corner. Camille and Morio were weaving some sort of spell against—oh crap, a bloatworgle. Hadn't we fought enough of these over the past few months?

It opened its mouth and sent a searing flame their way, and they broke apart, dodging left and right, disrupting the spell they'd been conjuring. Morio scrambled for his bag and pulled out a tiny coffin, about thirteen inches in length. Fuck. Rodney, the misogynistic bone golem he'd been given by Grandmother Coyote. But we needed all the help we could get, I thought.

Camille leapt to her feet and sent a blast of lightning toward the bloatworgle. It let out a shriek as the strike hit its distended belly, and its arms, too long for its body, flailed. But it did not fall. The buggers were dangerous because they were so hard to kill—and because of that mouthful of fire they had going for them.

I circled around, using the brush and weeds for cover, and then leapt on it from behind, my paws encircling its neck. I raked a paw full of claws across the demon's throat as Morio set Rodney loose to grow to full height. At the same time, the youkai-kitsune began to grow to full height. He could do far more damage in his full demonic form than he could in human form.

He lunged forward and raked at the bloatworgle's belly with long, black nails. I pulled back on the demon's neck as he did so, and the creature lost his footing, sliding to the ground on his back. Morio leapt on him, finishing the job as I looked around, trying to pick up Iris's scent.

Another noise startled me, and I turned to see Arial's ghostly shape racing toward me. I touched her nose.

What did you see?

There, in the house, snakes and a group of men tearing the place apart. And Menolly, and your friends the dragon and the incubus are fighting them. They need help.

Tregarts! Snakes . . . Damn—Stacia Bonecrusher's crew. We need all the help we can get.

I'll do what I can on the astral. She turned and vanished.

I shifted into my two-legged form so fast it hurt. Even as I let out a yowl, I was standing there in front of Camille and Morio and the dead bloatworgle.

"Tregarts in the house, and snakes. Fighting Menolly, Smoky, and Roz. Come on!"

We raced to the back porch. I took the steps two at a time and slammed open the back door, Camille and Morio hot on my heels. We burst into the kitchen, where the place had been trashed. Not stopping to ascertain how much damage there was, we raced on. By the time we made it to the foyer, the fight had spilled out onto the front porch. A group of biker look-alikes with chains and swords were holding their own.

Menolly was engaging two of them at the end of the porch, and one of them was holding a wooden stake behind his back.

"Get the fuck out of there! He's got a stake!"

Menolly didn't respond but instead leapt nimbly up on the railing and then over the side. The demons followed her, vaulting over the railing to meet her on the ground. Meanwhile, Smoky had dropped two Tregarts already, but three surrounded him as he fought his way down the front steps. Roz was grappling with a bloatworgle over by Camille's herb garden.

I waded into the fray, taking a running leap to bound over the railing and land on the ground near Menolly. Before he could turn around, I ran my dagger through the back of the Tregart carrying the wooden stake. He let out a yelp. As I pulled Lysanthra out, I twisted her, and that did the trick—he dropped the stake and fell to his knees, struggling to get up. Menolly gave him a kick to the jaw, and he went over, moaning. The other demon stared at us, looking for all the world like a Hells Angel with bad hair, but beneath that leather jacket there beat the heart and the soul of Demonkin.

Camille disappeared into the house, and I wondered where she was going, but I couldn't focus on what she was doing. There were still too many demons, too much danger standing beside me.

Smoky took one down, and then Roz finally got on top of his bloatworgle by stuffing one of his magical bombs down the creature's throat when he opened his mouth to breathe fire. The resulting inferno caught a nearby rosebush on fire, and Smoky swung around and let out a long breath, and an icy mist settled down over the flames, calming them.

In the dark of the night, illuminated by the lights from inside the house, all was chaos. I caught my breath and turned to help Menolly with the remaining demon she was facing. Together, we managed to corner him, and she ripped at him with her fangs while I sliced him cleanly between two ribs.

There was another noise, and I turned in time to see Wilbur, racing around the house, chasing two bloatworgles who were running for their lives. Whoa. Whatever he'd done had put the fear of magic in them—rare, because bloatworgles usually didn't scare easily—and they raced right toward us, their shouts echoing through the night. Rozurial dove out of their way as Smoky let loose with his talons and Morio engaged the other. They raged away while Menolly and I turned on the last Tregart.

I ducked in back of him, and when Menolly gave him a good kick that sent him flying toward me, I held out Lysanthra, and he landed right on the tip of her blade. His weight sent me reeling, and I landed hard on a rock in the crook of my lower back, with him on top of me. He was still, and I felt the flow of his blood spilling over me from the wound.

A moment later, all was quiet. I grunted as Menolly yanked the body off me and helped me up. As I wiped my blade in the grass and turned, I realized our front yard looked like a war zone. It was hard to count how many bodies there were in the dark, but the smell of blood, thick and metallic, rose to choke my lungs.

"Crap, that was nasty. Iris was right—we have to post guards here now. I hate this, but we can't leave the place unprotected. Speaking of . . ." I stood up and looked around. "Where is Iris?"

"She's not in the house," Camille said, slowly coming onto the porch. She was holding Maggie, who rested against her shoulder. "I looked everywhere, and she's not in there, guys."

"Fuck—turn on all the outside lights."

"I'll check the studio." Roz raced like Hel herself was on his heels, over to the studio. He adored Iris. We all did.

Trillian motioned to Morio. "Come with me, and we'll check the wild patch of woods out back." They hurried off.

Smoky said nothing but was away, heading toward the front perimeter of the land. I whirled and grabbed Menolly.

"Come on, let's check the trail down to Birchwater Pond." As we raced toward the tree line, I prayed under my breath that we'd find her. She'd be okay; everything would be fine. "She has to be," I whispered, as I caught a glimpse of Arial, on the astral, running beside us.

"Where could she be hiding?" Menolly stopped at the trail mouth, eyeing the path. "Would she be off path, or on?"

"Off, I guess. Let's just call her out. It's safe to do so now." I cupped my mouth with my hands like a megaphone and shouted, "Iris! Iris! It's safe to come out! Where are you? Are you okay?"

"Iris!" Menolly started calling, too, heading down the path. "You go off path to the left, and I'll head down to the pond. Iris!"

I climbed over the nearest tree trunk that was blocking the path and headed into the woods. A thought crossed my mind, and I pulled out my phone and called Vanzir's cell we'd bought for him.

"We took them out, but it was tough. You can bring Amber back now." I hung up as something caught my eye. Something sparkling, resting on the ground. I began to smell scorched earth amid the moss and mildew-thick forest. As I hopped over another tree trunk, then ducked under one that rested at neck height, I saw it. On the ground, a wand. Silver, with an Aqualine crystal.

Iris's wand. And what was it doing out here, without her?

CHAPTER 21

"Menolly! Get your ass over here. Now." I knelt by the wand and ran my fingers along the scorched ground next to it. As I brought my fingers to my nose, I could smell Demonkin scent . . . bloatworgles. Had to be. Had they killed her? If so, where was her body?

"What did you find—oh fuck." Menolly stared at the wand. "The ground's been charred."

"Go get Camille and tell her we need her to do a spell of finding right away. And I called Vanzir, told him to bring Amber back." I sat on one of the deadfalls, not caring that my butt was cold and that the continual drip of the boughs was hitting me and running down my collar.

Where are you, Iris? What happened to you?

This was all turning into one big mess. How the hell were we supposed to deal with everything coming at us? Had this been retaliation for our actions against Jaycee and Van? We'd trashed their lab, trashed their shop, and put an end—at least for the present—to them producing Wolf Briar. As I sat there, staring at the wand, my phone rang. I flipped it open.

"Delilah, get back up here to the house. Carter's here. We have another situation." She hung up.

Carter? He never left his basement apartment, as far as I could tell. Frowning, I grabbed Iris's wand and headed back to the house at a dead run. Vanzir drove into the yard as I looked up. Amber was still with him, safe and sound. I motioned to him.

"Take her into the parlor and make sure she's comfortable, then join us."

He nodded. "Will do."

Smoky and the guys had piled all the bodies to one side, and I skirted my way around them, then darted up the stairs and into the living room. Wilbur was just leaving, muttering about reruns on Nick at Nite, and how Martin was waiting for him.

Sure enough, Carter was sitting in the living room, his horns gleaming under the glow of the lamps. His foster daughter Kim sat next to him, but I noticed she was wearing some sort of chain around her waist and similar ones around her wrists.

Carter nodded for me to sit. We were all here—all except Iris—and I was frustrated, wanting to find her. *Now.*

"I hate to interrupt, but considering what your sisters have told me," he said, nodding to me, "it's imperative that I do."

"What is it?" I looked over at Kim, who sat unmoving, eyes cast down at the floor. A red mark on her cheek told me she'd been slapped and slapped hard.

"Remember how you were thinking there might be a leak in information? Someone feeding your moves to the Bone-crusher so she'd stay one step ahead of you?" His lips were tight, and I suddenly understood the chains around Kim.

"Oh, not you, Kim." I looked at her, but she wouldn't meet my eyes. I glanced over at Camille and Menolly. Both looked ready to kill. "Is this true?"

"It's true," Carter said. "I found her copying my notes, and she also had a tape—she's been recording our conversations and taking them back to her new mistress. My foster daughter has put you into grave danger. There's no way I can ever atone for her actions, but I can help you now."

"But why? How? I thought Kim was . . ."

"She doesn't have to speak to relay information. She's highly intelligent, can read and write with ease . . . she's mute, not mentally deficient. And apparently her mother's blood is stronger than her father's, because she's chosen to walk the path of the Demonkin rather than find her own balance within society."

Carter glared at her, and she shrank back, wincing. "I should kill you here, now, without another word. You ungrateful turncoat. You traitorous bitch. I treat you like my own daughter, and this is how you repay me."

The look in Carter's eyes made my stomach knot. He was furious, and I was afraid he'd make good on his threat. "We need to know what she told them. We need to know what she knows about them. Don't hurt her. Yet." I glanced at her, and she met my eyes then, contemptuous and sullen. "We can't trust her to give us the proper information, so what do we do? And she can't talk . . ."

Vanzir stood up. "You know I can get in her mind. Knock her out, and I'll go in and find out what she knows. I can dig through her defenses, and she won't be able to stop me."

A dream chaser demon, Vanzir could do exactly what he said. He could feed on her life force, too, if he wanted. I looked at Menolly and Camille. They nodded. We had no choice—we had to know what Kim had told Stacia. She'd probably listened in on every conversation we'd had with Carter and every bit of information he'd called us about.

"Do it. You can find out why she's chosen to align herself with them, too." I stood up and walked over to Kim, who flinched away. "Menolly, can you mesmerize her like you can an FBH?"

"I'm more than willing to try." She strode over to where Kim was sitting and yanked her to her feet, baring her fangs. "Don't resist, or I will do it the bloody way. Got it?"

The girl nodded, now looking petrified more than angry. Menolly leaned close and whispered something in her ear, grazing Kim's neck with her fangs, slowly slicing through the flesh to bite deep and hard. Kim gave a silent gasp, and a look of bliss washed across her face as Menolly lapped at the blood trickling out of the puncture.

After a moment, my sister pulled back. Kim was in a stupor, and Menolly said, "Sleep. Sleep until you are commanded to wake. Do not resist—open your mind, and slumber." Her voice was so hypnotic it made *me* want to sleep, but I shook my head and caught Kim as her knees buckled. We laid her out on the sofa.

"Do you need privacy?" I asked Vanzir.

"It would probably help. I'll let you know when I'm done. It shouldn't be too long." He flushed, and I remembered how much he loved to feed and how he did his best to avoid it. Life force was addictive, and Vanzir was a demon who didn't really like himself or what he did.

As we escorted Carter into the kitchen, Menolly opted to stay and guard Vanzir, just in case anything went awry.

I placed Iris's wand on the table. It looked forlorn, and I winced, hanging my head. "I can't stand that she's in danger. I can't stand that they may have her."

"I can't believe that Kim is a traitor." Camille leaned over and pulled Iris's wand to her. "I hope we're wrong. I hope Iris is just hiding someplace where she can't hear us. Carter, how did Kim fool you?"

He blushed, staring at his hands on the table. "Again, my apologies. I thought Kim was happy. I thought . . ." With a shrug, the demon leaned forward, resting his elbows on the table. "I came home today and found Kim listening to a tape. She didn't expect me till later, and she had all sorts of documents lined up on the desk—private, confidential documents. Not only about you but about other members of the Demon Underground here . . . the demons who all hope Shadow Wing will fail. When she saw me, she tried to hide everything, but despite my brace, I'm quick, and I'm powerful. I stayed her, and once I looked through the reports, it was obvious she was spying on my clients and me. I wasn't sure who for first, but then . . . then I found this in her purse."

He tossed a necklace on the table. A gold snake. "That's the symbol of Stacia's troops—the golden serpent. Only her most trusted confidants wear them, her spies and cronies. I recognized it from all the research I've done on her. Kim's been a spy for her since . . . well . . . I don't know how long. But long enough to muck things up for you."

"We talked about the ley line that ran through Harold Young's house into the graveyard in front of her—after you bought the land. Stacia must know we're the ones who broke her spell." I moaned, rubbing my head. "You tell us every time you've got a new sighting, but by the time we get there, she's gone. Kim's been warning her."

"No wonder we haven't been able to get to the bitch!" Morio grumbled, slamming his fist on the table.

"What are you going to do with Kim after we've got our information?" Camille caught Carter's gaze.

He met her eyes, unblinking. "Traitors are worse than enemies. There is only one punishment for treason. It can be quick, or it can be drawn out. I have no taste for torture, but I'm sure that if I told Stacia that Kim confessed she'd been spying, the Bonecrusher would love to have her little stool pigeon back. But there's an old adage among my mother's people: *Do not leave your enemy alive. They will return to bite you.* Kim is now one of the enemy. If I let her go, she'll come back to haunt us. As much as this whole affair pains me, I'm afraid I'll have to put her to death."

The words were cold but true. If we left her alive, she'd be so angry we found out that she'd do her best to run back to Stacia and do her best to help them against us. "How . . ." I wasn't sure how to ask what I wanted to ask.

Carter gave me a cold smile. "I have many powers from both my father, Hyperion, and my mother. Don't forget, I am of the Demonkin as well. I'll give her better than she deserves—a quick and painless end. But make no mistake: Kim has chosen her fate."

As Morio took Maggie on his lap, there was a shimmer in the kitchen. I pulled out my dagger, jumping to my feet, but Arial, who was padding around in her spirit shape, growled a warning.

No, don't attack.

"Arial says don't attack." I lowered my blade, waiting to see what was coming through. The men stood at the ready, waiting. As the shimmer grew brighter, a low sepia-toned mist spilled out from its center, and then, a brilliant light flashed as two figures stepped out of the roiling smoke.

Out of the mist stepped a man, a wave of energy rocking the kitchen. He stopped, his gaze fastened on me.

Shade.

And behind him raced a much shorter figure. *Iris.* As they materialized in the room, Arial quietly slipped away, brushing me with her astral tail. I smiled, content that I knew how to contact her now.

Iris gave one long cry of joy and threw herself into Camille's arms.

Smoky let out a low growl as he faced Shade, but I pushed past him. First, before anything, I yanked Iris into my own embrace and kissed her forehead.

"Thank the gods you're alive—we were terrified Stacia got hold of you. What happened? Where did you come from?"

I found her when I showed up, looking for you." Shade's voice, honey on peaches, washed over me, and I turned, sliding into his arms as if it were the most natural thing in the world. "I felt you put on my ring."

In a louder voice so everyone could hear, he said, "I came as soon as I could. I had no idea I'd show up in the middle of an invasion. Your friend was running from one of the beasts in the woods. I caught her up and shifted over to the shadow realm before she could be mauled by that mockery of a life-form."

"You're Shade," Camille said, stepping forward. "Delilah's new . . . her . . ." She stopped, blushing. "Welcome, and please, don't mind some of us who happen to be a bit churlish." She gave Smoky a long look. "We came home to find Iris missing and demons rampaging through the place. It's been one hell of a night, and we're suspicious about everything and everyone."

The others gathered in, greeting him and hugging Iris as I stood back, wondering how this was going to play out.

Smoky and Shade circled each other warily, eyeing one another like two male lions. Camille looked at me, then grabbed my hand and dragged me into the center between them.

"Listen, dudes—we have no time for your posturing. We have a crisis on hand, and if you two want to play king of the dreyerie, it will just have to fucking wait. Got it?" She rested her hands on her hips, glaring at Smoky.

His lip twitched, even as his gaze flickered over our heads to stare at Shade. A moment later, he let out a long sigh and backed off.

"My wife requests we give it a rest. What say you, Master of Shadows?"

Shade glanced at Camille, then at me. "Is her sister just as demanding?"

"In other ways, I'm sure. At least my wife doesn't turn into a tabby cat and play with my toes at night, as I've heard Delilah is wont to do." Smoky gave me a snarky grin, then abruptly sat down again, pulling Camille onto his lap.

Shade nodded to him, taking a seat and motioning for me to sit near him. "Have you told them, my dear?"

"Yeah, I thought it best not to leave you for a last-minute surprise." I laughed. "Of course I told them."

"Already she starts," Shade said. He turned to Iris. "Milady, did you suffer any damage traveling through the astral?"

Roz held out a chair for Iris, and she settled herself into it. "No, I'm fine. And thank you again for saving my life."

"How about you tell us what went down?" I gave her the once-over. She didn't look hurt. Shook up? Yes. But Iris was a lot tougher than she looked.

She picked up her wand, making sure it was all right, fingering the crystal reverently. "I was tending Maggie in the kitchen, when I heard a noise out front. I had a really bad feeling, so I ran Maggie to her playpen in Menolly's lair and then came back to see what was going on. I went outside and saw the Tregarts. I raced back into the house to get my wand and call you when I heard them coming through the front door, so I dropped out of my bedroom window—and let me tell you, that's a long drop for someone like me—and raced into the woods."

She sucked in deep breath, wincing. "I thought I was a goner. One of those beasts saw me. He followed me into the woods, and I got myself off the trail. He followed me and was using his fiery breath, but I hit him a good one with frost shards from my wand, and it stopped him. I started to run again but tripped and lost hold of my wand. By that point, he was coming at me again, and I left the wand and ran through the woods. I could hear him as I backtracked, trying to reach the path so I could move faster."

I could see it—Iris, racing through the undergrowth, trying to scramble over the tree trunks that were nearly as tall as she was, with a fire-breathing demon on her tail. The thought made me shiver. We'd lost friends. We could lose her, too.

"I'm so sorry—we should never have left you alone." Rage flooded over me. "Stacia can't have another one of our friends. She killed Henry, and it stops there. I promise, we'll make sure we leave you with a guard from now on. And we'll reinforce the house against the demons." A snarl rose up, and I wanted nothing more than to shift back into panther form and go rip up the nearest enemy—which happened to be Kim.

Shade reached over and placed a hand on my shoulder. I looked into his eyes and lost myself in the molten chocolate. His touch was like warm sugar on a cool autumn night.

Taking a deep breath, I shook off the desire to destroy and exhaled in a long, slow stream. "What happened after that?"

Iris bit her lip, drawing blood. "I made it to the path, and as I raced out of the wood, I ran smack into Shade here. I knew who he was immediately—you described him very well." She flushed, giving him a shy smile. "And he whisked me up and over to the realm of shadow. Anyway, Master Shade here, he saved my butt, and I will forever be grateful to him."

"My pleasure, Mistress Ar'jant d'tel." At her sharp look, he smiled gently. "Make no mistake, I see the cloak you wore— and you still wear in your aura. You cannot wield such power and expect to hide it from Dragonfolk, nor deny you own it. Can she, Master Smoky?"

Smoky let out a harrumph and cleared his throat. "I refrained from bringing it up because I believe it involves some painful memories, but yes. There is truth in what you say. I lived in the Northlands. You are steeped in the energy of the ice and snow, Iris, and anybody who's lived in the high ranges can sense it."

Just then, Vanzir came in, followed by Menolly. We all stopped, waiting.

"I know where Stacia is hiding." He motioned toward Menolly, who tossed a steno pad on the table. "We can get her, if we go now. We can take her down, because she won't be expecting this. She has no clue Kim's been outted. There's not a single cord connecting the two psychically. I also know her weakness—Kim observed it, though Stacia seems to have no clue that anybody else knows."

"Why . . . why did my foster daughter do this?" Carter started to stand, then fell back in his chair, his voice cracking.

This was tearing him up. I could see it, and it made me want to go over and wrap my arms around him and whisper that everything would be okay. Which it wouldn't, but the desire was still there.

"Kim wants to be powerful. She hates her human half, and she hates her mother for abandoning her. Stacia's a strong role model, if you like überbitches. Kim wanted to explore her demon heritage, and you never gave her permission for that. You raised her to be human. She despises what she perceives as her vulnerabilities." Menolly was reading off the steno pad. She looked up and shrugged. "I just took down what Vanzir told me."

Carter hung his head. "I was trying to raise her to be civilized. I would have eventually taken her to meet her grandfather and asked that he help her."

"Does she know who you are?" I asked.

He shook his head. "No . . . I had not yet told her. I didn't want . . . I didn't want her to grow up thinking she could have everything she wanted just by asking merely because she's the foster daughter of a half-Titan. I couldn't give her back her speech, but there are so many things I would have given her over time."

"I'm afraid it's too late." Vanzir let out a long sigh—whether of impatience or frustration, I wasn't sure.

"What do you mean?"

"Kim couldn't handle having me probe her mind. She went into a deep coma—so deep I couldn't reach her. When I disconnected . . . she died."

Carter let out a cry and pushed away from the table. For a moment I thought he was going to attack Vanzir, but he just limped past him, heading toward the living room. We could hear him sobbing.

"He really did love her." I glanced at the hallway. "Someone should go comfort him, but I'm not sure who would do best."

"Let me," Camille said. "I did this for you when Mother died. I'm used to it." She headed down the hall, and we could hear her voice, slightly muffled, settle into a soothing cadence.

Smoky frowned but said nothing.

Trillian shook his head. "Damn it . . . she shouldn't have

to do that. She's suffering enough right now, with her father disowning her. Speaking of which, I'd like to kill that fucking self-righteous bastard. I don't care what you"—he glanced at Menolly—"or you"—and then at me—"think about that. I won't touch him because Sephreh is your father, and Camille wouldn't forgive me, but the man makes me want to kick his ass from here to Dahnsburg."

"Camille gives help as a matter of course," I said. "I think it's part of who she is. And when she hurts, it makes her feel better to help someone else. A displaced way of soothing her own worries. We can talk about Father later, though. Right now, we need to plan out a strike on Stacia. Vanzir, do you really think it's possible?"

He thought for a moment, then nodded. "It won't be easy, that I can tell you—but I guarantee you, if we go in fully armed and with every person we can, we have a chance of taking her down."

"Then let's do it." I pulled over the steno pad and got out my laptop. "Tell us everything you know—and everything that we need to know. And don't leave anything out. When we walk out of her safe house, I want her head on a stick and her body sliced to ribbons. Leave no one standing."

CHAPTER 22

～⬥～

After Carter left, carrying Kim's body with him, we swung into action, printing out maps and raiding our arsenal as we gathered anything and everything we could take with us that might have an effect on the Bonecrusher.

Vanzir came through the door, leading Amber by the hand. Chase was right on his heels. "I called him," he said before I could ask why Chase was following him. "After I realized what Kim had done. I figured we'd be going for Stacia, and Amber would need to be protected."

Amber looked shaken. "All the dead bodies out there . . ."

"Demons. Raiding the house. Trust me, if they catch you, they'll strip that pendant off your neck and kill you. Or worse—and yes, there are worse things than being killed. Trust me." Menolly frowned. "Chase, can you take her down to my bar and stash her in the safe room? You know where it is. I'll give you the key. Nobody can get at her there."

Camille frowned. "Take Maggie, too. We're going to need Iris." She turned to Chase. "We're headed out to raid Stacia— we found the Bonecrusher."

Chase blinked. "Of course I'll take them. You think it will

be safe for me to take her, though? I don't have the firepower you do."

"I can solve this," Smoky said. "I'll take you both through the Ionyc Sea. It will take moments, and it shouldn't hurt your baby."

Chase picked up Maggie, cuddling her to his shoulder as Smoky wrapped his arms around the detective and Amber. Before Amber could say a word, they vanished. A few moments later, Smoky reappeared.

"They're safe. Chase will wait there for your call."

"That takes care of that," Camille said. "Let's get a move on. Get everything ready that might be useful."

According to the information from Kim's mind, Stacia was staying on the Eastside again—she apparently preferred it to Seattle's more crowded streets. Only this time instead of being near Marymoor Park, she had holed up in a house on the outskirts of Redmond, on three acres.

Roz picked up the magical stun gun from the table. "Is there a way we can recharge this without having to go down to the Energy Exchange? Camille? Can you do it?" He turned it over, stopping when he came to a panel on the bottom. As he flipped it open, we saw some sort of wiring, along with a mixture of various powders. "Holy crap—this isn't an Earthside weapon. Not totally. Whoever made this had to be from OW."

Camille took it, looking closely. "Correct. These compounds aren't found Earthside. That means somebody's come over here and set up shop selling a hybrid—the material this gun is made of definitely comes from over here. Who the hell would do that?"

"We don't have time to find out now, but we'd better mark that down on our ever growing to-do list." I regarded it quietly, then said, "Well, can you?"

"Can I what?" She gave me a quizzical look.

"Can you recharge it?" The stun gun was a powerful weapon and just might help us take down the Bonecrusher.

"I . . . I don't know. Maybe. Maybe if I take it to Wilbur's, he can help me. Morio, come with? I don't trust his wandering hands."

"Right behind you."

As Camille headed out with Morio, I turned to see Iris, freshly dressed in a pair of jeans and boots that came up to her knees. She'd put on a long-sleeve shirt and heavy leather gloves.

She grinned. "Snakes have a harder time getting through denim and leather. I'm no fool."

Smoky stepped to the side, discussing something in low tones with Shade. I eyed them suspiciously, but we didn't have time for me to eavesdrop. We'd just finished gathering our gear when Camille and Morio returned.

"Freshly charged, though it might not be quite as powerful a jolt as the ones the Koyanni threw at us." She handed the gun to Roz, who happily stowed it on his belt. "By the way, we're still going to have to deal with them after this is done. But if we can take down Stacia, we can take down just about anything."

I slid my arm around her waist. "If we can take down Stacia, then we'll have another wedding reception for you guys—a family one only. And we'll drink ourselves silly on Riellsring brandy and forget about Shadow Wing . . . even if for just a day."

As we headed out the door to our cars, I steeled my shoulders. I was lean, mean, and had a new hairdo I was quickly growing fond of. And—my gaze flickered to Shade—a new boyfriend who already felt like one of the gang. We were off to defeat Stacia; good times like this didn't come often enough.

The drive over to the Eastside didn't take long; there wasn't much traffic on the 520 floating bridge, and we sped along, late under the overcast sky, dodging raindrops and the occasional shower of hail pellets. We'd taken three cars—this time Shade and Iris were riding shotgun with me, while Roz and Vanzir caught a ride with Menolly, and Camille and her men took her Lexus. We were armed to the hilt, and I felt a stirring—always, now, before a battle, my blood began to rise and I felt anxious and eager.

We're warriors now, I thought. Unwillingly thrust into a war we didn't choose, but one that would risk the world if we let it happen. We were about to face our biggest foe yet, and I wasn't sure how we'd come through. But we were growing stronger and more cunning. We'd learned a few tricks along the way, and we were more ruthless, more willing to cross lines that had stalled us at first. We had to be. The stakes were greater; our enemies were too willing to use our friends against us.

As we swung right onto Leary Way, heading toward the Redmond Town Center, I glanced over at Shade, who seemed entirely unperturbed about sitting in the Jeep. "Have you ever been in a car before?"

"Several times." He flashed me a warm, easy smile. "Relax, I've been Earthside quite a bit. I am familiar with the customs. Perhaps more so than your brother-in-law, who's been over here longer. I'm more willing to integrate myself when necessary." He paused. "Lady Iris told me what you're facing. I knew about the demons already, but she filled me in on the lamia."

One less thing for me to do. "Iris said . . ." I glanced at her through the rearview mirror, and she nodded. "Iris said you're half shadow dragon?"

He nodded. "Aye. Yes. Half black dragon—which is the same thing as a shadow dragon—and half-Stradolan."

"What's a *Stradolan*? I want to know what you can do. It might be important in the upcoming fight."

Sucking in a deep breath, he let it out in a long, slow stream. "I can walk between worlds. I can move through the astral and the etheric without a problem, though I'm not very adept at shifting into the Ionyc Lands. I can enter the Netherworld and return. My powers are dilute because of my half-breed heritage, but I can, my lady, work with some forms of magic—shadow and illusion."

"Like the coyote shifters?"

Shade laughed. "They work with illusion, yes, but not to the extent I can. However, as I said, my magical powers are limited. I'm one hell of a fighter, though." Almost as an afterthought, he added, "Oh, yes. I can shift into dragon form, but only during the night in which there are shadows."

I glanced over at him, my heart swelling. Something about him spoke to me. He was a half-breed, like me. His powers were slightly skewed. He could transform, but he wasn't a full dragon nor full Stradolan. He was, for all intents and purposes, a misfit. *Like me.*

Turning right onto Eightieth, we followed the road as it

wound through Redmond, then into the suburbs of the city, finally merging into 172nd. A few winding S curves, and we were nearing the address. Stacia still lived in the suburbs, but the house had a nice piece of land attached to it.

I pulled to a stop a house or two away and waited for the others. As I stared over at the lot where Stacia and her cronies were hiding out, I knew in my gut this was it. Tonight would be the end. For her . . . or for us. She'd killed Henry, she'd destroyed Camille's shop, she'd subverted Kim and left Carter heartbroken, she'd taken control with Trytian's army, and while they might be working together against Shadow Wing, she was out for our blood.

And we . . . were out for hers.

I glanced over at Shade. "Tonight, we fight. You aren't a pacifist, I hope."

He reached out and gently covered my hand. "I have slaughtered more enemies that you can imagine in my time. I am far, far older than you think. Whether he knows it or not, I'm older than your dragon friend Smoky. Stradolan . . . we spend much of our time walking out of time, so to speak. I fought in wars before the Great Divide."

I met his gaze and saw the sands of time falling away, revealing an unending flow of centuries. How long had he been alive? And then I realized he wasn't anything verging on Fae. Or human. He was a half-breed, but he was the product of two great forces. How he even came to be perplexed me, but the warmth in his eyes was real, and so were the fingers that stroked my own. As I lost myself in the rich coffee of his eyes, Iris leaned forward and tapped me on the shoulder.

"We should go, Delilah."

"Right." I sucked in a deep breath, shaking myself out of the reverie. Whatever energy Shade was running, I wanted to be part of it. Whatever he was offering, I'd already accepted it.

As I climbed out of the Jeep, then helped Iris jump down, she whispered to me. "I like him. He'll be there for you, Delilah. No matter what happens, this one will be there for you."

I leaned down and pressed my lips against her cheek. "I know. I'm so comfortable around his energy that I want to curl up by the fire and never move."

She flickered her gaze over to where he stood, observing

the house, then back. "He bears your master's energy. If he's not an avatar of the Autumn Lord, he's the next best thing. I wonder how they came to be so linked. And how he knew about me."

"About that . . . what does *Ar'jant d'tel* mean?"

"Leave it for now. It's part of my story. When we win—not if, but when—and the dust has settled on Stacia's dead body, then I will tell you."

As the others joined us, I gauged the house. It was surrounded by a high fence, but that was nothing new in the suburbs. We couldn't get in from the back unless we managed to find our way through the thicket of trees that bordered her lot, and there were no roads back there. At least not close enough to give us an uninterrupted view of what was going on.

And last time, when we'd snuck in, we'd ended up almost getting blown to smithereens. We might as well just go in shooting, for all the good sneaking around had done us. I cleared my throat and mentioned my thoughts to the others.

"I say we attack on two fronts," Menolly said. "I can sneak in. So can Shade. Smoky and Roz can't because they don't know what's beyond the gates, doors. But let Shade and me get a head start, we'll come in through the back to try to keep them from escaping."

"I don't like splitting up," I said. "No. This time, let's just go in blasting. Kill anybody or anything that moves and looks remotely demonic. But our prime target is Stacia. This isn't her training camp, so I doubt if we're going to find humans around to get in the way."

Roz pulled out the stun gun. "Anybody want to use this? I have enough weapons to keep me happy for now."

Trillian held out his hand. "My skills are fairly adept with a sword, but that will give me a better edge till the charge runs out." He took the weapon, held it out to calculate the aim, and then nodded, hooking it on his belt. "I'm ready."

"Watch out for snakes," Camille said. "She's bound to have the place like an oven in there, and where there's a lamia and heat, there's bound to be snakes."

"I'll prepare one of my freezing spells. Smoky should do the same." Iris inhaled deeply, closing her eyes as the magic began to stir. I could see it, rising around her like a vortex. It was as if the past few months had ripped open her abilities, and the Talon-haltija could cast spells I hadn't had any clue even existed. Smoky took one look at her and followed suit. The temperature around us fell a good thirty degrees.

"Our turn." Morio looked at Camille, and they joined hands. *"Dust to dust, death to death, spell to spell, breath to breath . . ."*

Their voices rang softly through the air, chiming a note that sent a shiver of fear through me. They were growing more powerful, and their death magic scared the shit out of me. Until recently, I'd been worried. But now, I found something seductive about it.

Vanzir and Roz prepared their weapons—Vanzir had a nasty-looking sword, and Roz pulled out a handful of his magical bombs that I guessed were freezing from the icy white of their surface.

Shade looked at me and nodded. "I'm ready."

I longed to turn into my panther self but resisted. Once inside, I'd assess whether I could do more damage on two feet or four. With a glance at the others, I straightened my shoulders. We were ready. The die was cast.

"Menolly—go."

She blended into the shadows, running ahead to set off any traps that might be waiting. Except for Smoky—and perhaps Shade—she was the least vulnerable. As she covered the distance from gate to house, nothing actively moved, but Camille shook her head.

"They have wards, and she just activated them."

I licked my lips. "They know we're coming. Get your asses in there!"

As we plunged forward, Menolly kicked open the door and leapt to the side as a mass of Tregarts spilled out. The last time this had happened, Stacia had managed to escape while they distracted us. Not this time.

"Menolly, Shade—go left. Smoky, go right."

As they circled the house, the rest of us steeled ourselves against the oncoming attackers. The first wave hit like a whirlwind, but Camille and Morio were ready at the front. A wave rippled forward from their linked hands. The first four Tregarts were caught in the wake of the rolling energy, and my stomach turned as eager earthen hands reached out of the ground to grab the demons' legs and yank them, kicking and screaming, through the soil, deep into the earth, where they disappeared as if they'd never been.

I stared at the disrupted lawn. What the fuck kind of freakish spell was that? Did I even *want* to know?

It worked. Your sister is helping save your ass. My dagger whispered to me in the night, and I shook off my shock and dove in, looking for an opponent. It didn't take long to find one, as the second wave lurched forward. Zombies and bonewalkers. The walking dead. *Stacia's specialty.*

I narrowed my attention. One thing I'd learned from the battles over the past year: Never try to focus on everything that's going on. Fight your own battle, then glance around and move on. Otherwise you chanced ending up on the wrong end of a sword. I straightened my shoulders and assessed the skeleton coming my way.

The walking pile of bones would fight until broken to shards. That much I knew. I also knew that they weren't easily hurt by blades. Blunt objects were better, so I sheathed Lysanthra and, guarding my breath into a low, even rhythm, spun, my booted foot landing against the bone-walker's skull.

The skeleton's neck snapped back, and I kicked again, breaking the vertebrae. The head fell to the ground, but the bone-walker kept coming my way. Without the head, however, it was easier to jump out of its way and circle it. From the back, I pummeled it with a hail of kicks, breaking the tailbone in two.

The creature shattered, falling to the ground, and I pulled out Lysanthra and smashed the hilt through the skull, then severed the hands from the arm bones. One more smash to each hand ensured they wouldn't scuttle around, grabbing our ankles.

I turned around, quickly surveying the battlefield. Camille and Morio were casting another spell. A circle of light surrounded them, whirling like a vortex, and they walked forward toward a group of five bone-walkers. The creatures disintegrated into dust as the edge of the light hit them.

Damn, I'd like to have me some of that magic, I thought.

Roz, Vanzir, and Trillian were pounding their way through a couple of zombies and a Tregart. Trillian was wisely holding back on the stun gun. Good. When we came up against Stacia, perhaps it would do some sort of damage.

Iris was focusing her wand on the house—she was standing on the porch, and as I watched, a layer of mist began to flow out of the Aqualine crystal, in through the doors, turning to frost everywhere it touched. A layer of ice, a layer of cold. *Good girl.* That would take care of any snakes we might encounter inside.

I realized there was an opening to get to the door now and took it, racing up the steps, sliding on the frost right through the doorway. Morio, Vanzir, and Iris followed me while the others hung back, fighting the last of the front guard.

We'd rushed into what had once been a parlor but now appeared to be some sort of barracks. Cots lined the walls. My guess—they were for the Tregarts. I slowed. Stacia should be in here and—if we were unlucky, Trytian, too. I wasn't sure I wanted to take on the daemon. While he *had* tried to blow us up, my guess is that he would have left us alone if Stacia hadn't entered the picture. And he was fighting against Shadow Wing.

As I turned the corner, I stopped short. There, ahead, was a tall, lovely woman. Striking. Stunning. *Stacia.*

Oh crap. Where the hell were Smoky, Menolly, and Shade? I tried to slide back around the corner before Stacia noticed me, just grateful she hadn't shifted to her true form yet, but she turned as I was backing away. Her face—dark, brilliant eyes against an olive complexion—was beautiful, but the look in her eyes terrified me. There was no mortality there—no sign she'd ever felt compassion or mercy.

She smiled then. "I offered you and your sisters the chance to join my army." Her voice was soft, too gentle for the look on her face. "Remember that when you die. I'm not like my predecessor. He enjoyed playing with his food. I just get the job done—that's why I'm alive."

As she began to transform, I turned to yell for Iris and Vanzir, but saw they had engaged four zombies that had appeared out of the corner. And I found myself facing a very large, very scuzzy looking Tregart. *Crap.*

His fist slammed into my gut, and I doubled over. As he leaned down to grab me by the scruff of my collar, I managed to thrust Lysanthra straight up and stab him in the face. He shrieked and staggered back, and I forced myself to my feet. Stacia was midway through transformation—apparently it took time to turn into a twenty-foot anaconda woman.

The demon was bleeding like a stuck pig. I pushed forward, stabbing him through a gap in the leather jacket, managing to hit him in the gut as he tried to maneuver his eyeball, which had been dislodged, back into the socket.

At that moment, the front door—which I could see from my position—slammed open, and Smoky, Menolly, and Shade burst through. *High five! Backup had arrived.* As the Tregart writhed on my knife, I gave it another good twist and slid my blade out of him. He dropped to his knees, and I brought the dagger down on his head, giving him one final gash that did the trick. He keeled over, and I raced into the living room, where Stacia was just finishing up her shift into her lamia form.

"Remember, she's a necromancer!" I eyed the demon general, wondering just how the hell to kill this thing. She was twenty feet long, most of that in giant anaconda form. Her torso, arms, and head were female, grotesquely misshapen, with long fangs that dripped a dark liquid. Constrictor or not, I had no doubt that they contained some sort of venom.

Smoky let forth a low whistle, and frost spread from his breath, rippling through the room in a wave, freezing everything it touched. Stacia hissed at him, spitting some liquid toward his eyes. The dragon jumped back, dodging out of the way as the venom splashed against the frost and sizzled.

Shade began to walk toward her, shimmering so that it was hard to tell whether he was corporeal or not. She cocked her head at him, then struck, grabbing for him, but her arms went right through his image. Shit—he was walking in shadow, and that had probably just saved his ass.

I wondered why she wasn't tossing spells around—she was a powerful necromancer—and then a thought hit me: *Could she cast magic in her natural form? Or did she have to be in human form?* Necromancy wasn't an innate ability for her, so maybe she couldn't use it when she shifted back to her normal shape. Either way, I had to figure out some way to get behind her so I could hack into that damned long tail she had. Menolly joined me and pulled me to one side.

"I can vault over her head," she said. "A lot faster than she can catch me.

"Go for it. I'm trying to find an opening that isn't going to kick my ass."

"Be safe. We can't afford to lose you. Remember, we're all in this together—we don't have room for martyrs." She took a running leap and went soaring over the lamia's head in a flip to die for, landing near the end of Stacia's coiled tail.

Trillian took something out of his pocket, and I smiled. Of course, *he'd* be the one to figure that out. He slid a pair of shades on. Wraparound Ray-Bans, which looked stunning and would protect his eyes from her venom. He held up the stun gun and began to move toward her.

Stacia spit at him and at the same time slammed the tip of her tail into Menolly, knocking my sister against the wall. Menolly managed to grab hold of the tail, and she was using her long nails to claw her way up toward Stacia's back. At that moment, Iris came through the door, bloodied and bruised, and she took one look at Stacia and let out a long, terrible shriek.

"You killed Henry; you destroyed the shop!" Her eyes grew wide as she thrust her wand toward the lamia and let out a long string of chanting—I couldn't understand the words, but the power behind it was vast and terrifying, and I found myself backing away as the Talon-haltija sang her song.

Stacia started to home in on her, but right then Menolly made her way onto the creature's back and wrapped her arm around the lamia's neck. She began to squeeze. The lamia's tail was flipping now, smashing right and left as she reached up to try to claw Menolly from her back. Venom dripped from the demon's fangs, and she let out a long shriek.

"Do you realize how stupid you are?" Her eyes flashed. "Kill me, and you kill yourselves and this world. I'm your best chance to stand against Shadow Wing."

Iris let loose a spell that hit Stacia in the face. Energy crackled through the lamia, a web of forked lightning working its way down her body.

"We'll take our chances," I screamed, rushing in from the side. "If you're our only ally, then we're dead anyway." As I plunged Lysanthra into her side, Stacia backhanded me and sent me—and my dagger—flying against a buffet. Her tail swung toward me and coiled around my waist and I heard something in my chest crack. Moaning, I struggled to get free, but the pressure was too great, and I was beginning to pass out. *Crap,* I thought. *So close—I can't die now!*

Shade appeared then, at the side of the lamia, and he breathed a cloud of smoke on her. She screamed and rubbed furiously at her eyes. Shade let out a low rumble and began to shift, but he wasn't turning into dragon—no, he was turning into a creature of mist and shadow, a vaporous form. He enveloped Stacia within his sparkling clouds, and she clawed at her throat.

Menolly grabbed the demon's hair and began to pull, holding her neck bare and exposed. Shade quickly moved out of the way, and Smoky made a running pass, his talons ripping at the vulnerable flesh. He left five long, terrible gashes that immediately began to fountain blood.

Stacia let go of me, her tail thudding against the floor. I moaned as I hit the hardwood and dragged myself out of the way.

At that moment, Camille and Morio entered the room, followed by Rozurial and Vanzir. Vanzir pushed his way to the front and held out his hands. I knew what we'd see if we were on the astral—long tentacles coming out of his fingers, reaching deep within Stacia's mind to suck out her life force. His head dropped back, his rocker chic look dropping away to a mad fury as he let out a laugh that ricocheted through the room. His eyes grew wide, the kaleidoscope that made up one indescribable color whirling with passionate intensity.

"And I feed," he said, laughing again.

Stacia writhed, her heavy tail constricting in on itself. She grabbed for Menolly, but my sister leapt straight up, managing to avoid the tentacle of muscle. As she landed on the floor again, Menolly raced over to me, scooping me up to pull me out of the way. I screamed—the ribs that were fractured shifted, sending a paroxysm of pain through my body.

At that moment, Trillian stepped to the side so he wouldn't hit Vanzir and aimed at Stacia with the stun gun, hitting her dead center in the chest with the jolt of magic. He shot again and again, until the gun was empty.

Trillian broke off and backed up . . . his breath coming

in ragged pants. "She's done . . . get out of the way—I think
when she dies it's going to be messy."

We raced for the door, Menolly dragging me with her, but
before we could make it, there was a noise, and I turned to
look. Stacia wavered and went down, hitting the floor with an
earthshaking thud. As she landed, her body began to dissolve,
and snakes roiled out of her, hundreds of snakes. Constrictors,
vipers . . . all creatures from the serpentine world.

"Move! They're coming our way!"

And they were—at least three hundred of the coiling
beasts. I didn't mind snakes, but they'd been part of the lamia,
and I didn't trust that they weren't hungry and aiming for
whatever moved.

Iris let out a long shout and once again, a blanket of frost
raced through the room, slowing the snakes some. Smoky
joined her, and an ice storm raged through the living room,
beating hail and frost down on everything and everyone in
sight. The pellets hit exposed skin with a fierce sting, and I
heard Camille let out a cry—the pellets had to make the glass
wounds hurt like hell.

The snakes let out a collective hiss, and I realized they still
had Stacia's essence within them—they weren't just your
everyday pretty serpent.

"She's still there—in the nest of snakes! She'll heal if we
don't kill them."

I could barely breathe by now, my ribs were hurting so bad,
but I didn't care. We had to finish this.

Smoky pushed Camille into Morio's arms. "Get her and
everyone else out. I'll take care of this."

As Morio and Trillian herded everyone out, Shade swept
me up in his arms and carried me. We headed toward the front
of the yard as a loud rumble sounded, and the walls began to
shatter. Smoky was transforming into his dragon shape. As we
cleared the porch, a huge gust of wind blew us out, and then
snow began to fall in our area as a figure—tall and dressed
in the purest of whites—came striding out. Behind him, the
house creaked as it iced over. Another blast, and the timbers
began to fall in on themselves. Whatever he'd done, the place
was imploding.

Camille flipped open her phone. "Chase? Get a unit over

here now." She gave him the address. "We just killed Stacia . . . the house is gone. Tell them . . . tell them . . . hell, I don't know. Tell them Santa Claus paid a surprise visit, and he wasn't happy with Stacia being on the naughty list."

And as we watched silently, the Bonecrusher and her snakes vanished under the silent wash of snow.

CHAPTER 23

〜❀〜

"So, did anybody ever find Trytian?" I was sitting in the kitchen, my ribs wrapped tightly. Sharah had me on strict orders to rest for a good six to seven weeks. I'd heal faster than an FBH, but bones could only knit so fast. The kitchen was still trashed, there had been so much destruction, but most of the mess had been cleaned up, and the men were busy, trying to repair the damage done.

Iris was making tea, Menolly was hovering near the ceiling. Most of the guys were spread out in the living room except for Vanzir, Trillian, and Shade, who had joined us in the kitchen.

Camille shook her head. "No, and frankly, I'm willing to leave him alone if he leaves us alone. He's not out to take Shadow Wing's place like Stacia was. I wish there was a way we could let him know that." She leaned against Trillian, who wrapped her in his arms and kissed her head.

"I can make that happen," Vanzir said. "I'll put out a note through the Demon Underground, and it will spread. He'll hear. I have no love for the fucking jerk after he tried to blow us up, but if he's willing to let us do what we need to and tend to his own backyard . . . I'm willing to let it go."

"What about Van and Jaycee?" I hated ticking off the list of enemies we still had prowling around, but we needed to remember: They were out there, and they were gunning for us.

With a shrug, Camille said, "I don't know. We keep watch. We infiltrate the magic shops, spread the word we're on the lookout. And we hope they move on as soon as possible. My guess is that Stacia's training camp will either break up or Trytian will take over. We'll want to keep our ears out for whatever happens in that direction, too."

Iris brought a bowl of Cheetos to me, along with a glass of milk. "I take pity on you because of your ribs."

"You never did tell me your story," I said.

She shrugged. "You'll have plenty of time to listen over the next few weeks. And on the full moon, with those broken ribs, you're going to be confined to a room where you can't jump up on anything or hurt yourself. So get used to being an indoor-only for the next six weeks or so."

There was a knock at the door, and Menolly answered. She led Luke, Amber, and Chase into the kitchen. Chase looked weary.

"Call me, let me know what happens," he said. "Meanwhile, I'm needed back at HQ." I caught his gaze and smiled, and Chase smiled back then, and in that moment, everything was okay. What he would say once he knew about Shade was anybody's guess, but that was for another day.

After he left, Amber and Luke sat down next to me. Luke bit his lip when he saw the tight bandages around my ribs. "I'm sorry about that. But thank you—thank you all for saving my sister. I don't know what I would have done if you hadn't helped out."

"That reminds me, what are we going to do about the coyote shifters?" I popped a Cheeto in my mouth and savored the crispy cheese crunch, then licked my fingers.

"I think we should bring the Koyanni up on charges at the next Supe Community Council." Menolly patted Luke on the back—about as close as she ever got to a hug. "After all, they're breaking treaty by attacking the werewolves, and it doesn't matter whether or not they belong to the council. The wolf Packs do." She pressed her lips together, and I could tell she was pissed.

"I agree, Camille said. "Hand over everything to the council, and let them take care of it."

"Good idea. I just . . . I wish we could have caught all of them." I didn't like leaving matters as they were, but we had no choice. I was out of commission, and Sharah had made it clear to me that she'd strap me into a hospital bed if I tried to do anything more strenuous than channel surf.

Luke shrugged. "I'm just glad to have my sister back."

Camille glanced at me, her eyes pensive. "About that . . . Luke . . . Amber can't stay here if she's wearing the necklace."

"What necklace?" He glanced at her, then frowned. "Why not? What's wrong with it? Not fashionable enough?"

I let out a low sigh. "We have to tell you something. We've already told your sister, so she knows. You can never tell anyone else, but you need to know what's going on."

Over the next hour, we filled the two werewolves in on our mission, explaining from the beginning about Bad Ass Luke and Shadow Wing and the spirit seals and ending up with the Keraastar Knights. We did *not* tell them about our doubts or concerns over giving the seals to Queen Asteria now that we knew what she was planning to do with the spirit seals—a disaster in the making, in our opinions.

They sat, mouths open, shaking their heads. It was easy to see they were brother and sister, they looked so much alike.

"So that's what's going on with my necklace." Amber breathed a soft sigh. "And how will that affect my baby?" She curled an arm around her belly.

"I don't know, honestly. Queen Asteria's medics can probably help you with that—you can't tell anyone here about the problem, except Sharah." I hung my head. "Amber, you're going to have to either give us the necklace or volunteer to go to Otherworld and turn yourself over to Queen Asteria. I think you may have the genetic makeup she was talking about—to become a Keraastar Knight."

"This is sudden . . . I don't know what to do. I can't take off the necklace." She blinked, tears welling up. "I've never lived anywhere else . . . even coming here was so new for me."

"I'll go with you." Luke stood up.

She glanced up at him, eyes wide.

"I'm your big brother. I couldn't keep you from harm with Rice, but I can take care of you now. I'll go with you to Otherworld and make certain you're okay. I've nothing to tie me here except for my job, and Menolly can find someone to replace me. But you . . . you need family there. You need *me*."

"Thank you—but are you certain?" Amber looked over-joyed, but a flicker of fear still ran through her face.

"Yes. If Menolly and her sisters will volunteer to pack my apartment and put my things in storage except what we'll need over there." He glanced over at Menolly, who nodded softly.

"We'll take care of everything, Luke. You're a brave man—and loyal. Just like family should be." She smiled then. "We'll talk to Queen Asteria, make sure you have everything you need. And we'll visit when we can."

Just like family should . . .

"Luke, you're a good example," I said, motioning to Menolly. "And we need to follow your example. Tomorrow, we'll figure out just what we're going to say to Father about what he did to Camille. We're the Three Musketeers here . . . we stand united."

Camille said nothing, but her lower lip trembled as she smiled at me.

Menolly gave me a solemn nod, then called Morio and Smoky in. "Camille can travel to Elqaneve, though she can't set foot in Y'Elestrial. We're too near dawn for me to go. Why don't the three of you escort Luke and his sister and the sixth spirit seal to Queen Asteria. We'll send your things over later this week, Luke."

"Thank you," Luke said as they prepared to go. "We'll make you proud. We'll do our part in this war . . . because you're working to save our world."

Breaking the mood, Camille turned to me. "Hey, what about the hair? You going to let it grow out again?"

I frowned. Having most of my hair chopped off had been traumatic, but like everything that had happened lately, I'd found my peace with it. In fact, I liked it. The short, tousled, edgy look made me feel empowered.

"Actually, I'm going to keep it like this. The original color will grow back in, and that's fine with me—I could do without the blotchy orange effect, but I'm going to keep the style. It's . . . who I am now. And I'm really starting to like who I'm becoming."

Shade rubbed my shoulders. "My love," he whispered. "You are beautiful. Inside and out."

Iris glanced up at him. "Remember what Sharah said—no sex for a couple weeks. Delilah's ribs are cracked in several places and need to heal. For now, you sleep out in the studio with the Demon Twins and Shamas."

"No fair—" I started to say, but Shade put his hand on my shoulder.

"We have plenty of time, and I plan on being around for quite awhile." He leaned down and gently kissed my lips, and once again I lost myself in the glowing heat of his body. The mark on my forehead hummed, and I suddenly found myself standing in front of Hi'ran.

"Are you happy?" He reached out and cupped my chin, tipping my face up.

I gazed at him, my heart swelling. "He's part of you, isn't he?"

Hi'ran smiled then, softly, as the boreal wind raged around us. "He's *of* my season, but he is his own man in his own right. I told you, I am not a jealous master, as long as you remember that *I am your master*. When you touch him, I will know it . . . when he touches you, I will also be there. And when it's time, he will be the go-between for me to father your child."

I sucked in a deep breath—on the astral it didn't hurt—and slid into Hi'ran's arms. But this time, he simply held me, and I was content with that. I had a new passion in my life, and I wanted nothing more than to explore the burgeoning relationship with Shade. I knew him. He was part of me already, and for the first time in my life I believed in soul mates. At least, for me.

Chase and Zachary had been wonderful men, but I was a huntress, prowling the treetops, and I belonged to the Autumn Lord in spirit. And my heart . . . my heart belonged to the autumn, too.

I'd never expected to find my true self in the reflection of death and destruction, of fire and flame-colored leaves, but I'd grown up so much. This was who I was—this was who I would always be, and finally, I could accept my predator side and be happy with it.

"I love you, my Master," I whispered to him.

Hi'ran smiled. "I love you, too, Delilah."

I nodded. And then, with a blink, I was back in my body, home, safe for the moment, with my love standing by my side.

CAST OF MAJOR CHARACTERS

The D'Artigo Family
Sephreh ob Tanu: The D'Artigo sisters' father. Full-Fae.
Maria D'Artigo: The D'Artigo sisters' mother. Human.
Camille Sepharial te Maria, aka Camille D'Artigo: The oldest
    sister; a Moon Witch. Half-Fae, half-human.
Delilah Maria te Maria, aka Delilah D'Artigo: The middle
    sister; a werecat.
Arial Lianan te Maria: Delilah's twin who died at birth.
    Half-Fae, half-human.
Menolly Rosabelle te Maria, aka Menolly D'Artigo: The
    youngest sister; a vampire and extraordinary acrobat.
    Half-Fae, half-human.
Shamas ob Olanda: The D'Artigo girls' cousin. Full-Fae.

The D'Artigo Sisters' Lovers and Close Friends
Bruce O'Shea: Iris's boyfriend. Leprechaun.
Carter: Leader of the Demonica Vacana Society, a group that
    watches and records the interactions of Demonkin and
    humans through the ages. Carter is half-demon and half-
    Titan; his father was Hyperion, one of the Greek Titans.
Chase Garden Johnson: Detective, director of the Faerie-
    Human Crime Scene Investigation Team (FH-CSI).
    Human.
Chrysandra: Waitress at the Wayfarer Bar & Grill. Human.
Erin Mathews: Former president of the Faerie Watchers Club
    and owner of the Scarlet Harlot Boutique. Turned into a
    vampire by Menolly, her sire, moments before her death.
    Human.
Greta: Leader of the Death Maidens; Delilah's tutor.
Iris Kuusi: Friend and companion of the girls. Priestess of
    Undutar. Talon-haltija (Finnish house sprite).
Lindsey Katharine Cartridge: Director of the Green Goddess
    Women's Shelter. Pagan and witch. Human.
Luke: Bartender at the Wayfarer Bar & Grill. Werewolf. Lone
    wolf—Packless.

Marion: Coyote shifter; owner of the Supe-Urban Café

Morio Kuroyama: One of Camille's lovers and husbands. Essentially the grandson of Grandmother Coyote. Youkai-kitsune (roughly translated: Japanese fox demon).

Nerissa Shale: Menolly's lover. Works for Department of Social and Health Services and is running for city council. Werepuma and member of the Rainier Puma Pride.

Rozurial, aka Roz: Mercenary. Menolly's secondary lover. Incubus who used to be Fae before Zeus and Hera destroyed his marriage.

Sassy Branson: Socialite. Philanthropist. Vampire (human).

Shade: New ally. Delilah's lover. Part-Stradolan, part–black (shadow) dragon.

Siobhan Morgan: One of the girls' friends. Selkie (wereseal), member of the Puget Sound Harbor Seal Pod.

Smoky: One of Camille's lovers and husbands. Half–white, half–silver dragon.

Tavah: Guardian of the portal at the Wayfarer Bar & Grill. Vampire (full-Fae).

Tim Winthrop, aka Cleo Blanco: Computer student/genius, female impersonator. Human.

Trillian: Mercenary. Camille's alpha lover and husband. Svartan (one of the Charming Fae).

Vanzir: Indentured slave to the sisters by his own choice. Dream chaser demon.

Venus the Moon Child: The shaman of the Rainier Puma Pride. Werepuma. One of the Keraastar Knights.

Wade Stevens: President of Vampires Anonymous. Vampire (human).

Zachary Lyonnesse: Junior member of the Rainier Puma Pride Council of Elders. Werepuma.

GLOSSARY

Black Unicorn/Black Beast: Father of the Dahns Unicorns, a magical unicorn who is reborn like the phoenix and lives in Darkynwyrd and Thistlewyd Deep. Raven Mother is his consort, and he is more a force of nature than a unicorn.

Calouk: The rough, common dialect used by a number of Otherworld inhabitants.

Court and Crown: The *Crown* refers to the queen of Y'Elestrial. The *Court* refers to the nobility and military personnel that surround the Queen. Court and Crown together refer to the entire government of Y'Elestrial.

Court of the Three Queens: The newly risen Court of the three Earthside Fae Queens: Titania, the Fae Queen of Light and Morning; Morgaine, the half-Fae Queen of Dusk; and Aeval, the Fae Queen of Shadow and Night.

Crypto: One of the Cryptozoid races. Cryptos include creatures out of legend that are not technically of the Fae races: gargoyles, unicorns, gryphons, chimeras, etc. Most primarily inhabit Otherworld, but some have Earthside cousins.

Demon Gate: A gate through which demons may be summoned by a powerful sorcerer or necromancer.

Earthside: Everything that exists on the Earth side of the portals.

Elemental Lords: The elemental beings—both male and female—who, along with the Hags of Fate and the Harvestmen, are the only true Immortals. They are avatars of various elements and energies, and they inhabit all realms. They do as they will and seldom concern themselves with humankind or Fae unless summoned. If asked for help, they often exact steep prices in return. The Elemental Lords are not concerned with balance like the Hags of Fate.

Elqaneve: The Elfin lands in Otherworld.

FBH: Full-blooded human (usually refers to Earthside humans).

FH-CSI: The Faerie-Human Crime Scene Investigations team. The brainchild of Detective Chase Johnson, it was first formed as a collaboration between the Otherworld Intelligence Agency and the Seattle Police Department. Other FH-CSI units have been created around the country, based on the Seattle prototype. The FH-CSI takes care of both medical and criminal emergencies involving visitors from Otherworld.

Great Divide: A time of immense turmoil when the Elemental Lords and some of the High Court of Fae decided to rip apart the worlds. Until then, the Fae existed primarily on Earth, their lives and worlds mingling with those of humans. The Great Divide tore everything asunder, splitting off another dimension, which became Otherworld. At that time, the Twin Courts of Fae were disbanded and their Queens stripped of power. This was the time during which the spirit seal was formed and broken in order to seal off the realms from each other. Some Fae chose to stay Earthside, others moved to the realm of Otherworld, and the demons were—for the most part—sealed in the Subterranean Realms.

Guard Des'Estar: The military of Y'Elestrial.

Hags of Fate: The women of destiny who keep the balance righted. Neither good nor evil, they observe the flow of destiny. When events get too far out of balance, they step in and take action, usually using humans, Fae, Supes, and other creatures as pawns to bring the path of destiny back into line.

Harvestmen: The lords of death; a few cross over and are also Elemental Lords. The Harvestmen, along with their followers (the Valkyries and the Death Maidens, for example) reap the souls of the dead.

Haseofon: The abode of the Death Maidens, where they stay and where they train.

Ionyc Lands: The astral, etheric, and spirit realms, along with several other lesser-known non-corporeal dimensions, form the Ionyc Lands. These realms are separated by the Ionyc Sea, a current of energy that prevents the Ionyc Lands from colliding, thereby sparking off an explosion of universal proportions.

Ionyc Sea: The currents of energy that separate the Ionyc Lands. Certain creatures, especially those connected with the elemental energies of ice, snow, and wind, can travel through the Ionyc Sea without protection.

Koyanni: The coyote shifters who took an evil path away from the Great Coyote; followers of Nukpana.

Melosealfôr: A rare Crypto dialect learned by powerful Cryptos and all Moon Witches.

The Nectar of Life: An elixir that can extend the life span of humans to nearly the length of a Fae's years. Highly prized and cautiously used. Can drive someone insane if they don't have the emotional capacity to handle the changes incurred.

OIA: The Otherworld Intelligence Agency; the "brains" behind the Guard Des'Estar

Otherworld/OW: The human term for the UN of "Faerie Land." A dimension apart from ours that contains creatures from legend and lore, pathways to the gods, and various other places like Olympus. Otherworld's actual name varies among the differing dialects of the many races of Cryptos and Fae.

Portals: The interdimensional gates that connect the different realms. Some were created during the Great Divide; others open up randomly.

Seelie Court: The Earthside Fae Court of Light and Summer, disbanded during the Great Divide. Titania was the Seelie Queen.

Soul Statues: In Otherworld, small figurines are created for the Fae of certain races and magically linked with the baby. These figurines reside in family shrines, and when one of the Fae dies, their soul statue shatters. In Menolly's case, when she was reborn as a vampire, her soul statue re-formed, although twisted. If a family member disappears, their family can always tell if their loved one is alive or dead if they have access to the soul statue.

Spirit Seals: A magical crystal artifact, the spirit seal was created during the Great Divide. When the portals were sealed, the spirit seal was broken into nine gems, and each piece was given to an Elemental Lord or Lady. These gems each have varying powers. Even possessing one of the spirit seals can allow the wielder to weaken the portals that divide Otherworld, Earthside, and the Subterranean Realms. If the all of the seals are joined together again, then all of the portals will open.

Stradolan: A being who can walk between worlds, who can walk through the shadows, using them as a method of transportation.

Supe: Short for Supernatural. Refers to Earthside supernatural beings who are not of Fae nature. Refers to Weres, especially.

Triple Threat: Camille's nickname for the newly risen three Earthside Queens of Fae.

Unseelie Court: The Earthside Fae Court of Shadow and Winter, disbanded during the Great Divide. Aeval was the Unseelie Queen.

VA/Vampires Anonymous: The Earthside group started by Wade Stevens, a vampire who was a psychiatrist during life. The group is focused on helping newly born vampires adjust to their new state of existence, and to encourage vampires to avoid harming the innocent as much as possible. The VA is vying for control. Their goal is to rule the vampires of the United States and to set up an internal policing agency.

Whispering Mirror: A magical communications device that links Otherworld and Earth. Think magical videophone.

Y'Eírialiastar: The Sidhe/Fae name for Otherworld.

Y'Elestrial: The city-state in Otherworld where the D'Artigo girls were born and raised. A Fae city, recently embroiled in a civil war between the drug-crazed tyrannical Queen Lethesanar and her more level-headed sister Tanaquar, who managed to claim the throne for herself. The civil war has ended, and Tanaquar is restoring order to the land.

Youkai: Loosely (very loosely) translated: Japanese demon/nature spirit. For the purposes of this series, the youkai have three shapes: the animal, the human form, and then the true demon form. Unlike the demons of the Subterranean Realms, youkai are not necessarily evil by nature.

PLAYLIST FOR *HARVEST HUNTING*

I listen to a lot of music when I write, and when I talk about it online, my readers always want to know what I'm listening to for each book. So, in addition to adding the playlists to my website, I thought I'd add them in the back of each book so you can create your own if you want to hear my "soundtrack" for the books.—Yasmine Galenorn

Air:
"Napalm Love"
"Playground Love"

Beck:
"Farewell Ride"
"Nausea"

The Bravery:
"Believe"

Cat Power:
"I Don't Blame You"
"Werewolf"

Cher:
"The Beat Goes On"

Chester Bennington:
"System"

Cobra Verde:
"Don't Play With Fire"

David Bowie:
"Golden Years"

Deftones:
"Change (In the House of Flies)"

Evans Blue:
"Cold"

Everlast:
"What It's Like"
"Mercy on My Soul"

Fleetwood Mac:
"The Chain"

Gabrielle Roth:
"Black Mesa"
"Zone Unknown"

Gary Numan:
"Innocence Bleeding"
"Dominion Day"
"Down in the Park"
"Dream Killer"
"Hybrid"
"My Shadow in Vain"
"Prophecy"
"She's Got Claws"
"Stormtrooper in Drag"
"The Angel Wars"
"Tread Careful"

Gorillaz:
"Rock It"
"Spitting Out the Demons"
"Hongkongaton"
"Kids with Guns"
"Last Living Souls"

Heather Alexander:
"Fallen Angel"
"March of Cambreadth"
"Wolfen One"

Jace Everett:
"Bad Things"

Jay Gordon:
"Slept So Long"

Jethro Tull:
"Mountain Men"
"No Lullaby"
"Rocks on the Road"

King Black Acid:
"One and Only"
"Soul Systems Burn"

Ladytron:
"Ghosts"
"Burning Up"

Lee Dorsey:
"Give It Up"

Little Big Town:
"Bones"

Low:
"Half Light"

Nirvana:
"Lake of Fire"
"Plateau"

Oingo Boingo:
"Nothing to Fear"
"Home Again"
"Elevator Man"
"Dead Man's Party"

Ringo Starr:
"It Don't Come Easy"

Sarah McLachlan:
"Possession"

Simple Minds:
"Don't You (Forget About Me)"

Tangerine Dream:
"Beaver Town"
"Dr. Destructo"
"Grind"
"Hyde Park"

Tina Turner:
"I Can't Stand the Rain"

Tori Amos:
"Blood Roses"
"Muhammad My Friend"

Warchild:
"Ash"

Zero 7:
"In the Waiting Line"

And now,
a special excerpt from the next book
in the Otherworld series
by Yasmine Galenorn

Blood Wyne

Coming soon from Berkley!

"I can't believe I need *another* new bartender." I leaned back in my chair and propped my feet on the desk. Luke had left the bar for a good reason, but that didn't mean I had to like it. And his replacement—Shawn, a vampire—couldn't rise to the challenge. I'd fired him after two weeks of inept bartending and questionable customer service. When I caught him trying to put the fang on a couple of my regulars, I lost it and kicked him out. Nobody messes with my regulars, especially in *my* bar.

But that left a void. The Wayfarer was busy like every other place during the holiday season, and we needed every hand on board. I'd put up a fake tree in the corner, handed out bonuses already, but the main focus of Winter Solstice—and Christmas for my clients who celebrated it—was still ahead of us, and the parties were getting more frantic and raucous every night as people crowded in, exhausted from shopping and coping with holiday chaos.

Nerissa shrugged. "What can I say, doll? I'm sorry, but that's the way things go." Standing behind me, she leaned down and slowly trailed a line of kisses down my cheek to my neck. "I'd work for you if I didn't have the day job."

"You'd be such an awesome bartender, and you wouldn't accuse me of sexual harassment if I yanked you back here in my office." I sighed. "I know, I know—this is part of owning a bar, but it fucking sucks."

I tipped my head back and caught her full on the mouth, savoring my golden goddess's lips as she set off a ricochet of desire that shockwaved through my body. All I could think about was how much I wanted her. *Here. Now.* As I reached for her breast, my fingers sliding over the rounded curves of her body, a knock on the door interrupted us.

"Bad timing." I glanced up at her ruefully. "Rain check?"

"Always." She reluctantly stepped back to sit in the chair next to my desk.

A werepuma who reminded me of a slightly warped Aphrodite, my girlfriend was extremely good about knowing when I needed to present a professional appearance. She sat primly in the chair, her skirt-suit and tawny chignon making her look like a librarian waiting to bust out and go wild. Everybody knew we were together, but it wouldn't do for the boss to be sucking face when the help checked in.

"Come in." I waited as Chrysandra opened the door and peeked her head around it. "What's up?"

She glanced at Nerissa, then at me, and grinned. "Sorry to interrupt, Boss, but I've got someone out here looking for a job. I'm not sure about him, but you might want to talk to him."

"Supe?" I had instituted a policy of hiring only members of the Supernatural Community. The Wayfarer attracted far too many potential problems for me to take a chance on any more full-blooded humans. Chrysandra had gotten the hang of working around Supes of all kinds, but for a bartender, I needed someone who could also act as bouncer when I wasn't around.

Pieder, the giant, did a good job, but he worked during the day and I was hiring for the night shift. I probably should hire a second bouncer while I was at it, but since I worked most evenings in the bar, usually I could cover the void. Smart people didn't mess with vampires, and most of my regulars had quickly learned not to cross me.

She nodded. "Yeah, but I'm not sure what kind. He has an

odd feel to him." The look on her face told me that he either made her nervous or he was just so strange that she didn't know what to make of him. Chrysandra was, I had discovered, somewhat psychic for an FBH—full-blooded human—and she picked up on things easily.

"Send him in." I turned to Nerissa. "Sweetie, you mind giving me a little privacy to interview him?"

"No problem. You sure you want to talk to him alone, girl?" She stroked my cheek with her fingers. "I can stay."

"I can tear apart ninety percent of the creatures I meet if they bother me. Don't forget that I'm a vampire, sweetheart. Never, ever forget it." I took her hand, holding it for a moment. As much as I cared about her . . . all right, as much as I *loved* her . . . I never wanted her to forget I was a dangerous predator. It was my nature and I accepted it and, at times, reveled in it.

"I never do," she whispered softly, then followed Chrysandra out of the room, her skirt swishing in a way that drove me crazy. I wanted to slip my hands under the hem, to run them up her golden thighs. For so long I'd repressed my sexuality after Dredge was done with me, but Nerissa had woken it up, full-steam ahead, and there was no putting the Djinn back in the bottle.

I put my feet on the floor and straightened the papers on my desk. I had to start the inventory soon; we were coming up on the end of the year and I needed to do a full accounting of everything in the bar. I also was getting ready to open the Wayfarer to overnight travelers. We'd cleaned out the rooms upstairs and had space for seven guests. That meant hiring a maid and someone to run room service, carry bags, and take care of the needs of our Otherworld patrons in general. For the most part, that's who I expected to see. I already had decided that I wouldn't rent to goblins, ogres, or anybody likely to cause trouble.

Since the Wayfarer technically belonged to an OW resident, it was considered sovereign territory and I could discriminate for whatever reason I wanted. And letting creeps and miscreants stay in the bar wasn't my idea of security. Especially not when my sisters and I were waging a demonic war.

The door opened and a man cleared the archway. As

I glanced at him, looking him up and down, I was suitably impressed. At least as far as him being able to chuck people out of the bar.

Brawn, he had. That much was clear. The man—or whatever he was—stood around five-eight, but his biceps were works of art, and his thighs looked strong enough to crack a skull. His hair, jet black with a white streak, was held back in a thick pony tail, hitting about mid-shoulder. It set off eyes as green as my sister Delilah's. He looked mid-thirties, but if he was Supe, who knew how old he really was?

I could tell right off that he wasn't human. Chrysandra hadn't been kidding, this dude had some seriously powerful energy rolling off of him. I was about as headblind as you could get for someone half-Fae, but even I could feel it.

"How do you do? I'm Menolly D'Artigo. And you are . . . ?" I stood and walked around the desk. To someone my height, he seemed tall. I was five-one, barely, and petite, but I could probably take him out without blinking an eye. One of the perks of being a vampire: exceptional strength that belied any lack of visible force. Motioning him to a chair, I hopped up to sit on my desk.

"Derrick. Derrick Means." He took the chair and leaned back, eyeing me closely. "You *look* like a vamp," he said.

I blinked. Nobody had ever said that to my face, but what the hell. "Good. Because that's what I am, and anybody that works for me has to not only tolerate it, but actually accept the fact. What about you?"

He arched an eyebrow and folded his arms. "I'm from the Badger People. I'm a friend of Katrina's. She said you might be open to me applying for the job, even though you're a vamp. Said you'd hired a werewolf before."

Badger People? Weres and vamps didn't always get along, but I wasn't just any vamp—I was half-Fae as well as half-human. And Katrina was one of our friends, a werewolf who had started to fall for my former bartender before he ended up having to leave Earthside for Otherworld to protect his sister.

I frowned. I'd never met anyone from the badger tribes before and had very little clue what they were like, though if they matched their namesake creature, he wouldn't have any hesitation about tossing problem people out on their asses.

"Tell me about your experience. And are you part of a clan or a loner?"

"Used to be in a clan, until I decided to hit the city and see what life here is all about. I like Seattle, but there's not much chance to interact with my family since I moved. We keep in touch via e-mail but I don't get to see them often." He let out a long sigh that sounded suspiciously like a huff, and relaxed back into the chair.

"Experience?"

"I've got fifteen years bartending experience under my belt, I double as a bouncer no problem, and I've never been fired." He handed me a piece of paper. To my surprise it was a resume. A detailed resume. Usually people just came in and asked for a job. Or at best, an application.

"Why do you want to work at the Wayfarer?" I glanced over his CV. Everything seemed in order. No immediate alarm bells went off in my gut.

"Because I need a job. You need a bartender. And you won't get in my face about taking off the nights of the full moon." He leaned forward. "I'm good at what I do, I'm loyal, and I'll be here, sober, whenever you call. I don't hit on the women—at least not on duty. If you want to call some of my references, the numbers are there."

I stared at the list. Applegate's Bar, Wyson's Pub, the Okinofo Lounge . . . not upscale bars but not seedy holes-in-the-wall, either. They were solid and had a good clientele. I let out a long breath and glanced up at him. "Wait out front in one of the booths."

After he nodded and swaggered out of the office, I put in a few calls. Nobody had anything bad to say about him, and several of the bars praised him, though I could feel a definite tension there. Chalking it up to FBHs dealing with Supes, I made my decision and headed out front.

Derrick was nursing a Diet Coke and I slid into the seat across from him.

"You drink? Do drugs?"

He shook his head. "Drink beer and Scotch occasionally, but never on duty. Drugs and Badger People aren't a good mix. We have a temper; I am the first to admit it. I know my limits."

"Okay, here's the deal." I motioned at the bar. "I need

somebody and I need him now. So if you can start this week, preferably tonight, so much the better. Your shift is from four P.M. until two A.M., but you may need to come in to help with inventory at times during the day. I can pay you fifteen an hour to start. If you're as experienced as you seem to be, and you last ninety days, I'll raise that to seventeen. I'm the boss, you do what I say while you're here, and you keep your nose clean. What do you say? Want the job or not?"

He raised his glass in salute. "Here's looking at you, Boss."

At least one of my problems was over with. But it didn't take long for another to rear its head. As I was showing Derrick around the bar, watching how he handled the bottles and suitably impressed at how he handled customers, the door opened and Chase Johnson swaggered in.

My sister Delilah's ex-lover, and a detective who was as good as family by now, Chase dressed in Armani and perpetually smelled like a taco stand. He was also one damned fine detective.

After all the arguments we'd been through, I had to give him props. He'd managed to keep it together in situations that would drive the average FBH wacko. Oh yeah, one other little tidbit: Chase also was as good as immortal, at least in human terms. He'd been given the Nectar of Life in order to save his life, and that gave him a long leg up on the rest of FBHs.

He glanced at Derrick and nodded, giving me a quizzical look.

"This is Chase Johnson, detective and friend of the business. Close to being family. Treat him right." Derrick nodded. "Chase, this is Derrick—my new bartender. Derrick, give us a few minutes alone. Chase has something to talk to me about. Don't you?"

"Yeah, though I wish this were just a social call." He waited till Derrick moved off and then followed me to a booth. "Werewolf?"

"Badger People. Werebadger."

"Sheesh—is there a Were class for every animal on the planet?" Chase snorted and rubbed one perfectly coiffed eyebrow.

"Just about. What is it, Johnson?"

"Trouble. You have the time to take a little ride with me to headquarters? Vampire business, I think." He let out a long sigh.

Hell. Vampire business was so *not* what I wanted to hear, because when Chase came calling about vampires, it usually meant somebody was dead. Most likely murdered. There'd been an upswing in nocturnal activity lately, but since I was no longer privy to the scuttlebutt going around Vampires Anonymous, it was harder for me to ferret out secrets. I had to rely on what Sassy Branson could tell me, but she was growing more erratic every day. I'd been seriously considering taking my "daughter," Erin, out of the older vampire's care.

"Let me tell Chrysandra." I hustled over to my waitress and tapped her on the arm. "Keep an eye on Derrick. Help him learn the ropes. Chase needs me."

"Sure thing, Menolly. But are you sure? I mean, it's his first night." She looked a little worried. Normally, I'd chalk it up to nerves, but tonight I stopped and looked into her eyes, trying to get a feel for where her jitters were coming from.

"You have a bad feeling about him?" I cocked my head, waiting.

She glanced over at him, then slowly shook her head. "No . . . but . . . there's something about him. I can't put my finger on it. He's more than he appears to be, but I don't sense . . . he's not hostile, but I think he walks with danger."

I bit my lip, then said, "Get Tavah from the basement. Tell Riki to take over down there. If anything goes wrong, Tavah should be able to take care of matters." Tavah, another vampire, spent her nights in the basement of the Wayfarer, guarding the portal to Otherworld, and keeping track of the guests who came through. She kept the creeps out and let the paying visitors in.

"Okay." She ran down the steps as I hightailed it over to Derrick. "Listen, Derrick, I've got to go out. Chrysandra will help you out, and while I'm gone she and Tavah are in charge. I'll be back as soon as I can. Okay?"

He nodded, eyes on the drink he was mixing. "Not a problem. Got it."

And with that, as soon as Tavah appeared at the top of the stairs, I followed Chase into the icy night.

* * *

Winter in Seattle vacillates between mild and nasty, but the past couple of years had been pretty rough at times. Instead of the incessant rain, we'd actually seen snow—enough to stop the city in its tracks for a few days. Now, a week or so before Yule, it was cold enough to snow and I'd considered putting snow tires on my Jag.

The chill didn't bother me, but Chase buttoned his trench as we headed out the door. He held it open for me—he was, at heart, a gentleman—and we hustled to his car. I could tell he was cold; the breath puffed out of his mouth like clouds from a steam engine.

The streets were packed with shoppers looking for Christmas bargains. As we edged through traffic, Chase flipped on the radio and Danny Elfman's voice came out of the speakers, singing "Dead Man's Party."

"Man, I remember dancing to this at one of the local clubs almost fifteen years ago," he said offhandedly. "I was in high school and dating a girl named Glenda. She had hair a mile high and was in full retro mode. All she wanted to wear was spandex and look like one of the B-52 girls."

I glanced at him. "Do you miss those days? The days when you didn't know about us or the demons?"

He tapped his fingers on the steering wheel as we waited for traffic to inch forward. "Trick question. No way to answer that truthfully." Giving me a sideways smirk, he added, "Yes, I do, but only because life was much simpler then. Choices were black and white. But I have to say since you three entered my life, I've never been bored. Scared shitless, yes. Bored? Never."

Snorting, I leaned forward and turned up the music. "You ever want to, you can come clubbing with Nerissa and me, as long as we aren't hitting a vamp club. We're damned good on the dance floor."

Chase's turn to snicker. "Right, and while I'd be the envy of a thousand men, I don't think that would fit my style anymore. Hell, I have no clue as to what my style is now." He sounded lost, and a little frightened. "Look—Santa."

A sidewalk Santa was ringing his bell for the South Street

Mission in front of a small boutique. The winter was chill and cold, and a lot of people were out of work. Gauging from his expression, he wasn't having much luck.

"Santa's a freakass scary dude in reality. Camille met him when she was young." I stared at the pseudo-Santa through the window as we passed by and fell silent. *Santa, passing out presents.* Humans clung to their myths in the hope that they'd ward off bad luck, ward off evil. How little they knew about the truth that hid behind their fairy tales, or what monsters were *really* sliding down their chimneys.

I turned up the music as Ladytron replaced Oingo Boingo. A part of me felt sorry for Chase. We'd totally shifted his life and he could never go back to what he'd been, to the life he'd expected to lead. Collateral damage. We were leaving a nasty trail, and there'd be far more by the time this demonic war was over.

It took us another twenty minutes to reach the FH-CSI—the Faerie Human Crime Scene Investigation—headquarters. I knew this building all too well. It seemed like my sisters and I were here all the time, especially since our war against the demons was escalating.

Most of the building was underground—the bottom level was the morgue, in-house laboratory, and archives. Third floor down were the jail cells for the Otherworld magical and strength-enhanced Supes. Second floor down was the arsenal—containing a vast array of interesting weapons viable for use against anything from werewolves to giants. The main floor contained both police headquarters and the medic unit. Delilah had hinted that she thought there was another level below the morgue, but what it was or whether it really existed, we didn't know.

Chase led me straight to his office rather than to the morgue. A good sign, I thought. Straight to the morgue was *bad*. Straight to the morgue meant immediate danger, and right now, I wasn't in the mood for trouble.

But as I took a seat opposite his desk, I happened to catch a glimpse of the photographs spilling out of a file on his desk. They didn't look promising. In fact, they looked downright ghastly.

"That's your trouble, I take it?" I nodded to the pictures.

"Yes, and one I wish you'd take as far away from me as you could." He let out a sigh. "I don't know what to make of it. If it looked like straight vampire killings, I'd at least know what I was dealing with. But there's something else going on." He motioned for me to scoot my chair closer, and laid out the photos in a line for me to look at.

There were four women pictured, each with obvious puncture wounds in her neck. Vampire activity, all right.

"Looks pretty straightforward to me," I said.

"Yeah, you would think so, wouldn't you? But look again at the women. Look closely. Notice anything odd?" He frowned and leaned back in his chair, crossing his left leg over his right and interlacing his fingers. "I really want your honest opinion because I want to make sure I'm not just barking up a tree that doesn't exist."

I studied the photographs. Women, all pretty, all somewhere in their thirties, looked to be. All . . . Wait a minute. *Pattern.* There was a pattern.

"They all have long brown hair, layered. They all have brown eyes, and they all seem to be around a hundred thirty pounds. How tall were they?"

"All between five-six and five-nine. So you see it, too?"

"Yeah. Was there any connection between them? Any similarity to their deaths?" A nasty thought was forming in my head, and I had the feeling Chase had already come to the same conclusion.

"Well, obviously they were all exsanguinated, and they were all killed at night. Puncture wounds on the throat, though there's no way to prove for sure that they were killed by a vampire. All the women were murdered within a five-mile radius, and all four were hookers." He frowned. "I'm thinking we have a vampire serial killer. If it wasn't for the fact that all the girls look alike, I'd just chalk it up to vampire attack, but they look *so much alike,* they could be related."

I stared at the pictures. Chase was right. They did look like sisters. And even though he couldn't make the official call, I knew in my gut that it was a vampire—most likely singular—attacking the women.

"Do you have their bodies, still? I can probably verify

vamp attack, seeing that I am one, but I'd need to look at their wounds."

Damn, damn, damn. If it was a vampire serial killer, we had big trouble. Ever since Delilah decked him near Samhain, Andy Gambit—star reporter for the *Seattle Tattler*, a yellow tabloid that fed on the fears and titillation of Seattle residents—had been on a tear, doing his best to smear Fae and Supes of all kinds. He'd done such an effective smear job on Nerissa that she'd lost the race for city council, even though she'd started out with a decent margin and all signs pointed to victory. If word of a vampire serial killer got out, we'd be pouring gasoline on the fire.

Chase led me to the elevator. "So, are you guys ready for Yule yet?"

I grinned. "More or less. Delilah hasn't tipped over the tree yet, but then, we anchored it to the ceiling first thing. Camille and Iris have the house looking like a winter wonderland. All we need is snow for it to feel like the holidays."

"Does Otherworld get much snow?" he asked, holding the door open for me.

I swung in behind him. "Depends on where you're at. Y'Elestrial—yes, we get quite a bit of snow there . . ." I fell silent, biting my lip. Our home city was now sacrosanct and off limits to Camille. And to us, too. "I miss it. The city is beautiful, but now I wonder if we'll ever see it again."

"Queen Tanaquar and your father still won't relent?" He looked uncertain, like he thought he should pat me on the shoulder or something.

Shrugging, I shook my head. "When Delilah and I demanded they allow Camille to return to her full status, they told us we had two choices: abide by their decree or suffer the same fate ourselves. So we all went to work for Queen Asteria instead, and the OIA is history. At least for us. At least for now."

"They aren't talking to me, either," he said. "Ever since your civil war, it's like they've decided that we don't need to be kept in the loop."

"Join the club. Father tried to guilt trip us like crazy, but Delilah and I shut him out. He hasn't been by our sides, up

to his elbows in demon blood, wondering if Shadow Wing
is coming through next. He doesn't know how fucking hard
Camille's worked, nor the decisions she's had to make. How
could Delilah and I stand by and just watch them throw her
away?"

Chase nodded. "I get it. I really do. And I admire the choice
you made. You three—no matter what, no one will ever come
between you guys."

He looked wistful, and I wondered if he missed Delilah. He
was actually at our house more often now that they'd broken
up, and he seemed far more relaxed and happy. So did Delilah,
even though she was still finding her way with Shade, the half-
dragon, half-Stradolan. A part of the Autumn Lord's world,
Shade had walked into her life and they were slowly building
what looked like it could be the love match of the century. I'd
never seen Delilah's heart so free and easy.

"You okay, Johnson?" I tapped him on the arm.

"Yeah," he said softly. "And just in case you're wondering,
no—I'm not pining over Delilah. *I'm* the one who decided I
couldn't handle a relationship. And frankly, it's a good thing.
My moods are swinging like crazy now that my powers are
opening up. I'm happy one moment, pissed the next. Not good
boyfriend material. Sharah's found someone in town who's
going to help me learn how to channel the energy."

"Good, because unbridled psychic energy is dangerous for
all concerned." I stopped him as we stepped out of the elevator. "Truth time."

"What?" His dark eyes glistened and I resisted the impulse
to reach up and brush back an unruly cowlick—it was so out
of place on his perfectly coiffed head that it distracted me.

"Are you sure you're okay with my sister seeing someone
else? Because if you have any thoughts of a reunion later,
you'd better say something now. She's falling, Chase. She's
falling for Shade like I've never seen her fall before." I had no
intention of letting him put her on the spot later, forcing her to
make a choice she thought she'd already made.

He gazed at me, his eyes limpid, his expression torn. Then,
slowly, he asked, "She really loves this guy?"

"I think he's *the one*, Chase."

"Then I'll remain her blood brother, and I won't interfere.

Because I honestly don't know what the hell's going to happen in my life." He paused. "Can I ask *you* something now?"

So relieved by his reply that I would have granted almost any favor, I nodded. "Ask away."

"Do you think someone like Sharah might ever see me in anything but an official capacity?" He sounded hesitant, almost embarrassed to be asking.

I knew full well that Sharah was in love with the detective, but that was her place to answer, not mine. I gave Chase a soft smile. "Listen, you're a catch. You've had your share of screw-ups but, Johnson, you're okay, and I think you're going to make somebody happy someday. Could someone like Sharah could be interested in you? I don't see why not."

He thought for a moment, then nodded and led the way to the morgue. "We've kept the bodies. The families—of the two bodies we've been able to identify—know they've been murdered, but we've been vague on the hows and whys. I've got to tell them something soon, though, and release the bodies to them."

I stared at the brilliant white walls of the morgue, the shimmering stainless steel of the sinks and tables. This was my domain—the domain of the dead. Had Dredge not brought me back to life, I'd have walked the hallowed halls, crossing over to the Land of the Silver Falls.

Every time I came face-to-face with mortality, I remembered my own immortality and once again had to face the fact that I was a predator. A creature who belonged in the shadows. Never again would I walk under the sun, not until the day I was ready to give it all up and go home to my ancestors. Until then, there was only the moon for me.

Four bodies were laid out on tables, covered with white sheets. Spotless sheets, like freshly fallen snow against a barren background.

"I take it you've watched them for any signs of rising?"

He nodded. "Yeah. Nothing. I think they're truly dead."

I approached the first one and pulled back the sheet. She was unearthly in her silence, in her stillness. Like a statue, or a figure frozen in ice, she lay there, pale from the lack of blood. I leaned down and examined the puncture wounds on her neck. *Vampire.* I could feel him. *Smell* him. The vamp who killed this woman was male and fairly young. That much I could tell. Quickly, I checked the other bodies, startled by the similarity of their looks. They could have been sisters.

In a way they are, I thought. *Sisters in death.* They were killed by the same vampire. I could smell him on them, his breath, his scent, his . . .

Oh crap. I jumped back, trembling. Very little set me off but this—this did. It was too familiar, still too stark in a memory that I'd never, ever shake.

"Did you check to see if they were raped?"

Chase looked at me, his expression slipping from neutral to pained. "Yeah, we did. I was hoping I wouldn't have to tell you. I know what that does to you."

"They were, right? You wouldn't find semen, but they were torn and bruised. I can smell it. I can smell the bloodlust . . . not just around the puncture marks." Feeling the room spin, my fangs came down and I began to panic. I had to get out of there. "Chase, I have to get up to the surface. Now."

"Come on." He guided me out but wisely didn't touch me.

When we came to the elevator, I held out my hand. "You'd better not ride up with me. I'll meet you out front."

He didn't question, just stood back, letting me board the car without him. I punched the button for the main floor and counted the seconds as they ticked by. The elevator wasn't slow, but by the time it reached the main floor and I managed to haul ass outside, it felt like it had been a thousand years.

A thousand years of memories, a thousand years of wanting freedom, a thousand years of wondering if we had another Dredge on our hands.

NEW FROM *NEW YORK TIMES*
BESTSELLING AUTHOR

Yasmine Galenorn

BONE
MAGIC

**"Galenorn's kick-butt Fae ramp up the
action in a wyrd world gone awry!"**
—PATRICIA RICE

Another equinox is here and life's getting more
tumultuous for the D'Artigo sisters. Smoky, the
dragon of Camille's dreams, must choose between his
family and her. Plus, the sisters can't locate the new
demon general in town. And Camille is summoned to
Otherworld, thinking she'll reunite with her long-lost
soul mate, Trillian. But once there, she must undergo
a drastic ritual that will forever change her and those
she loves.

penguin.com

Don't miss the new series from
New York Times bestselling author

YASMINE GALENORN

NIGHT MYST
An Indigo Court Novel

Eons ago, vampires tried to turn the Dark Fae in order to harness their magic, only to create a demonic
enemy more powerful than they imagined. Now Myst,
the queen of the Indigo Court, has enough power to
begin a long-prophesied supernatural war.

Cicely Waters, a witch who can control the wind, may
be the only one who can stop her—and save her beloved Fae prince from the queen's enslavement.